T0283711

A COLD, HARD PRAYER

A COLD, HARD PRAYER

A NOVEL BY JOHN SMOLENS

Michigan State University Press | *East Lansing*

♾ The paper used in this publication meets the minimum requirements
of ANSI/NISO Z39.48-1992 (R 1997) (Permanence of Paper).

Michigan State University Press
East Lansing, Michigan 48823-5245

Library of Congress Cataloging-in-Publication Data
Names: Smolens, John, author.
Title: A cold, hard prayer : a novel / by John Smolens.
Description: First edition. | East Lansing : Michigan State University Press, [2023]
Identifiers: LCCN 2023001799 | ISBN 978-1-61186-478-6 (cloth) |
ISBN 978-1-60917-747-8 (PDF) | ISBN 978-1-62895-512-5 (ePub)
Subjects: LCSH: Orphans—Fiction. | LCGFT: Novels.
Classification: LCC PS3569.M646 C655 2023 | DDC 813/.54—dc23/eng/20230123
LC record available at https://lccn.loc.gov/2023001799

Cover design by David Drummond, Salamander Design, www.salamanderhill.com
Cover photo by ArtMarie via iStock

Visit Michigan State University Press at *www.msupress.org*

For the Sunday Zoomers
Linda • Peter
Elizabeth • Aron
Allard • David • Megan
Berta • Michael
Ellen . . .
And Papi

ACKNOWLEDGMENTS

My thanks to the staff at Michigan State University Press,
especially Kristine M. Blakeslee, Catherine Cocks, Amanda Frost,
Elise Jaguga, and Nicole Utter.

And to Ellen Longsworth, who helped me get from the first sentence to the last.

Beware, O wanderer, the road is walking too.
~Jim Harrison, Poem #37, *After Ikkyū and Other Poems*

June 14, 1919
Sister Superior
St. Ann's Orphanage /
Youville House
12 Granite Avenue
Worcester, Massachusetts

Andrea Selinski
c/o Fr. John Nolan, S.J.
St. Mary's Church
St. Ignace, Michigan

Dear Sister Superior,

I was given your name as a result of inquires conducted on my behalf
by Father John Nolan, S.J., at the Church of St. Mary's, here in St. Ignace,
Michigan. (Father Nolan is assisting me with the composition of this letter.)

My full name is Andrea Magdalena du Casse Selinski, the sister of Louisa
Mae du Casse. She gave birth to a baby girl, who, I believe, is currently in your
care at St. Ann's in Worcester. The child would now be twelve years of age, and
I am given to understand that she goes by the name Mercy. I do not know what,
if any, surname has been assigned to her.

Louisa and I were brought to the United States from Jamaica when we were
quite young. I believe I was six or seven and she was two years younger. Our
parents moved a great deal as our father sought employment, mostly as a laborer
or in factories. When we were in our early teens he disappeared; he ran off, and
we never heard from him again. Our mother supported us working primarily as
a seamstress. We lived in New York City, Providence, and then Boston, where
she died of tuberculosis.

Louisa and I found employment in textile factories in several Massachusetts
towns. We were living in Clinton, a mill town on the Nashua River, working
the looms in the Bigelow Carpet Company, when Louisa became pregnant. She
was about fifteen years of age. She would never reveal the exact circumstances,
though I am certain it was not of her own volition. She never mentioned the
father's name, but I am quite sure it was a man who worked as a laborer named
Henri Boursard, who had come down to New England from Quebec Province.

During the last months of her pregnancy, Louisa resided in a home for unwed
mothers in Framingham, which was sponsored by the Boston Archdiocese. As

soon as she delivered her baby girl the child was taken and placed in St. Ann's Orphanage. Louisa recalled that the nuns commented on the child's mixed heritage. Just before they left Louisa's bedside, they said they would call the child Mercy, as though such information would sufficiently assuage any doubts my sister might have about giving up the infant.

If at the time my sister had consented to giving the baby away, she was in retrospect plagued by deep regrets.

In subsequent years Louisa and I moved numerous times, looking for employment and a tolerable place to live. We continued west, living for a time in Rochester, New York, and then eventually arriving in Detroit and then Lansing, Michigan. At this point we were in our twenties, and we found work in one of the new Ford Motor Company manufacturing plants.

The rigors of factory work precipitated a decline in Louisa's health; and, like our mother, her constitution was susceptible to tuberculosis, complicated by other ailments. In 1914, I accepted the sacrament of holy matrimony, and Louisa lived with my husband and me, until she passed away October 4 of that year. I nursed her during the final stages of her illness and, though she was prepared to enter into the care of our Lord, she was increasingly distraught over the fate of her child Mercy.

Louisa's last wish, her most pressing request, was that after her passing I would locate her daughter and make arrangements to take her into our home. My husband, Raymond Selenski, and I, who unfortunately have not yet been blessed with children of our own, were more than willing to fulfill Louisa's desires.

Father John Nolan has helped me discover that Mercy most likely had never been adopted and is currently residing in St. Ann's Orphanage. Raymond and I wish to begin whatever proceedings are necessary that would allow us to bring her to live with us here in Michigan. (We have since moved from Lansing to St. Ignace in Michigan's Upper Peninsula, where Raymond is a cook in the kitchen of the Grand Hotel on Mackinac Island during the summer season, and the rest of the year he works on fishing and transport vessels that operate on the Great Lakes.)

I wish to inquire after Mercy's health and trust that you might help us bring my sister's daughter home, where she will be loved and live in the presence of our Father.

Yours in Christ,
Andrea Selinski

1

Nau Farm 1924

One

Only children boarded the train, accompanied by three adults. October sleet pelted the windows as they pulled out of Haverhill, a mill town on the Merrimack River, north of Boston. More children were put on the train in Worcester and Holyoke, dozens of them, orphans ranging in age from nine to their late teens. For some, it was the first time they'd ever ridden on a train.

As they headed west, the snowy Berkshires gave way to the gray landscape of upstate New York. The children were in the charge of Mr. Trent, along with two women who saw to their personal needs. It was no secret among the orphans that Mr. Trent was a priest in a bowler and tweed wool suit, a ploy necessary to thwart distrust of Catholics. The elderly nurse Mrs. Yarborough lugged her valise through the carriages, dispensing pills, ointments, and elixirs, and often probing the children with a terrifying assortment of stainless-steel instruments. Her young assistant, Miss Irene Lansdowne, was considered kindly if a bit touched. Periodically the train would stop in a village, and the children would be herded out on the station platform, where townspeople would look them over. "Like horses," a boy named Arnie whispered. "Or cattle." He was taken by a widow in Herkimer, the first stop after Albany.

The strong ones went first, and the pretty ones. Those who hadn't been taken were considered too scrawny or physically defective. More than half the children had been taken by the time the train reached Ohio. "Claimed" was the word Mr. Trent often used, as though a child's selection was part of the Lord's design. Most of the children went eagerly, though tears were often shed as they were separated from friends on the station platform.

In a village outside Cleveland a Negro couple arrived in a wagon drawn by a mule. When they indicated that they wanted the girl known as Mercy, she sat down on the platform. The others looked down the line of the children at the girl. Slight, undernourished, she wore a long wool coat with stitched sleeves, and her russet hair was tied up in a tattered scarf. Her large green-yellow eyes seemed to possess a defiant light. From the beginning of the journey, she had been deemed contrary by Mrs. Yarborough, and the other children often ridiculed her. On the train, she kept to herself. She was the last one likely to be taken, but this tall man with a gentle smile, a farmer in what appeared to be his Sunday suit, took her by the arm to help her to her feet. She turned her head quickly and bit his hand, causing him to release her.

"She's no good," the farmer's wife said. "You can see she's mixed."

The boy standing next to Lincoln Hawser glanced up at him, as if to ask what the woman meant. Lincoln shook his head, the smallest gesture. The boy understood and looked straight ahead, didn't move, making himself inconspicuous. He took Lincoln's hand, seeking his protection. The little ones often did.

The couple walked down the line of children and stopped in front of the only black boy in the group. "We'll take this one instead," the wife said to Mr. Trent.

When they were herded back on the train the children were quiet, as usual. It seemed providential, how they had been spared, though it was really a matter of being passed over, rejected repeatedly, village after village. There was, too, uncertainty and fear. Mr. Trent had declared that Chicago was their final destination, inciting a rumor that any children still on board were customarily deposited at the Union Stock Yard, where they were fed to the hogs.

Mercy's behavior at the station incensed Mrs. Yarborough, who insisted that she would go without supper. She stared out at the passing countryside, while the children were ushered forward to the dining car. Lincoln ate quickly and returned, sitting across the aisle from Mercy. He wasn't sure why, but he admired her refusal to be claimed.

"Why wouldn't you go with them?" he asked. She continued to stare out the window, now streaked with rain. "Mr. Trent and the nurse," he said. "They think you're defying God's will."

She turned her head, her eyes hard on him now, as if to say, *Why are you even speaking to me?*

"Divine providence, and all that." He looked over his shoulder to be sure no one was entering the carriage, and then took the napkin from the left pocket of his coat and held it out to her.

"What's this?"

"Dinner."

She stared at the folded napkin in his hand, then, reluctantly, reached across the aisle. "I know why you keep your other hand in your pocket. What happened?"

"An accident."

"Divine providence." No smile. Her eyes might even have been accusing, the way they bore into him.

"You could have gone with them."

"Just because I'm not white?"

"They looked like good people."

"No," she said. "This is Ohio."

"So?"

"Michigan. It's where I'm going."

"God's will?"

"No." For the briefest moment there was a hint of a smile. "Mine."

She unfolded the napkin and examined the chicken leg, the slice of bread, and a small wedge of cheese. When she looked up at him again, her eyes seemed less guarded. "Do you dream?" she asked.

"I suppose so. Why?"

"What do you dream about?"

"I . . . I'm not sure. I usually forget them when I wake up. Don't you?"

"No, though I wish I could." She picked up the chicken leg from the napkin. "Maybe it's because there is no difference between dreams and being awake?" She looked up the aisle toward the front of the carriage. "This train. I have dreamed about this train. Before we even boarded it, I knew this train." Her slender fingers raised the chicken leg to her mouth.

While she ate, he turned his head away, a matter of decency, and watched night fall on the land.

•

By the time they departed Toledo, five children were left on the train as it made its way along the Michigan-Ohio border. Smaller crowds gathered at the railroad depots, as though instinctively they knew that what children remained would not be worth the effort of a trip to town. Rather than a horse or a cow, Lincoln felt like a turnip or an onion. Too ripe, too bruised to be edible. They stopped at Adrian, then at Cold Water, but there were no takers. In a village called Otter Creek the children lined up on the platform, facing just one couple. Mr. Trent addressed them cordially as Mr. and Mrs. Harlan Nau.

Harlan Nau held his wife's arm in courtly fashion as they walked down the row of five children. His crushed fedora hat seemed to mimic his sunken cheeks and his jaw didn't line up properly with the rest of his face. She was a good foot shorter and much heavier than her husband.

Mrs. Nau inspected each child with a severe, dismissive eye. They stopped in front of Mercy. The woman seemed to be holding her breath as though she feared contagion. "Will you look at that skin?" she muttered in disgust. "And those eyes?"

"Mixed blood, no doubt," her husband said. "How old is she?"

"We figure seventeen," Mr. Trent said.

"You got a name?"

At the orphanage in Worcester, the nuns often gave the children their names. There were boys named Peter, Paul, and Ignatius. Girls were named for Joan of Arc and Saint Chiara, and too many were named Mary. The nuns' thoughts gravitated toward virtues, which led to girls named Prudence, Felicity, and Submit. Many had no last name. She knew her mother's last name, but she couldn't let on that she knew. It was her secret. "My name is Mercy."

"Mercy, indeed," his wife said. "Awful scrawny. Underfed, and probably sickly from that foul air back in them cities with all those factories." She shook her head as she turned to study Lincoln. "This one looks strong. Where you from?"

"Haverhill, Massachusetts."

"Never heard of it," Mrs. Nau said. "What's wrong with him? How come he ain't been taken already?" Though she didn't look around, her question was directed toward Mr. Trent, who had followed behind the couple like an usher.

Mr. Trent nodded but Lincoln didn't move. Nurse Yarborough hissed, "Show them." When he still didn't move, she said, "This is the last stop before Chicago, Rope."

Lincoln removed his right hand from the pocket of his corduroy jacket.

The woman gasped.

"What happened to your fingers?" her husband said.

"I worked in a shoe factory in Haverhill. A machine that stamps out leather took them."

"You can see he's strong," Mr. Trent offered. "Going on seventeen, and he's got the might of these three other boys."

"Ain't got nothing but a thumb and stubby things on that hand," the woman said. She considered the other three boys. "I don't know, Harlan, these others are all the runts of the litter."

"Right you are, dearest. Best we wait till another train comes through."

"That likely won't be till spring," Mr. Trent advised.

"Sure could use some help before winter sets in," Harlan Nau said. "Come, Estelle."

He began to steer his wife away, until Miss Landsdowne stepped out from behind Mrs. Yarborough. "Pardon, but might you reconsider if you knew that Mercy here can sew real good? And cook? She has a real way with a pie crust. And Rope, like Mr. Trent said, he's strong. But mild in nature."

Mrs. Yarborough took this imposition as an affront, which was nothing new. She often reprimanded Miss Landsdowne for speaking out of turn.

"Both of them?" Harlan said.

Mr. Trent cleared his throat. Lincoln knew what was coming. He had heard it in all its variations since leaving Massachusetts. "We do understand that to feed, clothe, and house a child is a not insignificant financial burden, but it should be deemed an investment in the future, that is the future of your farm and household and, indeed, in the future of this great God-fearing country of ours." The God-fearing part always led to the pitch. "We only ask that you contribute what you can, which helps defray the costs incurred during our long and arduous train ride, not to mention the medical attention we have provided, and then too some documents must needs be processed, for we are only interested in a transaction that is right and legal. We recommend a minimum contribution of five dollars."

"Five dollars?" Harlan Nau said.

"But of course," Mr. Trent added, "As regards your contribution to our worthy cause—why yes, I believe we'd accept a special accommodation."

"Two for the price of one." Harlan spoke slowly, a man who appreciated a bargain. He said to Lincoln, "What he call you, Rope?"

"Yes, sir."

"Why?"

"My name is Lincoln Hawser."

"Hawser." The man's crooked jaw worked sideways in a fashion that seemed painful but unavoidable. "I see, like a ship's rope."

"We'd have to fed 'em both," Estelle said.

"I reckon." Harlan nodded. "Where'd your name come from, Lincoln Hawser? You be an orphan. How do you know?"

Rope glanced at Mr. Trent, as though requesting permission to speak. "I don't know, sir. It's just the name I was given, I guess. It's on my official papers."

"Well, dear," Harlan said to his wife, looking at Rope's right hand. "That mule kicked my jaw, and I've gotten by all these years. I suppose this boy will do with what he's got."

"But a mulatto," Estelle said, spitting the word as if it were a curse. "Under our roof?"

"Mulatta," Mr. Trent corrected gently.

"She's but a child." Harlan Nau said. "The girl will mind, you'll see." When his wife's objection was not forthcoming, he turned to Mr. Trent, who had removed his bowler. "Two for the price of one. Mister, you and your worthy cause got yourself a deal."

Two

arlan and Estelle Nau's farm was a half-hour's drive by wagon south of the village of Otter Creek. Sixty acres, bordered on one side by the Michigan Central tracks and on the other by the woods that lined the Little Otter Creek, which fed Otter Creek farther west. Mercy was confined to a room in the attic, while Lincoln slept in the shed attached to the back of the house. Chores began at five. Meals were plentiful but bland.

Mercy's cot was next to a window that looked out on pasture that ran to the trees that lined the creek. At night the panes often rattled in the wind, and branches scratched the roof. Days she cleaned the house, scrubbed clothes, assisted in the preparation of meals. She'd sometimes go an entire day without getting outdoors, while Rope spent most of his time splitting and stacking wood or tending to the animals.

One afternoon she went outside the house to hang the laundry on the line. Rope had been mucking out stalls and stood just outside the barn door, rake in hand, and watched her hang clothes on the line.

"What you looking at?" she said.

"Nothing."

"No?"

"Didn't mean nothing by it."

"Good."

Harlan's union suits looked like flat white men on the line, headless, dancing in the breeze.

"This is not what I expected," he said.

She finished pinning a large pair of bloomers on the line. "What did you expect?"

"I don't know. Not this."

"Why don't you run away? They lock me in the attic, but you're out in the shed off the kitchen. You could just walk away at night."

"I've considered it. But Harlan talks about the woods."

"What about them."

"There's bears and wolves. And what he calls big cats. Says you want them to kill you clean before they start gnawing on your innards. And then, where would I go?"

"You could look at a map," she said. "I'd go north."

"North?" Like he'd never heard of it. "What's up there?"

"St. Ignace."

"What's that, a place?"

Her laundry basket was empty. She picked it up, adjusting it against her hip.

"On the train you said you wanted Michigan. Why here?"

"That's my business, isn't it?"

She walked back toward the house.

•

"You ain't naturally left-handed, are you?" Estelle observed at dinner toward the end of the first week. "But I can see you figured out how to use that one 'cause you don't look about to starve to death."

"He does all right with it in the field and the barn," Harlan said. "Going to take some getting use to being around so many animals, though."

"We got to place a limit on how much he eats," Estelle said. "They said he was quiet, but that's because he usually has his mouth full. Two helpings, hear?"

"Yes, ma'am."

"What about the girl?" Harlan asked. "She don't eat much."

Estelle glanced at Mercy. "She could use some fattenin' up. Have another potato."

At night Rope lay on his cot, surrounded by farm implements. The wind swept the fields that ran toward the creek, and after dark there came the howling and cries and shrieks of animals. The shed possessed an odor he could not identify, until he found the remains of a dead rodent that had chewed its way into a burlap sack of some sort of grain.

A daily routine had been established, and occasionally Mercy was allowed to set foot outside the house in daylight. She would hang laundry, feed the chickens. She usually ignored him. Her face had a tawny hue with a saddle of freckles bridging her nose. Harlan once called her skinny, but then he grinned crookedly as though he meant something else. "But she does her work."

One day an automobile arrived in the yard. A man in a long wool coat and a fedora entered the house, toting a black leather satchel. Rope was splitting and stacking firewood next to the barn. He watched the house, expecting something, a sound, a cry, but there was nothing until after perhaps a half hour Mercy came out toting the laundry basket on her hip.

Rope continued to split and stack wood but finally looked over toward the clothesline. She was facing him, her arms raised to hang a bedsheet. "She sickly."

She'd never spoken to him first before.

"He a doctor?"

"Hm-hm." Her lips were wrapped around a clothespin, like she was smoking a cigar. She removed it from her mouth and nudged it down to fasten the sheet to the line. "Talking about female aliments and an operation in a hospital in some placed called Lansing."

"It's the state capital of Michigan, I think."

She picked up the empty laundry basket. "Never seen someone split logs one-handed before."

"Takes a sharp blade and an eye for the grain."

"I suppose." She headed back across the yard toward the house.

Two days later a Ford truck arrived. Estelle had a valise packed and was waiting by the kitchen door. All she'd said at breakfast was, "Harlan don't like his chicken undercooked."

Harlan stood in the yard watching the truck take her out to the road. When the vehicle was out of sight, he went into the barn.

Rope knew what he was up to—he'd smelled it sometimes, usually in the late afternoon. He kept splitting and stacking wood. After about a half hour, he went into the barn to sharpen his axe on the whetstone. He tucked the axe under his right arm and cranked the handle till the wheel got up some speed, and then with his left hand he held the blade at an angle to the spinning rim. The sparks reminded him of fireworks he'd once seen above the Merrimack River. It was the Fourth of July, and the streets and riverbanks in Haverhill were crowded. American flags everywhere. The fireworks reflected off the river, doubling the light. There was a way that the embers descended in the sky and hissed in the water that resembled the sparks coming off the point of contact between the axe blade and the spinning stone.

Harlan came out from behind the partition that supported his workbench, bottle in hand. "You always lived in an orphanage before taking that train out here?"

"Yes, sir. Several of them. When I was twelve then I got work at the factory."

"Until you lost your hand."

Rope turned the axe handle over and began to grind the other edge. Nothing shone new and pure like freshly honed steel. He was drawn to, and afraid of, such sharp edges. The moment when the machine's cutting edge came down on his fingers never seemed far off. A moment swift and decisive, his bloodied fingers lying helpless on the polished metal plate.

"Know anything about your family, who your people were?"

"Nothing much," Rope said.

"Irish. You look like you could be Irish. Catholic?"

"I was in orphanages run by nuns. Many of them are."

"I hear they're taking over the cities back east. Irish, Italian. All them Catholics."

"They come into Boston on ships." Rope took the axe away from the wheel. The rotation of the stone slowed, droning until it stopped. "They were starving, wherever they come from."

"Everyone around here's near starving, and we don't pack up and go elsewhere." Harlan took a swig from his bottle. He went back around the partition, dragging one foot slightly the way he did. When he tried to sit on the stool by the workbench, he fell over on to the packed earth floor. He seemed to find it funny. But then, angrily, he said, "You come here and help me up."

Rope went around the partition and looked at the man, lying on his back. He had managed not to spill too much, holding the bottle up in a gesture of victory. Rope held the axe handle across his right forearm for a moment, and then he leaned it against the workbench. He reached down with his good hand and took hold of Harlan's shoulder and pulled him up.

Harlan offered the bottle. "Want a touch?"

"No thank you, sir."

"Well then. Back to work. This house requires a lot of wood to keep warm."

Rope took up the axe and went back out to the woodpile. It was beginning to snow.

•

"Whatcha put in it?" Harlan's face was inches above his plate, the result of several hours of drinking out in the barn. "Tastes different. Smells . . . strong." He picked up the leg and bit into it. With his mouth full, he said, "Is this black chicken."

Mercy had a way of looking off as a form of self-defense. "I found some thyme in the pantry." Her russet hair was tied up in the kerchief she wore when cooking, making her jaw and cheek bones sharp angles in the failing light.

Harlan put the leg on his plate as though it were diseased. "Estelle never used no thyme."

The chicken was, to Rope's taste, far more tender than anything Estelle had put before him.

Mercy looked at him briefly, acknowledging that Harlan's drunk may have reached the point where it could take him any which way—he could turn belligerent, gleeful, morose, or he might just fall asleep at the table.

This required some kind of a distraction. Rope said, "Ever eat moussaka?"

"Say what?" Harlan asked.

"Or spanakopita?"

"The hell're you talkin' about?"

"Greek cooking."

"Never heard of it."

"You'd like the lemon chicken soup." Rope said to Mercy, keeping it easy, conversational. "Usually with rice, sometimes orzo."

"Orzo." Her lips formed the syllables as though she were tasting something for the first time.

"It's Greek," Rope said. "Where I came from, the Merrimack Valley, there's a lot of Greek families."

She appeared willing to play along. "Sure. Immigrants. Up and down the East Coast. You hear all sorts of languages and accents."

Harlan raised his head, alert as though he smelled something from afar, fire or perhaps manure. "You're an orphan," he said pointing his fork at her. "Know where your people come from?"

"Momma was from Jamaica." Mercy's slender fingers stripped meat from the bone.

Keenly interested now, Harlan asked, "How do you know that?"

"I found some information at the orphanage in Worcester. I wasn't supposed to see it."

"And your daddy?" When Harlan sneered it was as though an invisible hand were pushing his jaw over to align with his right ear. "A white man who took a fancy to her, eh?"

"Fancy," she said. "That's an interesting way to put it."

"Pro'bly some damn immigrant just off the boat." Harlan glanced at Rope. "Some Harp. Or maybe one of these Greeks that puts lemons in their soup."

"My father wasn't Greek, and he wasn't Irish," she said. "I know that much."

Harlan slapped the table and laughed. "He was hot for your momma is what he was!"

For the first time anger surfaced in Mercy's pale green eyes. "No, he was . . ."

Leaning forward, Harlan said, "He was what?"

"French-Canadian. He was from Quebec."

Harlan sat back, stopped cold. "If you're an orphan, how do you know that?" When she didn't answer, he looked about ready to slap her. "Asked you a question."

"Because I just do."

"An orphan ain't got no family. Till now. We are your family. We took you in. We tell you what to do, when to do it, and you don't put no thyme in the damn chicken." Harlan pushed off the table with both hands and stood up, the chair scraping on the wood floor. "Trouble with children is they ain't grown up." He was unsteady on his feet as he left the kitchen and climbed the stairs to the second floor. They could hear the bedsprings thwacking and singing when he collapsed in the bedroom.

•

Midmorning the truck came into the yard, the same couple that had taken Estelle to the hospital in Lansing. The woman had to be Estelle's sister.

Rope was emptying buckets of slop over the fence into the hog pen. Despite the grunting pigs, he could hear some of the conversation as Harlan stood with one foot on the running board of the truck.

"The doctor called." The woman's voice was high and shrill, much like Estelle's. "She's . . ." The wind tore away whatever she said, but it was clear she was distressed.

"So how long they gonna keep her up there?" Harlan asked.

Rope could not hear the response. Until Lyle said, "You ought to get yourself one of these telephones."

"Don't need no telephone," Harlan said. "Got something to say, you say it to my face."

The wind shifted, bringing the sound of an approaching train across the fields. When Harlan took his foot off the running board, Lyle turned the truck in a circle and headed out toward the road.

Rope returned to the barn with the slop pails, listening to Harlan's footsteps as he came into the barn. He went to the workbench, emerging a few minutes later with the bottle in his fist. Rope was hanging the pails on their wall hooks and Harlan leaned a shoulder against the nearest stall gate. He'd been hungover at breakfast, but after nipping from the bottle during morning chores he seemed much revived.

"Mason liked the hogs. Merle took to the cows and milking, and she had a pony, but it got sick, and we had to put it down. Near broke that little girl's heart."

Reluctantly, Rope said, "Your children?"

"Both lost to the influenza. Took a lot of folks around here. Ours were twins." Harlan raised the bottle to his mouth. "Mason and Merle were going on fourteen when they took ill. Them pigs is smarter than both of them, but they did what they were told." He sounded reasonable, determinedly so, as though relating an age-old argument. He saw something in Rope's face that caused him to say, "It's important to recognize a thing for what it is. There ain't no good or bad, there's just what is. That's what separates us from pigs—they know it and we don't." Another pull on the bottle. "Estelle's not been the same since we lost them kids. They cut the woman all out of her, but they just don't know how she'll fare. And now they don't know when she'll get out of that hospital."

"Why don't you pay a visit?"

Harlan peered at him through raw suspicion. "You'd like that, wouldn't you? Me going up to Lansing so you—" he nodded toward the house.

"What?" Rope said.

He smiled, his jaw moving to one side. "I ain't going nowhere. Staying right here." As though it were a curse, or maybe a sacred oath, Harlan gazed toward the house again and whispered, "Women."

•

Harlan's drinking continued into the third day. Sometimes it made him talk, often near tears, but by evening he turned contrary. Mercy was plenty busy tending to the house, knowing Estelle would inspect everything upon her return. She tried to keep clear of Harlan. The following day, Lyle and Hannah stopped by to tell him that Estelle was going to be released from the hospital the next day. They would drive up to Lansing to collect her.

Harlan drank through the afternoon, spending most of the time in the barn. He didn't come in for supper. Twice Mercy sent Rope out to tell him that she was putting their plates on the table, but Harlan stayed in the barn.

"He just sits there, muttering to himself," Rope said as he sat down at the table and looked at his dinner. "You used thyme again."

"Once more before she returns. It's my black chicken recipe." She glanced out the window toward the barn.

"What is it?" Rope asked.

"Nothing." She leaned over her food. "Don't like being alone in the house with him is all."

"He bother you?"

"Suppose he'd like to. The liquor fuels the urge, then more liquor kills it. I found him at the foot of the attic stairs this morning, curled up like one of the barn cats."

"Can you lock your door?"

"Flimsy latch is all. No lock. He'll likely sober up once she returns."

"I suppose."

"She don't allow drink. She told me that. She told me lots of things. You know about their children?"

"The influenza took them both," Rope said. "Mason and Merle."

"Merle, hm."

"What about her?"

She shook her head. "It was Estelle's idea to see what came through on the orphan train."

"He wasn't for it?" He had a steady gaze.

"Not at first. She said she had to pester him about it." She touched her forehead, tucking strands of hair beneath her kerchief. "But then we were a bargain. Two for one."

•

After supper Rope went out to the shed and lay on the cot beneath two blankets. He'd been mending fence all day in a raw wind spitting sleet, and he fell asleep immediately.

The voices were part of his dream.

No. They were pressing down on him, pulling him up out of sleep. Voices, muffled by the blankets covering his head. Sitting up, he realized it came from above, in the house.

He got up and went outside—he'd only managed to pull his boots off before lying on the cot—the frozen ground slippery beneath his wool socks. His axe leaned against the kitchen door frame. He picked it up and entered the house, went through the parlor, and took the stairs two at a time. He'd never been on the second floor of the house. Two rooms off a hall, and at the end was an open door and a set of narrow stairs, steep as a ladder. At the foot of the stairs, he stood listening, axe in his left hand, the head cradled in the crook of his right arm. They were gasping for air, desperate, urgent.

Rope climbed the stairs, rising into a familiar smell. Thyme. The attic was illuminated only by two candles. He could barely see them on the cot.

Three

When the Otter Creek police car, a Chevrolet, arrived at Nau Farm, there was a Ford truck in the yard. Lyle Nesbitt came out of the house and approached the car. "Captain Kincaid," he said in greeting, and looking across at the driver, he added, "Milt."

Kincaid looked up at the farmhouse, its white clapboards in need of paint. "What we got here?"

"Best come have a look for yourself," Lyle said.

They walked up to the house and Lyle opened the door but paused before stepping aside. "Estelle just got back from the hospital. She's feeling poorly." He seemed embarrassed. "Her operation was difficult. Female troubles, and such."

When Kincaid led the other two men into the kitchen he had to duck under the lintel. He could smell coffee. Hannah Nesbitt stood by the stove, a mug in her hand. "Care for a cup, Captain?"

"Not just now, Hannah, thanks. How's your sister?"

"She's in bed. Very upset, you understand. Coming home from the hospital and all." She glanced at her husband as though seeking permission to continue. "We didn't know where Harlan was. Nobody was around."

"Finally," Lyle said, "I looked everywhere. Found him in the attic. Touched not a thing."

"Why don't you stay here while Milt and I have a look."

Kincaid walked into the parlor and began climbing the stairs, his holster creaking with each step. Behind him Milt passed wind between his teeth, not exactly a whistle but notes in search of a melody.

"What's that song?" Kincaid said as they went down the hall toward the attic stairs.

"'A Pretty Girl is Like a Melody.' You know, Irving Berlin?"

Kincaid paused at the bottom of the stairs. "Even Irving would fail to recognize that tune."

Kincaid started up the stairs, which required both hands as though climbing a ladder. The air seemed to get thicker with each step up toward the attic. There was only light coming from the windows at both gable ends of the house. The attic floorboards groaned beneath his weight, and he had to be mindful of the slanted roof timbers.

"Fragrant in here," Milt said when he got up the staircase.

Toward the window to their left there were boxes and crates stacked, and a clothes rack with hanging garments. A transparent bag protected a wedding gown.

"Long time since Estelle fit in that dress," Milt said. Kincaid glanced at him. "You weren't around these parts when we all were growing up. Was a time when she and Hannah were, you know, pretty as a melody."

Kincaid had to admit they were stalling. Neither of them was eager to look toward the window at the other end of the attic.

He turned around and saw it on the bureau drawers: arcs of blood flung against the chipped white paint, and rivulets that had run down over the wooden knobs. Harlan Nau was silhouetted against the pale light from the window. He was on the floor, his back against a cot, both arms extending down to his legs, where his hands lay on his bare thighs. His overalls were bunched about his feet. Wool socks, no boots.

It was difficult to see. Kincaid stepped closer. The axe had entered Nau's skull almost dead center. Deep. The handle protruded, its length making him think of a bird's beak.

"Never seen an axe murder before," Milt said. "You wonder if death is instantaneous, or if you have a moment to consider your prospects." He snorted, a sure sign he was about to attempt a joke. "I'm of two minds which I'd prefer."

Kincaid ignored him and leaned toward Harlan. His head was tilted down, seemingly from the weight of the axe. His mouth was open and his bloody tongue visible. He seemed to be staring at his hands, which were both palms up, as though in supplication.

"They got a telephone here?"

"Harlan? Doubt it."

"Lyle must have gone down the road to their place to call us. We'll have to get Doc Evers out here."

Milt looked at him.

"Well, go on. If there's no phone here, drive over to Lyle's and use their phone."

Reluctantly, Milt went down the staircase. Kincaid found a stool by the bureau, checked to see that it was not bloodied, and sat on it. Such furniture always made him feel inordinately big, like a grownup trying to sit on chairs made for children. He realized that, in fact, the stool and the bureau were designed for a child, a girl. It must have been their daughter's—her name, it didn't come to him immediately. Then he got it: Merle. And the boy Mason, both taken by the influenza. Looking about, he realized that the cot, the bureau, the wash basin, they all must have belonged to Merle, and had been moved up here after she died.

Slowly, Kincaid reached out and placed his hand around the end of the axe handle. It was wedged in there tight, and rigor mortis had locked down Harlan's muscles so there was no give in his neck or shoulders.

Kincaid took his hand off the axe.

•

Downstairs he found Lyle and Hannah seated on dining room chairs at the end of the bed in the room off the parlor. Estelle lay back against the pillows, pressing a handkerchief to her watery eyes.

"I wouldn't mind that cup of coffee now," Kincaid said to Hannah.

"I'm brewing a fresh pot. Be just a few minutes."

After she left, he went to the window and looked out at the fields. "You found him, Lyle?"

"Just like he is now. And then I went up the road to our place and called it in."

"Who's living up in the attic?" Kincaid asked. When Estelle didn't answer immediately, he turned around. She had her arm extended as she said to Lyle, "Reach me those papers on the stationary."

Lyle went to the desk and picked up an envelope. When he offered them to her, Estelle motioned toward Kincaid. Lyle came around the bed and handed him the envelope.

"Two children," Estelle said. "We took two orphans off one of those trains that come out from the east. Boy and a girl." She looked up at Kincaid, saucer-eyed. "So many of us lost kin to the influenza. I expect you understand, Captain." Looking away, she added, "What information we got's in those papers they gave us at the station."

"Who slept in the attic?"

"The girl. And the boy out in the shed off the kitchen." She closed her eyes, exhausted. "Both lit out."

"Together?"

"How'm I supposed to know?"

"So, while you were up in Lansing Harlan was here alone with the two of them." Kincaid looked at Lyle, who seemed to know where this was going. "And he was up in the attic where the girl stayed."

"I know what state he was in," Estelle said. "Lyle told me. He was into the liquor, that hooch the Dingley brothers make in their still somewhere out there in the woods. I knew he would get into that while I was in the hospital. The girl, she lured him up there." She turned her head away, and hissed, "I knew that little black bitch would be trouble."

"She's a Negro?"

Estelle turned her head on the pillow. "Half. That makes it even worse, you ask me. She's got this reddish hair, broad nose, and those lips. And her eyes. Light. I tell you it's ungodly. But we gave her an opportunity. Nobody wanted her, and we got her off that train."

"And the boy, he's—"

"A damn cripple," Estelle said. "Missing fingers so one hand's a might useless."

"He black?"

"No, no. He looks like one of those Irish lads. They breed them by the dozen and most of them end up in an orphanage. According to those papers, both of them from Catholic orphanages."

"You can send 'em all back to Ireland," Lyle said, "and the darkies can stay down south."

Hannah came in with a cup of coffee that rattled on its saucer. Out the window Kincaid watched Milt turn the Chevrolet into the yard. Some days he thought the best part of his job was having use of that machine.

"Thanks all the same, Hannah," Kincaid said, "but I'm going to have to move on. Doc Evers will be out here shortly. He'll make the necessary arrangements. I am sorry for your loss, Estelle, and hope you're feeling better soon."

"They won't get far, will they?" Estelle said. "Couple a kids looking like that, on the lam in Michigan?"

Since becoming police chief, Kincaid had learned not to make promises. "Hard to say."

Four

E arly November. Vapors lifted off the frosted ground, the mud-bound roads shrouded in fog and shallow dawn light. Mercy kept to the trees, where she could hide from wagons or those Ford jalopies that banged over ruts and potholes. Angry crows wheeled overhead, assaying her passage. Deer, grazing in the corn slash, fled at the sight of her.

Always, insatiable thirst, an eternal hunger. And the chill air, hard and constant. She'd been cold ever since she arrived in Michigan. Since leaving Nau Farm she'd slept in barns and outbuildings, bedding down on straw or horse blankets, alive with bugs and skittish rodents. Exhausted, she fell asleep to the sound of teeth gnawing in sacks of grain or boring into wood. She ate oats from a feed bag, carrots spilled from a slop bucket. She pilfered eggs from a coop, slipping through the shadows so quietly the hens weren't alarmed.

Two days after running from Otter Creek, Mercy came to a town in the early evening. She kept to the back alleys until she found a train depot, empty and warm. She lay down on a pew, the smell of oak reminding her of church services at the orphanage in Worcester. Pulled her coat about her and slept. In the early morning she discovered a lunch pail under a bench, left behind by a conductor or a member of the track crews. She ate the half sandwich, ham on a crusty rye bread with a sharp horse radish mustard, while staring at the map of Michigan on the wall. The Lower Peninsula was shaped like a hand, or a mitten. At the very top, across a narrow band of water called the Mackinac Straits was St. Ignace in the Upper Peninsula.

At dawn, she went out on the platform, beneath a sign that read *Ovid*. She had no idea where this was, wondered if the sign was a misprint. Wasn't Ovid an ancient poet? She only knew she was in the Lower Peninsula, and she needed to head north to the Upper Peninsula. She walked the tracks, her boots slippery on dew-covered ties that smelled of creosote. As the sun rose above the trees to her right, she had found her bearings: north.

She carried nothing. Her dress, torn at the shoulder, was held together by too few buttons and a safety pin. She kept the letter in the inside pocket of her overcoat. She'd had it since she wasn't quite twelve, since the night she had stolen into the main office of the orphanage. There was a cabinet behind Sister Marie's desk that contained the files, one for each of the children. By candlelight, Mercy found her file and opened the folder. Her mother was Louisa Mae du Casse, who on August 4, 1907, gave birth to a daughter in The Home for Women of Faith, Framingham, Massachusetts. Named Mercy by the nuns, the child was first housed in an orphanage in Boston—she didn't remember it—and over the course of several years there followed a series of transfers.

Lumbering footsteps echoed out in the corridor. She could tell it was Mr. Mills, the janitor, who lived in the basement of the orphanage, making his nightly rounds. He had a flashlight, its beam splintered on the frosted glass in the office door. Mercy glanced down the page in her file but only saw medical history. A tooth. Tonsils. Measles. Inoculations. As the footsteps approached, she blew out the candle. She had marked the place in the file drawer with a pencil from Sister Marie's desk. As she slid the folder back into the drawer, something fell on the floor. She picked it up, an envelope. Tucking it in the pocket of her jumper, she pushed the drawer back into the cabinet slowly, removing the pencil just before the latch clicked shut. She put the pencil on Sister Marie's ink blotter and crouched down so she could crawl under the desk, waiting until Mr. Mills's slow footsteps passed down the corridor and around the corner leading to the east wing.

The envelope contained a letter from her aunt, written by a Catholic priest in Michigan. Always there was the expectation that she would be called to Sister Marie's office and questioned about a letter missing from her file. But Sister Marie never called her, not for that. Infractions, warnings, reprimands, yes, but the letter, no. Once the sister concluded, "You've been moved around so much, but you don't fit in anywhere, not with the whites or the coloreds. And you're quietly defiant. The most dangerous sort." Perhaps she'd forgotten that the letter had been placed in Mercy's file. Perhaps there were so many such letters that if one had gone missing it would not be noticed.

When she heard a train approaching behind her, Mercy climbed up the embankment and into the woods. The Michigan Central train seemed eternal. Box cars bound, she imagined, for Canada. Flat cars piled with tree trunks. She sat on a rock in the woods, listening to the clatter of the passing train, and took the envelope from the inside pocket of her overcoat. When she wanted to know who she was, she read the letter. When she wanted to remind herself why she'd agreed to board that orphan train, why she wanted to come to Michigan, she read the letter. She had read it countless times since that night in Sister Marie's office, so many times that she knew it by heart. She didn't really read the letter now, but she loved to look at the script. It was like gazing at a work of art. She felt that she could see her aunt sitting at a table, dictating the letter to Father John Nolan. He had a beautiful hand. Mercy had been taught the Palmer Penmanship Method by the nuns, but she had never acquired such grace. Father Nolan's ovals were perfect, and throughout the letter there were small flourishes—tails and squiggles to the capital letters—that lent elegance to the words.

After the train had passed, she folded the letter carefully and slipped it back into the envelope, which was coming apart at the corners. Around her, the silence of the woods was not really silence. There were rustlings and movement amid the brush. Maple leaves drifted down, tapping gently on those already covering the ground. Occasionally, there was the sound of the wind as it passed through the needles high in the pine trees.

She got up off the rock and walked to the top of the embankment. Looking left and right, she saw no movement. She concentrated on the tracks leading back toward the station in Ovid. There was nothing, only a few crows pecking at the gravel bed beneath the railroad ties. But Mercy sensed it again. There was someone back there. Someone was following her. She must keep going, moving north.

She descended the embankment and resumed her course along the rails. How far could it be from Ovid to St. Ignace in the Upper Peninsula? Why did Sister Marie put the letter in the file cabinet and never respond to Mercy's aunt? And

Mercy's letters. Twice she had written to Father Nolan at St. Mary's Church, asking him to inform her Aunt Andrea that she was there in Worcester, that she was waiting for something to happen, whatever it was, a miracle, perhaps, that would bring about her release so she could go and live in the place called St. Ignace. She had studied the map of Michigan in the library's atlas, the two peninsulas, surrounded by the lakes, divided by the Mackinac Straits. Could she swim across to St. Ignace, a holy place, named after a saint? But there was no response to her letters. Months passed, years passed, and there was no mail from Michigan.

Mercy turned around quickly, peering back down the tracks.

There was nothing. No one. Just crows.

•

The trick was to not let on. Milt Waters despised the man. Three years earlier, when he had learned that the town council was interviewing James Kincaid for the position of sheriff, Milt saw how it would go down: they would take the job Milt had been in line for and give it to this outsider Kincaid. He was a veteran, serving in France during the war. After returning to Michigan, he had married a local girl, Allison DeVries, who had been a couple of years ahead of Milt in school. Daughter of a county judge. That's the way it works.

But things don't work out the way they're planned. In three years, a lot had changed since Kincaid joined the force. Death, divorce, you name it. But the one constant was the search for stills. The Dingley brothers produced much of the whiskey in the county. Sometimes Kincaid and Milt would find one of their operations and shut them down, but soon another would crop up elsewhere.

The morning after they had examined the murder scene at Nau Farm, Kincaid and Milt were driving out south of town to see about a still that was reported to be operating in the woods. It was the Dingley's still no doubt. Milt took pride in providing the insider's perspective, and he was going on about competition between various bootleg operations in Detroit and Chicago, and then about how the Ku Klux Klan was making its way up into Michigan from Indiana, when Kincaid raised his hand off his knee, indicating that he wanted Milt to stop talking.

Kincaid said, "I prefer that you refrain from using those words while on duty."

"What words?" Milt said. "Oh. Those words. Well, what would you have me call those people?"

In his patient, even manner, Kincaid said, "I fought in the war with some of those people."

Milt attempted a laugh. "France is thankful for that. Did they send them—those people—back here? Or maybe they liked 'em so much they decided to keep them there in Paris."

Kincaid was staring at him now.

That's how it was with Kincaid: *I would prefer that you refrain.* He often used words—refrain—that Milt found offensive. "So tell me, Captain, what words would you prefer?"

"They are Negroes. They are Jews. They are Catholics. Are they not?"

"Well, yeah." Milt navigated the car around a particularly threatening looking pothole. "But you don't go around calling people like you and me Caucasians, do you?"

Kincaid had a hand on each knee. His trousers were freshly pressed, his hands were large. He was a big man, tall and fit. Fit. That was the word the town council used: Kincaid was a very fit candidate for the job.

They drove the rest of the way in silence.

And found evidence of the still up in the woods south of town. Abandoned.

As they walked back to the Chevrolet, Kincaid mused, "Perhaps Owen and Mink Dingley knew we were coming, and they packed up what they could and lit out. Wonder if someone tipped them off."

Milt kept his mouth shut.

"Any ideas?" Kincaid was not one to let a thing go. "Someone who might know we were going to ride out here informed them of our intentions. You were raised here. You know these people. What do you think, Milt?"

"No one comes to mind."

Kincaid took this with one of his lengthy silences.

Halfway back to the station, Milt couldn't stand it any longer, and said, "Car's due for an oil change."

Kincaid might not have heard him. He continued to stare out at the passing woods, until he seemed to come up out of some place deep and thoughtful, and said, "Where do you take it, Lyle Nesbit's garage?"

"That's the one." Like there were a dozen to choose from.

Kincaid thought about this awhile. "Fine."

"Now? It might take a while. I could drop you off at the station first."

Kincaid lifted a hand off his knee again, as though weighing his options carefully. "No, let's go. I can always walk over to the office, it's only a few blocks."

Milt glanced at Kincaid, who continued straight ahead with the concentration of a bird dog. Then, turning at the next corner, he pulled up to Nesbit's Garage and Livery.

Lyle Nesbit was shoeing a bay gelding. Milt's father had been a farrier, and he always loved the sound of a nail being driven into a horse's hoof. Wasn't the same sound as wood. It was hard, but a living thing, a hoof. When Lyle released the horse's leg, he couldn't quite conceal his surprise at seeing Kincaid with Milt.

"This an arrest?" he said.

"Depends on what you charge for an oil change," Milt said, backing it up with a chuckle.

Kincaid didn't smile. He looked around the shop, as though he'd never seen one before.

Lyle went to the door to the office, and said, "Billy, pull the Chevrolet into bay two and change the oil. Check the radiator, the tires, the works."

"How's your sister-in-law fairing?" Kincaid asked.

"Ain't been easy," Lyle said, removing his farrier's apron, the pockets weighted with tools. "The operation and all. Hannah's over there with her most of the time."

Kincaid stared across the street. "Good that she has family at a time like this." He didn't speak for a bit, long enough that Milt and Lyle exchanged glances. "It's one of the reasons why we came here, family."

There was a silence, until Lyle said, "Blood relations is everything. Got to stick to your own kind."

Kincaid turned to him, as though he didn't understand what had just been said, but then he seemed to let it go. "How long will it take?"

"What, the car?" Lyle asked. "Oh, Billy will have her done in no time. Half hour, forty minutes."

Kincaid looked across the street again. He watched a man come out of the Van Nal's tailor's shop buttoning up an overcoat. "Well, then I think I'll go back to the office and do some paperwork."

"I'll bring the car back as soon as possible." Milt spoke a little too hastily.

Kincaid didn't seem to notice, still concentrating on the shop across the street. He turned up his coat collar and left the garage. Lyle produced a pack of

Luckies, and he and Milt both smoked as they watched the captain walk down the sidewalk and turn the corner.

"Think he knows?" Lyle asked.

"He was suspicious. You warned the Dingleys?"

Lyle nodded.

"Kincaid's something else, I tell you."

"The way he was eyeing Van Nal's," Lyle said. "Think he's figured it out?"

"Hard to know what that man knows," Milt said.

Lyle went to the workbench at the back of the garage. "Well, here, let me change your oil." He reached up to a shelf, moved aside some cans, and took down a brown bottle. There were several coffee mugs on the bench. He poured whiskey into two of them and came back to Milt, who was running his hand along the horse's flank. Handing one of the mugs to him, Lyle said, "Owen and Mink Dingley are making a killing with this stuff."

Milt took a sip from the mug, and gasped. Lyle laughed.

In a hoarse voice, Milt said, "Our police chief objects to kikes being called kikes, and he has a rare appreciation for coloreds. He seems particularly fond of crossbacks—oh, I mean Catholics."

"How do you know?"

"Told me I ought to refrain from using certain words, at least while on duty," Milt said. "I heard him this morning on the telephone with the state police about that girl and boy out to Nau Farm. He doesn't think they're doing enough. You and me know they got better things to do."

"Like track down bootleggers and confiscate their booze so they can resell it."

"Right. Both kids, orphans. Most of those orphanages back east, you know, they're run by Catholics or Jews, and they think they can just get rid of them by shipping them out here. He describes the girl as mulatta, never uses any other word. Says they're under suspicion and need to be apprehended. See, that's your difference right there: he wants to apprehend these two kids, and I want to catch them." Milt braced himself and downed his slug of whiskey. "Jesus," his voice barely a whisper. "Catholics. Jews. Mulattas."

"Whatever you call 'em," Lyle said taking Milt's empty mug and placing it on the workbench, "we can't let 'em going around burying an axe in no white man's skull in his own house."

Five

Rope lost sight of Mercy when the train came through, so he sat up on the embankment, watching the sun rise over a field of corn slash. After the train finally passed, he saw her descend the embankment farther along the tracks. She was heading north. Something determined about the way she went about it, like she had a destination in mind. Fog hovered over the land and after about a hundred yards he lost sight of her. He'd give it some time before he'd follow her.

When he'd climbed up into the attic, he couldn't see clearly in the candlelight. He heard rapid, frantic breathing and, as his eyes adjusted to the faint light, he saw them on the cot. Harlan's overalls were bunched around his ankles, and he was on top of her, driven by a relentless urgency. Her dress appeared to be torn, exposing a breast, and her leg was cocked so that the skirt was up around her hip. The rise and fall of her thigh reminded Rope of a horseback rider, but her leg kicked not in union with Harlan's thrusting backside but in resistance as her hands repeatedly slapped his face and shoulders.

Harlan stopped abruptly and turned his head to look at Rope. "The hell you got there?"

"You get off her."

"You get on outta here."

"Get off her."

Harlan began the process of disentangling himself from Mercy, who pushed him away. "Hear what I said?" Harlan managed to stand, naked from the waist down.

He took a step toward Rope, but his feet were caught in his overalls, and he fell to his knees. As Rope lifted the axe with his left hand, raising it above his head, Harlan gazed up at him. To Rope's surprise, the man appeared relieved, as though he'd been anticipating this moment for a long time. Now he almost seemed grateful that it had finally arrived.

•

Ahead in the ground fog, Mercy spied a shack in the woods, with old railroad ties stacked against the wall. She went around to the bushes behind it, unbuttoned her overcoat so she could hold her dress aside as she squatted to urinate. The morning air was cold and damp. She was wearing nothing under her dress and she could see goosebumps on her bruised knees.

When she finished, she heard the footsteps on the railroad gravel. She remained still, crouched behind the bushes. The fog was burning off in the sun, but there were still horizontal rags of smoke drifting above the tracks. At first it looked like half a man walking past the shack, just legs below the fog, and then she saw the rest of him.

Rope.

Mercy wanted to stand up and call him out, shout at him, tell him to go away, leave her be, quit following her. But she remained concealed behind the bush, watching him continue along the tracks.

•

The morning fog had burned off. Ahead, Rope couldn't see any movement on the tracks. Maybe she'd gone up into the trees in search of a town. But there were no houses, no buildings on the horizon, only fields and trees, and the occasional distant silo. He stopped walking, thinking he should go back. Maybe he'd gotten ahead of her.

He turned around, and there she was, some fifty yards behind him. Walking on the ties, kicking gravel as she walked straight for him, her hands stuffed in the pockets of her overcoat.

"What you want?" she said. Before he could answer, she nearly shouted, "What you following me for?"

"I just . . ." But words didn't come. He'd always been plagued by the inability to find the words at the right moment.

She stopped in front of him, her green eyes bright with anger. "You keep away, hear?" She took a step forward, forcing him to back pedal.

"I just . . ."

"You just keep *away!*"

Her leg came out, swift and forceful. She kicked him just once, and that was all it took. He was lying on the ties, curled up, holding himself, the pain radiating from the very center of his being. She walked on, her feet crunching gravel.

•

Kincaid took the call at his desk.

"Sergeant Pease here, up in Kalkaska. I understand you're looking for a black girl and a white boy. Something about a murder down your way."

"We had a homicide here, yes, Sergeant."

"One of our troopers stopped to help a trucker who was stuck in mud—this time of year our roads are something terrible. He says there was a girl in the truck. He didn't think anything of it until he came into the office and saw the bulletin we posted. Said she had reddish hair. Didn't get a good look at her, but he believed she wasn't entirely white."

"The trucker say anything about her?"

"Nope. Could have been his daughter, though in retrospect he didn't think that was likely. Earl's a good fellow but sometimes it takes a moment for him to fit two and two together. Probably a hitchhiker, he figured after the fact."

"What direction was the truck heading?"

"North."

"Where was this, exactly."

"Oh, a few miles outside Kalkaska, on the way up to Bird Lake. Earl and the girl pushed the truck until the driver managed to get out of the mud. Then she climbed back in, and they went on their way. Earl said the truck bed was stacked with wooden crates."

"The girl, she had reddish hair."

"Sorta frizzy, yeah."

"I see." Kincaid waited but the sergeant didn't add anything else. "Any print or signage on the truck?"

"Nope. But then Earl's not the most observant set of eyes, either." The sergeant waited, and when Kincaid didn't come back with another question, he chuckled and said, "Axe murder, I hear. Haven't had one of those in a while. The girl's name isn't Borden, is it?"

Kincaid wanted to ask if the sergeant had ever seen the victim of an axe murder. But he just said, "No."

"Well, that's all I got. Hope it helps."

"It does, Sergeant Pease. Thanks for your call. And let me know if you hear anything else."

•

Milt leaned against the door jamb to the coffee room as he watched Kincaid take the phone call. There was an efficiency even in the way the man sat at his desk. Straight up, no slouch. Always at the ready. When he first started talking to the caller, he jotted something on a notepad, but then he put the pencil down and never bothered to write anything else. It was hard to distinguish between his expression of tolerant indifference and keen interest, but the tautness in his posture reminded Milt of a well-trained hunting dog.

After hanging up, Kincaid left his desk and went to the bulletin board on the wall. Above the board were official portraits of Michigan governor Alex Groesbeck and President Calvin Coolidge. They both looked like bank executives. Kincaid, hands on his hips, stood before the map of Michigan.

Milt gave it a moment. He poured a second mug of coffee—he knew Kincaid liked his black no sugar (he was fit)—and then ambled over to the bulletin board. Kincaid accepted the mug of black with a nod as he studied the state map.

"Planning a trip?" Milt asked.

Kincaid sipped his coffee. Same as when he was on the phone: no difference in his expression. Good coffee, bad coffee, too hot, too cold, didn't make a dent. "You could take care of things here for a few days."

"I could hold the fort down."

Kincaid glanced at him. Perhaps he'd sounded sarcastic. Best to double-down. "If Ohio invades," Milt said, "I'll be the last man standing."

"Look, Waters, I know how you feel, really. You thought you were in line for this job." Now he turned to Milt, his eyes genuinely sympathetic. "I understand that. We all have our disappointments. In the army, I felt I was due a promotion sooner than it happened, but eventually I became captain. Such disappointments—" he paused, rethinking how he was going to address this. "It's what you do with them. It's how you respond. That's the true measure."

"The true measure," Milt said.

"You can look after things while I'm gone," Kincaid said. It was as though he was giving a kind of benediction. Milt might have bowed his head or genuflected like some Papist, some crossback.

Kincaid was not a man to dwell. Said what he had to say. He turned back to the map.

"Where you headed?" Milt asked.

"North. Other than that, I'm not sure. Haven't been up there in years."

"The roads are bad everywhere in Michigan. We build cars here, so you'd think the roads would be better." Kincaid continued to stare at the map, his thoughts elsewhere. "You're going looking for those kids? Can't leave it to the state police, that's for sure." He waited, but still Kincaid gave no reaction. "We can't let axe murderers just run off, can we?"

"Alleged."

Milt was about to take a sip from his coffee mug, but this gave him pause. "You don't think they did it?"

"We don't know who did what. That's why we need to find them."

Something moved around in Milt's mind that he knew he ought to control. That ferret-like impulse, the one that had been getting him in trouble all his life. "Right. The process of the law." Sarcasm, no question. "Give 'em court-appointed lawyers on the taxpayers' dime, who cook up all sorts of alibis and excuses. They're young. They're orphans. Lord knows what these poor children have been through. Run this by a jury of twelve citizens, appeal to them as mothers and fathers. Get 'em off with a slap on the wrist, which for the boy will be really light seeing that he's got but the one good hand."

"Evidence will be examined and presented in court," Kincaid said evenly. "Witnesses will be called. That's the way it works, yes."

"Evidence? That boy buried that axe yay-deep in Harlan's skull, then he and the girl ran for it." Milt waited. "Unless you think the girl did the deed. I wouldn't put it past that little n—oh, sorry, the Negro."

"We have a bloody axe handle," Kincaid said. "No fingerprints, just smeared blood."

"Fingerprints," Milt said in disgust. "There's another of your new ideas that's only going to help a lawyer get some guilty defendant off."

"Not in this case," Kincaid said. "Neither the boy nor the girl have fingerprints on record."

"Why would anyone fingerprint an orphan? They come out here on a train to find a home. Harlan and Estelle take 'em in and look what the thanks they get. You been out to the farm lately?"

"No, I haven't."

"I have," Milt said. "Estelle's in a state. Between Harlan's death and the operation where they cut out what's left of her womb, I don't know if she's going to survive it all. Far as I'm concerned, we may be looking at a double homicide. Does the court ever consider that? What a violent crime does to the victim's family?"

"I'm sorry to hear about Estelle."

"Yeah, well don't go talking about the process of the law around her. Or Lyle and her sister Hannah."

"You have a better method?"

"I do. Track 'em down and string 'em up. Right then and there. It's called an example, one that's instructive, one that just might keep someone else from wielding an axe."

Kincaid put his mug of coffee on top of the file cabinet in the corner. He hadn't taken one sip, as though he knew it would be bitter and cold. "Our job is to find those kids, not try and punish them. Finding them is not going to happen by sitting here waiting for the phone to ring."

Milt nodded toward the map on the wall. "So, you're gonna run around in Michigan's great northern wilderness, looking for them. The state police, they supposed to do that." He shook his head. "No, you got a point there. They won't do much. They're too busy tracking down bootleggers—that's where the money is, if you know what I mean."

Kincaid gave it a moment. "As I said, Milt, I'll be gone a few days." He started to move.

"I was them, I'd get myself across the border into Canada."

Kincaid hesitated. "That's a fair assumption."

"What you don't know is if they're smart enough to make a fair assumption." Kincaid nodded, giving Milt that even stare. "I know how to find 'em."

"Do you now?"

"I do. And how to deal with 'em."

"I see." Kincaid studied him a moment. Taking the true measure. Let him, damn it. "I'm going home to pack." He began to walk back to his desk.

•

Ellie Landis, the police department secretary, habitually went outside the station for a cigarette at three o'clock. She could smoke at her desk, but at that point in the day, with another hour and a half to go, she maintained that she needed to get outside those four walls, regardless of the weather.

Milt was returning to his desk when the captain's phone rang. Something about telephones Milt still didn't trust. He didn't get how a voice coming from miles away could squeeze through that little wire. He lifted the receiver, leaned forward, and spoked loudly into the mouthpiece. "Otter Creek Police."

"This is Sergeant Pease. Is Captain Kincaid there?"

"No. He's out of the office. This is Deputy Waters. I can leave a message."

"All right. Tell the captain that after our conversation earlier I had another chat with the trooper who helped that trucker out."

"Yes, sure. This was up in . . ."

"Kalkaska."

"Of course. What did the trooper say?"

"Well, he remembered something. The captain had asked if there was any writing on the truck. Nothing on the truck but the trooper remembered some crates. They were stamped Mackinaw Fish Supply."

"Uh-huh. That's Mackinaw, spelled with a w, not a c. I never understood why you have the two spellings."

"Yes," Pease said. "Mackinaw, with the w, not the island."

Milt wrote it down on the captain's notepad: *Mackinaw Fish Supply.*

"Don't know if that'll help Captain Kincaid but I thought I should pass it along."

"The captain will be glad to have this, really. Thanks, Sergeant Pease."

"Don't mention it."

As he hung the receiver in the hook, Milt looked out the front window again. Ellie must weigh close to two hundred pounds now. She never wore a coat when she went out for her three o'clock cigarette. Always complaining about being too hot, even on cold days when the station windows were rattled by gusting wind and snow, and the drafty air passing through the room could flutter paper lying on a desk.

Milt tore the top page off Kincaid's notepad, balled it up and, as he walked back to his desk, tossed it into his wastebasket. "I won't," he said.

•

They ate dinner in the kitchen. Now that it was just the two of them, Kincaid's mother-in-law rarely set their places in the dining room. Lois DeVries's culinary efforts were consistently plain and substantial. Ham, baked potatoes, peas, biscuits. There was only the sound of their cutlery on their plates, the wall clock ticking above the sink. When he started the job as police chief, he and Allison moved into her parents' home and began looking for a house of their own. When they learned that Allison was pregnant, the house search was postponed until after the baby was born. When Allison came down with a severe case of the influenza, the house she grew up in was like a hospital ward, until she died, two months before the baby was due. The loss of his daughter, their only child, enfeebled Judge DeVries, whose health was already fragile, and for the next few months Lois nursed him until he died of what Doc Evers determined was pneumonia. He told Lois he could not in good conscience write *A broken heart* on the death certificate. Kincaid considered getting a place of his own, and at times he thought it might be best if he sought work in law enforcement elsewhere. But a fresh start didn't feel right; more to the point, it didn't feel possible. And Lois would be left alone in the family home, with her plain and substantial meals. It had been this way for going on three years.

Now, buttering a second biscuit, Kincaid thought she was waiting. Somehow, she knew. She could sense these things. Allison had been the same way. When he put down the butter knife, he said, "I have to go out of town tomorrow. Need to drive up north."

"Where?"

"I don't know exactly. I might be a few days."

"This about those orphans?"

He nodded.

"In town, it's all anybody talks about." Her voice, hollowed out from smoking Pall Malls for decades, was dry yet musical, until it often deteriorated into a hacking cough. "An axe murder? In Otter Creek? It's fear. They're afraid. There's always been this fear of outsiders. Strangers."

"I know."

"You're an outsider. You, the police chief."

"I'm reminded every day."

Since the loss of her husband and daughter, she seemed to wither, lost in her outfits, this evening a cable sweater and a gray flannel skirt. She was the kind of woman people had often referred to as vivacious, but now her face that had gone haggard and slack. "Fortunately, there are enough people around here who saw who you are, what you are, and had the nerve to say we need that here. And it brought my daughter back home. But it's more than fear. There's something else here, something that's pushing them. I don't know. Hatred? Two kids. Teenagers. They came on a train from the east. No family. Nothing. Where do all these orphans come from? Prostitutes, some. But also unwanted children, for whatever reason. I have to admit I feel some anger toward the parents, whoever they are. How could they let this happen, their child abandoned, raised in some institution, and then carted across the country and auctioned off like that?" She looked at him, her blue eyes hard now. "I saw it once, you know. Last fall I went down to the station when one of these trains came through. They line the children up on the platform, and couples look them over like . . ." She looked away, shaking her head.

"I need to find them," he said.

Lois gazed toward the corner of the kitchen as though noticing something most people overlook, something essential. "Yes. That's your job. But if you find them, and you bring them back here, what then?"

He shrugged. "It's out of my hands."

"That's what I'm afraid of." She leaned toward him now, speaking quietly. "That's what we are afraid of. What this, this thing will do. You go up north and bring those children back here, you really believe they'll get justice? Even the Judge, who had utter faith in the courts and the rule of law and the wisdom of a jury of your peers, even he would have doubts. There are crimes of passion, he would say. But what was done to Harlan Nau is something else entirely."

"You can't let them go free."

"No, I suppose you can't. But don't call it justice."

One small piece of ham remained on his plate. He stared at it. They didn't speak, for how long he did not know, the silence fathomless and inescapable.

"So." Finally, her voice broke through, quiet, resigned. "You leave in the morning. You'll want to pack a few shirts. Suitcase or your old army rucksack?" She already knew the answer. "Rucksack."

2
North

Six

Dusk. Long shadows of trees darken the tracks. Rope lay on the gravel bed, curled around the pain. When he heard the train approaching, he managed to get to his knees. The engine's headlight gleamed off the rails as the whistle sounded twice, followed by one long ireful blast.

He struggled to his feet, though he couldn't stand up straight, and he managed to hobble down the gravel embankment. There is nothing like a train, the noise, the force of its passing. He crouched and inhaled deeply. If anything, the train was a distraction from the pain.

After it passed, Rope began to walk, watching the caboose disappear around the bend. The first mile or so he would have to pause and wait out a spike of pain. Once, he stopped at a bush, thinking he needed to vomit, but nothing came up. There wasn't anything to come up. The last thing he recalled eating was a bruised apple, found on the ground outside Ovid, the last town he walked through, where he'd caught sight of Mercy as she came out of the train station.

He kept walking. He had no choice. It seemed to help and after several miles the pain became more confined, whereas at first it seemed to radiate up through him. Occasionally, he'd look around to see if another train was coming, but the tracks were clear. He imagined a slow-moving train. He imagined hopping a boxcar and riding the train wherever it would go. He imagined, with luck, the train returning to Massachusetts, where he would drop down off the boxcar within sight of the Merrimack River. He would walk, straight up by then, crossing the bridge between Bradford and Haverhill, and then descend into the cavernous streets beneath the brick factory buildings. On Essex Street there was a bakery, and the smell of fresh bread would lure him inside, as it had many a day as he walked to work. He could go in the store because he had a few coins in his pocket and when he would place a nickel on the glass counter the woman in the white apron and cap would bag two rolls, their warmth coming through the paper bag in his fist. Throughout this transaction she spoke Italian to the man, also wearing an apron and cap, who could be seen in the back room. He was her son, or maybe a nephew—it didn't matter, everyone who worked in the bakery was family. They stocked the shelves, worked the big ovens, and handled bread using large wooden paddles. The woman behind the counter was warm and soft, like the bread, and sometimes, if he said *Grazie*, she'd smile and say *Prego*. He imagined her calling out to him as he reached the door, and saying to him, *After your shift, you come back, okay? You come upstairs and stay for supper. We have a nice spaghetti tonight, with tomato and basil, alio, and parmesan. You come, we eat, okay? Now vai, vai, don't be late for your shift.* And he would eat one roll as he walked around the corner to the entrance of the factory, finding it difficult to save the other roll for his lunch break, and throughout the day the work would go well, no problems, no foreman shouting at him, the hours like boxcars racing by, until the shift whistle would sound, he would punch out, go back around the corner, and climb the flight of stairs to the apartment above the bakery, where he would sit at the table with the family. He would not understand much of what they were saying, but it didn't matter because they were laughing and smiling, and the woman, who now smelled like tomato, basil, and parmesan, kept replenishing his plate with piles of steaming spaghetti.

But there was no slow-moving train that would take him back to Haverhill. Only these tracks that seemed to run endlessly through woods and fields. The air was so raw he could see his breath, and it smelled like snow. As he walked, he stood up straighter, and by nightfall the pain was a faint memory.

He left the tracks and stood on the roadside. When a car or a truck approached, he stuck out his left thumb, reaching across his body, hitching with his good hand. When people stopped to pick him up and asked where he was headed, he simply said, "North." As he moved north, as the hours passed, time seemed measured in how the air was getting colder, how the sky and the land seemed to lose color, how the world became shades of gray.

Finally, a long ride with an elderly man and his wife who talked constantly about their children and grandchildren, until they pulled over, saying they were turning west here. He thanked them and got out of the automobile, which struggled at the turn in the road, where ice had formed in deep mudholes. Up ahead he could see a town clustered around two church steeples on land so flat he had to walk a good mile before he reached the first houses. People came and went from the stores, bags and packages in hand. Horse-drawn wagons and machines passed slowly in the street. Out of habit, Rope kept both hands shoved in the pockets of his coat. It wasn't that people didn't notice him but that they didn't see him. He was invisible, and he did not know the name of this town somewhere in Michigan where it was beginning to snow.

At the next corner he looked to his right and saw a Ford Huckster backed up to the warehouse. A man finished stacking the last crate and slammed shut the tailgate to the truck bed. He climbed in behind the steering wheel, and as he turned out into the street the Model T engine reverberated off the warehouse brick. The man smoked a cigar and wore a hat with the earflaps down. He was speaking to Mercy, sitting next to him in the cab. As the truck passed by, she looked out at Rope for a moment, and then she turned her head away.

The crates in the truck bed were all stamped *Mackinaw Fish Supply*.

·

As Kincaid drove north the roads, like the weather, became worse. Sleet, mud, and ice. Wind gusts rocked the Chevrolet, and the roads were strewn with stranded cars, trucks, and horse-drawn wagons. He'd stopped twice to help someone out of a frozen, muddy culvert. He considered turning back and had to remind himself that his task was to track down two adolescents on the run. He was out of his jurisdiction. The state police could take this on. But they wouldn't, not the way he would—the murder had taken place in his town. He could not sit in Otter Creek and wait, hoping for a call from a trooper about two orphans who fit the description that had been issued throughout the state of Michigan. And there was something else: being the lone hunter suited him. Out here, on the trail, one might find uncertainty but also possibility. He stopped for the night at the Osceola Hotel in Reed City.

In the morning, he had steak and eggs for breakfast and read a three-day old edition of the *Lansing State Journal*. Out the front windows he observed the passage of two trucks. Men, women, and children were crowded in the back of each vehicle, tattered coats drawn tight against the cold.

"Migrants," the waitress said, arriving at Kincaid's table with the coffee pot. A plump girl in her teens with buck teeth. "Heading back, now that harvest is done."

Kincaid put his hand over his cup. "Three's good, thanks. Back where?"

With a shrug she said, "South? Alabama, Mississippi? Mexico?"

Another truck rumbled down the street, so full that some of the passengers in back only had room to stand, clutching the wood slats that fenced them in.

"Where do they stay when they're up here?" Kincaid asked.

"There are camps outside town. Depends on the farm, the crops. Some stay through the winter, if they can catch on to a job. Day work, or the processing plants when they're going full tilt." She smiled. "Anything else?"

"No, thanks." As she placed his receipt on the table, he said, "Well, I do have a question. An Exalted Cyclops. Do you know what that is?"

"A what?"

Kincaid gestured toward the newspaper next to his coffee cup. "He's quoted in this article."

"Cyclops. Doesn't he have one eye?"

"In mythology, yes."

She glanced at the paper, wary. "What does he say?"

Kincaid took out his billfold and handed the girl a dollar. "That the aliens are here in our midst, and we must be vigilant." She was perturbed, as though she'd never seen a dollar bill before, or perhaps wasn't sure what vigilant meant. Getting up from his chair, he said, "That was a fine breakfast. Please, keep the change."

He went to the front desk. After settling his bill, he crossed the lobby to the phone booth. When he closed the folded door, the confined air smelled of cigarettes. During the war he smoked almost constantly, but since returning home he had desperately tried to avoid them. He put a call through to the Kalkaska police and asked for Sergeant Pease, who was not a man to exchange pleasantries.

"You're on the way to Mackinaw City?"

"Excuse me?" Kincaid said.

"You got my message?" Pease said. "From your deputy."

"I haven't spoken to him, no. What about Mackinaw City?"

"Well. That girl you're looking for. She found a ride with a trucker, as I told you yesterday. I called back and told your deputy that my trooper here remembered something about the truck. There were crates in the bed. They were stamped, the name of some outfit called Mackinaw Fish Supply."

"You told Waters? Yesterday."

"That's right. I called back not long after you and I talked on the phone. He said you were out, but he would pass this information on. Maybe he couldn't reach you?"

"Thank you, sergeant. Thank you again."

Kincaid sat in the phone booth, thinking about Milt Waters, his veiled resentment. He realized that since leaving Otter Creek he'd also been haunted by his mother-in-law's tired, acrimonious eyes as he left the house. Being out on these roads heading north, being in pursuit, it was a welcome form of deliverance.

He left the phone booth, slinging his rucksack over his shoulder, and walked out the front door of the hotel. There had been sun early in the morning, the hard, angled light of November, but now there were lowering clouds bringing a cold wind that smelled like snow.

•

Milt was so hungover in the morning that the sunlit frost seemed to burn his eyes. When he stopped at Nesbit's Garage, Lyle took one look at him and got the bottle of hootch down from the shelf.

"A touch in your coffee will set you up."

Milt accepted the mug and took a swallow. Bitter, lukewarm black coffee, but fortified. He took another sip and then realized there was someone else in the garage.

Owen Dingley tipped his head in greeting. "Deputy Waters." He looked at Lyle. "Thanks for getting to my car so quickly."

Lyle appeared to bask in the recognition. "The brakes will be done by noon."

"Good. I need to get moving." Owen seemed to have a second thought, and said to Milt, "Listen, I could use some breakfast at Jake's. How about you?"

Milt shrugged.

Owen said to Lyle, "I'll be back by noon," and led Milt out into the street.

They walked around the corner to Jake's Diner and sat in a booth. When Jake's wife Nora came over with the coffee pot, both men ordered two breakfast specials.

"I understand Captain Kincaid is out of town," Owen said as he added sugar to his coffee mug.

"I'm holding the fort down," Milt said.

"You sound . . ." Owen nearly smiled, indicating he was attempting a joke. "Like a martyr."

"A what?"

"Aren't you Catholic?"

Owen's eyes were difficult. Unflinching.

"Was," Milt said. "Was Catholic. Raised, but converted when I got married. Sophie, my ex-wife, she's a Methodist."

"And you're still a Methodist."

"I'm not a Catholic."

Owen nodded, accepting this fine distinction. "So perhaps you're one hundred percent."

"Perhaps?" Milt waited. Owen sipped his coffee. "You know a lot about me."

"Did a little research," Owen said. "It's my job. Last month I went down to Indiana for a few days. Met with some very interesting people, important people. I am now what's known as a G-2 man."

Milt shook his head. "I'd have to research that."

"It's . . ." Owen leaned back as Nora delivered their breakfast specials. Three eggs, sausage, potatoes, biscuits. After she went back around the counter, he said, "I recruit people."

"For the Klan."

Owen nodded.

"So you need to know if I'm . . . one hundred percent?"

Owen's fork speared his first egg, bleeding yoke into his sausage and potatoes. "You're not, I'm afraid."

"I told you I converted."

"Because your ex-wife was Methodist."

"I'd know if I was Catholic. And I'd say so."

"I expect you would." Owen cut into his sausage. "You understand the objection to Catholics?"

Milt decided to concentrate on his scrambled eggs. He'd never cared for runny yokes.

"They're not American," Owen said, chewing. "They're here at the behest of the pope. The things that go on in seminaries and the convents, it's . . . well. You understand the dangers they represent? They want to undermine our values. They're corrupt. Their vestments and habits and rituals, it's all a distraction. The pope has designs on America. All these immigrants. It's not by chance there are so many Catholics coming in from these countries. You see it in the cities, the population changing. It adds up to political power. The police department, the fire department. That's what they go after first. And then one of them is elected, ward chief, city councilor. Mayor, even. They move up. It's because of their numbers. It's the flaw in democracy. You have the numbers, you can put anyone in power, and then you see the erosion of the basic freedoms we associate with democracy."

"Nobody wants them here," Milt said. "Most folks in Otter Creek have worked the same land for generations. Good, hardworking people."

"Protestants," Owen said, seeming content that they had finally come to agreement. "So your captain, Kincaid, he's gone after those two. An axe murder, here, in Otter Creek. Catholic boy, and that girl—you don't even know for sure what she is. Kincaid, he wants to bring them to justice."

Milt looked at his plate. His sausage was gone, and he didn't even remember eating it. Finally, he said, "Are you saying they should get away with this? Kincaid shouldn't go after them?"

"I'm saying: there's justice, and there's justice."

"Ah. I know," Milt said. "It'll all get bent and twisted in a courtroom. I told Kincaid that. But you have to understand a man like him. He just sees it as his responsibility: bring them in. What happens to them after that is somebody else's business. He means to do his job."

"His job." Owen put his fork down. He appeared to have lost interest in his breakfast. "How did he get his job?"

"You tell me."

Owen seemed to accept this as a legitimate request. "He's widowed. Allison DeVries was from here. She and I graduated from high school the same year. Her father practiced law, sat on the bench. Judge DeVries was well-connected, pulled some strings. Cheated you out of the job you had every right to expect was yours. There's justice for you."

Milt decided silence would be confirmation enough. He worked on his potatoes. More than all the cups of coffee, a good breakfast before noon was what his hangover needed.

"Are you a moral man?" Owen asked.

Milt stopped eating. "Am I what?"

"Moral. Your behavior. Your values. Are they upright?"

"You're talking about a little moonshine on occasion? It comes from your own still you and your brother have out in the hills. That your idea of moral?"

Owen waived his hand over his plate as though shooing away a fly. "Temperance won't last forever. Prohibition days will pass, you'll see."

"And you find them quite beneficial."

"It's a matter of demand and supply. The dry laws, I don't support them, so Mink and I decided to provide a community service. A man has the right to his own council. I do not judge. You want a drink, I'll provide it."

"I'm obliged. Most of us are."

Milt resumed eating, as did Owen. They didn't speak for a few minutes.

"A G-2 for the Klan. That's a big deal?"

Now Owen put his knife and fork down with a sense of finality. With a thumb, he pushed his plate to the side of the table. He looked up the length of the diner, which was filling up with lunchtime customers, and spoke quietly. "When Lyle finishes working on my car, I'm going out on the road, recruiting throughout the county. Our network is growing, throughout the state. I'm going to put the word out about these runaway kids. No one wants them in their town. We've got to haul them in."

"If you found them, then what?"

"Well, that remains to be determined. We would like to see justice done, Milt. True justice. We want to lead by example. Actions speak louder than words. But let us suppose for a moment that Kincaid runs into difficulties. His search proves futile. Two criminals remain at large. Or, even if he finds them, something happens. Something that might prove to be an embarrassment to Otter Creek's law enforcement community. Something that sets the wrong example." Owen waited. "What might be the result?"

"It would be on Kincaid's head."

"Exactly. He might be deemed incompetent, unworthy. The powers that be here would have to make amends for their original error. They'd need to replace him. You and I know that a lot of folks around here have always felt that you deserved to be captain."

"I'll not deny it. I have my supporters."

"People don't forget," Owen said. "The Klan doesn't forget." His eyes now seemed bright, but he waited until Nora came and took away their plates. "I have a list of recruits and referrals. Good people. Town administrators, local clergy, members of the school board, teachers, and even the school superintendent. Since the Klan's rebirth, it's been happening in other places—Indiana, Ohio, Chicago and now it's coming to Michigan. In a few years you're going to see a dramatic change in this state." Owen gave it a moment, delicately changing the direction. "But there's a problem. An issue that is unfortunate but must be recognized." Owen paused, and then said, "You are not one hundred percent."

"I told you, I'm no Catholic. I'm Protestant."

Owen stared at him, his eyes earnest and perhaps sympathetic, and for the first time he appeared reluctant to speak, but then he said, "Your mother, she was Canadian. You were born—correct me if I'm mistaken—in Ontario."

Milt sat back in the booth. "My father was from here. My mother was from across the border, and she had returned to her parents' place in Simcoe, Ontario. My understanding is this was a good month before she was due. She planned to return to Michigan, but there was a blizzard, and she couldn't get back . . . so she had me on her parents' farm. I have dual citizenship. I'm a U.S. citizen."

"True. But foreign born. Listen, I do not make the rules or the requirements for admission to the Klan. We have established certain standards, which make us what we are." Milt was about to speak but Owen raised a hand. "In our resurgence we have developed into a very complex institution. We know that there are foreign-born residents in America who can make a meaningful contribution to our cause. But there are requirements regarding admission that cannot be breached. Standards that must be maintained. Afterall, this is America." He took a pen from inside his coat and wrote something on Milt's paper napkin and folded it over once. "There is a branch of the Klan specifically designed to accept individuals like you. You would be eligible for this. I would personally sponsor your application." He pushed the napkin back to Milt's side of the table. "I have to collect my car and get on the road. Let me go up and pay Nora for this fine breakfast." There was a hint of a smile. "And you have another cup of coffee and think about our conversation." He reached across the table and shook Milt's hand, firmly, his eyes steady, unflinching, and then slid out of the booth.

Milt did not watch him go. He looked out the window a moment, and then down at the napkin. There had been so many disappointments over the years. A marriage that walked out the door. Being passed over for the position he rightly deserved. The daily indignities he endured at the station. People would come in or call, people who had known Milt since he was a boy, but they would insist on talking to Captain Kincaid. Maybe it was necessary to suffer and survive such embarrassments. Maybe Milt's time was yet to come.

He opened the napkin and looked at the two words Owen had written with his fountain pen: *American Krusaders.*

Seven

Mercy woke beneath a scratchy wool blanket on a cot. She didn't open her eyes but held the image of the train in her dream a bit longer. It was cold on the train, which was full of children, so cold that she could see their breath, rising above their heads, looking like ghosts.

She opened her eyes and, seeing the unfamiliar room she was in, immediately tried to sit up, but a woman seated on a chair next to the bed gently placed a hand on her shoulder, keeping her down. She said something in Spanish, and two men came into the room.

The older of the two men wore a tattered wool vest over a collarless shirt. His fine, white hair fell to his narrow shoulders. "How do you feel? Do you remember what happened?"

There was a dull pain in Mercy's right knee. The older man said something in Spanish to the others, and as they left the room, he eased himself down on the wooden chair. "You must rest."

"There was an accident," she said.

"*Sí,*" he said. "The truck, out on the road north of Kalkaska. You knew the driver?"

"No. He gave me a ride, is all. His name was Gus something. We were going to Mackinaw City."

The man nodded. "Why there?"

Mercy looked around the room. Cracked plaster walls and one small window up high. The only decoration was a crucifix, with dried palm fronds stuck behind it. "The icy road," she said. "The truck, it skidded, spun completely around, and then tipped on its side in the field. What happened to Gus?"

The man had sunken cheeks in a face scored with deep creases. "My son Pedro, he saw it happen. He was out hunting, and he saw the truck slide off the road. The crates spilled out and broke open. The police took Gus in."

"Why?"

"You do not know what was in those crates?"

Mercy shook her head. "He said something about delivering fish."

The man's long bony fingers rubbed his chin, his whiskers crackling. "Fish. *Dios mío.* Pedro knew immediately. The smell came across the field."

"What smell?"

"Whiskey. Dozens of bottles."

"That explains it," she said.

"Explains what?"

"Gus said that if the police stopped us, he would say I was his niece."

The man nodded. "He thought having you in the truck would make him less suspicious. Bootleggers don't usually drive their routes with girls along."

Mercy shifted in the cot. "How did I get here?"

"After the truck crash you climbed out and ran. Limped. Pedro was in the woods and watched you cross the field. But you collapsed when you reached the trees, just as the police arrived. It was dark by then. He carried you here."

"Where is here?"

"This is our camp." He turned on his stool and spoke Spanish loudly and the woman in the next room responded, calling him Javier. Turning back, he almost whispered, "Do you like grouse?"

"Is that a bird?"

He nodded. "A very pretty bird, with fine meat."

"I've never had it."

He studied her face. "Where are you from?"

"A place where people don't eat grouse. Long way from Michigan."

He smiled. "We all are."

•

Rope had hitched two rides, getting to another town by midafternoon. In the warmth of the train station, he sat on a bench, trying not to look like he was staring at the coat, which lay on the bench by the door. On the wall above the ticket window there were towns listed: Boyne City, Petoskey, Harbor Springs, Mackinaw City. People came and went from the waiting room, and nobody took notice of the coat. After about fifteen minutes he got up, picked up the coat, and continued out the door.

A navy pea coat, a bit large. In one pocket, a watch cap and a pair of wool gloves. In the other, four crumpled dollar bills and a quarter. He bought a ham and cheese sandwich and an apple and then began walking north out of town. The broad lapels, turned up against his cheeks, helped block the wind, and the snug wool hat came down over his ears. Wearing the gloves, his right hand almost looked normal, as he walked backwards with his thumb out. Long spells would go by without a vehicle passing. The cold wind coming off the fields never let up. He wished he had some idea how big Michigan was, how far north he'd have to go to reach Mackinaw City. What really irked him was that he didn't understand why he needed to find Mercy. He kept thinking of her eyes. Their color, their light. The way her eyes exposed him. Something happened down at Nau Farm, and he just knew he had to find her.

A farmer gave him a ride to the next town, which hardly was more than a cluster of small houses and a general store. Midafternoon he was thumbing north out of the village when a car pulled over, a Chevrolet.

"Where you headed?"

"Mackinaw City."

"That so? You're in luck. So am I. What's up there? Family? Job? School?"

The man wore a wool overcoat and a gray felt hat with a broad satin band and a wide brim pulled low over his forehead. He was clean shaven and looked like a man who seldom missed a day using a razor. Rope found it difficult to determine an adult's age, but he thought this man wasn't yet forty. Men who worked in the Haverhill shoe factories could look fifty well before they reached forty. Often it was the dark skin around the eyes, or an invisible weight from years of labor that seemed to settle into their shoulders. This man had never spent a day on the factory floor, but there was a scar below his right eye that appeared to be the result of a deep gash that required stitches.

"I'm looking for someone," Rope said.

"In Mackinaw City."

"I think so."

"Interesting," the man said. "So am I."

.

"My name's Kincaid, Jim Kincaid."

At first it seemed that the boy hadn't heard him. "Thank you for the ride, Mr. Kincaid."

"Not a problem . . ."

"Lincoln."

"Lincoln." Kincaid waited but no last name was forthcoming. "It's cold out there, Lincoln."

The boy nodded.

"I can turn the heat up if you're cold. The heater in this car works pretty well."

"I'm all right, thanks."

Kincaid figured he was still in his teens. But he seemed older. There were boys who had lied about their ages to get in the army. He reminded Kincaid of them. Once they got overseas, they were no longer boys.

"Where you from, Lincoln?"

Again, the boy didn't seem to hear. He was calm, considering his answer. "I'm from out of state."

"Really? Where?"

"A bunch of places. Mostly back east." He cleared his throat. "I came out here on a train and I lost my luggage. Or it was stolen, I'm not sure. That's why I'm hitching, and I don't have any luggage. It was stolen."

"I see. You have any money?"

"Not much."

Kincaid kept his eyes on the road as the boy turned his head and looked at him.

"When's the last time you ate, Lincoln?"

"A ways back."

"I'll tell you what. When I stop for gas, we could get something to eat."

"Oh no, Mr. Kincaid, that's not necessary, thank you." He took an apple from his coat pocket. "I have this. I'm fine."

"Well, we'll see when we stop. You might change your mind."

Kincaid let it go for a while. The boy gazed out at the fields and woods. Finally, he asked, "What do they grow here?"

"Depends," Kincaid said. "Corn. Winter wheat. There are apple orchards, and cherry orchards farther north. Around here I believe they grow onions. Over in the Thumb beets do well."

"The Thumb?"

"That's right, you're not from Michigan. Hold up your right hand."

"Excuse me?"

Kincaid took his right hand off the steering wheel and held it up, palm facing him. "This is map of the Lower Peninsula, see? The thumb is well over to the east of here. We're driving north up the ring finger. Mackinaw City is at the very tip of the middle finger." The boy kept his right hand in his coat pocket. "Pretty convenient, having a map in your hand like that, huh?"

The boy cleared his throat again. "I don't, sir."

"Really?"

"No, I don't have a map." He took his right hand out of his pocket but kept the glove on. "I had an accident and lost four fingers."

"I'm sorry. Back east?"

"Yes, sir. In a factory."

When Kincaid had asked Estelle about the boy and the girl she and Harlan took off the orphan train, she spoke mostly about the girl, how she had reddish hair and was of mixed race. According to the papers Estelle showed him, the girl's name was Mercy. Estelle only said that the boy, whose name was Lincoln Hawser, was strong, and he had fair hair cut short. Almost as an afterthought, she mentioned that he was missing some fingers, though she couldn't remember with certainty which hand.

"I haven't been up this way in years," Kincaid said. "Next town, we'll gas up and get a bite to eat." He looked at the boy. "You might be hungry by then. Don't worry about paying."

He cleared his throat. "Thank you, sir."

They stopped for gas, and Kincaid asked the attendant for directions to the police station. It was only a few blocks away. Lincoln sat perfectly still in the car, a stillness that could only come from nerves. It was the mention of the police, no doubt. Estelle also said that her husband called him Rope.

As the car pulled out of the station, Kincaid said, "That café up the ahead, we'll stop for something to eat."

"The tip of the middle finger," the boy said. "How far is it to Mackinaw City?"

"It's not a matter of distance. Depends on the weather. Up here, winter comes early."

Kincaid drove a block up the road and pulled over in front of a place called Betty's. There was a telephone sign above the door. He turned off the engine but didn't get out of the car. "On second thought," he said, "we should keep going. How about if we get some sandwiches and eat them as we drive."

The boy seemed uncertain.

Kincaid took out his billfold and gave him a couple of dollar bills. "Listen, we go in, you order the sandwiches while I call home. Anything you like. And pie. A place like this usually has good pie. Get us a couple of slices. Then we can get moving."

The boy took the bills. "All right. Thank you."

"And." Kincaid reached under his seat and picked up his thermos bottle. "We'll need coffee."

Eight

Javier sat across the table from Mercy. Beyond him, several children were gathered out in a hallway, peering through the open door at her. "You liked the grouse," he said.

Mercy nodded as she wiped her mouth with the small towel provided with the plate. "I've never had anything like this. Grouse. And the beans and rice . . ."

"It's the chili."

"Funny name for something so hot."

"I suppose so."

"I must thank you," she said.

Javier smiled, waited.

"I must be going now."

"You are going to walk? On that knee?"

"Yes."

"Interesting. And where are you going?"

"Didn't I tell you?"

"At my age I forget easily. Tell me again."

"Mackinaw City."

"Why?"

"Because that's how to get to St. Ignace."

"Are you asking me or telling me?"

"I have never been there. Is that right? St. Ignace is across the water from Mackinaw City?"

"This is so," Javier said. "What is in St. Ignace?"

Mercy folded up the towel and placed it on the table next to her plate.

"You do not wish to tell me, I understand," he said. "But even if you do, I will not remember." He smiled. "I do not remember yesterday, and tomorrow I will forget today. It makes every day . . . new. I believe this is why I have lived so long on this earth." He waited.

"I have family there. An aunt."

"Ah. Family is good." Javier tugged at the loose skin beneath his right eye for a moment. Turning to the doorway, he said something to the children. The oldest of them, a girl with a long plaited braid, ran down the hallway. The building they were in felt large, designed to house many people. Mercy could hear voices and sounds from other rooms, babies crying, doors closing. She could see the girl enter a kitchen where several women were preparing dough for some sort of bread, their hands and arms and aprons dusted with flour.

"Pedro, he often drives up to Petoskey." Javier's legs were crossed, his hands folded in his lap. There appeared to be nothing but bones inside his clothes. He seemed to be speaking out loud to himself, not to her. "Sometimes I go with him. Petoskey is on the way to Mackinaw City. He may get you that far, and perhaps he may find someone who can take you the rest of the way."

Pedro came down the hallway, eating a rolled-up wad of dough. He leaned against the doorjamb while he and Javier spoke Spanish. Pedro seemed concerned, while Javier was consoling. Mercy assumed that Pedro frequently resisted his father's counsel.

Javier finally leaned toward the table in an attempt to see her better. She suspected that one eye might be blind or nearly so. The pupil had a milky quality. "This accident you were in," he said. "The bootlegger is in custody. The police may be looking for you, thinking you know something about their operation."

"I only rode in the truck. I had no idea those crates contained whiskey bottles."

Javier nodded. But he seemed doubtful now.

"You come to Michigan to work in the fields," Mercy said. "You don't return home after the harvest?"

"Home? Some of us stay on, if there's work. Some work in a cement factory or the canning plants. Pedro makes deliveries in his truck."

"He is not a bootlegger?"

"Pedro is not one of those. Canned goods, grain, lumber, anything. We invested in a truck."

"I must get to St. Ignace."

"I understand. You have family there. But you have never been there before."

"No." She watched Pedro, who turned and walked back down the hallway, followed by the children. Clearly, he was not pleased about something. "I have never been there. The water, how wide is it?"

"The Mackinac Straits?"

"Can I swim across?"

Javier was startled. He gazed at her, his head turned so his good eye took her in full. "The water is very cold, and there are winds and currents. It is miles across. No, I would suggest you take the ferry to St. Ignace." Javier spent a moment buttoning up his wool vest. Though it was soiled it had been a fine garment long ago and she could tell he took great pride in it. He got to his feet slowly. "We must get started," he said.

"You? You are going, too?"

He finished buttoning his vest. "I am going."

"Why?"

"Well. Pedro speaks little English so it would be difficult to have a conversation. And his wife insists that I accompany you. She knows Pedro too well. All these children. He has this urgent desire to make them. I will be your chaperone."

"I have heard this word, but I'm not sure what it means."

"It means you should not be alone with men who have urgent needs. Old men like me, you need not worry. We have only our memories." His smile made her feel that she had known him a long time and that in his presence she would be safe. "Now, we must be going."

•

The snow came and went, and Kincaid called them squalls as he shifted gears often, keeping the Chevrolet centered on the road that wound through the forest. Rope was mesmerized by the way the big flakes drifted through the headlight beams. He'd never seen anything like the purity of the trees, their branches edged in white. In Haverhill, snow blew in off the Merrimack River, and wagons that passed beneath the factory windows turned the streets to slush often tainted with horse dung.

They reached Petoskey, where Kincaid said they would stay for the night at the Hotel Perry. Rope did not mention that he had never been in a hotel before. He sat on a sofa in the lobby while Kincaid requested two rooms at the front desk. Oriental rugs, chandeliers, oak woodwork, potted ferns. The clerk assumed Rope was Kincaid's son. Kincaid didn't correct him.

They ate steaks in the dining room, took turns bathing in the claw-foot tub at the end of the hallway. Exhausted, Rope didn't remember falling asleep in his enormous four-poster bed. In the middle of the night, he was awakened by the sound of distant waves. He thought of the man who came to the orphanage when he was no more than four or five. Rope had been asleep and was awakened by one of the nuns. The man beside her wore a starched collar, and his oiled hair seemed painted on his skull. He removed something from his pocket and handed it to Rope. At first, he thought it was a stone, but it was too smooth, and there was an image etched into its polished white surface. Boat, Rope said. Schooner, the man said, and then he was gone.

One of the nuns told him it was whalebone, and the etching was called scrimshaw. Rope kept it for years. Until it was lost. Or stolen. Rope reached the age where boys fought often. They worked in gangs, packs. He wasn't a joiner, so they picked on him until he got big enough to fight back and beat them, and then they let him be. The scrimshaw man, for that's how Rope thought of him, never returned, though for several years he would receive a package at Christmas. Always something that seemed foreign, exotic. A small knife with a carved wooden handle, which the nuns immediately confiscated. A tiny lion in green stone. Also lost or stolen. Then there were no more presents.

In the morning, Rope and Kincaid ate again in the dining room with lace curtains. A wide bay stretched across to snowy hills.

"That's Harbor Springs across the way," Kincaid said, cutting into his ham. He pushed the meat through the yoke running from his poached eggs. "When I was a boy, growing up near Port Huron, I'd come up this way to fish with my father and grandfather. Sometimes out there on Lake Michigan, but he preferred the smaller lakes. Charlevoix and Walloon, sometimes Burt or Mullet

Lake. I haven't been this far north in years. We used to come up by train. Now we drive automobiles."

"The clerk at the front desk," Rope said. "He thought I was your son."

Kincaid paused over his breakfast. He appeared caught, trapped, and then he resumed eating.

"What name did you give?"

"Mine, of course."

"For me."

"I don't even know your full name," Kincaid said. "You just said people called you Lincoln."

"Hawser. It's Lincoln Hawser. Sometimes people call me Rope."

"I see."

"What name did you put in that book?"

"The register." Kincaid finished his breakfast by wiping his plate clean with the last of his bread. "I wrote down the name Eliot Kincaid."

"That's your son? How old is he?"

Kincaid's eyes changed, just for a moment. He did not strike Rope as an indecisive man, but briefly he seemed uncertain. "No," he said vaguely. "Eliot was my father's name, is all. First thing that came to mind."

Rope had already finished his breakfast, and the waitress came to take their plates away. She smiled at him. "Would you like anything else?" She was about his age, pale lashes and skin that may have never been in the sun.

Kincaid looked away as though he were witnessing something intimate.

Rope merely shook his head.

"Just coffee," Kincaid said to the waitress. "Black."

After she left, Rope said, "So you don't have a son?"

"No." Kincaid continued to stare out at the bay. "Influenza, it took my wife when she was pregnant."

"I see," Rope said. After a moment he said, "I didn't know my father. Maybe some men aren't meant to be fathers." Kincaid stared at him. He didn't seem angry, but extremely alert. "I'm sorry about your wife," Rope said. "And the baby." When the waitress returned, Rope said, "I'm not a coffee drinker but I think I'll try a cup."

"We make it strong here," she said. "Maybe with a little cream?"

"Fine, thank you."

She went to the sideboard and returned with a cup of coffee and a tiny glass pitcher of cream. "Shall I pour for you?"

"All right."

She poured cream into the coffee until it achieved a color that looked familiar. "And if this is your first cup, maybe a teaspoon or two of sugar?"

"Thank you. I guess I can manage the sugar myself."

After she left, Kincaid observed, "You have a way with the ladies." He smiled when Rope didn't say anything. "I have some fresh shirts in my valise. You could wear one, just in case."

"Just in case of what?"

"Another pretty young lady takes a shine to you."

Rope pretended he didn't hear or understand what Kincaid had said. He added one and then two teaspoons of sugar. Stirring his coffee, he said, "This color, they call it 'regular coffee' where I grew up."

"Back east?"

"How'd you know that?"

"Your accent."

"I have an accent?"

Kincaid nodded. "You're not from Michigan, that's for certain. I'd say Boston, thereabouts. It's your broad A. *Baahstin.*"

"I'm from a town north of Boston. This coffee, it's the color of the snow after the wagons and trucks have been through the streets. When it snows you have to watch your step for the hidden road apples."

Kincaid sipped his coffee and leaned back in his chair. "I was in Massachusetts once. During the war we shipped out of Boston for France. We were there for a couple of days. Mostly drunk. I remember a place called Scollay Square."

Rope tried the coffee, which was hot. He took another sip. He liked it. "I think I met my father, once, when I was very small. He never took me fishing."

"You grew up in an orphanage."

"I think my father was a sailor, and he gave me the name Hawser. Maybe it was his name, maybe he just made it up."

"And your mother?"

"No idea. The kind of woman who finds herself with a sailor. I think she's dead, maybe when she gave birth. Who knows? She's dead and he went to sea. And here I am." Rope picked up the coffee cup again, feeling emboldened.

Something about the coffee, the sugar. "Mind if I ask what your business is, Mr. Kincaid?"

"Care to guess?"

"I was thinking maybe a truant officer."

"Close." The dining room brightened, the sunlight illuminating the lace curtains backed by the blue bay. "This'll melt the snow," he said, "and the roads to Mackinaw City should be clear."

•

Mercy sat between Pedro and Javier in the truck. When Pedro shifted gears, she had to move her leg over to the right. She was wary of how his wrist would rest briefly against the side of her thigh. But she liked leaning into Javier and eventually fell into a half-sleep, her head against his bony shoulder.

She saw again the attic. The dim light from the gable end windows, and at night, candles. After Estelle went to the hospital in Lansing, Harlan climbed up to the attic every night. Always drunk. The first few nights he sat on the floor and rambled on about things she had difficulty following. He talked about family, about his sister-in-law Hannah and her husband Lyle, who ran a garage and farrier service in the village. And about their children, a boy and a girl who had died in the flu epidemic within days of each other. Since losing them, Estelle had been sickly. They would have no more children of their own. Mercy came to understand that she and Rope were taken off the orphan train as a means of compensation.

While his wife was in the hospital, Harlan indulged in whiskey he kept out in the barn. In the attic he talked more to himself than to her. But the night he came to her cot, Mercy held still. She was wearing her dress, with the blanket pulled up to her throat. That night he was drunk but not as talkative. He moved as though he had come to a hard realization. He unfastened his overalls. They slid down around his boots. He only wore a collarless shirt, nothing below. He smelled of the barn. As he yanked the blanket away, his hand tore the left shoulder of her dress. She tried to gather up the material to cover herself, but his weight came down on her. The cot's wooden frame articulated the struggle, creaking and groaning. His fingers clutched at her undergarments until they ripped, and she felt him against her skin. The liquor on his breath was sour, and his hips lurched as he tried to spread her legs apart, but something else was happening, she wasn't sure, footsteps climbing the stairs, and then she saw Rope standing there, the axe held across his body, the head supported by his damaged right hand. Time seemed slow. Harlan was standing, and she managed to get off the cot, her dress falling off her shoulders. She pulled what she could up over her as she began to move toward the stairs.

"I could kill him," she said as she walked past Rope.

When she reached the kitchen, she managed to button up her dress enough that only her left shoulder was exposed. She pulled on her boots, took her overcoat off the hook, and left the house.

She awoke when they reached Petoskey, where the truck was unloaded at a warehouse. Because of the snow, Javier said they would stay the night. The men working in the warehouse let them sleep in a room heated by a stove. In the morning, Mercy awoke lying under a blanket, warmed by the fire in the potbelly stove. Javier and Pedro came into the room and said that they had a shipment of lumber to deliver to Mackinaw City. After Pedro went out to help load the truck, Javier squatted down on the floor in front of the stove, holding his hands toward the heat.

"You talk in your sleep," he said. Mercy sat up. "You said something about a train, and then later, 'I could kill him.'" From his pocket he took a biscuit and handed it to her. "Kill who?"

"It was just a dream."

He nodded.

When the truck was loaded with lumber, they left the warehouse, the cab smelling of pine tar. The sun was out and, though it was cold, the snow had melted in the streets. Below the town there was an enormous bay. Mercy liked gazing down the streets toward the water. As they passed a hotel, she saw him. The boy, Rope. He followed a man down the steps to a sedan. She turned her head and watched through the rear window.

"What is it?" Javier asked.

"Nothing." She looked out the windshield. "How long to Mackinaw City?"

Javier conferred with Pedro in Spanish and then said, "We will be there by noon, provided we don't get any more snow. It is unpredictable the way it comes in off Lake Michigan."

"That's a lake?" she said. "It looks like the ocean."

•

Milt was invited to dinner out at Nau Farm. Around Otter Creek they were called Mercy Dinners. Since his wife Sophie had moved out, Milt never turned down an invitation. Before dinner, he and Lyle paid a brief visit to the barn on the pretense that Lyle needed to see how some hoof plaster was setting up. He knew where Harlan kept his stash of Dingley's up behind the turpentine.

After they had a couple of pulls off the jug, Milt took the paper napkin from his coat pocket. "'American Krusader.' Because I wasn't born here?"

"I don't care if you were born in Canada." Lyle seemed embarrassed as he gazed out the open barn door and across the fields of corn slash. "I know Owen talked with you about this. We need you, we need people like you. We all got to be prepared to contribute. Big plans for Otter Creek."

"Owen, and the Klan."

"He's lining up lots of recruits. He's met the Old Man down in Indiana, the Grand Dragon. Owen wants him to come to Michigan, and we want to establish a Klavern in Otter Creek. You know, in some towns the entire police force are Klansmen. They call us vigilantes. Owen says the answer to that is work with law enforcement, not against it."

Milt took a last drag on his cigarette and crushed it out on the ground. Lyle did the same, and they left the barn. Cold wind cut across the fields.

"Kincaid, he still up north?" Lyle asked.

"Far as I know. He called the station today, just checking in."

"He find them kids?"

"Don't know but I doubt it. Ellie took the call. He don't tell much."

"Axe murdering orphans," Lyle said as he opened the kitchen door. "People round here can't believe it. Word's been sent out. Kincaid don't find them kids, we will."

Estelle was laid up in bed, which unfortunately left the cooking to Hannah. Fried chicken, a might heavy. Still, it was better than whatever Milt could rustle up for himself.

After dinner he went in to sit with Estelle before heading into town. She lay on her back, gazing at the ceiling. He'd never seen anyone so pale, as though all the blood had been drained from her.

"You know what I want to hear, Milt." She could barely whisper.

"All I can tell you is we're looking for them."

"That girl, I didn't trust her from the get go. Nobody's said so directly, but I got a good idea what state Harlan was in when they done the deed. Harlan was a good man, but he had his weaknesses like any other. That girl played 'em both. She had that boy twisted around her you know what, and Harlan was just an old fool, especially when he got some of that barn juice down his gullet."

She fidgeted with her blankets a moment, lost in thought, which lead to the faintest smile. "You wouldn't believe it to look at me now, but both Hannah and I used to turn boys' heads."

"What you need, Estelle, is rest. Hannah and Lyle, they're taking good care of you."

No smile now. Her face hard, murderous. "I just want to look them two ingrates in the eye."

Nine

As they drove north from Petoskey, the country felt elevated, the hills closer to the sky. Rope had never seen such a density of trees. Mackinaw City was a village overlooking the straits. Five miles across, Kincaid said, was St. Ignace on the Upper Peninsula, which ran north to Sault Ste. Marie on the Ontario border, and hundreds of miles west to Wisconsin. Michigan's Upper Peninsula, Wisconsin, Ontario: living in New England you don't give much thought to such places. Now, to be so close, they seemed exotic, despite the cold, the snow, the gray sky.

"There was a British fort here," Kincaid said, "and the town started out as a trading post. There's still a lot of hunting and fishing up here." He steered the Chevrolet around a corner, and they could see down several blocks of clapboard buildings that ended at a pier running out into the lake. "Ferry to St. Ignace." He parked and turned off the engine. "So, now you're here." Was he saying goodbye? "You're looking for someone."

"Yes, sir."

"So am I. How you going to go about it?"

During the drive from Petoskey there were long periods when they didn't speak. Rope thought about Kincaid, who wasn't a truant officer but "close," and he realized that, as much as he had come to like the man, he needed to get free of him. It wasn't that he didn't trust him, but that he couldn't determine his purpose. And it was clear that he had a purpose.

"I guess I can ask around."

Kincaid considered this approach a moment. "Might work: canvasing neighbors and merchants."

"I might take the ferry to St. Ignace."

"What's over there?"

Rope didn't answer.

"Well, good luck in your search," Kincaid said.

Rope looked out at the straits. Halfway to the far shore a thick column of smoke angled into the sky: the ferry, returning from St. Ignace. He was suddenly overwhelmed with uncertainty. Moments earlier he was concerned with exactly how he was going to get away from this man and his Chevrolet, but now he was frozen with reluctance. He gathered that Kincaid expected him to simply get out of the car and walk away.

"My shirt," Rope said. "I mean your shirt. I'm still wearing it. I need to return it."

"It's a bit cold for that right now. Why don't you keep the shirt? You can owe me one."

"All right." Rope opened his door, but then said, "And good luck in your search."

"Thanks. I probably have less to go on than you." He did not sound perturbed about this predicament. It was more an intriguing idea, a challenge he welcomed. As if to confirm that Rope was free to go, Kincaid reached over and offered his hand, his left hand. Rope shook it, a firm handshake, one meant to instill trust without undue obligation. In Rope's experience, few men offered him their hand. He assumed it was because of his maimed right hand, but also because they saw him as an orphan, not someone to befriend.

Kincaid said, "Good hunting, Lincoln Hawser."

"Thank you, sir."

•

Pedro's truck was unloaded at a lumber yard in Mackinaw City. For their return load of shingles, they needed to cross the straits to St. Ignace. As they drove down to a pier and out on to the ferry, Javier seemed to sense her apprehension.

"You wanted to cross the straits, *sí?*" he asked.

"I need to get to St. Ignace," Mercy said.

The ferry was packed with cars, trucks, and dray wagons. She could not believe that this enormous steel vessel could float on water. Alarmed, she felt a strong vibration shake the truck as the dock appeared to slide backwards. They must be sinking. She felt not so much afraid as rushed in her preparations for death. But the ferry didn't sink, and its engine droned on as the vessel pushed out into the straits. Wind gusts blew coal smoke down on the row of vehicles and the ferry bucked against surging white caps. Mercy felt disoriented and lightheaded, like when the train had first pulled out of the station in Worcester, Massachusetts, causing the earth to move backwards.

"I've never been on a boat before," she said. "It's making me a bit . . ."

Javier pointed toward their destination. "The thing to do is watch the shore."

"Why don't they build a bridge?" she asked.

"Five miles of water? With the wind and the currents?" Javier said. "Never happen."

"I need . . ." she said.

Javier and Pedro seemed to understand her urgency and quickly got out of the truck. She climbed down to the vibrating deck and started to walk toward the railing, leaning into the wind, until Pedro took her by the sleeve of her coat and turned her around. "Other way. Not into wind." It was the first time she'd heard him speak English.

She staggered down to the railing on the left side of the ferry and threw up. She felt better then, and she did not let go of the railing all the way across the straits. Their destination looked to be an infinite forest of trees beneath hovering clouds. As the ferry approached the pier, she could make out a village. Roof tops, chimneys, a church spire. She had never seen a place so remote, so isolated. Yet she had family here. It almost felt as though she were returning.

Docking the ferry was a slow, elaborate process, which distracted Mercy from her nausea. Crewmen wielded thick ropes that were tied to the pier. There were shouted commands, and the ship repeatedly sounded its horn to boast of its successful passage. It all seemed orchestrated by mysterious forces, subject to dynamics and principles that did not apply on land. And the enormous cordage used to secure the ferry reminded her of the boy on the farm. Rope was aptly named, and she was not surprised that he had followed her. She didn't exactly regret kicking him where it hurt, but she wondered if she might have reasoned with him, or cautioned him, to leave her be. That she had seen him on the hotel steps in Petoskey was confirmation that even pain and discomfort would not deter him. They had that in common. That, and Harlan Nau. She realized that her recollection of what had happened in the attic might be distorted. Had she spoken to Rope before she descended the steep attic stairs? *I could kill him.* Perhaps she had said nothing. She was tired, exhausted, cold, and hungry, and her memory might be playing tricks on her. She might have just thought *I could kill him.*

•

Kincaid knew it was a gamble, letting Rope go. The boy and the girl, apparently, both possessed a kind of fortitude that was as rare as it was admirable. It had gotten them this far. Hundreds of miles north, into country they didn't know, in a season that would force many to turn back and seek a place that would be forgiving and safe. Shelter. Kincaid let the boy go, boarding the ferry that would take him across the Mackinac Straits. He might never see him again. He might have held the boy, taken him back to Otter Creek, and let the girl go. Most people would assume such a murder would not be the work of a teenage girl. But Kincaid had traveled north in search of the two of them. The boy, he happened upon by chance. Set him free, wait, and then follow. Something about this boy called Rope suggested that he would find the girl. He had a determination, a relentless, quiet determination. He would not give up, and he would find her, and then, Kincaid believed, he would find them both.

He went to the police station. It appeared that Mackinaw City's squad was only slightly larger than his own in Otter Creek. There was a sergeant at the front desk who led him into Captain Meacham's office. They looked like a father-son outfit. The captain's uniform seemed inflated, and he had three chins and a shaved head. The only evidence of hair was an attempt at a mustache, designed to conceal a hare lip. Bud Meacham leaned forward, his hands folded on his desk, as he listened to Kincaid.

"We have two other men out on patrol," Meacham said. "I have alerted them. A white boy and a girl . . . of questionable race. This is a small town, particularly in the off-season, after people stop coming up here to cross over to Mackinac Island." He leaned back in his swivel chair, folding his arms over his expansive belly. "Where'd you say, Otter Creek? Never been there, but then I hardly ever get south of Grayling." Meacham smiled faintly, as if to say that's all he could do, and he was a busy man.

Kincaid stood up and reached across the desk. Reluctantly, Meacham shook his hand, a light, wet grip.

On the way out of the station, Kincaid walked around the front counter. The sergeant, who had to be Meacham's son but with two chins, looked up from some paperwork. "I read about this axe murder."

Kincaid hesitated at the door. "That so?"

"You come way up here? You don't think the state police can handle this?"

"You think they're looking very hard?" Kincaid asked.

"It's their job."

"If it happened here, would you sit back and wait for them to track down the suspects?"

The sergeant considered this a moment. "Axe murders." He busied himself unscrewing the cap of his fountain pen as he leaned over his paperwork. "Makes you wonder what this country's coming to."

Kincaid let himself out on to the porch. The wind was up.

•

"I seen her," the woman said. "Maybe two hours ago."

Rope hadn't known what to do, so he walked from one store to the next asking if anyone had seen a redhaired girl in a long overcoat. He had worked his way down the street that led to the ferry. No one had seen such a girl.

But this woman, who was stocking shelves with canned goods in a grocery, pointed toward the front window. "They were unloading a truck over there at the lumber yard. Couple of spics. And this girl. Red hair, you say? I could see from here she wasn't, you know, entirely white." She was a heavy woman with enormous breasts bundled inside her apron. Then she tipped her head, indicating the direction of the straits. "They went down to the water."

"How often does the ferry run?"

"Depends on the time of year, the conditions in the straits. There are two ferries, one for cars and such. And the other ferry takes the train across to St. Ignace."

"Thank you, ma'am." Rope turned to leave the store but stopped and fished the money he had in the pocket of his peacoat. "What can I buy to eat for, say, fifteen cents?"

She studied the shelves. "Loaf of bread. Can of beans. Or a half dozen eggs."

He put a dime and a nickel on the counter and looked at the shelf. There were Heinz, Campbell's, and VanCamp's Boston Baked Pork and Beans. "VanCamp's, please. And would you mind opening the tin?"

"Sure, honey." She took a can down from the shelf. "This here's twelve cents." She indicated the bread box on the counter. "How 'bout if I throw in a couple slices, too?"

Rope left the store and sat on a low stone wall between two clapboard houses. At first, he dipped the bread into the can, but eventually he found it easier to pour beans out on to the bread. He picked the chunks of pork fat out with his fingers and ate them separately. Nothing had ever tasted so good.

When about a third of the beans were left in the can, he stuffed it in his coat pocket, open end up, and started down the street toward the piers. The wind gusted out of the east, and the first snowflakes were horizontal. Out on the straits he could see a ferry boat making its way back toward Mackinaw City.

Ten

I n your language," Mercy said, "you say thank you . . . *gracias?*"
Javier leaned on the fender of the truck. "And in response we often say, *de nada*. It was nothing."

Pedro took a bundle of shingles from the truck and balanced it on his shoulder. He looked like he was born to tote such weight. He muttered something in Spanish and then carried his load to the shed and dropped it on the stack of bundles.

A moment of displeasure caused Javier to shake his head. "My son, he has these notions." Then he brightened as he touched the brim of his hat. "It is good to be on a journey, to be searching for what you need. I wish you success."

"*Gracias.*"

"*De nada.*"

With reluctance, Mercy turned from the old man and walked up an alley between two shingled walls. In the snowbound street there were mostly horse-drawn wagons and carts in front of the stores. Few automobiles and trucks. She felt as though she'd stepped back into an earlier time, a time before the sound of a Model T engine. She continued uphill through the snow toward a church. Her overcoat was heavy, the collar turned up against her throat, but beneath she only wore her dress. She was so cold her legs trembled, and the chill in her back caused her to shudder. Her bruised knee was stiff, causing her to limp. She was hungry. She'd been hungry before but never like this, never when she felt she didn't have the strength to take the next step.

She stopped once, placing her hand on a wagon for support. The church steeple, now barely visible in the snow, seemed no closer. She feared she would never reach her destination. She continued on in the snow, and the second time she paused, she leaned against the wrought iron fence in front of a large brick house. A child gazed out a window, a girl who seemed fascinated by the sight of her. Then there was the sky, spinning as Mercy fell on her right side into fresh snow, and the swift descent into darkness.

Until hands lifted and carried her through the snow, up a set of stairs, into the warmth of a house. She was laid on a cot and covered with blankets. Though her teeth chattered, she began to sweat. She could not keep her eyes open, and she was baffled by a language she did not understand. Not Spanish but something else. French? Yes, French, spoken in a curt, familiar tone which reminded her of the orphanage in Worcester. Women giving instructions that were to be followed without question.

But there were children's voices, too. Whisperings not in French, but in another language.

•

After paying the fare, Rope had three dollars and change left. When the ferry powered away from the dock, he was standing at the bow, peering into the snow. The far shore was no longer visible. He spread his legs for balance as the vessel moved out into the straits. There was a rhythm to the oncoming waves, and he made a point of not gripping the railing in front of him, but letting his legs do the work, anticipating the rise and fall of the deck. He had always suspected that his father was a sailor, but now he was certain. Something about the man came clear as the ferry pushed into the wind and snow. His father had signed on for the voyage. He had been at sea since he was young—perhaps as young as Rope was—and he was less concerned with his destination than the work that was necessary to get the ship there. There was always the threat of weather, of shoals, of collision, of sinking, but that only gave the cruise greater meaning. Being on the water required a sense of order and purpose. There was freedom in having set a course. In the harbors near the mouth of the Merrimack River, mariners always seemed ill at ease while ashore. They were often drunk, looking for a fight, looking for women. Looking for something to sustain them until they went to sea again. This must be how it happened. This must be how he happened. Rope's mother met the sailor. It may have been a tavern or grog shop, an inn or a brothel. What transpired between them was urgent, driven by need. Maybe she loved him. Maybe he loved her. Maybe they lied to each other, or maybe they knew better. They shared a certain knowledge, an understanding about water, about living on the water, about surviving in a harbor town where sailors and women seemed stranded together. There must have been something between his mother and father, something that lasted longer than the moments of their coupling. Otherwise, how would the sailor know she was with child? Why would he show up at the orphanage? It was the not knowing that had always been a torment. But now, standing on the ferry's deck, breasting a savage November wind on the Mackinac Straits, Rope understood this one truth. He was the son of a sailor.

•

Cars and trucks lined the pier, and Kincaid would have to wait for the next ferry. He stood next to his Chevrolet and watched the crew release dock lines. Despite the driving snow he could see the boy standing at the rail just as the ferry began to move out into the straits. The wind-driven snow turned his thoughts to a hot noonday meal, and Kincaid walked up the street, looking for a place to eat. He would then catch the next ferry.

He entered Eula's Homestyle Cooking, where the chalkboard in the front window proclaimed today's special: Chicken Fritters. Inside, he sat in a booth and occasionally glanced out the window at the car parked across the street. Two men sat in the front seat, both wearing fedoras with their coat collars turned up. They made no effort to conceal the fact that they were watching the restaurant.

Kincaid ate his lunch, and as he was finishing up the two men got out of the car and walked toward the restaurant. When they came inside, they shook snow off their hats and came to his booth. One of the men was tall and wiry, while the other was balding, early forties, with a well-honed, dead-on stare.

"You paid a visit to the local constabulary." He sat down in the booth opposite Kincaid, while the other man leaned against the window frame and gazed out at the snow.

"This police business?"

"I'm not with the police, Kincaid." By way of introduction, he said, "Ben."

"What line of work are you in, Ben?"

"I work for Mackinaw City."

"Town employee?"

"Not exactly."

Kincaid pushed aside his plate. "So, this is town business."

"In a manner of speaking."

"I never quite understood what that meant, in a manner of speaking."

"I understand you're here looking for a boy and a girl, perpetrators of that heinous crime downstate."

"News travels fast."

"Having any luck?" Ben asked.

"I'm alone. What's that tell you?"

"You were down at the pier."

"Missed the ferry. With this weather, maybe it's for the best."

"You think they crossed the straits?"

"I don't know. Why?"

"You're looking all by yourself." Ben folded his hands on the table. "Perhaps we could help."

"I appreciate the offer," Kincaid said, "but this is police business."

"If these criminals are up here, it's our business," Ben said. "We want them apprehended quickly. For the benefit of the town."

"I understand."

"Do you?" Ben turned and looked at the other diners. Most of them were concentrating on their lunches, trying not to appear interested in what was transpiring at the booth by the window. Some of them seemed afraid. "Let me ask: if you find them, what will you do?"

"Take them back downstate, where they'll be charged."

"Ah. Remand them to the custody of the courts. The process of the law." He spoke as though this were a logical but flawed plan. "How? How exactly does one man take two people—purportedly violent criminals—hundreds of miles to be charged? My question is, how do you restrain them?" He opened his hands, a gesture of sincerity, even compassion. "Do you handcuff them? Hold them at gun point while you drive? Exactly how do you get them from here to there?"

"Funny you mention handcuffs," Kincaid said. "It just occurred to me that I only have one pair. That was poor planning on my part."

Ben opened his hands again, this time as if to say *So you see my point.*

The man staring out the window said, "You could use our assistance."

"You have a set of cuffs you could lend me?" Kincaid asked.

"No," Ben said. "Luke is suggesting a different approach." He waited a moment. "Go home. Turn around and go back down to, what is it, Otter Creek?"

"I thought you wanted to protect your town from these criminals."

"We do," Ben said. "And that's my point. Let us take care of it. You've had no success in finding them, so go on back. You're not to blame. You tried. Besides, I'm not quite sure of the legal aspects of this, but you might be out of your jurisdiction?"

"That's an interesting point," Kincaid said. "I thought I was sworn to serve the state of Michigan. Maybe I should consult a lawyer."

"Lawyers are most often a waste of time."

"Quite often that's true, but they do serve a purpose," Kincaid said. "Are you saying that this is your jurisdiction? I didn't think you were with the police."

"We're not. Not like you think. Our concern is not a mere court conviction, but true justice." Ben took a pair of gloves from his coat pocket and began to pull them on, working the leather down each finger. "No, our sense of jurisdiction reaches far and wide, Captain."

"I think I can manage on my own," Kincaid said. "But I thank you for your offer."

Ben nodded. "We knew they were coming up here before you showed up at the police station. Our lines of communication are exemplary. It's quite possible they have crossed the straits. So we have already sent someone across."

"You heard from people down my way?"

"Modern times. This would not have been possible before the telephone," Ben said. He slid out of the booth and yanked his fedora down snug on his head. "Telephones, telegraph, electric lights, machines. The world is changing, is it not? This was the Northwest Territory, very wild, but pure, in its own way. And in some ways, it still is, and we want to keep it that way." He leaned over, his gloved fists resting on the table. "Let us take care of this, Captain Kincaid. Best for all concerned."

Luke opened the door for Ben, and they both went out into the snow.

•

Several children stared at Mercy, lying on the cot. Curious, wary, but not afraid. One girl looked like she wanted to reach out and touch Mercy's face and count the freckles straddling her nose. Another seemed mesmerized by her hair.

Mercy couldn't recall having ever seen an Indian before. Their faces were smooth, their eyes brown, their dark lustrous hair cut short, unevenly in some cases. They had timid smiles, and she didn't think she'd ever seen such beautiful children before.

"What are you?" The eldest of them was a thin girl in her early teens.

"What am I?"

"Where do you come from?"

"That is not an easy question to answer," Mercy said. "Massachusetts."

The children looked at the elder girl. "It's a state," she explained to them. "And how did you get here?"

Mercy tried to sit up, but she realized she was not only weak but lightheaded. "That is even more difficult to explain. What is this place?"

"St. Mary's," the girl said.

"In St. Ignace."

"Yes."

"The church?"

"Next door. We live here."

"You are orphans?"

The girl seemed perturbed by the word. "No. We're Ojibwe." She added, "That's our tribe."

One of the younger children spoke in another language, and then several of them shushed her as there was a knock on the door. The youngest of them, a boy, rushed to open it, and a nun, stout and elderly, entered, carrying a tray. The children all backed away from the cot.

"Oh, you mustn't bother her," the nun said.

"They weren't," Mercy said. She managed to sit up this time, resting her back against the wall.

The nun placed the tray on Mercy's lap. A bowl of soup, a tin cup of water, a thick slice of brown bread. "Chair, Theresa."

"Yes, Sister Regina." The eldest girl brought the straight-back chair from the table across the room and positioned it next to the cot.

Sister Regina appeared relieved to ease herself down on the chair, which creaked under her weight. "Now, you must eat, but not too fast."

The soup was hot. Barley, carrots, potatoes, onion. No meat.

"You are mulatta," Sister Regina announced. "Where do you come from?"

"The state of Massachusetts," Theresa said.

Sister Regina did not have to look at the girl to register her displeasure. "It is not a state," she said, causing all the children to turn to her with wide, troubled gazes. "Massachusetts is a commonwealth."

Theresa appeared mortified, but looking at Mercy, who nodded, she seemed to accept this distinction. "What's the difference?"

"Not now." Sister Regina nodded at the tray on Mercy's lap. "I said, eat slowly."

Mercy broke the bread and dipped it in the soup. "Yes, sister."

Sister Regina's lungs seemed to be filled with fluid, her breath audible and moist. Her starched wimple made a scratching noise every time she spoke. "And what is your purpose for this long journey from the Commonwealth of Massachusetts?"

Mercy waited to swallow her bread soaked with soup. No doubt, Sister Regina would reprimand her for speaking with her mouth full. She drank some water, considering whether she should fabricate a story. "I was in an orphanage in Worcester, Massachusetts, and came to Michigan with other children aboard a train. I am searching for my aunt, who wrote to me from here."

"From here?"

"Yes, sister, from St. Ignace." Mercy took up a spoonful of soup.

"What is your aunt's name?"

"Andrea du Casse. She is married to a man named Raymond Selinski."

Sister Regina rubbed her forehead just beneath the coif. "No, I know of no one here by that name. But then I came here from Canada only a year ago."

"The letter was written in 1919," Mercy said.

"Five years ago." Sister Regina shook her head slowly. "I will inquire of Sister Superior."

The mention of Sister Superior caused some of the children to look alert, perhaps even frightened. One of them whispered something Mercy could not understand.

Without turning her head, Sister Regina said, "English."

On behalf of all the children, Theresa said, "Yes, sister."

"This aunt," Sister Regina said to Mercy, "how is she related to you?"

"She is my mother's sister."

"You know your mother? I thought you were an orphan."

"I only know what my aunt has told me about her. She died some years ago."

Sister Regina blessed herself and the children followed suit. "And was she the Negro? Or was your father?" When Mercy didn't answer, Sister Regina said, "I guess it doesn't really matter."

"My mother was from Jamaica."

"And your aunt, her sister, is here? Do you know anything about her husband?"

"I know his name, Raymond Selinski. He worked as a cook on a place called Mackinac Island, but he also worked on fishing boats."

"Seasonal work is common," Sister Regina said. "Lumberjacks, fishermen. They come and go."

"The letter," Mercy said, "it was written for my aunt."

"Perhaps she has not been blessed with literacy." Sister Regina said this for the children's benefit.

"Maybe, I do not know why." Mercy hesitated and Sister Regina eyed her expectantly. "The letter was written for her by a priest. Father John Nolan. He was here, at St. Mary's, I believe." She looked at the children. "You found me in the snow and brought me inside, here, next to St. Mary's. It's . . ."

"A miracle? Perhaps," Sister Regina suggested. "Perhaps we should notify the Vatican?"

"I'm very grateful," Mercy said. "If you hadn't found me lying in the snow and brought me inside . . ."

Sister Regina turned her head and looked out the window. Mercy could not see her face, only the tip of her nose, which protruded beyond the edge of her broad white wimple. Across the room, the girl Theresa was leaning over the table, where there were books and paper tablets. She was writing something, looking very intent.

"There is no such priest here at St. Mary's, not now, anyway," Sister Regina said. "They come and go, too, like the seasonal laborers." She turned her head, her wimple making an awful dry sound, and regarded the tray in Mercy's lap. "You were hungry."

"Yes, sister. Thank you for your kindness."

The old nun got to her feet with difficulty. "At least this orphanage in Massachusetts managed to teach you some manners." She picked up the tray. "You see, children, how one responds? 'Please' and 'thank you,' these are the keys to civilization. And prayer may get you into heaven."

Her back was to the children, and the boy who had opened the door made a face. To conceal her smile, Mercy put her hand over her mouth and cleared her throat.

"I must report this 'miracle' to Sister Superior." Sister Regina moved toward the closed door, where she waited. Theresa rushed to open it for her. As the nun went out into the hall, she said, "Back to your lessons now, children. Downstairs we go, in file. And quietly so as not to disturb our guest, who needs to rest."

The children obediently lined up in twos and followed Sister Regina across the hall and down the stairs. The boy picked his feet up as though he were a soldier marching in formation, until the girl next to him slapped him on the back of his head. Theresa, the last to leave the room, gazed at Mercy a long moment before she pulled the door closed.

Eleven

Rope was sorry to get off the ferry. After being on the water, land seemed a disappointment. St. Ignace, a smaller settlement than Mackinaw City, consisted of a few streets lined with clapboard houses on a hill overlooking the straits. The wind and snow were accompanied by a grinding sound, a rumble that suggested the earth was breaking up. He walked down an alley toward the water and saw the cause: ice floes, driven by the wind and current, piling up against the shore.

When he turned to go back to the street, he found a man standing in the alley. His graying beard covered much of his broad chest, and he was holding a bottle in one fist.

"You don't look lost exactly, but you're clearly not from around here." He had a raspy voice and an accent Rope couldn't place. Irish? If so, not like a Boston Irishman. He guessed Scottish.

"I just got off the ferry," Rope said.

"Did you now? So did I, Laddie. The U.P. and these lakes, they're no easy place to get to, but it's harder to get away. It tends to take you in, body and soul. You plan on going back anytime soon? The trip across will be tough until this weather abates." He took a swig from the bottle.

Rope thought he knew what abates meant. "I'm looking for someone."

"Aye. Aren't we all?" He offered the bottle to Rope, who took it in his left hand. He wasn't sure what kind of liquor it was, copper-colored and burning all the way down. "Warms your insides, don't it now?" The man laughed as he took back the bottle. "What's your name, lad?"

"Lincoln Hawser."

The man laughed again, louder. "You're a rope, are ye?"

"Yes, that's what they call me sometimes."

"Well, you look like the bitter end of a strong braided rope at that." He turned and started to walk back up the alley. "Whyn't we get in out of the cold then?"

Rope followed, and said, "Well, thank you, sir, but I must continue to . . ."

"Oh, right, you're search." He leaned close, smelling of the liquor and tobacco. "Well, then, be off with ye." Halfway up the alley the man stopped at a door to the dilapidated house. "I happen to know that this place is abandoned. There be quite a few of them in St. Ignace. I'm going to get in out of this blasted wind. Good luck to ye, lad."

The warmth from the open doorway was enticing, and Rope hesitated.

"Perhaps you'd like to step inside for just a minute and get warm?"

"Yes, I would. Thank you, sir."

The man led him inside to a room with only one window, which was covered by a heavy curtain. "You kin stop with the sir business. I'll be looking round for the gentleman standing behind me, if you don't. It's Angus MacLeod. Was a time when it was Captain MacLeod, but that time is past."

"Thank you, Mr. MacLeod."

"Angus, fer Chrissake." MacLeod sat on a wooden crate by the wall that was missing large sections of plaster so that the lath underneath was exposed. "So who would you be looking for in the Upper Peninsula during a blizzard?" He tipped the bottle up to his mouth, which was barely visible amidst his whiskers. "No, let me guess. Is it your mother? No. Is it your father? No. Someone who owes you money? Now that's a possibility. I'd like to find the bastard myself. Or . . . wait. Or is it a lass?" MacLeod slapped the bottle with his other hand. "That's it! You're looking for a girl. And she no be your sister, am I right?" Leaning forward on the crate, he whispered, "Is it any girl? Because if it is, I could outfit you with one who might suit your needs. There's this house not far from here that's full of pretty girls, and I venture that you'll find what you need in no time." MacLeod sat back against the wall, thoughtful. "It no be a particular lass you're seeking?" Disappointed, he said, "Oh, that's a terrible shame. Indeed, a terrible shame. But then you're so young you're bound to be smitten."

Rope wasn't sure what smitten meant.

"I was never so smitten when I was your age." MacLeod slapped his knee and bellowed, "But I did smote a few times!"

Rope had no idea what smote meant.

Angus MacLeod extended his arm, the bottle in his large fist with the hairy knuckles. "Take a nip, lad. Fortification against the coming winter."

Rope hesitated, and then accepted his offer.

•

The room was cold. Mercy stood at the window, her overcoat buttoned to her throat and a wool blanket from the cot about her shoulders. The snow was so heavy she could barely see the clapboard houses across the street. Downstairs the children were singing. The sister would blow into her pitch pipe, and they would sing a line or two, and then she would stop them by clapping her hands and chastising them. Harmony, she wanted harmony in three parts. In Worcester, the children sang many of the same hymns, and Mercy hummed along when they sang, "And my dying words shall be, Virgin Mary pray for me."

On the table by the window there were tablets and books. The alphabet, verb conjugations, the phonetic spelling of the French lyrics to "Frére Jacques." Sketches and drawings. Ships on the lake. Children outside log cabins. Ponies, dogs, a bear. Dark nuns and a priest in black soutane. The sun rising above a stand of trees, with a church steeple bearing an oversized crucifix. Scrawled inside the cover of a tattered dictionary, the word *Ojibwe.*

Mercy leaned over one tablet, trying to read it upside-down. With cold fingers she turned the tablet around and read:

~~Father~~ John Nolan

The word Father had a bold pencil stroke through it.

The girl Theresa, she had written this while Sister Regina was in the room.

Mercy heard footsteps on the stairs. She tore the top sheet off the tablet, folded it, and stuffed it in the pocket of her overcoat as she rushed back to the cot. The footsteps approached her door, paused in the hallway. Mercy lay down and closed her eyes. The door opened, creaking gently. Mercy remained still until her observer pulled the door shut. She heard a jangle as keys were sorted through until one was inserted into the lock. The bolt closed, hard and fast, and the footsteps descended the stairs.

•

The ferry was about halfway across the straits when the constant throb and vibration that ran through the deck of the *Chief Wawatam* ceased, bringing an eerie lack of purpose to the vessel. The smokestack, which had been belching a vast column of black smoke, now emitted only a light gray residue. Kincaid, standing at the port rail, found the abrupt silence disconcerting, much like the sudden cessation of shelling across a battlefield. The vessel quickly lost its persistent forward momentum, and he could see that she was drifting westward, surrounded by ice floes that knocked dully against each other in the waves. Astern, Mackinaw City had disappeared in the snow, and ahead the Upper Peninsula shore was faintly visible. Crewmen broke the calm as they hustled about the deck in response to bellowed orders.

The nearest passenger at the rail, a man in a long fur coat turned to Kincaid and said, "Now isn't this an adventure? I cross the straits frequently. We've had delays and cancelations. But those coal-fired engines keep turning." He pointed with his cane, which appeared to be made of polished mahogany. "Look, despite the helmsman's efforts at the wheel, the stern is falling downwind. We'll be bow to the weather soon."

A woman standing nearby called out, her shrill voice cutting through the wind, "What has happened, Dr. Uccello?" She had her arm about a small boy in woolen knickers and a floppy tweed cap.

"My dear Mrs. Salo, not to worry. I'm sure it's not a question of being out of fuel. Just the other day, from my office window, I watched them refill the coal chutes. They will drop anchor to keep us from drifting too far off-course." He pointed his cane at the boy, looking inordinately cheery. "Jonas, pretty exciting, eh? Why don't you take your mother inside where it's warm and dry?" As the boy led his mother toward the cabin door, the doctor said, "That's a brave lad."

The doctor came down the deck and reached inside his massive fur coat. "A little adventure like this calls for medicinal intervention, eh?" He produced a silver flask, unscrewed the cap, and filled it with whiskey. "Might I prescribe a touch of Canadian courage?"

Kincaid had not had a drink since he took the job in Otter Creek. Drink had got him through the war, and drink had sustained him in the aftermath, but he told Allison that upon taking the new position in her hometown, he would give it up. It was only fitting that the chief of police upholds the laws regarding Prohibition, even if he didn't agree with them. But it was more than that. It was the place the drink took him back to, the place he was determined to abandon. In its own way, liquor was a vessel adrift in blinding, wind-driven snow.

As Kincaid stared at the proffered silver cap filled with whiskey, there came a loud grating sound of metal coming from the bow of the ferry.

"They're dropping anchor." Snowflakes dusted Dr. Uccello's luxuriant eyebrows, the brim of his felt hat. His mustache had long waxed ends that twisted up into tight, symmetrical loops. He appeared to enjoy it all. "If she doesn't hold fast, we could drift across the northern reaches of Lake Michigan and end up in Green Bay!"

Again, Kincaid considered the cap in the doctor's hand.

•

By nightfall the snow was at least a foot deep, the drifts higher. For such a large man, Angus MacLeod kept a good pace as he led Rope through the deserted streets of St. Ignace.

Only once did he pause, leaning against the side of a clapboard house to take a long piss in the snow. When finished, he drained the whiskey bottle and tossed it aside as they continued along the snowbound road. "A girl, you're looking for a girl. Tell me, is she a raven-haired beauty? No? Let me guess . . . red, her tresses are possessed by the fire of the gods. Ah! I'm right, I can see by your eyes, laddie. So. We are in search of a redheaded lass. And where might we find her?"

Rope shook his head.

"Well, I know where we might look. The Four Winds! It would not be the first time a stranger to the straits ended up in the employ of Madge Dancer. But listen, we don't hurry we'll miss the races."

"Races?"

"The boat races," MacLeod bellowed into the wind, laughing. "Winters are long up here. There are but few diversions. Actually, only three that come to mind. Drink and women, of course. And the races."

"Out there, in the straits?"

MacLeod's stride hesitated as he looked at Rope in awe. "Good Lord, you are green!" He pointed up the road as he resumed walking. Ahead Rope could make out the steeple of a church and several small buildings, their roof shingles edged with snow. They walked toward the church, and then turned down a side lane that led to a house with candles burning in every window. The sign hanging over the door bore the faded image of a compass rose above the name, carved into the wood: Four Winds.

Inside there was pure havoc. Long tables filled with sailors, fishermen, lumberjacks, and tradesmen attended to by women who wore scant and frilly outfits. Everyone seemed to know MacLeod, and the din of the place required shouting. Glasses and mugs were frequently raised in a toast to Prohibition. The drinks and banter flowed. Rope lost track of time, and he didn't care.

When MacLeod clutched Rope's shoulder in a firm, avuncular grip, he pointed toward two girls, one serving drinks, and the other sitting on a patron's lap. "There, a couple of sirens. Would either be the lass you seek?"

Rope shook his head.

"How about that one there?" MacLeod asked, steering Rope around until they were looking toward the end of the bar. "I saw her staring at you with what could only be a come-hither look."

"A what look?"

"She's not the one you want, eh? That's too bad because she has a rare talent for—"

A small man stood on one of the tables and fired a pistol into the ceiling, causing the crowd to fall silent so that the plaster dust could be heard as it sifted down on his top hat and frock coat.

"Finally," McLeod whispered. "It's Charters."

"Ladies and gentlemen," Charters announced solemnly, "Let the races commence."

The room exploded with cheers. Rope was handed a fresh glass of whiskey. He had drunk liquor before, but nothing like this. If at first the whiskey burned his innards, he soon was quaffing the stuff as though it were water.

He was assigned to a crew, along with MacLeod, several fishermen and one lumberjack. They referred to themselves as the Whitefish. Like the other crews, they were provided with a small box containing sticks and paper and were given a fair amount of time—a half-hour, or three drinks, Charters declared—to build their boat. One of the fishermen, Landon, used his filleting knife to carve the wood until he fashioned a sleek hull. A round of drinks later, two masts were inserted into holes bored into the hull, and sails were bent on, curved sweetly, or so Landon proclaimed, so the vessel appeared to be in perfect trim. When Rope inquired what he meant by trim, the fisherman laughed and said, "The wind." And another said, "That be you, boy."

Eventually, Charters doffed his top hat and proclaimed it was time for the first race. Several tables were cleared of mugs and glasses, and a pair of long wooden troughs were placed on them. They were filled with water, which was subsequently christened by Charters, with great ceremony, with a dram of whiskey. The Whitefish crew placed their boat in the end of one trough, and another crew, the Walleyes, placed their boat in the other. There was much debate regarding the design of each boat. Challenges were settled by Charters, who essentially claimed that if the boat came from materials found in the box and it floated, it was a legal contender. When the arguments subsided two life jackets were produced, one for each crew.

MacLeod went first for the Whitefish. He finished his most recent drink and donned the life vest, which Charters inspected, to be sure that it was properly fastened. Then, at the crack of the pistol, MacLeod leaned over the table and blew on the crew's boat, pushing it down the watercourse, while the Walleyes' crewmate did the same in the other trough. The room reverberated with cheers, and Charters accepted monies and recorded wagers in a small ledger.

MacLeod clearly had a reputation for being full of wind, and indeed he blew his sailboat to the far end of the trough well ahead of his opponent. There, he quickly unfastened the life jacket and passed it off to his crewmate, the boat architect Landon, who donned the jacket, laced and buckled it up properly to Charters's satisfaction, and began blowing the boat back down the trough. The Walleye crew was more efficient in their life jacket transfer, making up lost time and reaching the far end of the trough slightly ahead of the Whitefish boat. Again, the passing of the life jacket was conducted to the amusement of the crowd, and a new crewmate blew his vessel down to the far end amid cheering that intensified as the two boats fell into a dead heat.

On and on the boats sped, back and forth in their troughs. MacLeod, the self-designated Whitefish skipper, bellowed commands and determined the order in which his crew would don the life jacket. Despite his protests, Rope was saved for last, the anchorman, which apparently was an initiation rite all new crewmembers had to endure. As he put the vest on and struggled with its belts and laces, the Walleye's anchorman embarked on his last lap down the trough. Once he was inspected and approved by Charters, Rope leaned down so his head was behind the sails of the Whitefish's vessel. He blew, long and hard. Landon, walking behind him, offered advice regarding technique and wind direction and strength. "Long, steady breezes are best! Pace yourself, son!" he shouted. "Save something for the final dash to the finish line!"

At the far end of the trough, MacLeod sat on a bar stool, arms folded, observing with a cocked head that aimed a critical eye down the length of the two troughs. The Walleye boat was well ahead, being blown down the course by a fellow who wasn't much older than Rope. He was barrel-chested, and there seemed to be no limit to the amount of wind his lungs could produce.

When Rope was approaching the halfway point, the Walleye boat was nearly at the finish line. The cheering suddenly stopped, turning to an anguished groan, as both masts on the Walleye vessel toppled over and the paper sails immediately shriveled up in the water.

"She's foundering!" Angus MacLeod hollered as he rose off his stool. "Blow, Laddie! Blow!"

Rope leaned over and inhaled a great draught of air, so deep that he felt something pop and release from his chest. He looked about, alarmed.

"You've busted a belt," Charters observed, a model of neutrality. "Your ship may not proceed until your life jacket is properly fastened and passes inspection."

There was much shouting and confusion. Both boats were adrift, virtually bow and bow.

Though her sails were down and soggy, the Walleye ship was advancing slowly as the winded crewmate summoned what little oxygen he had left in his lungs.

From the pocket of his overcoat, MacLeod produced a coil of rope. He wrapped it around the vest twice, attaching it to the loose buckle with an elaborate knot, which he presented to Charters for examination. Despite protests from the Walleyes, Charters nodded his approval.

Rope climbed up on the table and crawled on all fours as he blew his boat across the finish line. He was lifted up by his crewmates and carried toward the bar.

Then the fight broke out.

Rope had no idea why. Some dispute regarding true wind and apparent wind? Whatever the reason, everyone entered into the fray. Rope found himself on the floor, in danger of being trampled on, and he crawled toward the door.

Outside, he staggered up the lane, wind and snow at his back. He was still wearing the life jacket, and his icy fingers could not untie MacLeod's knot. Just as well. The vest was insulation against the cold gusts. He reached the main road and looked to his right, where the church steeple rose into the darkness. Straight ahead there was a small brick building, surrounded by a high wrought iron gate. He made his way toward the gate, thinking that he might hold on to it for a moment until he got his bearings.

Someone came to the second story window, holding a candle. It was difficult to see through the snow, but he thought he recognized the hair, the way it framed her face. She had a blanket draped about her shoulders and as she stared down at him, he felt the world turn unexpectedly. He lay in the snow, his arms outstretched, staring up through the bars of the fence at the window which was now dark.

•

The passengers on the *Chief Wawatam* had been sequestered in a large room referred to as the saloon. It was barely warm but a comfort as the wind rocked the ferry and hurled snow against the darkened windows with such force that it sounded like pebbles. Deckhands distributed sandwiches and coffee, compliments of the ferry company. They reported that two anchors were holding fast while the crew worked on the ship's engines. If repairs could not be made by daybreak, boats from Mackinaw City would be sent out to tow the ferry ashore. Shortly after nine o'clock, they issued blankets, and passengers began to stretch out on the long benches in the saloon.

Dr. Uccello finished the contents of his flask but showed no ill effects. His fingers instinctively maintained the waxed points of his mustache. He surmised that Kincaid had served in the war. When he learned that Kincaid was now a police officer from downstate, the doctor asked if he would be arrested for possession of contraband spirits. Kincaid assured him he would not. The doctor passed the time with stories of other difficult crossings.

Around ten o'clock one of the ship's officers entered the saloon. He knew Dr. Uccello and asked if he would come below to look at an injured member of the crew. Minutes after they left, a young deckhand came into the saloon and asked

Kincaid to accompany him, saying that the doctor had requested his assistance. The young man led Kincaid below, taking stairs and passageways toward the lower regions of the stern, until they reached the engine room, where another young crewmate with oil smudges on his face and hands lay on a blanket. His right arm appeared to be injured, and he was in considerable pain.

"I figure you saw your share of the wounded during the war," Dr. Uccello said. "Most of these fellows down here are mere boys, and they're busy trying to get the engines started."

"What do you want me to do?"

Dr. Uccello reached inside his fur coat and took out a flask, a different one. He filled the cap and offered it to the injured boy. "Son, you might want some of this. Captain Kincaid here is going to hold you steady while I set the bone."

The boy had straight blonde hair, and he didn't look to be twenty years old. He sipped the whiskey, but it ran down his chin as his eyes watered. Then he tossed the rest of it back like a veteran drinker and handed the cap back to the doctor.

"How did this happen?" Kincaid asked the boy.

"I was adjusting a valve when a wave rocked the boat and threw me against the bulkhead."

The doctor took a long pull of whiskey, screwed on the cap, and tucked the flask inside his coat. "Are we ready? Captain, if you could help our young friend sit up, and then take a hold of him from behind, it will help me to rectify . . ." The boy was shaking. "It's all right, now. We'll get that arm set and you'll feel better."

•

Two nuns gazed down at Rope. One whispered something in French.

"What are you saying?" he asked.

"It was serendipitous that Sister Agnes chanced to look out the window and see you lying beyond our fence—before the snow covered you up. Otherwise, you'd be dead before morning."

The other nuns said, "It means you're alive by the grace of God."

Rope closed his eyes. He was exhausted and still inebriated. For as long as he could remember, he had been in the presence of nuns. They ran the orphanages. They taught in the schools. When he was very young he thought of them as a breed of human that was separate from the children in their charge. Their stark black and white habits gave them a remote authority. They spoke in their own language, French and occasionally Latin, and sometimes Rope thought of them as a kind of bird, a flock of crows or ravens, most likely. They gave the orphanage its sense of order, meting out an exacting discipline sanctioned by God Almighty. They were feared. They were hated. They were needed.

Rope opened his eyes. The nuns were still whispering in French. "Where am I?" he asked.

"St. Mary's." The older nun was clearly in charge.

"Mary," he whispered. "Again, it's always Mary."

"What?" The other, Sister Agnes, said. "What do you mean?"

He remembered the boat races, the drinking, the fight, and then suddenly finding himself staggering through the snow. Abruptly, he sat up and leaned over. Almost by instinct he knew that there was a porcelain bowl on the floor beside the cot. There was a vile yellowish vomit in it, and he disgorged more, burning in his throat and nostrils. The nuns stepped back, careful of their laced-up shoes.

"Theresa." The older nun used that voice reserved for commands.

Rope had not noticed the girl standing by the door. "Yes, Sister Regina."

"Bring this young man a towel and a bowl of water with which to cleanse himself."

"Yes, Sister Regina." The girl slipped out the door.

Sister Regina said to Sister Agnes, "We must let him rest. And then . . ."

Despite the foul smell rising from the bowl, Rope smiled as he fell back in the cot. The unfinished line, the implied consequences. "And then what, Sister?"

This she took as a mild, harmless affront. "We shall see, won't we? In the meantime, we shall pray for the health of your body and that your soul finds its way back to the state of grace."

She turned and led Sister Agnes and the girl out of the room.

He closed his eyes and minutes passed, until he realized that the girl had returned with the bowl of water, a towel draped over her arm.

"It's . . . Theresa?"

"Yes."

"You're . . ."

"Ojibwe."

"What's that?"

"My tribe."

"And you live here. You're an orphan?"

"No."

"Why don't you go home, back to your family or your tribe?"

Her eyes were hurt, momentarily angry. "You don't understand."

"No, I guess I don't."

"You should wash." She folded the towel and laid it on his blanket. "And then I am to take you down to meet with Sister Superior."

He picked up the towel. She didn't move. He leaned over and dipped a corner of the towel in the bowl of water, which was ice cold. She was still standing next to the cot. "What?" he said.

She whispered, "The girl, upstairs . . . she saw you from the window. She knows you."

"Does she have reddish hair, and freckles, here?" He indicated his nose and cheeks.

Theresa nodded. "Like I have never seen before."

Rope wiped his mouth with the damp towel. "Her name is Mercy."

"She has a message for you." She appeared to struggle with what she was about to say.

To give her time, Rope rubbed his face with the towel. "What did Mercy say, Theresa?"

"That she's sorry."

"Sorry?"

"I don't know why," Theresa said. "She said you would. Do you?"

He began to fold up the towel. "I do, yes."

Twelve

Mercy heard the morning bell, followed by the sound of children being ushered into the dining hall downstairs. Before breakfast, they said prayers, recited the Pledge of Allegiance, and sang a hymn.

Her door remained locked, and the room was cold. She sat on the cot in her coat with the blanket around her shoulders. When the key turned in the lock, Theresa came in with a tray. A bowl of oatmeal, a glass of milk, a cup of tea. No sugar.

"You spoke to him?"

"He was drunk. Very."

"Do you think he understood?"

"Yes. What were you sorry about? He wouldn't say."

"I kicked him. Hard." She watched confusion blossom on the girl's face. "I saw what you wrote." Mercy nodded toward the notebook on the table. "Why cross out Father?"

"Because John Nolan's no longer a priest," Theresa said. "I think they made him leave."

The tea was barely warm. "Where did he go?"

"He still lives here, outside St. Ignace." Theresa appeared reluctant to continue and looked toward the window. The snow had stopped during the night, giving way to brilliant sun and gusting winds that rattled the loose panes.

"Why would they make him leave the clergy, Theresa?"

"He lives with a woman." The girl pulled the arms of her sweater down over her hands. "One of us."

"Ojibwe."

"Yes, Anishinaabe."

"What's that?"

"Different name for us. They rarely say these names, and when they do it's as though they are curses. It is a sin for John Nolan to live with any woman, but with one of us . . ."

"I must talk to him. You know where his house is?"

Theresa now looked terrified. "They have children. They are like you, only different. A little bit of both the mother and father. It makes them beautiful in an interesting way. John Nolan is old. Sickly."

"You must tell Rope to help me get out of here. And tell me how I can find John Nolan." The girl shook her head. "Please, Theresa."

"Only . . ."

"Only, what?"

She watched Theresa's cold fists work inside the frayed sleeves of her sweater. "Only if you take me. I can show you where he lives." Theresa looked toward the door as though a nun were eavesdropping in the hall. "They trust me," she whispered. "I do things for them. They call me their little angel. They think I will join their order."

"So you want to run away. I understand that, Theresa. I did, all the way from Massachusetts to here. A long journey. You meet strangers, and it's hard to trust anyone. The land is unfamiliar. You find yourself in a hard place. Once you start it's not easy to stop. If you run away, Theresa, you must be sure."

"I have been sure for some time."

"Where would you go?"

"To the Keweenaw."

"What's that?"

"A peninsula west of here. Hundreds of miles. I have family there. I know people along the way. This is what it means to belong to a tribe. They will help me. I can show you how to get out of here, but you must take me with you, and then I will continue on to find my family."

"But first you will take me to John Nolan."

"All right." Theresa went to the door but paused. "His name really is Rope?"

"No but that's what people call him."

"He is strong. He is braided, like good rope. And he followed you way up here?"

"He is not like other boys," Mercy said. "He is . . . very persistent."

"You should marry him."

"What?"

"You need to marry him."

"Go. Get out, now."

For the first time the girl smiled as she turned to open the door.

•

Kincaid had never encountered such a deep affection for a boat. During the night Dr. Uccello described the salient features of the *Chief Wawatam*, which had served as railroad ferry between Mackinaw City and St. Ignace since 1911. Her steel hull, built in Toledo, was 351 feet long, with a beam of 62 feet, and she drew 20 feet by 6 inches; she had two stern screws and one in the bow to break up ice. She could carry up to twenty-two railcars, with a combined weight approaching 3,000 tons. At dawn, her engines were still moribund, so a tug ran out from Mackinaw City and towed the ferry against the eastern current to the St. Ignace pier. Dr. Uccello and Kincaid had only managed a couple hours of sleep. Along with setting the young crewman's bone, Kincaid had assisted Dr. Uccello when he pulled an abscessed tooth from the mouth of a railroad lineman who lived in Trout Lake.

When they came off the ferry, a Model T was waiting for the doctor.

"You travel to the U.P. regularly?" Kincaid asked.

"Every week or two. Francois drives me to places like Brevort, Epoufette, DeTour. We're going north to the Soo, which is where I'll see patients before I return to Mackinaw City tomorrow night, provided the ferry is operating again," the doctor said. "I'm a Roman Catholic. I've lost Protestant clients since the Klan has begun their campaign. They're burning crosses all over the Midwest. There's a bill in the Michigan state legislature that would ban all Catholic schools. On the north side of the straits, I treat lumberjacks, Indians, people who rarely travel out of the U.P. and don't concern themselves with my religious affiliations." He climbed into the car. "Can we drop you somewhere?"

The weather had cleared. It was windy and the sun was bright on the new snow. Kincaid gazed toward St. Ignace, a village overlooking the straits, with serpentine islands in the distance. "Thanks, but I think I could use the walk. Besides, I don't know exactly where I'm going."

The doctor turned to Francois, who wore a wool cap pulled down over his ears. "He's an officer of the law, looking for two adolescents, a boy and a girl who are on the run from some trouble downstate."

Francois appeared hungover. "A boy was at the races last night. Part of Angus MacLeod's crew."

The doctor smiled at Kincaid. "The Upper Peninsula is the biggest small place you'll ever find."

"The races?" Kincaid asked, leaning down to the window for a better look at Francois.

The driver said, "At the Four Winds, in the village. Down a side street near the Catholic church. You can't miss it. The boy disappeared when the fight broke out."

"What fight?"

Francois shrugged. "*Mon Dieu*, there's almost always a fight, eventually."

"What did this boy look like?"

"Strong." The man rubbed his stubbled chin a moment. "*Ses doigts.*"

Kincaid recalled little French from the war. "His fingers? What about them?"

"*Manquant.* He was missing fingers on one hand."

Kincaid looked at the doctor. "That's him. Francois, what about a girl. Was he with a girl?"

"There are many girls at the Four Winds. Who can keep track?" Francois shrugged again, though now he appeared to be recalling a pleasant memory. "But this young man was engaged in the races. I saw no girl draped all over him."

"*Merci*, Francois," Kincaid said.

"No ride to the Four Winds?" Dr. Uccello asked.

Kincaid shook his head.

"See, Doctor?" Francois said. "He prefers to walk behind his nose, like a bloodhound."

Dr. Uccello took a business card from his coat pocket and handed it out the window to Kincaid. "If you're passing through Mackinaw City, here's where I am." He smiled. "I can always use a good assistant."

They shook hands, and Kincaid watched the Model T move slowly down the road.

•

After breakfast, Theresa came to the room Rope had slept in and walked with him down a hallway past paneled oak doors and fluted columns. She explained that the Catholic church had bought the house from the widow of a Canadian lumber baron. From one of the rooms children could be heard reciting the times tables, while in another they were singing a Gregorian chant. Theresa stopped when they reached the door at the end of the hall, which was flanked by a statue of Joseph and the Virgin Mary.

"Sister Superior," Rope said.

Theresa nodded. She didn't exactly look frightened but alert, as though she sensed lethal danger was near, a wild animal or a ghost.

"When I was little," Rope said quietly, "I used to watch statues, expecting them to move. Sometimes I think I imagined that one would blink, or the head would turn slightly."

"Me too," Theresa whispered. "I know they're watching us." She backed away, cautiously. "Knock just once. Sometimes she doesn't answer right away, but if you knock again, it sets her off. Good luck. I'm to wait for you." She went back down the corridor and sat on a scarred church pew.

Rope knocked on the door once. Immediately, a woman's voice inside said, "Enter." As he turned the glass doorknob, he looked down toward Theresa, who smiled in an attempt at being reassuring.

Sister Superior's office was spare and tidy. Shelves were lined with large leather-bound books, and a life-size statue of Jesus stood in the corner. At first, it was difficult to see Sister Superior, sitting at her wide oak desk, because of the sunlight coming in the window directly behind her. She was a substantial woman, broad shoulders with a jaw to match, but he could barely see her eyes above the half-frame reading spectacles that seemed about to drop off the end of her nose.

"I'm told they call you Rope," she said. "What is your baptismal name?"

"Lincoln Hawser."

"Mr. Hawser, I understand that you were found in the snow outside last night, inebriated."

"I expect so, Sister."

"You were wearing a life vest? Are you off one of the fishing boats?"

"No, Sister."

"Well, the life vest would not have saved you. You were so inebriated that you would have frozen to death had we not brought you inside."

He decided to neither confirm nor deny this.

"Are you prepared to die, Mr. Hawser?"

"Excuse me?"

"Had you died in that drunken state, would you have gone to heaven?"

"I don't know."

"Is your soul in the state of grace?" It had been a while since he had heard such a voice. Firm, direct, allowing no room for debate. "I said, do you think you are in the state of grace?"

He wanted to say he thought he was in the state of Michigan but decided that flippancy might actually lead to a paddling or a spanking, which was frequent punishment in the orphanages. "I hope so. I haven't committed a . . . a mortal sin, I don't believe."

"I am told by Sister Agnes that you said you are a baptized Catholic, raised in an orphanage. So you know the difference between venal and mortal sin?"

"I believe so, yes."

She inhaled, exhaled. This was intended to say *What are we to do with you?*

"Sister, I appreciate that I was brought in and given shelter for the night. I would like to be on my way and not be a bother to you anymore."

She leaned back in her chair. Raising an arm she massaged her forehead a moment, fitting her hand inside the starched white hood of the wimple that surrounded her face. For a moment, he could see her eyes better. Gray. Large. The eyes of a woman who does not sleep well at night.

"I am free to go?" he asked.

"Free?"

"Yes, Sister. I would like to be on my way, if there is no objection."

She lowered her arm and folded her hands on her ink blotter, which was barren. No papers, no pens, nothing. He imagined her sitting that way when she was alone, sort of like a dog that sits at the door, waiting to go out and herd the flock. "On your way where, if I may ask?" she said.

"Well, I can't say exactly."

"Can't or won't." She waited only a moment. "Why are you here, Mr. Hawser?"

"Here? In St. Ignace? In Michigan?"

"Why are you on this earth?"

"Well. I'm not sure I know the answer to that."

"Do you think you should? Know the answer?"

"I suppose so. I came to Michigan on a train full of orphans. I hitchhiked up here, and I walked a good ways, too. And, of course, I took that ferry across the water to get here."

"Jesus walked on the water." She said this with great sincerity. "He walked on the water because he knew his purpose, he knew why he was here on this earth. He revealed many things to us. One was that we must strive to know why we are here."

Rope had to check the impulse to say something he knew he'd regret. That he might try to walk back across the water to Mackinaw City, but he'd probably drown and go to hell. Or that he might try to swim across. Or that he'd wait till the straits froze, which might be in a matter of days, though it was still only November, and then he'd sure as hell walk across the ice. He used to do this at times in the orphanages, get fed up with the nuns and talk back. They would call it sass. You have a lot of sass. Or obstinate, they would say he was a hopelessly obstinate boy. It would lead to a paddling. It would lead to punishment, sitting alone in a room for hours, no food or water. Sass and obstinacy never got him anywhere but in trouble.

Sister Superior seemed to understand that he was holding back, that he was exercising caution. She almost sounded conciliatory. "Perhaps, Mr. Hawser, you would benefit from some time to reflect on this question?"

"You mean stay here longer?"

"Were you not comfortable last night?"

"I was, and I appreciate your letting me stay."

"Then maybe you should stay on with us and see if it helps you arrive at . . ." Now she turned her head, staring toward Jesus. She was never really alone, there in her office, with the statue of Jesus standing in the corner. "You would benefit from further meditation in the presence of our Savior. Perhaps it would lead to a clearer understanding of your purpose."

He wanted to say that he had spent years in orphanages, and his sole purpose was to get out. When he managed to do that, he found himself working on the floor of a factory in an enormous brick building overlooking the Merrimack River. He wanted to tell her that he boarded the train in Haverhill willingly because it would get him out of all that. And when he went to live and work on the farm in Otter Creek he had hope—at the beginning—that this might lead to his finding what she called his purpose on this earth. But it didn't work out, just like everything that had gone before back in Massachusetts hadn't worked out. He wanted to tell Sister Superior that there was always someone that did something that reminded him that evil was everywhere, that all the prayers and the sacraments and the masses, all the vows and novenas and holy water and Gregorian chants didn't do a thing about it, there was still evil, and people did hurtful things to one another. He wanted to tell her about climbing into the attic of the farmhouse and finding Harlan Nau with Mercy, describing it just as he saw it, the man's overalls around his feet, and Mercy getting up off the cot, her dress torn. But most of all he wanted to tell Sister Superior that something happened to him as Mercy walked toward him, covering herself as best she could, and then when she said something to him, it changed him. Forever. He believed he was changed forever, and though he couldn't say exactly how or why he was changed, he knew that she was the reason he had come north, had crossed the water to arrive in St. Ignace. Following that girl who had fled the farm was why he was on this earth. That was his purpose, and nothing would change that, not Jesus, the Virgin Mary, or Joseph, and certainly not another night in this place full of children singing hymns in a language that was not their own.

But he didn't say any of those things and just stood there before the wide oak desk, expecting that the statue of Jesus to his right was watching him. Jesus didn't scare him. The wrath of God didn't scare him. The nuns had wanted him to be scared, but he wasn't. He honestly didn't know what to make of Jesus, but he knew He wasn't a mean person, He wasn't a threat. The sisters could be a threat, some of the priests could be a threat, but not Jesus. In fact, he always felt he shared an understanding with Jesus, that they both knew a secret that the nuns and priests either didn't know or refused to acknowledge. Rope said none of this, believing that Sister Superior would not understand, that she would take it as blasphemy, arrogant and unforgiveable. Worse than obstinate.

"Well," Sister Superior said. "You know about venal and mortal sin. So you also must know about free will. You have a free will. You are not detained here against your will, thus you are free to go." She lowered her head and seemed to gaze at her folded hands. They might have been held together by invisible manacles.

Rope cleared his throat. "Jesus," he said, causing her to look up. "He didn't need a life jacket."

"Excuse me?"

"When he walked on water, he wasn't afraid of drowning."

"Young man, are you being facetious?"

"No, Sister." He glanced at the statue, half expecting it to nod in agreement with what he was about to say. "He wasn't afraid. He wanted us to know there is no reason to be afraid in the world."

Sister Superior looked down at her hands. She didn't know what to say.

"I would like to stay one more night. If you don't mind. I would be grateful."

"Very well." Her hands parted, as though her invisible bonds had been broken, miraculously. "So be it."

"Thank you, Sister."

He left the office and pulled the door closed gently.

Theresa was still on the pew. "You survived," she whispered. "I prayed you would."

"Thank you for your prayers." He sat next to her.

"I saw them." She nodded at the statues outside Sister Superior's office. "Mary and Joseph, they both glanced at me. It was very quick."

"Damn, and I missed it."

She stifled a laugh. Getting to her feet, she whispered, "We have a plan."

"We? You. And Mercy?"

"Yes."

He got up and they started to walk down the hall. "Good. When?"

"Tonight."

3

A Cold, Hard Prayer

Thirteen

When Milt arrived at the station in the morning, Ellie didn't acknowledge his presence as he walked past her desk. It was, he thought, as though she knew how bad this hangover was and believed her silence would be the best reprimand. He was in no mood for one of Ellie's reprimands.

He poured himself a mug of coffee and went to his desk.

Ellie didn't move, didn't look around, but took the piece of paper she'd been reading, turned it over and continued to read. Until she stopped reading and sat up. She seemed to be weighing her options. When she turned around, she wore that expression she reserved for people who came into the station making petty claims and demands. Complaints about dogs and neighbors, about getting gypped by a merchant at the store. "What are you doing, Milton Waters?" she asked.

Milton. It was going to be bad.

"What do you mean, Eleanor?"

"What I mean is I knew your mother, your grandmother, and I even remember your great-grandmother. Your father was a no-good, and I know he disappeared when you were young, but your mother she was something else again."

"I know. An angel."

"That's right, an angel."

"Maybe even a saint. Who played the organ at church Sundays . . ."

"Who didn't raise you to come in here hangdog every morning the captain is away. You're supposed to know better. Whatever that stuff is you're drinking, it's doing a real number on you. Most likely, it's that stuff the Dingleys make out in the woods that's going around town like a contagious disease. It's vile, poisonous, and it's illegal. This is the police station. Right now, you are the law. You're the officer on duty, the only one we got since in its infinite wisdom the parsimonious town council decided it would be fiscally prudent to cut back on funding for the police department. If I wore a badge, I'd arrest you and take you back there and lock you in one of the cells until you sober up."

"I am sober, Ellie."

"Well, you could have fooled me. I watched you come up the steps out there. You can hardly walk a straight line."

"Yeah? Well, your coffee is doing me wonders."

She had a pencil in her hand and now she slammed it down on her desk and got to her feet. "My husband Mitch can hardly stand after taking another fall down the stairs, and the dog ate something he shouldn't have, and he was puking his guts out all night long. I got maybe two hours of sleep, and I got to come in here first thing in the morning, see that you're late again. And hungover. That is not my idea of a good morning howdy-do."

"You want to be careful about bringing up the women in the Waters family, Ellie. My mother, the angel, used to say that when you were kids you sold peeks at your hooters to boys."

"She did not."

"Did too. They used to call you Peek-a-Boo."

Ellie looked like she was prepared to come around his desk and gouge his eyes out. Instead, she went to the coat rack by the front door. As she pulled on her jacket and fussed with her scarf, she swore under her breath. When she was buttoned up, she went out on the porch, slamming the door behind her.

As Milt listened to her navigate the steps to the sidewalk, he removed the flask of Dingley's from his coat pocket and topped up his coffee.

•

Sister Regina, accompanied by Sister Agnes, brought lunch to Mercy's room. Fish chowder. Bland, in need of salt. A piece of bread with a crust hard as slate.

"Why is my door kept locked?" Mercy asked.

Sister Agnes stood by the door, like a guard, while Sister Regina sat at the table, which Mercy had pulled over next to her cot.. "Sister Superior's instructions," she said.

"But why?" She looked at both nuns and settled on Sister Regina.

"That, I cannot say."

"Does it have to do with what I told you about my aunt? Or about the priest, Father Nolan?"

Sister Regina's eyes avoided meeting Mercy's, and she tended to stare at the pine floorboards. Finally, she said, "You are stronger today. The food, the rest, it is working. Had you gone out in this weather, who knows what would have become of you?"

"I am being held against my will."

"We want to be sure you fully recover," Sister Regina said.

From the door, Sister Agnes said, "It's a question of your safety."

"My safety? No one's ever concerned for my safety." Mercy finished the chowder. She could have eaten another bowl, as well. The bread was another matter. She pulled clumps from the middle that had not gone stale. "The children here, they are all Indians. Ojibwe? And there's another name they use—"

"Anishinaabe."

"So. Why are they here? Don't they have families?"

"They need an education," Sister Regina said. "They need spiritual instruction. You don't understand how it is with them. Their ways are not like ours. Here, they learn to speak our language, properly. There are matters of hygiene to consider—"

"They are prisoners." Mercy stood up, crossed the room, and placed the tray on the table. "I am, too."

Sister Regina got to her feet and stood behind the chair, as if ready to use it to defend herself. From the pocket of her habit, she produced a set of rosary beads made of wood. She held them as though they would protect her. "Won't you pray with us?"

"No."

"Well. Jesus wants you to have these." She placed the beads on the table.

Mercy picked them up and held them out to her, the cross dangling from her fingers. Sister Regina looked at her hand. Mercy had seen these eyes many times. It was her skin. The woman was afraid to touch her outstretched hand.

"Keep them," Sister Regina said.

Sister Agnes, said, "In case you change your mind."

"I don't need beads to pray."

"But you do?" Sister Regina said. "Pray?"

Mercy reached out with her other hand and took Sister Regina's wrist. There was a moment when the woman tried to pull away but then she seemed to accept that she was in the presence of a force that might easily overwhelm her. She relented, meekly, like a martyr and opened her fist. Mercy placed the beads in her palm, held her wrist a moment longer than necessary, and then released it.

Sister Regina tucked the beads away in her pocket buried in the folds of her habit, and then picked up the tray. "Pray, my child," she said. "Pray and you will find peace."

"I am not your child, and I need that door unlocked."

The nuns retreated to the hallway, Sister Agnes pulling the door closed. A key was inserted, bolting the lock.

Mercy sat down on the cot, pulling the blanket tightly around her shoulders. Theresa had told her that the doors leading outside were always locked. She said the nuns saw it as a means of protecting them, the children, from harm. From evil. One of the nuns often described this old house as a boat adrift on the Straits of Mackinac, and that the water surrounding it was deep and cold, and that if one stepped outside there was the danger of being swept away by the current.

Mercy suddenly felt tired. She wanted to sleep, to be ready for the night, for the plan she had made with Theresa, but she was disturbed by her refusal to say the rosary. She used to pray. In Worcester, she would get on her knees and pray, not only when the nuns expected her to do so, which was often throughout the day, but on her own she would bless herself and place her hands together and pray. There was a time when she considered the nuns as her protectors. She thought she might even become one of them. The convent might be a safe haven: the habit, the life of sacrifice, of contemplation and prayer, of working with the poor and sick, perhaps even working with orphaned children. But she was quite young, and as she got older she saw that they were not all at peace, really. Some, yes. Some did good works and were content, but most of the nuns were riven with jealousies and resentments, the nature of which she did not understand. Some of them, she came to believe, were not of their right minds. They were afraid, and it was only the strict rules, the regimental orderliness of their days, that kept them from drifting into a suppressed and irrevocable state of madness.

Pulling the blanket about her face, she closed her eyes. She no longer prayed, no longer said the rosary, the Lord's Prayer, the Hail Mary, the Act of Contrition. Instead, there was something she did that seemed truer, something honest and forthright. She spoke to God. In her mind, she talked to Him. She asked Him to look out for her, to give her strength. She apologized for her failings, for when she did things that might be considered a sin. She didn't ask for forgiveness, but just that He would help her to avoid doing such things again. She asked Him about her mother, about her aunt. He didn't respond, and yet . . . and yet she had come to believe that she was meant to make this journey into this frozen place in northern Michigan.

Michigan.

She had never given thought to the word before but, like Massachusetts, she assumed it was from the language of one of the tribes that had inhabited this land long before European settlers arrived. A place where the children of those tribes were now provided religious instruction and prohibited from speaking their own language. And she had come to Michigan because it offered a chance to find family. She did not know exactly what family meant. It was something other people possessed, and they assumed you had one, too. Family, its name, its place, was the first thing people mentioned when describing who they were, but for her family was a missing piece, a dark, empty void. So, she came here, to Michigan, a cold, hard prayer.

•

Barber shops were often a source of local information, and Ned's Parlor proved to be no exception. The precision of Ned's thin mustache gave the appearance of a phalanx of ants marching across his protuberant upper lip. When Kincaid entered the shop, Ned was preparing to shave his only customer, a rotund man in a three-piece tweed suit who was smoking a cigar, a man who looked like he'd perfected the art of leisure in his every gesture. The aroma of tobacco blended with the scents of aftershave and lather, and while honing his razor on his strop, Ned asked Kincaid, "Haircut or shave? Or the works for four bits. Canadian currency excepted. The wife's from Blind River, Ontario, and she uses it when she goes up to see her dear old mum."

A practiced pitch, no doubt. The thought of having his face shaved and wrapped in a hot towel was inviting, but Kincaid said, "Right now, I'm looking for information."

"That'll be one dollar."

Ned's recumbent customer, bearded in white lather, emitted a robust chuckle.

"Angus MacLeod, know him?" Kincaid asked.

"That's too easy. I could not deign to take your money, kind sir." Ned considered the straightedge in his hand a moment. "Everyone around here knows the man. He moves back and forth between Mackinaw City and St. Ignace. He's the Great Lake's most reputable reprobate, and we have a few, wouldn't you say, Roger?"

Roger grunted his agreement.

With the precision and delicacy of a surgeon, Ned drew his blade down through the heavy lather on Roger's face, exposing a clean swath of pink skin. "Charming, at times, McLeod is, but a deadbeat. If you curry his disfavor, there's an untamed animal lurking within, one that is in constant search of prey. It can be a fearsome thing to witness. You'll recognize Angus by his size and his beard. He stiffed me once too often, and I refuse to shave him. That was some time ago, and he now sports a substantial beard. But listen, friend, if you're passing through, I could give you the closest shave of your life."

"Thanks, perhaps another time. Where might I find MacLeod?"

Together, Ned and Roger said, "Four Winds." Ned added, "Continue down this street toward the water. You'll see the church on your left. Walk toward it and turn right just before you reach the church. The Four Winds is at the end of the lane. Nobody's ever sure where MacLeod resides. Cellars, attics, abandoned warehouses on the wharfs. Summers he can be found sleeping it off in a fishing boat and in warm weather he reeks of salmon and walleye."

"Appreciate it."

Roger, whose vest girdled an enormous belly, turned his lathered face toward Kincaid. "If he's not there, Madge Dancer at the Winds might know where he's holing up. Rumor has it they once formed a union, whether they were legally married is a point of conjecture. She threw him out long ago, but she still looks after him like a stray, leaving him scraps." The cigar wedged between his stubby fingers sent a thin blue line of smoke toward the tin-molded ceiling. "They say she's got the prettiest girls this side of the Soo at the Four Winds."

"That's what they say." Ned's pinky finger stroked the corner of his trim black mustache. "But then we're married men, so we lack any empirical evidence."

"Indeed." Roger nodded solemnly. "Haven't had any empirical evidence since the Taft administration."

"Roosevelt," Ned corrected.

"Was it Teddy?" He sighed. "I suppose it was. We're getting on, Ned, getting on."

Kincaid let himself out into the cold wind that came off the straits. Collar turned up, he walked several blocks past stores and shops, and then turned into the street that led to the church. Catholic church, shingled steeple, topped with a cross, green with verdigris. The newspapers frequently reported cross burnings in Michigan. It was curious how the KKK used the cross—burning them—to announce their arrival in towns and villages. All in an effort to eradicate the non-Protestant. No Catholics, no Jews, no Negroes. The Klan seemed to have run its course back in the decades following the Civil War, and then their appeal flagged. Until recently, when a reconstituted Klan emerged in Indiana and quickly spread into other Midwestern states. The push was on in Michigan. Kincaid liked to think that Michiganders would reject such populist chicanery—there was plenty of evidence that with the purchase of memberships and the sale of KKK robes and paraphernalia someone was getting rich from playing on the public's fear and prejudices—but the frequent newspaper accounts about the cross burnings, parades, and patriotic public events (Protestant only) were proving him wrong. Kincaid's mother, who as a young girl had come to America from Ireland, and who employed language and accent in a most beautiful and unorthodox fashion (to her son's ear) would call what the Klan were up to codswallop. He could hear her say, *No better than tinkers selling pots and knives of suspicious origin, and the only good'll come of it will be the lining of their own pockets. Codswallop, pure and simple.*

It had been years since Kincaid had been inside a Catholic church. As a boy, his Scottish Presbyterian father tolerated what he referred to as his wife's Popish ways. Sunday mornings, she would herd the four children, dressed in their finest, to Mass, and sometimes, as a gesture of familial unity, the old man would accompany them. Throughout the service he would mutter caustic annotations, despite his wife's elbow jabs. *If they served single malt whiskey instead of wine, I'd convert in a moment. They have to ring the bells to announce the miracles.* But after she died, when Kincaid was eleven, his father said that it was the end of their churchgoing.

Gazing up at the steeple, Kincaid felt a hint of regret. The vestments, the incense drifting into the rafters, the sacred rituals of the Mass, they held great significance for him when he was young. But what he truly missed was his mother's lilting intonation as she sang the hymns, a rich mezzo-soprano. As cancer withered her vocal cords, her voice became thin as the pages in the family missal. To the end, though, she had perfect pitch.

Turning down the lane just before the church, Kincaid saw the house with a signboard: *Four Winds.*

Angus MacLeod sat alone at the bar, nursing a mug of coffee laced with whiskey. He had a split lip and a swollen left eye that was various shades of purple and black. His right earlobe was caked with blood, and he held a towel filled with melting snow on his head, which caused his hair to hang in snarled curls that fell to his massive shoulders. He did not smell of fish, as had been suggested in Ned's Parlor, but of whiskey and dried vomit, which had encrusted the lapels of his wool coat. Kincaid imagined that a bear waking from winter hibernation would look more sober and alert.

"I've seen the lad you're talking about," MacLeod said. "I'd like to find the little bastard myself." He removed the towel from his head and pressed it tenderly against his swollen lower lip.

The bar in the Four Winds was in a state of disrepair. Tables tilted on their sides, chairs knocked over. Two girls, perhaps not twenty years of age, were cleaning up. The one with the broom said, "Angus, Madge will be downstairs any minute now. You best be on your way before she finds you, eh?"

"Madge," Kincaid said. "Your ex-wife."

MacLeod removed the soggy towel from his mouth. "Now there's a fine bit of investigative work. You really must be a policeman. Where'd you say you were from?"

"Downstate. Almost to the Ohio border."

"Ah. The Toledo Strip. Imagine if the Upper Peninsula still belonged to Ohio. It would be tragic." MacLeod finished his coffee and got to his feet with great effort. "We best be moving on. Don't want these girls to catch it from Madge for harboring old Angus. They dote on me like a father, but Madge doesn't take kindly to her ex hanging about. She's all business. When I bring customers in the door at night and money is spent, everything's fine, but otherwise . . ."

He lurched across the room and waved to the girls who both offered him sweet smiles. "Later, darlings." Outside, he stopped and took in a great draught of cold air. "That's what I needed. A snootful of a fresh lake breeze." He continued up the lane, favoring his right leg. "We had a bit of a donnybrook during the races last night. It happens quite often, ye know. Passes for entertainment around here. Winter days, they're short, and the nights they be long."

They walked up the lane toward the church on the main street, but MacLeod stopped before a dilapidated house on the corner. "This one should do."

He led Kincaid around to the side of the house and pushed a door open. The kitchen cabinets were charred, the ceiling plaster had collapsed, exposing scorched joists. MacLeod stepped over the rubble and into what must have been the parlor and fell on to a sofa that had been burned at one end. "Fire here a week or so ago. It'll do till it's time to go back to the Winds."

"Tell me about this boy you met last night."

"Would he be in a wee bit of trouble? At his age, what lad isn't? What do they call him?"

"Rope."

"That's right. Well, Rope was part of our crew during the races. Had a good set of lungs on him, he did, but when the fight broke out he up and disappears. I know I had four dollars and change on me, but it's nowhere on me person now. You're a lawman—you ain't after him for thievery, are ye?"

"No." Kincaid went to one of the two windows in the room. The broken panes were stuffed with wadded rags, but he could see through wavy glass across the street to a weathered brick house. There was a wrought iron fence about the place, and children were playing in the snow, with several nuns standing guard. "I don't think this boy is a thief."

"Somebody stole me money. You could help me retrieve it, Officer."

"Could have been one of your other mates. Or the girls?"

"No, no. Not the girls."

"I see. You trust them."

"Indeed. I'm a very good judge of character, having no such thing myself."

The nun standing on the front porch had a set of wooden clappers, which she smacked together twice, a signal that made all the children stop their running about. They froze in place, standing in awkward positions, feet raised out of the snow, arms held up toward the sky. As though it were a game. Upon the second set of claps, they all quietly scurried to the middle of the yard, where they lined up in a column of twos. Upon the third clap, they marched through the snow, up the granite steps, and into the house.

"Savages," MacLeod said. "Indians, that's bad enough. But, my Lord, Catholic Indians?" Kincaid turned and watched MacLeod reach under the sofa and remove a bottle. "You care for a touch?" MacLeod held the bottle out to him.

"No, thanks."

MacLeod shrugged and tipped the bottle up to his mouth. "Been living on the hard since my last ship went down. Use to skipper ships that worked the lakes and all the way up the St. Lawrence. I'll captain no more. Who'll hire me?"

"You lived here, before the fire?"

The man took up half the sofa, the less burned half. He looked about as though trying to orient himself, and then shook his head. "Possibly. I move around, ye know, both sides of the straits. If this Rope lad's not a thief, what are you after him for?"

Kincaid gazed out the window again. The children had filed into the house, and the nun with the clappers was just pulling the front door closed behind her. The sky was clouding over, and the street seemed forlorn in cold November light. "Looks like it may snow again."

"That's the safest bet in the U.P." After another pull on his bottle of whiskey, MacLeod said, "Must be something serious the lad's done for a lawman to follow him all the way up here, eh?"

"That may be the case. He wasn't with a girl, was he? He's up here looking for a girl."

"No, I didn't see a girl with him. But he mentioned something about one, and that's why I took him to the Four Winds. Girls that wander, they often end up at the Four Winds, or places like it. It's a matter of survival, ye know. But he didn't see the girl he was looking for there." With the drink, the man sounded more assured, but edging toward belligerence. "No, the lad was alone, and me money's gone missing. If I sniff out this lad before you do, and I find that he stole me four dollars, there won't be much left of him to take back down to wherever you come from. Or maybe you should just let it go, leave the boy and this girl to their miserable fates. This far north, there is not much law but there is true justice."

"True justice. Now that sounds familiar."

"Does it?"

"An out-of-work skipper, you were on a mission."

"A mission, you say?"

"Why'd you crossed the straits yesterday?"

"I move back and forth frequently."

"I understand that." Kincaid waited until he had MacLeod's full attention. "In this case, were you sent?"

The shift in MacLeod's stare was barely perceptible. Caution, cut with a vicious sizing up of his quarry.

"A fellow named Ben, and the other one, they came into to the restaurant where I was eating lunch." MacLeod said nothing. "You know them?"

"I know most everyone who lives on both sides of the straits. Ben? Sure, I know him."

"He sent you across to look for two kids. You found one, the boy, and lost him."

MacLeod inhaled deeply, preparing to set things straight. "I lost me four dollars. All the capital I possess at the moment. And I aim to get it back." He took a swig from the bottle. "If I was sent, as you say, it was for good cause."

"I heard all about that from Ben and . . ."

"Luke."

"Right. Luke."

"I also know a stranger here, when I see one. Do you know what you're dealing with up here, Captain Kincaid?" MacLeod didn't wait for an answer. "'Cause if you don't, you need to consider your priorities."

"That could mean any number of things."

"I think you know what it means, and I don't have to spell it out. Soon as the ferry's operating again, you want to get yourself back across the straits." MacLeod got up off the sofa and pocketed the bottle. "Now I've got to make my way out back to the privy for a few moments of quiet reflection, so you best see yourself out."

"The ferry's repair," Kincaid said. "That could take some time."

"You never know up here. Time is different this far north."

"I see that. There a hotel nearby?"

"Yes, but it's famous for its lice. Better to stay at Mrs. Schuller's boarding-house, three blocks south of here. She's a bit stern but keeps a clean establishment." He hobbled toward the burned-out kitchen, bumping a shoulder against the doorjamb on the way, muttering, "When the ferry's ready to make a passage, she'll sound her horn. You want to be on it, Captain."

Fourteen

Keys are not the problem," Theresa whispered, her mouth so close Rope could feel her warm breath on his ear. "I know where a spare set is kept." She held out her hand, presenting the key ring. "The problem is the vestibule down on the first floor. A nun sits in a chair by the front door all night. She can see down the length of the hall, and she's looking right up the staircase. We call her our guardian angel. It's a form of punishment. Tonight, it's one of the novitiates. She's on guardian angel duty three nights. We need to get to the cellar, where we can climb out a window."

It was after midnight, and the house had been in slumber for hours. Yet the old house was far from silent. Wind caused glass panes to rattle in their sashes, and the walls and the roof constantly creaked and groaned in response to sudden gusts. There were occasional footsteps and doors closed. More than once, Rope had heard water filling a chamber pot.

"A house like this," he said, "there must be back stairs."

"Yes, the servants' stairs. The third floor has tiny cells where they lived when the house was owned by a lumber baron named Blaine Larson. I sleep up there now. The door to the back stairs is locked at night, but I have the keys."

"So how do we get to the cellar?"

"First, we get Mercy out of her room down the hall, and then we'll take the Miracle."

"The what?"

She put her fingers to her lips, indicating that they must stop talking, and led him out the door and into the second-floor hallway. She walked toward the back of the house, her hand running along the top of the oak wainscoting, passing by closed panel doors. Once she hesitated and pointed at the floor and walked around a section. Despite her care, the floorboards creaked occasionally. The wind, the noise it created, helped disguise the sound of their footsteps. When she stopped at a door and sorted through the keys, Rope could hear movement inside the room.

Theresa unlocked the door and opened it slowly. They stepped inside, closed the door, and looked at Mercy, who stood in her overcoat, holding the one candle that lit the room.

"Hello," Rope said.

Theresa glanced up at him, disappointed. "You need to do better than that."

"Hello," he said again, with what he hoped was with greater feeling. "I hope you are well."

Theresa shook her head in disappointment.

"Why did you even think to follow me from the farm?" Mercy whispered.

Rope didn't know how to put it into words. He tried to smile, which seemed to anger her. She had a wool hat pulled down over her hair, and her eyes held the candlelight. The angles of her face were made for such shadows. He thought she might be pleased to see him, but she looked like she was prepared to kick him again.

"So, what now?" he asked Theresa. "The Miracle?"

"Larson had a gasoline generator," Theresa whispered, "and there was a small elevator installed in the back of the house. The elevator was removed long ago. It's called the Miracle of the Hoopskirt. His wife, she either was forgetful or she was drunk, probably drunk, and she once opened the door to take the elevator downstairs and fell down the shaft, but was saved by her hoopskirt, which opened like an umbrella and caught in the walls of the shaft. It took hours to get her out of there. The shaft goes to the cellar."

"Fine, we'll need hoopskirts and another miracle to get down there," Mercy said.

"No," Theresa said. "We'll take the Mistress Ladder. It runs the length of the shaft. Larson had many visitors in the night. Maids from the third floor, as well as his friends' wives, and even their daughters. I once heard two nuns talking about it. They can be terrible gossips." She leaned forward and blew out the candle in Mercy's hand. "Now, you must follow me, stepping exactly where I step. The back hall to the shaft will be very dark. I have a box of matches, but we cannot use them until we get to the cellar. We must hold hands. Me first." She took Mercy's hand.

Mercy put the candle down on the table, hesitated, and then held her hand out to Rope. He took hold of it with what remained of his right hand. He had never touched her skin before. They were rough hands, strong from doing chores. She let go and took firm hold of his wrist.

Theresa led them out into the hall, dimly lighted by a lamp at the foot of the front stairs. They walked slowly toward the back of the house, turning a corner, and entering near darkness. Theresa moved in a zig-zag pattern, avoiding creaking floorboards. Periodically, they stopped and listened. The wind buffeted the house. Deep snoring. A cough. Finally, they reached a door at the end of the hall.

"This was the hardest part," Theresa whispered. "It's a very old lock." She handed the key ring to Rope. "The big skeleton key, like something to a dungeon."

He found the keyhole with his right thumb and inserted the large key. It didn't turn either way, at first, but after several tries the lock opened.

"The rungs are bolted into the wall on the left side," Theresa said. She stepped forward into near pitch dark. "I've climbed them before. Most of them are bolted tightly."

"Most of them," Mercy said.

"One, I'm not so sure about. I have to count as we go down, and we shouldn't step on it." Theresa began to descend into the shaft, her shoes on the metal rungs echoing faintly.

Mercy looked at Rope. "You next."

"You sure? I doubt I'll catch you if you slip."

"I do, too."

Rope reached into the shaft, his left hand finding a metal rung. As he hooked his right hand over the rung, he set one foot and then the other on a lower rung. He began to follow Theresa down the shaft, which was pitch dark. Mercy got on the ladder above him. Once her foot came down on the knuckles of his left hand.

"Thank you," he whispered.

"Shhh." Theresa said. "Now, here's the loose rung." She put a hand around Rope's boot. "Two down. You have to not step on it but lower yourself to the next rung. Then we are almost to the first floor. Very quiet because the shaft is between two of the sisters' bedrooms."

Rope bypassed the loose rung and, taking hold of Mercy's boot, guided her safely below it as well. Cobwebs clung to his face. It was so dark it was better to descend with his eyes closed.

Above him, Mercy stopped.

"What is it?"

"My coat, it's caught on something." There came the sound of tearing fabric, and then she continued to climb down.

They all stopped when they heard snoring. Theresa whispered, "Go. We must keep going."

When they were below the first floor, a faint light came up from below. Rope could see just enough to make out two beams near the bottom of the shaft, forming a cross. "What's that?"

"I'm not sure," Theresa said. "Maybe the shaft needed to be shored up? We have to squeeze through."

The space was tight, but Rope got through without snagging his coat. Below, Theresa stepped off the last rung on to the dirt floor. She got out a box of matches and lit one. Above him, Rope could see that the hem of Mercy's coat was caught on a protruding nail. He lifted the wool free and, as Mercy lowered her foot, he slid the knuckles of his left hand out of the way just before she stepped on to the rung.

Rope climbed down three more rungs and then his first foot, followed by his second, touched packed dirt. Mercy's foot missed one of the last rungs, and she fell away from the wall with a little yelp. Rope caught her, awkwardly, and eased her down until she was standing on the cellar floor. Her elbow had struck his nose, sending pain back through his cheekbones, and he tasted blood that ran down from his right nostril.

Theresa lit another match and said, "This way." But she didn't move.

They heard footsteps overhead—two sets of footsteps in the front hall. Theresa waved out the match just as a door opened, sending a dim oblong of lantern light down a steep set of wooden stairs. Two nuns stood in the doorway. One of the sisters leaned down for a better view into the cellar.

"I didn't hear it," the other said.

"I thought it was from down there."

They both sounded young. Novitiates.

"It's probably the wind," the first said.

"Or rats."

"Rats?"

"Rats making little rats."

"Oh."

Slowly, the door closed.

Theresa lit another match and led them along a stone wall until they came to a small window up just beneath the joists. "This one," she whispered. "I unlatched it months ago."

"Why did you wait?" Rope asked. "Why haven't you already run away from here?"

"I tried," Theresa said. "I have come down the Miracle several times, but I get this far and then I'm afraid to go out by myself. I don't know why. Maybe I was waiting for you?"

"Are you sure you want to do this?" Mercy asked. "I told you, running away is hard."

Theresa's eyes were large, fearful in the light from the match. "I know. But this time, with you, I must go. I can't stay now. If I do, the sisters will know I had something to do with it. They have trusted me so. I couldn't face their disappointment. And Sister Superior's anger. So, we must go. Now. There is no turning back." She waved out the match. "Can you lift me?" she said to Rope. "With your hand like that, can you lift me up to the window?"

He took hold of the girl about the waist and picked her up. Thin beneath her coat, so light he could raise her above his head. Mercy helped, supporting Theresa's foot with both hands.

When she swung the window open, cold air and snow, smelling of freedom and uncertainty, blew down on them.

•

Milt sat up and rubbed his forehead as he gazed out the windshield of his truck. It was dark, the road ahead lined with bare trees. It took a moment to realize that he was just east of town, and the question was: *How did I get here?*

It had been one of those quiet days at the station. Ellie had walked out in the morning, disgusted by his spiked coffee as much as the way her day was going. When she had returned to the station, Ellie ignored him, pretending to do paperwork throughout the afternoon. No one came to the station. No one called. No complaints. No arrests. A perfect day of law enforcement in Otter Creek Township. Milt sipped Ding's from his mug while playing solitaire on his desk. A tune in his head all afternoon. Hummed it, sang it, just to irritate Ellie. Somebody stole my gal, somebody stole my pal. *Somebody came and took her away. She didn't even say she was leavin'.* Singing it over and over brought a discernable tension to Ellie's shoulders. Shuffled the stack of cards with a flourish. *The kisses I loved so, he's gettin' now, I know. Dum-dee-dum-dum, that broken-hearted pal, somebody stole my gal.* By four-fifteen, she'd had enough. Without a word, pulled on her coat and left the station.

And then what? More solitaire, more Dingley's. Few crimes after seven p.m. in Otter Creek Township, nothing that couldn't wait till the station opened in the morning. Late night complaints could be taken up with the county sheriff's office. Otter Creek used to have a round-the-clock police force, six men rotating twenty-four hours a day. As a rookie Milt was usually put on the night shift. Rarely a call. Maybe some domestic incident resulting in a bruise or a shiner, or the occasional dispute over a cow that had wandered into the wrong pasture. When the town council determined that budget cuts were necessary, the force was reduced to two police officers and one secretary. The joke was: cutting the force reduces crime.

He closed up the station a little before seven. Took the bottle of Dingley's out to his truck and did the rounds, like the old days. Cruised by stores and shops, closed for the night. After turning down Cedar Street, he pulled over to the curb a couple of doors from Ted Kunkel's house. Dr. Ted Kunkel, DDM. Little one-story. Tidy yard, freshly painted shutters and trim. Sitting in the truck, sipping a touch of Ding's, Milt had a view of the side of the house, the ceiling light in the kitchen. *Somebody stole my gal.* Sophie came to the sink, her head lowered, doing dishes, cleaning up after dinner. She'd gotten her hair cut, and the light from the ceiling created a halo-effect. *Somebody stole my pal.* One thing he had to admit, nothing wrong with her cooking. Fried chicken, pork loin, steaks. Mashed potatoes. Pies with that lattice crust. Since she moved out, he'd lost his appetite. Now it was a can of this and that or whatever was on special at Jake's Diner. Sophie picked up a towel and gazed out the window as she wiped her hands. No way she could see him in the truck parked down the dark street. Still, there was a moment when it felt as though they were staring right at each other. Milt sat perfectly still, until she turned away from the sink, ran a hand through her hair, and smiled as she said something to Ted. And then she was gone from the window and the kitchen went dark.

Milt put the bottle on the floor and drove down Cedar, slowly, past Kunkel's house, and then continued his rounds. For how long? An hour? Two? What difference what time he'd get back to his house? He drove the streets, late enough that most houses had gone dark.

•

Mercy's overcoat was torn in two places from the climb down the elevator shaft. But they were free. They stood in the snow outside the wrought iron fence, the sound of waves coming in on the wind. She had always liked the dark, its isolation, its ability to harbor and conceal. But here, she felt exposed, not just to the cold gusts coming off the Mackinac Straits that caused a shiver in her spine, but her sense of purpose. She was close now.

"John Nolan," she said to Theresa, who did not look cold at all, "this former priest."

The girl smiled, but then appeared determined to establish some ground rules. "I will take you to him. In a few hours, when it's light. And then I go away from this place. Forever."

"How you going to get there?"

"How does anyone get anywhere? How did you get here?" Theresa shook her head. "I am not worried. I know people. They will take me. I'll be so far from here they'll never know where to look." She smiled at Mercy. "No convent for me."

Mercy did something that surprised her, something impulsive. An instinct, maybe a desire. She placed an arm around Theresa, and the girl responded by falling against her side, burying her face against her shoulder. "Theresa, when we were in that shaft, in the pitch dark, I had my doubts. We could get caught. We could fall. I didn't think we were going to make it out of there."

Rope was looking at her as though seeing her for the first time. The trick had always been not to expose yourself. Keep everything hidden. Don't look vulnerable. Stay strong. She'd been wrong about this boy. He was quiet, determined, and she believed that he was true and honest. Theresa saw this, too. *You should marry him.* What did a twelve-year-old girl know about such things? *You should marry him.* Still, it was a frightening thought.

She looked back at Rope. Really looked at him. He seemed revealed, embarrassed, timid. Frightened, too. Good. Feel this? *Feel what I think I'm feeling? If you do, realize what it means. The weight of it. What it asks of you. What it will give to you.* She wanted her eyes to say this to him.

He looked back at her then. Wary, at first. But then there was a moment—his eyes, she saw it there, what would make a boy follow her all this way up to this cold northern place. She didn't have a name for it, but it was something they both felt, both needed. Something earnest, forthright, maybe something to be shared.

But then he became distracted, looking past her, his face softened first by doubt and then alarm, and he turned and began running, disappearing into the heavy snow.

Mercy and Theresa looked around at the sound of heavy, lumbering footsteps as a large man appeared out of the dark. Shaggy hair and beard, enormous shoulders. Theresa clung tightly to Mercy's coat for protection.

"You—you stay right here!" he shouted at them as he ran after Rope.

•

Mrs. Schuller, a substantial woman with a tight bun and loose jowls, gave Kincaid the bedroom at the end of the hall on the second floor. He paid for two nights, six dollars, which included breakfast and dinner. When she asked him his business in St. Ignace, he said it was a police matter and he would need the use of the telephone in the vestibule. The other guests at dinner were a traveling cutlery salesman and an elderly couple from Escanaba who were waiting for repairs to be completed on the *Chief Wawatam* so they could cross the straits and visit an ailing relative in Charlevoix. Mrs. Schuller cooked with an excess of lard, and the meat was laced with gristle.

According to house rules all was quiet by nine o'clock. Though he was exhausted, Kincaid lay in the single bed beneath wool blankets that smelled of camphor, listening to the wind. He was finally dropping off to sleep when a knock came at his door. He had gone to bed in his clothes—the room was that cold—and when he opened the door Mrs. Schuller stood in the hall in her bathrobe, hands on her broad hips. "House rules," she said. "No guests after nine o'clock, but I guess this might be an exception, you being up here on police business."

"Excuse me?"

Mrs. Schuller started down the hall, her slippers shuffling on the floorboards. "He's downstairs in the parlor. I can smell the liquor on his breath, so maybe you should arrest him and do all of St. Ignace a favor." She went into her room and shut the door firmly.

Kincaid went downstairs and found Angus MacLeod standing in the parlor, gazing at framed portraits on the wall. "I found your lad," he said without looking away from the wall, "the fella you call Rope."

"Where?"

"I saw him up by the Catholic church. He was in front of the old Larson house, which the church owns now. I chased after him, but he got away in the snow and dark. The way he bolted there's no question he's got me four dollars." MacLeod turned away from a portrait of a man with long side-whiskers. "I mean to get it out of him. If I get my hands on him, he will be much worse for wear."

"You say he ran off."

"Aye. They all did."

"Who?"

"The two girls."

"Two girls?"

"One of the darker persuasion, I think. And a girl, looked like one of the Indians the nuns harbor there in the Larson house. The nuns think they can bring the little savages to Christ, make 'em civilized." He snorted.

"You have any idea where they'd go, in this weather, in the middle of the night?"

"No. There's any number of abandoned houses and warehouses down by the water. I know 'em all. They could hole up any one of them. Four dollars. May not seem like much to you, staying here all snug in Mrs. Schuller's house, but it's all the money I've got."

"That's all you're in this for, four dollars?"

MacLeod had strutted into the vestibule but paused at the front door. "Four dollars. Where I come from, a man can get killed for less."

"What about those two over in Mackinaw City, Ben and Luke? What do you get if you turn those two kids over to them?"

"That be my business."

Kincaid dug into his pocket for his wallet and pulled out a five-dollar bill. "Does your business take the highest bidder into consideration?"

MacLeod stared at the bill in Kincaid's hand. He cleared his throat, preparing to make a declaration of some import. "There's the satisfaction of justice, which has no price."

"Of course, justice," Kincaid said, as he began to put the bill back into his wallet. "I have the greatest respect for such principles."

MacLeod stepped back into the parlor, eying the wallet. "Would that be a down payment then?"

"It would," Kincaid said. "Five now. And twenty if you deliver them."

"Twenty? No." MacLeod said. "You came a long way to find them. Twenty-five, each. The lad, and the lass." When Kincaid looked at him, he smiled. "Kincaid? That name wouldn't be from one of the highland clans with a long history of cattle theft and horse trading?" He plucked the bill from Kincaid's fingers and went into the vestibule and opened the front door. "For all I know, we might be related. Distant cousins, like." He pulled the door shut, cutting off the bite of the cold wind that rushed into the parlor.

Fifteen

When Milt entered the station in the morning, Ellie was at her desk, conducting business as usual. This was as close to forgiveness as she ever got. She was a big-hearted woman who believed in bygones.

"You just got a call from Doc Evers," she said. "Because he got a call from Lyle Nesbit. He and Hannah are out at Nau Farm. Estelle passed early this morning. Doc Evers says his car won't start so he wants you to drive him out there."

The doctor was dangerously thin, and a perfectly trimmed white mustache was his only extravagance. He had the ability to sit still in Milt's truck to the point where he seemed to have been cast in bronze. It made Milt nervous. As they drove out to the farm, he tried to bring up the weather, the change of season, but the old doctor simply stared out the windshield as though he could see clear into the next life. He'd acted as county coroner for years. Around Otter Creek, you weren't dead until Doc Evers said so.

Milt was not prepared for the blood. The blankets, bedsheets, and Estelle's nightgown were saturated. Coagulated blood so dark it was fairly black. Her withered, gouged arms lay palms up.

"Where's the knife?" Doc Evers demanded.

"On the floor, over there." Hannah's voice always had the slightest quiver, but now it sounded as though she were trying to speak while some unseen force shook her violently. She so resembled her sister that since childhood they were often mistaken for each other. They were only a year or two apart, and Milt couldn't remember which one was older. Now, confronted by the mortal image of herself, Hannah looked like she was about to die of fright.

Milt walked around the end of the bed, where a steak knife lay on the pine floorboards. He ventured a glance at Estelle's wrists, the jagged incisions running halfway to her elbows.

Doc Evers looked like he'd been swindled. "Lyle, where were you?"

"We set up a bed in the room off the parlor," Lyle said. "Asleep, didn't hear a thing."

"Cuts like that," Hannah said, barely able to get the words out. "You'd think we'd hear her cry out. Nobody realized how tough my sister was. She got it from . . . from Momma." She turned, sobbing, and fled the room.

The doctor, unmoved, said, "The knife, you just gave it to her?"

"Well, you know, Doc, we brung her dinner in here, like always. She must have kept the knife, and we just didn't take notice when we took the tray away."

Doc Evers placed the back of his hand against Estelle's neck. "Cold. Rigor mortis well established." He glared at Lyle. "Reminds me of my moribund automobile. You had it in the garage four days ago and now it won't start."

"I adjusted the distributor. Must be something else," Lyle offered.

"You think it's something else now? You going to charge me again to fix that?"

"Doc, I'll come over today and tow it back to the shop. We'll deduct the other bill from whatever the charges are. I wasn't planning on opening the garage today, what with all this, but I'll have you up and running by tomorrow morning."

The doctor ran a finger along his trimmed mustache. Milt couldn't help but notice it was the same hand that had just touched Estelle's skin. The doctor might have been discreetly trying to detect a scent. "Deputy Waters here is starting a side business, providing a taxi service for doctors who need to make their rounds." He turned his vengeful stare on Milt. "I reckon you don't have anything better to do?"

There was no advantage to challenging Doc Evers. "I could give you a lift, I suppose," Milt said.

The doctor's irritation did not seem diminished. "And our chief of police, he's still off somewhere hunting down those two orphans?"

"He's up north, yes," Milt reported.

"You want to know how this works? Well, let me tell you," the doctor said. "Captain Kincaid finds them, brings them back down here, and there will be a trial. That boy and girl are minors in the eyes of the law, but then what was done to Harlan is no minor offense. Nothing like this has happened in Otter Creek, not since I began practicing medicine here over forty years ago. At the trial I will be expected to offer testimony." He raised his voice. "Hannah, you might as well hear it now." In the kitchen, she stopped crying. Nearly shouting, he had a rich baritone and the cadence of a preacher who could spread hell, fire, and brimstone to the very back of the tent. "If you choose to attend said trial, which I would not recommend considering the history of heart ailments in your family, you will most certainly hear it then. That axe? The one used on Harlan? The blade was buried four inches deep in his skull. That's what I will say under oath." He looked at Milt, and then Lyle. "I tell you it was a mighty swing."

•

They spent the night in St. Mary's Church. Theresa said that Father Lalonde, the current pastor, did not believe in locking the house of the Lord. They stretched out on pews toward the back of the church, listening to the creaking rafters announce gusts off the straits. A couple of men staggered in during the night and took up residence in pews near the altar. One of them snored loudly, rhythmically, keeping time through the night.

At first light, Theresa led Mercy and Rope through the slumbering village to a road that wound up a steep hill. They walked several miles, passing through woods and pastureland, until Theresa stopped at a fork in the road and pointed at a small white house on the ridge.

"John Nolan lives there," she said. "I'm going that way." She pointed toward a stand of gray woods that ran to the gray horizon.

"You're not coming with us?" Mercy asked. "But—"

"I'm headed that way, west, across the U.P."

There was a moment's hesitance before she stepped into Mercy's arms. Then she came to Rope and put her arms around him as well. Such displays only embarrassed him. Theresa held him about as long as he could stand it, and then she grabbed his shoulders so she could pull him down close and whisper in his ear, "She wants to marry you. She doesn't know it yet, but I've fixed it." As she released him, her smile was proud and duplicitous.

She walked off along the west fork in the road, never once looking back, her boots pushing through the fresh snow until she disappeared in the trees. Mercy gazed at the woods long after the girl was out of sight.

Finally, Rope turned toward the house on the ridge and said, "Why are we here?"

"I ask myself that every day," Mercy said. "I haven't come up with an answer. Yet. I keep thinking today is the day. But the answer doesn't come. Or if it does, I don't recognize it. Listen, you don't have to go up there, you know. You can wait here. Or go back down to the village." She started walking toward the house perched on the high edge of a white plane of snow, smoke rising from its chimney.

"Or I could just wait out here," he said. "Until I freeze to death."

"In this weather, you could, yes."

It was like the moment in the attic, though its opposite. There, it was warm, and she was barely clothed. Here, they were in this cold, barren expanse, an unforgiving landscape. Harsh, bitter air, but he liked how it was empty. No, not empty. Open. The land, the sky, they were open. She walked away from him then, at Nau Farm, and she walked away from him now. This terrain had something to do with all this, in a way that Rope couldn't fully grasp. It was a wild, merciless place, woods and fields, and long views across water to islands and distant shores, that seemed the geographical embodiment of eternity. No beginning, no end. As he watched her walk through it, he felt both drawn and captive. But chosen, too.

He began to follow her up toward the ridge, planting his boots in the footsteps she left in the snow.

•

The house, cluttered but orderly, smelled of smoke, and of cooking, aromas and scents Mercy could not identify. There was a woman who answered the door, Ojibwe, like Theresa, and clinging to her shawl were two children, a boy and girl. John Nolan lay on a daybed by the stone fireplace. Mercy did not think he had the strength to get to his feet without assistance. His tired eyes reflected the light from the burning logs, creating a glazed stare that seemed both saintly and demonic. He lay on his back beneath a blanket with bold geometric lines, red, black, azure, one hand stroking his beard that extended down to the high mound of his stomach. He did not seem surprised when Mercy explained who she was, but he was impressed.

"You have come all the way from Massachusetts?" he said as he gestured toward two wooden milking stools. "Please, sit. What a long journey! Yes, I can see her in you. You could be Andrea's daughter. Your aunt was greatly distressed when your mother died. And it wasn't long, three or four years after, when her health began to decline."

"My aunt, too?" Mercy lowered herself to the stool. "When?"

He turned his head toward the woman who had let them in the front door, who now stood at the cast iron stove. She had ladled soup into clay bowls, which she brought to the two children sitting at the table. "Naomi, how many years since Andrea died?"

The woman, tall and sinewy, had black hair, graying at the temples, tied in a braid that hung to her waist. Mercy could not understand her response. Ojibwe. The language the nuns had forbidden the children to speak. Mercy had never heard it before coming to St. Ignace. Writing *Ojibwe* in the notebook was an act of rebellion. She thought of Theresa, making her way to a far-off place called the Keweenaw Peninsula, where she believed she would find freedom. Rebellion was the same in any language.

John Nolan's grimy fingernails raked his beard. He might have been grooming a cat. "Well, the years go by. I lose track, too. I was still wearing the collar. Your aunt worked in the rectory. She cleaned and cooked for us. Priests are like inattentive husbands. When it comes to domestic activities, they can't help themselves. She was underappreciated and yet, bless her heart, she called it God's work." The faintest smile appeared beneath his whiskers. "She and your mother were from Jamaica, right? Her cooking could be rather spicy for some of the priests more accustomed to boiled chicken and poached whitefish. Our pastor at the time, Father Tremblay, when I told him I was leaving the priesthood, he said he wasn't surprised, only disappointed. "You are too fond of that spicy food,' he told me. 'It's a sign that you've lost your sense of self-denial. So you'll go off with that squaw you have your eye on—I've seen it, we've all seen it—and you'll make babies, little brown babies, and you will get fat eating the way you do, and making those babies will sap your strength, and you'll die young, and when you do God is going to ask you one question: Why didn't you continue with the Lord's work? And tell me, Father Nolan, what will you say to that?'" He laughed now, laughed until he was overcome by a hacking cough. Spittle clung to his whiskers. "Old Father Tremblay, he proved himself a prophet! But eventually he was assigned back to a parish in Montreal. A monsignor by then. Until the influenza took him, like so many others. And I don't know. What *am* I'm going to say to God? 'Monsignor Tremblay was right?' That, he was. I did like the spicy food your aunt from Jamaica made for us in the rectory, and maybe that's what led to my downfall, my desire for earthly pleasures. Or maybe it was Naomi here, who granted me the privilege of being a father, this kind of a father." Again, he looked at Mercy, the firelight in his eyes. They were the eyes, she believed, of someone who knew he did not have long to live. "I'm sorry to be the bearer of such sad news, and I'm sorry you came all this way to learn that your aunt died some time ago. But you don't seem surprised."

"I guess I'm not," Mercy said.

"You both came all the way up here because of that letter I wrote for your aunt?"

"I came," Mercy said, "because she was the only family I have. If it weren't for the letter you wrote for her, I wouldn't even have known about her, or anything about my mother." She glanced at Rope, who sat on the stool beside her. "He has his own reasons for coming here."

John Nolan gazed at Rope a long moment, and then nodded. "I see. Yes, I see that." Looking at Mercy again, he said, "Your aunt was disappointed that she couldn't bring you up herself. She wanted so badly to have children of her own but that never happened. Eventually, her husband—Raymond Selinsky, that was his name—he went off. We heard that he was working in lumber camps farther out in the U.P. And then we heard that he had died. Killed when a tree came down wrong. We learned this when she was sickly, and it only made her go faster. In one way, Andrea was a most fortunate woman. I've never known anyone to welcome death the way she did. That's a real gift, you know. But you, she had promised your mother that she would take care of you, and I think that, more than losing her husband and not bearing children of her own, that was the hardest on her."

At the stove, Naomi had ladled soup into two more clay bowls and the older child, a boy of about five, brought them over, two trips, first to Mercy and then to Rope. He walked with slow dutiful purpose, careful not to spill. He might have been distributing a sacrament. No spoons. Mercy held her bowl in both hands, the heat penetrating her cold fingers. The broth was salty, with carrots, onions, and beans. It was spicy, and it went down hot.

Next to her, Rope took a sip from his bowl and then put it down on the floor next to him.

The little boy remained standing before them. He stared at Mercy as though he didn't know what to make of her. His mother said something Mercy didn't understand, but the boy didn't move. The second time she spoke more sharply, and reluctantly he began to return to the table, but his father's arm came out and stopped him. John Nolan spoke in Ojibwe, his bony hand clutching the boy's shoulder. When he released the child, he went around the table and into the room at the back of the house.

"And you," John Nolan said to Rope, "you also came out from Massachusetts on one of those orphan trains?" Rope nodded. "And you agreed to accompany Mercy on this journey north."

"Agree?" Rope said. "I wouldn't exactly put it that way."

"She asked you to?" John Nolan urged gently. "Accompany her up here?"

"No, I . . . followed her."

"I see."

The woman spoke as she began clearing bowls from the table. John Nolan stared at the fire as he listened to her. "She thinks you are in some trouble." When neither Mercy nor Rope responded, he glanced at them. "I see," he said again.

The boy came back into the room and brought a leather satchel to his father. He whispered to the boy, who then returned to help his mother clear the table. His fingers seemed to lack the strength to open the tarnished hasp on the satchel, but finally he raised the flap and removed an envelope. "When your aunt was ill, I visited her daily. The last time I saw her, only hours before she died—it was the last time I performed Extreme Unction, the last time I anointed someone who was dying. Strange, perhaps, but it was my favorite sacrament. I did not care so much for hearing confession. You tell someone they are absolved of their sins, but somehow the weight of those transgressions stays with you. My father was from Ireland, and he used to talk about the sin-eater in their village, the man who came to the house during a wake and he would 'eat' their sins, and bear them away, along with his compensation, a crust of bread, a tumbler of whiskey, a bit of coin. I find that tradition preferable to confession. I knew I wasn't long for the priesthood when I began to question whether one person can absolve another's sins. But to eat them, consume them, that is another matter. And there is a forthright honesty to Extreme Unction. You bless the body and soul before they separate. It can provide the soon to depart valuable comfort. That last time, after performing the sacrament, when I was about to leave your aunt, she gave this to me." He tapped the envelope lying on his massive stomach. "She wanted me to send it to you. But first I wrote another letter to the orphanage. They never replied."

Mercy put her empty bowl down on the floor. "They never gave me any letters. They kept the one I have in a file cabinet. I'm not supposed to have seen it, but I found it. And I kept it. It's why I'm here."

"A single letter—such power, to bring you all this way," John Nolan mused as he picked up the envelope. "When I received no response from the orphanage, I didn't know what to do. I wasn't going to send another letter to Massachusetts unless I was certain it would reach you. But then, well, things at the rectory became difficult, complicated. I knew I had to leave, but for some of us it is not so easy to just walk away. Has it been easy for you?"

"Nothing is easy for me," Mercy said.

"Of course," John Nolan said. "But you did leave. This trouble, whatever it is, when trouble arises you have no choice. If we didn't encounter trouble, I wonder if we would ever move. It is how we learn who we are. There is nothing like being chased." He stared at Mercy, and then at Rope. "You are, aren't you? Being chased."

Rope sat forward, resting his elbows on his knees. "I think you could say that, yes."

"I see."

"How?" Rope asked. "How do you see this? How do you know?"

John Nolan ventured another brief smile. "You have the look of prey. Seeking shelter but afraid to stop, eager to keep moving."

Rope thought about this for a moment. "No. I am not afraid. Mercy is less so."

"We have done nothing wrong," Mercy added.

"I did not say you had. But still, you are being pursued. Guilt or innocence has nothing to do with it. If Christ taught us anything, he taught us that. What do you intend to do?"

"I wish I knew," Mercy said.

"I'm sorry, that is a broad question. I fear that you have no plan, no direction."

"My direction has been to find my aunt. It's been my only purpose. I have come this far to learn that she's dead." Mercy paused, realizing that she sounded like she was rebuking him. "Now, I don't know."

"Indecision plagues us all," John Nolan said. "*Come uno che esprima la propria volontà e poi la modifichi, cambiando idea a ogni capriccio mutevole, finché tutte le sue migliori intenzioni si riducano al nulla.*"

"Latin?" Rope said.

"Italian, an old form. You speak Latin?"

"Altar-boy Latin. *Mea culpa, mea culpa, mea maxima culpa.* That's about all I remember. English, Ojibwe, Latin, Italian, how many languages to you speak?"

John Nolan gazed at the fire, calculating. "I can get by in French and Gaelic, and a little Polish. My mother was from Kraków. I don't know enough. There hasn't been time. Language is one of the true treasures in this life, no?"

Mercy wasn't about to disagree with him. "What does it mean, what you said in Italian?"

"It's from Dante, the *Divine Comedy.* 'As one who wills, and then unwills his will, changing his mind with every changing whim, till all his best intentions come to nil.' Something like that."

"Indecision," Rope said, "will get you nowhere."

"Yes. Very astute, young man."

"When you left the priesthood," Rope asked, "how did you make a living? As a teacher?"

John Nolan smiled broadly now, revealing missing teeth, as he handed the envelope to Mercy, a gesture that seemed to require all of his strength. "This is all I have of your aunt's," he said. "I have long regretted not getting it to you. So it's quite miraculous that you have made your way this far north. To come out here by train, and then north . . . hundreds of miles. And here you are. You walked into our house. Just in time."

She held the manila envelope in her hand. "What is it?"

"Something you should have," he said. "I hope it will make you feel your journey was worthwhile."

She opened the envelop and removed a photograph. The card was stiff and cracked: sepia image of two girls in white dresses standing beneath a palm tree. "My aunt, and the smaller girl, my mother."

"She said it was all she had left of their childhood, before they came to America," John Nolan said. "I can see the resemblance. Her face, your hair . . ."

Mercy looked at the photograph a moment longer, at her mother's eyes, the eyes of a girl who can imagine none of the hardship she would face, and then she slipped the card back in the envelope. For a photograph, she'd come all this way for a photograph. "Thank you for saving this."

"Your aunt gave it to me the day she died. For the longest time I resisted opening the envelope," John Nolan said. "But I finally succumbed to temptation. I was curious and couldn't resist." He chuckled and, staring once more at the fire, he began to laugh. A robust laugh, one that Mercy imagined often burst from him before he had become so ill. "I have come to believe that God is not some dour, gray-bearded old man. If so, He would be made in my image and likeness. No, I suspect that if He resembles a man or a woman in any way, He is quite the jester," he wheezed, "and we must see the humor in all things." More laughter, which led to coughing, until he managed to catch his breath and whisper, "Until I finally gave in and opened the envelope, I thought that maybe it might be her spicey Jamaican recipes!"

•

When they got up to leave, Rope watched Mercy lean down and kiss John Nolan on the cheek. There was such poise and dignity to the way she bent toward the dying man. Her face hovered above his for a moment, and then she whispered, "God bless you for writing my aunt's letter." She began to straighten up, but then hesitated. Her voice even softer, she said, "You have a fine hand." John Nolan gave the slightest nod.

After Mercy moved toward the door, Rope went to the daybed, and John Nolan took hold of his left hand. His grip was surprisingly firm, considering his condition. Nolan gave a slight tug, and Rope obliged by leaning down to the man.

"You take care of her now," John Nolan said. And then he said something that Rope believed to be in Latin, or maybe Italian, an invocation, a blessing.

Rope didn't know what to say. The more he thought, the more he felt. At times, when the two seemed to converge and boil inside of him, he was rendered mute. All he could do was grip John Nolan's hand and look him in the eye. He hoped it was enough.

He went to the door, where Naomi was helping Mercy pull a long wool sweater over her dress. "No wonder you're cold," Naomi said. "This dress, it's too thin for this far north." She helped Mercy put her overcoat back on and then wrapped a scarf around her neck.

The two children, the boy and his younger sister, both touched Rope, their small hands probing his coat. He reached inside his pockets. There was an apple, which had been there for several days. He removed it and held it out to the boy. "Share," Rope said. "It's for both of you." The boy nodded and then put his arm around his sister and held the apple to her mouth so she could take a bite. A small gesture.

Rope turned to Naomi. "Sometimes I wonder if I have brothers or sisters somewhere."

"That is good, very good." But she seemed intent on a more immediate matter. She held out a pair of wool gloves. "These are John's. He no longer goes outside. You should have them."

They were much thicker, heavier than the pair of gloves Rope had been wearing since he'd found the pea coat in the train station. "Thank you."

Naomi went to open the front door. As the cold air rushed in both she and Mercy gasped, and then they ran out into the snow. Rope followed, pulling the door closed and followed them out on the plane of white, where about fifty yards down the hill lay a body. Rope knew, but he couldn't be sure until they reached her. Theresa was on her back, staring at the overcast sky. She struggled to sit up, so Rope took her by the arms and brought her up to her feet and held her. She was shivering and she said something in Ojibwe to Naomi.

"I must get her inside," Naomi said.

"What happened?" Mercy said.

"That man," Theresa said. "Big, with the beard. He followed me. He must have seen us leave the village. He followed me and caught up with me in the woods. I told him you had decided to go back across the straits. He hit me, and then left me. I tried to get to the house, but . . ." She looked at Rope. "He said you have his money. But he wants both of you."

"I don't have his money," Rope said. "Where is he now?"

"He went back down to the village. He moves like a bear, a drunken bear."

Theresa raised her head, her eyes rolling, and fainted. Rope caught her before she fell in the snow.

"She has been out in the cold too long." Naomi held her arms out. "I will take her. I know this girl."

"She does not want to go back to the nuns," Mercy said.

"I know. They all want to get out of there," Naomi said. "This bear of a man, it is Angus MacLeod. So, this is your trouble."

"Part of it," Rope said.

Naomi whispered something in Ojibwe, a prayer, an oath, or perhaps a curse. Then she said, "I know this girl, have seen her in the village."

"And you know MacLeod," Rope asked.

"Everyone here knows Angus MacLeod." Naomi shook her head. "Get away from this place. Go. Give her to me, and we will take care of her. You must go. Now."

Rope placed Theresa in Naomi's arms. She turned and walked through the snow back toward the house, carrying the child. She might have been bearing a gift, a sacrificial offering. The boy pulled open the front door, she disappeared inside, and the door was pushed closed.

"What's this about money?"

"I don't know," Rope said. "The night at the races, he must have lost money in a bet or maybe someone picked his pocket."

"The races?"

"I don't have his money."

In the distance, came the sound of a horn from the docks on the straits, a deep plaintive moan.

"The ferry," Rope said. "We need to get across."

"Do you have any money?"

"A little. Enough for two tickets."

"We should go down to the ferry," Mercy said, looking toward the snowbound path they'd taken up from the village. "We need to be around people, can't let him find us alone." She began walking, quickly, awkwardly in the snow, and looking over his shoulder, she hollered, "Come on!"

•

Kincaid went from one shop to the next, inquiring about Angus MacLeod.

Yes, they knew him. No, they hadn't seen him.

"Does he owe you money?" the hardware merchant asked.

"He's not allowed in here anymore." Dottie's Bakery.

When Kincaid entered the St. Ignace police station, he received a different reception from the one in Mackinaw City. As Sargent George Redfield shook his hand, he said, "I hope you find MacLeod, Captain, and St. Ignace would appreciate it if you'd take him back down to the Other Peninsula with you." He said Other Peninsula as though it were the proper name of a most undesirable geographical location. Redfield had an enormous gut, which caused him to lean back to counterbalance the weight. "We've locked him up so often we should charge him room and board. But I haven't seen him lately. What's he done now?"

Kincaid explained that he was searching for two orphans wanted in Otter Creek, and somehow MacLeod believed the boy stole four dollars from him, all the money he had.

"I've heard about that murder. A bad deal that brought you way up here. We have a small squad, but we'll keep a look out for Angus and these two kids."

"Thanks. I'm staying over at Mrs. Schuller's boardinghouse." Kincaid began to button up his coat, but then said, "Mind if I use your telephone?"

"Not at all."

Kincaid put a call through to the station. It took the operator a few minutes to make the connection. Redfield brought a mug of coffee to the desk where Kincaid sat.

When Ellie answered the phone, she said, "Any luck?"

He wanted to tell her that the coffee he was drinking was better than what they usually had at the station in Otter Creek. "No," he said. "The kids have probably moved on by now."

"When are you coming back?"

"As soon as the ferry is repaired. Should be back there by tomorrow."

"Good." And then she said something else that was lost amid the static on the line.

"Say again?"

Ellie spoke slowly. "The sooner. The better."

"What's happened?"

"Estelle Nau's dead. Slashed wrists. And if you want to talk with your deputy, I'll have to wake him."

"It's almost noon."

"While you've been gone, it's been hard for Milt. He lacks adult supervision. That Dingley's hooch is bad news. He doesn't look so good. Want me to wake him?"

"No. Tell him I'll be back soon."

"It will be my pleasure." Ellie cleared her throat. "There's more."

"More?"

"Your neighbor, Myra? She stopped in to see Lois this morning and then called the station. Said your mother-in-law isn't doing too well." Ellie paused to clear her throat again. She wasn't telling him everything.

"What's the matter with her?"

"I'm . . . not sure. I sent Mitch out with some soup. And I called Doc Evers."

"She ill?" Kincaid asked. "Take another fall?"

Ellie cleared her throat once more. "I don't know."

Then he understood. "I'll be back as soon as I can."

Kincaid hung up the telephone and looked out the small vestibule window at the snowbound street lined with dark, somber houses. Nothing moved except the wind that swept snow into small, twisting cyclones, white phantoms that rose into the night sky and then vanished.

4

Grand Dragon

Sixteen

Milt and Lyle used a wheelbarrow to move Estelle out of the house to the bed of Milt's truck. They drove into town, where Doc Evers got out at his office, and then went to Poole's Funeral Home. Sidney Poole's twin sons put Estelle on a gurney and took her to the embalming room. Sidney led Lyle and Milt to his office, where he poured them glasses of Dingley's. Maroon velvet curtains, mahogany paneling, leather chairs and sofas, Sidney's office had to be the most well-appointed room in Otter Creek. He settled behind his broad desk, cleaning his round spectacles with his gray necktie. His egg-shaped head was devoid of any hair, and Milt suspected that he shaved his eyebrows as a matter of consistency.

Two drinks in, they concluded the business of arrangements for Estelle's funeral and internment. As Sidney screwed on the cap of his fountain pen, he said, "I'll check with the Reverend Sneed, to be sure there's no conflict."

"Good point," Lyle said.

After a moment, Milt said, "Conflict? With what?"

Sidney and Lyle exchanged a glance. "It's best not to schedule the funeral the same day as the parade," Sidney said. "It's going to be hard enough on Hannah, as it is. The funeral can wait a few days."

Lyle sipped his whiskey in a gesture of confirmation.

"What parade?" Milt said.

People in Otter Creek referred to Doc Evers and Sidney Poole as the Rock and the Hard Place, but the two men couldn't be more opposite. Where Doc Evers could be blunt and, at times, aggressively exercised, Sidney Poole's calm, professional demeanor had been described as "even as paint on a wall." He inspected his manicured fingernails a moment, and then said, "We've obtained the permit from the town clerk's office."

"Permit?"

"For the parade," Lyle said. "Didn't I tell you, Milt?"

"No, you didn't tell me."

"Thought I had. Or maybe I thought that being police you'd be informed, you know, through official channels." Lyle attempted a smile. "But then you've been shorthanded, with Kincaid out of town, so maybe word didn't get to you."

"A parade?" Milt said. "When?"

"This weekend," Sidney said. "Considering it's November, weather's supposed to be good Saturday."

"Yeah, cold but dry," Lyle added. "None of that sleet like we had the other day."

"Let me guess." Milt finished his glass of whiskey. "The Klan."

Sidney folded both hands on his ink blotter. "They'll be coming in from all around. Some have already arrived, I understand. A big deal for Otter Creek."

"So, the rumor, it's true?" Lyle asked, leaning forward.

Sidney said, "It's no rumor." He removed his glasses and pinched his eyes a moment with his fingers, apparently an effort to control his emotions. "He's coming. He's really coming here."

"Who is?"

Lyle turned to Milt, pausing a moment as though to prepare him for a shock, though from the look on Lyle's face it was unimaginably good news. "The Grand Dragon. In Otter Creek. Can you believe it?"

"The Old Man." Sidney shook his head, solemnly. "They almost never refer to him by his name. I tell you, that's respect. Owen Dingley pulled it off. Don't know how he did it."

The leather-topped table next to Milt's chair had a coaster on it, something rarely seen in Otter Creek. He placed his empty glass on the coaster, embroidered material that matched the maroon drapes, and got out of the leather chair. He went to the nearest window and stared out at Main Street. "Saturday," he said.

"We'll march right by here to the west end of the village," Sidney said, his voice a reverential whisper. "The Grand Dragon will ride in the parade and then conduct the ceremony in the fairgrounds."

•

After buying two ferry tickets, Rope had less than a dollar in change left. They joined the long line of passengers waiting on the pier and shuffled toward the gangplank as the snow blew in from the east. He regretted having given the apple away. "You hungry?"

Mercy shook her head. "Better if I have an empty stomach while we're on this boat."

"It's only five miles," he said.

"It might as well be fifty." She did not appear reassured as she looked out at the straits. "Some distances aren't measured by . . . distance."

He followed her up the gangplank, and they walked around to the other side of the deck, where it was less crowded and more protected from the wind. When the ferry sounded its horn and began to move away from the pier, she gripped the railing with both hands. "It's supposed to help to stare at land," she said, "but with this snow pretty soon we won't be able to see it." She looked at him, her hair, which had come free of her wool cap, streaming across her face. "You love it." The ferry's engines were accelerating, causing the steel deck to vibrate. She had to shout. "This. You love being on the water."

He leaned toward her so she could hear. She didn't seem to mind. "My father was a sailor."

"You knew him?"

"He came to visit me when I was little. Just once. He said something about shipping out. I didn't understand what that meant. I received a few postcards from places I had to find on a map. Barcelona, Athens, Constantinople. And then there were no more cards."

"Your mother?"

"Not sure, though one of the nuns suggested she paid for her sin while in labor. Like I was responsible."

Mercy stared out at the ice floes on the gray chop. The wind was getting stronger as the ferry moved out into the straits. She said something he couldn't understand. One word, sounded like quilt.

"What?"

"Guilt! It was their biggest weapon." Her face came so close their noses were almost touching. "Where are we going?"

"You asked that before."

"I'm asking again. This is such a cold place."

"We are crossing the straits to the Lower Peninsula. There's something about water. You set a course . . ."

"And?"

"Your destination doesn't seem so important. You maintain your course."

"And eventually you get there? I'm not sure about that. Maybe . . . maybe you just keep wandering!"

He didn't know what to say to that, and he wanted to stop shouting. "Want to go inside and get warm?"

She nodded. As they crossed the rolling deck to a door, she leaned against him, and he placed his arm around her back. In this moment, leaning into the cold wind, he felt something within him turn and it seemed to rise, filling with pride and hope. There were times when he would look at couples, men and women, young or old. It was curious how their lives entwined, how easily they navigated together without saying much, as though they were of the same mind, or understood the same signals, a kind of private Morse code that only they created and only they could decipher. Simple things. A man opening a door for his wife. A girl taking hold of a boy's hand. He'd never known that, caring how someone else fared. If they were hungry, if they were cold. He had always walked alone, been alone. Had never wanted to ask someone what they needed. Now, wanting to ask changed his very dimensions. He felt swollen, as though a new being might emerge, too large for his skin.

"Please, allow me?" He opened the steel door with a courteous bow.

"Thank you, kind sir." She laughed, and then pulled her coat tighter about her neck as though it were an elegant garment.

They took shelter at the top of a narrow metal staircase, pulling the door shut. The engines' rhythmic knocking reverberated through the structure of the vessel, a steel pulse, and the warm air felt greasy and smelled of smoke. They kept their heads together as they looked through a porthole in the door at the windswept swells.

"Better?" He didn't have to shout.

"As long as I don't have to throw up."

"That's the first time I ever heard you laugh. Or make a joke."

"On dry land I'm a hoot," she said. "The nuns didn't have a sense of humor. When I'd be sarcastic, they'd punish me." She turned her head and looked at him. "I've never really known where I was going. It's always been a matter of looking back, glancing over my shoulder, like I'm getting away from something. The orphanage, that farm, St. Mary's. It's always a matter of escape."

"I know."

She gazed out the porthole, as though she were looking at her past and suspecting that laughter might never be possible again. "In the attic . . ."

"You don't have to say anything."

"No, I do. I knew what he wanted. Each day his wife was away he'd get drunk and say things to me. I was going to run away. I was going to do it that night. But he came up to the attic and . . ." She looked at Rope, her eyes green with yellow the color of straw. "Fortunately, he was too drunk. And then you came up the stairs. I said something as I walked by you?"

"You said, 'I could kill him.'"

"If I had that axe, that's what I would have done. But my dress, it was torn. I had to get out of there. What did you do after I went down the stairs?"

"Does it matter?" he asked, leaning toward her until their foreheads touched. "What's done is done."

Slowly, she turned her head to one side and kissed him, at first unsure, their lips barely meeting, and then they fell into each other, their arms clutching, and their kiss seemed to bring up a warmth that had long resided within them both, a heat that they'd harbored throughout their cold journey north.

•

Kincaid settled up at Mrs. Schuller's boardinghouse and with his rucksack slung over his shoulder walked down through the village to the pier. Because ferry service had been postponed due to repairs, a substantial crowd was lined up to board the vessel for Mackinaw City. He was one of the last passengers to climb the gangplank to the deck, and he found a seat on one of the long benches in the saloon. As the vessel pulled away from the dock, St. Ignace disappeared in the snow.

He got up from the bench and walked to the counter at the front of the saloon, where he bought a mug of coffee. The ferry surged through the waves, though the rolling motion was not nearly as bad as when he'd crossed the Atlantic aboard a troop ship. Coffee mug in hand, he made his way to the leeward side of the large room to look out the bank of windows at the straits. He passed a door and through its window saw a set of stairs that led down to a lower deck. There, at the top of the stairs, a young couple were embracing. The boy had his back to Kincaid, and the girl had red hair.

When Kincaid opened the door, they parted hastily. Kincaid's first impulse was to apologize for disrupting such intimacy, but he said, "Hello, Rope."

"Sir." The boy sounded resigned, as though he expected to be caught sooner.

"You found her, I see," Kincaid said.

She had stepped away from Rope until her back was against the door that opened on to the deck. Where the boy seemed calm and accepting of the abrupt change in their circumstances, her eyes were frantic, angry. A slight girl, in a large, soiled coat. "Who is this?" she asked Rope.

"Mr. Kincaid, he gave me a lift on the way up here."

She now looked at Kincaid as though ready to strike. "You a copper?"

Rope turned to her. "What?"

"She's right," Kincaid said. "Police chief, Otter Creek Township."

"You are?" Rope asked.

Kincaid nodded. "I've been looking for you, both of you. We are going to return to Otter Creek, where you will be charged with the murder of Harlan Nau." He saw it in Rope's reaction. Bewilderment, disbelief. "The axe," Kincaid said. "With one swing it was buried in the man's skull."

The girl came away from the door, her feet spread apart to compensate for the roll of the deck. At first, Kincaid thought she was going to leap at him, but instead she threw her arms around Rope and pressed her face into his shoulder. Now Rope looked trapped, not so much by her embrace but by some struggle within, and he was about to protest.

Kincaid raised a hand. "I would advise that you say nothing at this time."

"But . . ." Rope pleaded, and then looked at the girl. "Mercy, I . . ."

"You will be afforded legal counsel."

"Soon as his wife was off the farm," Mercy said, letting go of Rope and turning toward Kincaid, "that farmer was trying to get at me. He was drunk every day, working up the nerve. Attempted rape. You have laws against that?"

"You'll have an opportunity to explain the circumstances, but this is not the place. Hold this, will you?" Kincaid handed his cup of coffee to Rope and reached inside his overcoat. "My immediate problem is due to a lack of preparation on my part." He removed his set of handcuffs. Rope and Mercy stared as though they needed an explanation for the purpose of such a contraption. "I didn't think to bring two pair, so we must make do with the one."

He took hold of the girl's arm and clamped the cuffs on her left wrist. "Seeing as you're already well acquainted, I hope you don't mind holding hands on the rest of our trip." He stared at Rope. The boy understood, and calmly offered his arm. Kincaid locked the other cuff about his right wrist. "There," he said, taking back his coffee mug, "that's done. Now let's go back in the saloon where it's warm."

As he opened the door to the saloon, Kincaid felt again the temptation to apologize. He knew something about this boy, and believed he already had a sense of the girl. They were fortunate to have found each other. It was so seldom one saw love in its most raw and primal state. They didn't even seem to know it yet. Rope took the girl's hand, and they proceeded through the door ahead of Kincaid. People seated on the benches took little notice of the young couple holding hands, though a few scrutinized the girl's face with evident disdain.

·

Rope held Mercy's hand as the ferry crossed the straits. She did not seem disturbed by the touch of his damaged fingers. He knew by her stillness that she was trying not to reveal her discomfort at the ship's erratic movements. "It helps to lean with it," Rope whispered. "It's like riding a horse."

"When have you ever ridden a horse?" she said through tight lips.

"Well, I hope to one day."

"Let me know when you do. Let me know if it's like being on this boat."

Kincaid, sitting on the other side of her, said nothing. His face maintained a blank neutrality that was impossible to decipher. The man was police, but the way he had treated Rope didn't square with it. In Haverhill, coppers were to be avoided. They carried nightsticks, and they didn't hesitate in using them as they ushered people through the cavernous streets along the banks of the Merrimack. The police were notorious for demanding bribes from shopkeepers, and some had reputations for forcing favors from women who worked in the factories. Kincaid had driven Rope north on snowbound roads, put him up for a night in a hotel, bought him meals. One thing was clear to Rope: Captain

Kincaid was dogged and tenacious, and he would only be satisfied when he had them both in his custody.

Kincaid had said that the axe was buried in Harlan's skull. He cautioned against saying anything now, that it would be better to wait until they had legal counsel. When Rope had climbed up into the dark attic, he found Harlan on the cot with Mercy, both gasping with effort. The farmer's sense of heat and urgency. Her torn dress. The frantic strength of her limbs as she fought him off. The light of a candle. Rope's heart raced so fast that he could feel its pulse in his temples. His hands shook. Sex was something boys at the orphanage referred to in whispers, out of range of the nuns. Magazines and photographs were passed around, depictions of women in blissful abandon. But here on a farm in Michigan Mercy resisted with her arms, pushing and shoving Harlan. Angered by Rope's intrusion, Harlan managed to get to his feet, overalls bunched about his feet. Mercy got up and crossed the floor, holding up her dress. *I could kill him.* The axe handle was in Rope's good hand, its head resting on his other forearm. He had watched her doing her chores, hanging the laundry, cooking, and cleaning. He couldn't resist looking, watching her. He didn't know what it was about her. Her bearing, her eyes, *something* that drew him to her. But to do what Harlan Nau had done, to force himself upon her, was unimaginable. And when they saw Rope with the axe, Harlan's lust turned to outrage, and Mercy fled the attic holding up her torn dress. *I could kill him.* Beyond that, Rope couldn't trust his memory.

"I remember," Rope said, causing Kincaid to lean forward and look past Mercy at him. "It all happened so fast. I remember the axe. I used it to split wood."

Mercy whispered, "He said not to speak."

"But in the attic, you said—"

"Don't."

"When you passed me, you . . ."

Overhead there were two blasts of the horn as the ferry slowed down as it approached the dock. Passengers gathered their belongings and crowded toward the saloon doors.

"It's curious," Kincaid said. "You're heading back across the straits. I figured you'd be in Canada by now. Not going south again." He stood up. "My car is nearby."

•

If anything, it was worse on land. The ground pitched and yawed beneath Mercy's feet, and she leaned against Rope for support as they followed the passengers down to the icy pier. It was nearly dark as Kincaid led them into a side street lined with warehouses. He stopped at a Chevrolet, produced keys, and unlocked the door.

"We will drive for a while," he said. "If this weather doesn't get too bad, we should make Petoskey tonight, where we'll stop for the night."

As he opened the passenger door, Mercy turned her head at the sound of footsteps behind her. A man—the same large, bearded man who had chased them in St. Ignace—came up to Kincaid and struck him on the head with a club. One good blow, which left Kincaid lying in the bloodied snow.

"MacLeod," Rope said. "What are you doing?"

The bearded man bent down and picked up the set of keys that had fallen from Kincaid's hand. "You see, mate, you don't abandon MacLeod's ship. It be mutiny, y'know. Now get in the car, both of you." When he saw that they were handcuffed, he said, "Good. It might make you think twice about running off again." He went around the car and got in behind the steering wheel. As he sorted through the keys, he said, "You don't have me four dollars, do ye, lad?"

"What? No."

"Well, no matter." He inserted one of the keys into the ignition and started the car. "The two of you will fetch a good price."

Seventeen

Mercy held Rope's damaged hand. Time seemed to have accelerated. On the ferry she had kissed him. He'd kissed only a few girls before, usually in the shadows of the factory buildings in Haverhill, girls who smelled of cigarettes and machine oil. But Mercy had kissed him in a way that confirmed something he could not name. Something between them, a tie, a bond, a reason for their being on that boat, crossing the straits. And then, there was Kincaid, who turned out to be a policeman, and they were bound together by handcuffs. From then on, holding hands was not a matter of affection. He could not tell from the feel of her hand what she felt. Uncertainty? Dread? They had been caught by Kincaid, who all the way back to when he had first given Rope a ride must have known that this was his goal: to find them both. Until MacLeod appeared, seemingly out of the dark, leaving Kincaid bloody, lying in the snow. So now Mercy was holding Rope's hand, more tightly than when they'd first been handcuffed on the ferry. Her fear of the water seemed now to be replaced by something far greater, a dread that could not be defined.

MacLeod handled the wheel of the Chevrolet as though they were being chased, causing the tires to swerve and skid on the dark, snowbound roads.

When they reached a farmhouse surrounded by fields, MacLeod pulled up to the back door and stopped next to a truck with a wooden enclosed compartment built into the bed, something used to convey farm animals. He shut off the engine, and said, "Get out."

Rope opened the passenger door, and he and Mercy climbed out into the snow. MacLeod got out and came around the car. He grabbed her by the arm and pulled them both toward the house. Before they reached the steps, the door opened, and a man in a leather jacket let them into a kitchen lit only by a kerosene lantern. Another man sat at the table, smoking a cigarette.

"See, Ben? Told you I'd find them." MacLeod let go of Mercy's arm.

Ben got up from the table. He only glanced at Rope but came up close to Mercy and looked her over.

"So," MacLeod said.

"So," Ben repeated. "You want to settle up."

"I had a better offer."

"Did you now? Let me guess. That would be from Kincaid."

"He gave me five down and offered me fifty dollars for the pair of them."

The other man, standing by the door, whistled softly.

"I had to borrow the money for the ferry ticket," McLeod said. "We need to settle up. I've already lost four dollars on this."

Ben turned to him, surprised. "How'd a thing like that happen?"

"The Four Winds, anything can happen. I thought this one—" MacLeod nodded toward Rope, "I thought he stole it but maybe not. Anyway, fifty is the going price. Can you top it?"

Ben looked at the man standing by the door. "What do you think, Luke?"

"That's quite a sum," Luke said. "I sure don't have it. We'll have to wait."

Ben seemed satisfied with this. "That would be best."

"Wait for what?" MacLeod said.

"Owen Dingley. He's coming up from down there where this all started. I'm sure he has cash like that."

"You expect me to wait for this bloke?"

Ben said, "He's a G-2 man. In charge of recruitment."

MacLeod could barely contain himself. "MacLeods don't wait for G-2 men or whatever. We settle up."

Ben went back to the table and sat down, taking his time. "We can't. We don't have that kind of money on us, and we don't have—" he glanced over at Luke again. "The authority. You know how the Klan is. See, it's a question of authority, and we don't have the authority."

MacLeod took Mercy's arm again. "Well then, I'll just hang on to them until you find the authority." He started to push her and Rope toward the door.

Luke had been leaning against the jamb, arms folded. He didn't move. "Why don't you all wait here. Dingley called earlier from Grayling. The snow is letting up and he should make it tonight."

"Besides," Ben said. "You go back to that cop Kincaid, Owen Dingley will not be pleased."

"I don't care what pleases Owen Dingley," MacLeod said.

Luke turned and looked out the window in the door. "That car. A Chevrolet. It looks like Kincaid's. You stole it from him?"

MacLeod smiled. "It's on loan. A down payment. Kincaid offered fifty, and he has the authority to pay me what he promised. That's more than you two have."

Ben and Luke gazed at each other, both seeming to consider this a reasonable if unfortunate assessment. "Are your feelings hurt, Luke?"

"My feelings? No. The man makes a good point."

Ben nodded, sadly. "I thought MacLeod saw the larger implications here. But it only appears he's in it for himself."

"Don't give me your larger implications," MacLeod said. "There are no larger implications." He snorted. "That's your business, lads. Fine. But it's going to cost you fifty dollars. That's the going rate."

Ben and Luke nodded again, as though there were nothing left to say. Ben said, "The fact remains, we have to wait for this G-2 fellow. I'll bet he'll be here in an hour or two." He gazed at MacLeod, hopeful. "That's not too much to ask, is it? We separate them. You have the key to those cuffs? We'll put him in a room, handcuffed to the bed. The girl we'll stick here in the pantry closet. No windows. No escape. And listen, we've got some steaks. Have a little dinner, and once Owen arrives, we settle up, and you're on your way. Plus, you've got that nice car out there. Maybe it's on permanent loan. It must be worth something, no?"

MacLeod looked from Ben to Luke. "Steak?"

Luke smiled. "How do you like yours done?"

•

Dr. Uccello held a hand up within inches of Kincaid's face. "Follow my finger."

Kincaid's eyes followed the finger as it moved from side to side, up and down. "How did I get here?"

"A couple of the ferry crew found you in the snow a few blocks from my office. I don't think you have a concussion, and you don't need stitches. But you're going to have a pretty good lump back there. How's it feel?"

"These crewmen, they say anything about my car? Or the two kids who were in it?"

The doctor shook his head. "Just said you were lying in the snow. Every year up here we have people die on winter nights. They get drunk, walk home, and pass out within sight of their front door. Or they slip on the ice and hit their head, and nobody finds them until it's too late. It's only November, but with the windchill tonight's going to get down below zero."

The office smelled of disinfectant and pharmaceuticals, undercut by a hint of whiskey on the doctor's breath. Paper crinkled as Kincaid sat up on the examination table. "I need to find them. And my car."

"These kids, they're why you took the ferry across to St. Ignace. They stole your car?"

Kincaid shook his head, a mistake. He touched the swelling on the back of his skull. "It wasn't them. I didn't see who did it, but I know who it was, or I'm pretty sure. You know this Angus MacLeod?"

Dr. Uccello shrugged. "Everybody does."

Kincaid started to climb down off the table, but the doctor placed a hand on his shoulder. "I need to—"

"What? Wander out in the cold and dark? And go where? No. Come with me."

The doctor turned and walked out the door of the examination room. Kincaid followed, navigating the hallway as best he could, and then they climbed a set of stairs with an elaborately carved oak banister. They were in an old house that now did not look like a doctor's office.

"You live here alone?"

"Since Muriel died. Our daughter and her family live in Winnipeg." The doctor opened a door to a bedroom and switched on a lamp on a nightstand. "Stay here tonight. Let me see how that lump is in the morning. I made soup earlier today. Minestrone soup is the best medicine there is."

"But—"

"You need to eat."

"What I need is . . ." Kincaid looked around the room. It didn't smell like a doctor's office up here, but a place that had not been used for some time: old furniture, lace doilies, glass figurines crowding shelves. It felt like a museum. "A car. Something I can drive."

Dr. Uccello said, "You lie down. I'll bring your soup up. Maybe I can do something about a vehicle for you. But not till morning."

As the doctor moved toward the door, Kincaid asked, "Were you on the ferry earlier?"

"No." The doctor turned and leaned against the jamb. "I had office hours yesterday and had to get back to this side of the straits. This happens, the ferry service shutting down. I can always get a ride on some fishing boat." He reached for the doorknob. "Up here, we find a way."

After the doctor closed the door behind him, Kincaid lay on the bed, careful not to put pressure on the swelling on the back of his skull. He stared up at a plaster medallion on the ceiling, and the room was silent until the radiator emitted a serpentine hiss.

•

The pantry was dark except for the line of lantern light that seeped under the door. Mercy sat on the floor, and the rope that bound her hands behind her back was tied to the frame of the shelves that were filled with canned goods and jars of preserves. She had heard them take Rope upstairs, and she assumed that they used the handcuffs to lock him up as well.

She wasn't sure about time, how much had passed. She was exhausted and may have dozed briefly. Finally, the man they referred to as Owen Dingley arrived, and she could hear it in his voice, the way the others responded to him. He was in charge, he had authority. He acknowledged that MacLeod had done them a great service. Before MacLeod could raise the issue of money, Owen assured him he would be properly compensated. MacLeod did not sound satisfied.

They moved from the kitchen to the parlor, but she could only understand an occasional word, a phrase. A few times MacLeod raised his voice, and it was clear that he wanted to be paid and on his way. Dingley's calm murmur always prevailed. Eventually, MacLeod hollered, "Otter Creek? Where that copper comes from?"

A chair was knocked over and there was the shuffling of feet, which led to a struggle. Someone was thrown against a wall, hard enough that it jounced the floor in the pantry. There were several blows, sickening thuds, until it was silent in the parlor.

·

Rope was on his knees, handcuffed to an iron bedframe in a room on the second floor. When the one called Luke had taken him upstairs, he said as he left, "Your mistake is messing with a girl like that. Should have stuck to your own kind."

The floorboards were cold, and his knees ached. As he listened to the men in the parlor directly below him, he wondered about Kincaid, left lying in the snow. MacLeod had hit him on the head with a club of some sort, and now his voice rose up from the parlor as the men argued. When they began to struggle, Rope yanked on the bedframe, causing it to move slightly, the legs banging on the floor. He twisted and yanked on the cuffs, succeeding only in bruising his wrists. Downstairs, something had happened, bringing a heavy silence, until Ben and Luke, and the new one, Dingley, spoke with an urgency. Rope didn't hear MacLeod's voice.

After several minutes, there was the shuffling of feet, the opening of doors. Something heavy was being dragged into the kitchen and outside: MacLeod.

They came back into the kitchen. Dingley gave orders, no questions asked, and then footsteps came up the stairs. Ben and Luke opened the bedroom door and unlocked the handcuffs. As soon as Rope was on his feet, Ben locked his wrists in the cuffs again.

"What's happened to MacLeod?" Rope said.

"Shut your mouth or do you want the same?" Ben said.

Luke pulled a revolver from his coat pocket. "Not a word."

They took Rope down the stairs, through the kitchen, and out into the yard. It was snowing lightly. He was pushed toward the truck, which was parked next to Kincaid's Chevrolet. Ben opened the rear door in the back, grabbed Rope by the arm and forced him to climb in, where he fell over MacLeod's body lying on a wood floor covered with straw and smelling of chickens.

"What about Mercy?" Rope said.

"What did I say?" Ben said. "Kids like you don't listen too good."

The door was shut, locked, and one of the men climbed into the cab. The other got in the Chevrolet and led the truck away from the farmhouse. It was dark in the back of the truck, which had one small window in the door. The vehicle moved slowly on country roads, rutted and snowbound. Rope could hear the Chevrolet up ahead. MacLeod's body rolled and swayed. He was out cold, or he was dead. After a few miles, both vehicles stopped, and Rope heard the two men come to the back of the truck. When they opened the door, Luke held the revolver and Ben pointed the flashlight at Rope and MacLeod.

"Out," Ben said.

When MacLeod didn't respond, Luke tapped his boot with the revolver. "Out, you hear?"

Rope climbed down from the truck, which was parked in a field near a stand of woods.

Ben pocketed the flashlight and began to pull on MacLeod's legs, but he couldn't get him out of the truck.

"Help him," Luke said to Rope.

Rope pulled on MacLeod's other leg, and slowly he and Ben managed to yank his body toward the open rear door. MacLeod sat up then, his boot coming up and catching Ben's jaw. He pushed Rope aside, causing him to slip and fall in the snow. MacLeod lunged toward Luke, and they grappled in the dark, until the revolver was fired twice.

Rope got to his feet. He could barely make out the three men in the snow. No one moved, and he considered taking his chances and running for the woods.

"Help me up, Laddie."

Rope took hold of MacLeod by the arm and helped him to his feet. He was bent over and breathing heavily. He had the revolver in his hand. On the ground, Ben rolled on his side, groaning, and Luke slowly got up on his hands and knees. MacLeod considered them a moment and then shot each once in the head.

Looking toward the Chevrolet, its motor rumbling deeply, he said, "You know how to drive?" he asked.

"Yes." He held up his cuffed hands. "The keys, they're in the car."

MacLeod held his side as blood dripped into the snow. "Get me to town, Laddie. I'll be needing a doctor."

Eighteen

The pantry door opened on a dry hinge. The man the others called Dingley came in holding a kerosene lantern, which he placed on one of the shelves. Droplets of melted snow glistened on the shoulders of his wool coat. His smile was warm but threatening, as though he'd long waited for this moment. He untied the rope that bound Mercy's hands and pulled her up to her feet.

"Where are they taking them?" she demanded.

"Be thankful you're not going on that ride. Would you like me to have sent you with them?"

"Bastard."

"Funny, coming from the likes of you."

"Bastard."

He might not have heard. "You'd rather stay here, alone?" he asked as he coiled up the rope and stuffed it in the pocket of his overcoat. He had a calm intensity that seemed impenetrable. "It could be a good while before Ben and Luke come back. You prefer that? Stay here with the two of them, alone?" She shook her head. "That's what I thought."

"What now?"

"Now," he said, taking hold of her upper arm, "we have a long drive ahead of us."

They left the house and got in Dingley's car. Mercy was thankful that it had a good heater because they drove in and out of snow squalls, which after a couple of hours gave way to a steady rain.

"We're driving out of the snow," she said. "We're going south."

Dingley nodded without looking away from the road.

"Where?" When he didn't answer, she said, "Otter Creek?"

"Nearby."

"Rope and that bearded man—"

"Forget them."

"They're both dead?"

"And buried. Or maybe they'll just be left to the wolves."

The wipers kept frantic time as the rain became even louder on the roof of the car. She remembered during their first days at Nau Farm, Rope had mentioned the animals in the woods, the screeches and howls that surrounded the house at night. Rope, dead. Buried somewhere in the woods in a shallow grave, or his body being torn apart by beasts. He couldn't be dead. Perhaps it was because he was so young, younger even than she, and there was something about him, his persistence that would push him beyond ordinary limits. She did not trust boys, and certainly not men, but Rope seemed different. The one thing, the one good thing that had come out of this journey to Michigan was this quiet boy who rarely used his real name. Rather than sorrow she felt anger, a deep outrage that left her speechless. The car kept pushing ahead into the night.

Finally, she said, "What do you mean 'nearby'?"

"Near Otter Creek. I want you to meet someone. We have work to do before—"

"Work," she said. "Having people killed, that's your work?"

"You have a sharp tongue, when you choose to use it. You have been educated to a degree. That's a dangerous thing. You do not need an education. It's a waste."

"What then? What do I need?"

"You need to be useful."

"Useful."

"That's what you people are good for. It's why you exist. It's in the Bible. The sons and daughters of Ham. Canaanites. You were defeated and are meant to be in bonds." He shook his head as a means of reconsideration. "But one of your parents was white. In one sense that dilutes your role, I suppose. But in another way, it's worse. This is what makes you truly dangerous. You are what happens when we allowed the races to mix. You are young, nubile. I'll bet you know what that means. A bit scrawny, maybe, but few men could resist such temptation. They'd be curious, you know, about a mulatto."

"Mulatta," she said.

"See what I mean about education? You dare correct a white man? Mulatto, mulatta—do you know where the term comes from? I'll tell you. It goes back centuries and is a reference to the offspring of a horse and a donkey: a mule. You are a mule. A young, nubile beast, as it turns out, but still a beast. More dangerous than a mule because they are usually infertile. You have many childbearing years ahead of you. Women like you could only lead to the further mixing of the races, the dilution of the Caucasian race. That is the ultimate threat. That is the danger you pose."

"I asked what you meant by 'nearby,' and you give me a lecture about mules."

"And this is what I mean about your sharp tongue." But he seemed to be enjoying their exchange, as though it provided a distraction from the tedium of driving in the rain at night. "The people in Otter Creek, people everywhere, they are horrified about what happened to Harlan and his wife Estelle. I travel around Michigan and when I tell them I'm from Otter Creek, I see it in their eyes. There must be justice, they want justice."

"What happened to Estelle?"

"She was in such a state of remorse after her husband's brutal murder, she killed herself."

"I had nothing to do with their deaths."

"You were taken in at their farm. You were there when Harlan was killed."

"I was there when he came into the attic and tried to rape me. I ran away."

"Lies. All lies."

"The truth," Mercy said.

"No," he said. "There are larger truths here. Otter Creek must be purified."

"How do you intend to do that?"

He didn't answer immediately, then he said, "You're from back east somewhere."

"I came here from an orphanage in Massachusetts."

"A Catholic orphanage, no doubt. That explains it. People don't talk like that out here. People read the Bible here. The nuns, they fed you the pope's lies with his catechism, and all that Latin."

"I have read the Bible. We had to memorize passages."

"You learned by rote. This is not a true education. Reciting the Bible is not the same as reading it, taking it to heart. You've heard of the Klu Klux Klan?"

"Of course."

"What have you heard?"

"After the Civil War. They wore those hooded outfits and rode their horses about at night, threatening people, carrying torches. They burned crosses. They lynched people. Ex-slaves."

"For offenses, crimes committed," Dingley said.

"What crimes?"

"Crimes such as despoiling white women. There is no such thing as an ex-slave." He steered the car around a bend in the road, and then asked, "Do you know who was the white one, your mother or father?"

"My father."

He nodded as though this made sense. They drove in silence for a few minutes, until he said, "We're coming back. The Klan. We're moving into the northern states. We're becoming stronger. Our membership numbers are growing. Thousands are joining. Pure Americans, 100 percent Americans. We call them citizens."

"This is your work?"

"I am a recruiter, yes. I work for the Old Man."

"I don't know who that is."

"We rarely even mention him by name. A very influential man. He's the Grand Dragon of Indiana."

"Never heard of this . . . Dragon," Mercy said. "What makes him so grand?"

"He's the head of the Klan in Indiana. Very powerful, nationwide."

"What exactly does a recruiter do?"

"I determine who in a community might be eligible for the Klan."

"Not everyone is qualified, not pure enough?"

"Only those who are 100 percent."

"I heard this before, this idea of purity."

"Have you?"

"Yes, when I was being what you call educated. The nuns and priests, they constantly talked about the purity of your soul, being in the state of grace. This is why we pray, why we have the sacraments and the Mass, because—"

Dingley lifted a hand off the steering wheel, a signal to stop. "We are growing incredibly fast. In just a few years the Klan has become a significant force. Government administrators, police, teachers, judges, people with influence."

"You recruit them," Mercy said. "Because of people like me."

"To preserve our way of life, our jobs, our values."

"Values." Mercy considered this for a moment. "Are you really afraid of me? People like me?"

"That is an interesting question. I wouldn't say it's fear, but an awareness based on—"

"Yes, I know it's right there in the Bible."

Dingley didn't answer but stared out at the road.

"What do you plan to do with me?"

"It depends."

"On what?"

"On . . ." Dingley thought a moment. "Harlan Nau was murdered, a white man in his own home. It's because you and that boy were sent out here. This must be addressed. It must be rectified." He nodded, as though in agreement with some fleeting realization. "It depends on the Old Man."

"You actually believe in this Dragon?"

"Absolutely." Dingley seemed pleased as he stared out at the rain sweeping through the headlights. "The Grand Dragon has come to Otter Creek for the parade."

"What parade?"

"The Grand Dragon. He'll determine what to do with the daughter of Ham."

"Parade? Dragon? What is the matter with you?" When Dingley didn't answer, she said, "You going to feed me to your Grand Dragon?"

He laughed. A strange baritone laugh.

Quietly, Mercy said, "And this makes you useful."

"You might say that. I am useful," Owen Dingley said. "And being useful can be very lucrative."

•

As a car pulled up in front of Dr. Uccello's house, Kincaid recognized the sound of the Chevrolet's engine. He got off the bed, which caused the back of his head to throb, and went to the front window. Down in the snowy street, Rope aided MacLeod as he got out of the car. The man was buckled over, injured. Dr. Uccello came out of the house and helped them up to the front door.

Kincaid went downstairs and found them in the doctor's examination room. MacLeod was lying on his side on the table. There was a great deal of blood.

"Gunshot at close range, it appears," Dr. Uccello said.

"What happened?" Kincaid asked.

"After he knocked you out, sir," Rope said, "he took us to a farmhouse." He looked down at his shirt, covered with blood. "I'm afraid this shirt you gave me is ruined."

"Don't worry about that. Are you injured, too?"

"No, sir," Rope said. "There were three men. Two of them took us out to the woods. They would have killed us, but MacLeod was stronger." He turned to the doctor. "Is he going to live?"

Dr. Uccello was pressing a folded towel against the wound. "I'm afraid it's most likely. There's a long history of attempts on this man's life, yet he plagues us still. This will not be the first time I have stitched him up." Leaning down to inspect the wound, he said, "It appears the bullet passed through, which may be a good sign. Captain, I would like you to assist me again and press down on this towel."

Kincaid went around the examination table, rolling up his sleeves. As he put pressure on the towel, he said to Rope, "Where's the girl?"

"The other man. He was the boss, it seemed. They said his name. Owen something."

"Dingley," Kincaid said.

"That's it. He has her. They may still be at the farmhouse, but I doubt it. When he and the other men were talking, he mentioned Otter Creek."

MacLeod opened his eyes. "He's a G-2 man. Recruits for the Grand Dragon."

"Grand Dragon," Dr. Uccello muttered, as though putting up with the fantasies rendered by a child. He wiped blood away so he could inspect MacLeod's wounds. "Small caliber," he noted.

MacLeod glancing up at Kincaid. "Please accept my apologies for tapping the back of your head. Clearly, you have a Scotsman's noggin. Hard, like briar burl?"

"I survived," Kincaid said.

"And my intention, truly, was to deliver both these young culprits to you," MacLeod said. "Might your offer of a reward still apply?"

"The deal was for the two of them," Kincaid said. "And it appears that Rope delivered you."

"Not even half?" MacLeod's voice was barely a whimper.

"If I gave you anything, you should turn around and give it to this culprit," Kincaid said.

The doctor looked up from the wound. "He has a point. You could have bled to death. That boy probably saved your life."

MacLeod turned his head away. "And I thought you, Captain, were an honorable clansman!"

"Earlier you thought I descended from cattle thieves." Kincaid looked at Rope. "Go upstairs. The first bedroom, you'll find my rucksack. Clean yourself up and get another shirt, and when you're finished bring the rucksack downstairs."

Rope hesitated.

"What?" Kincaid said.

"Dingley," Rope said. "If he has taken her with him, I need to find her."

MacLeod turned his head so he could study the boy. He winced as the doctor inserted the suture needle, but then he chuckled, causing the doctor to pause after he pulled the thread through the wound. "I suspect, gentlemen, that we are in the presence of true love. I have seen many of its mutations, but I believe this is the real gold crown. I am grateful to have lived long enough to witness it."

•

In the late afternoon, Dingley drove through Otter Creek. Mercy recognized the stores from when she arrived on the train. They continued through the village and soon were out in the country again. After several miles, he turned on to a two-track that ran up to an old stone farmhouse. There were at least two dozen men in the yard, some in street clothes, others in white robes with tall, pointed hats. The yard reverberated with the sound of saws and hammers as a structure was being built out of scrap lumber. When Mercy got out of the car, men paused to stare at her, and they appeared satisfied that her hands were bound with rope.

Dingley took her by the arm and walked her into the kitchen, where more men stood about in groups talking quietly in the haze of cigar smoke. They parted for Dingley, and Mercy refused to look at any of them as she passed by. Several large men in robes appeared to be standing guard at the foot of the stairs.

"The Old Man doesn't want to be disturbed," one of them said.

"He'll want to see her, Weiss," Dingley said.

"She's the one?"

Dingley nodded.

Weiss nodded and they allowed Dingley and Mercy to climb the stairs.

When they reached the second floor, Mercy asked, "Is this your Dragon's den?"

"No, it's my house. Our granddaddy built it with the rocks and trees he dug out of the land."

They went down the hall and stopped before another robed man, this one wearing a mask draped loosely over his face. He opened the door and Dingley entered, leaving Mercy out in the hall. The guard folded his arms over his chest and didn't move. His robe was of fine silk material, which reminded Mercy of the vestments a priest wore during Mass. The holes in the mask were uneven in size and shape, as though cut out by a child, and she could barely see his eyes, peering at her from the dark.

Dingley came out and said, "The Old Man wants to see her."

The man looked her over one last time, and then nodded.

Dingley untied the rope that bound Mercy's wrists, stuffing the cord into his coat pocket, and then he knocked on the door before opening it. He guided her into the room, stepped back into the hall, and closed the door behind her. There was only a single bed, piled with a tangle of sheets and blankets, and by the window, a man sat in a straight-back chair. Still, as though he were part of the furniture. Short hair, chubby face, dimpled chin, white shirt, gray tie, which matched his double-breasted suit. The jacket was too tight, as was the collar of his shirt. She never understood why men did that, wore shirt collars that made their necks bulge. He held a glass in his pudgy hands, and a bottle of whiskey stood next to him on the floor.

He didn't speak, didn't take his eyes off her. Some of the nuns used to do this, try to use their eyes and silence to intimidate the children. Mercy stared back him.

Finally, she said, "What is this?"

He might not have heard, the way he looked her up and down. "The coat," he said, "take it off." When she hesitated, he said, "I said . . ."

She unbuttoned her coat and draped it over the end of the iron bedframe. He nodded, indicating the sweater she had been given by Naomi. Reluctantly, she pulled it over her head and placed it next to the coat.

"That, too."

"My dress?" When he didn't say anything, she shook her head.

He just looked at her. It was different than when Harlan Nau looked at her. His gaze was a matter of appraisal. Evaluation. But there was impatience, too. "You want me to do it for you? Or should I call the fella in the hall to help out?" When she shook her head, he nodded. "All right then."

It was his eyes, the way they bore in on her. She reached across her chest and took hold of the safety pin that held her torn dress together at her left shoulder. But then she dropped her arm to her side. "No. I don't care what you do."

He leaned over and picked up the bottle, removed the cork with his teeth, and poured more whiskey into his glass. There was something methodical about his movements, as though he had to think everything through carefully. He placed the bottle on the floor, being particular about how it was positioned next to his worn leather shoe. Then he drank the whiskey. First, two deep draughts, and then he tipped his head back and drained the glass. When he gazed at her again, there was a sense of accomplishment, of pride, even, as though he expected recognition that he had just performed an astounding magic trick.

"Turn around," he said. When she didn't move, he added, "Slowly."

She turned part way and faced the wall. Cracked whitewashed plaster, with divots. Then she turned again, looking at the door, and then another quarter turn.

Out of the corner of her eye she watched him take a pack of cigarettes from his coat pocket and tap one out. His face, it had the same pallor and texture as the plaster wall. "You know, it wasn't that long ago when a girl like you would be stripped and put up on an auction block." He lit his cigarette, gazing at her, disappointed. "To bring a fair price, you'd need to be fattened up." He exhaled smoke, and then leaned forward, placing his elbows on his knees, staring out the window.

She turned again and faced him. He might have been alone in the room as he smoked, seemingly deep in thought. "You. You're the Dragon," she said. "The Grand Dragon. From Illinois."

"Indiana," he said, placing his empty glass on the windowsill. Like the bottle of whiskey, he was careful about how the glass was positioned, turning it just so. "Dingley said you were smart, got what passes for education from one of those cities teeming with babies that should never have been conceived. They send you out here to the Midwest by the trainload."

"Nobody sent me."

"You may be smart, but you don't even know your purpose."

"My purpose?"

"The pope, he sent you. Like missionaries. Come out here, infest our towns. It's the great hypocrisy. The Roman Catholic Church preaches abstinence, the rhythm method, and yet there are all you foundlings." He seemed to think of something that was humorous. "Why do you think they call it the missionary position?"

"The pope didn't send me."

"We are at war, and you are a soldier. A missionary soldier. Like that Jesuit."

"Saint Ignatius."

"See?"

"See, what?"

"See, you know more than need be."

"I know that you have no right to keep me here."

He looked at her now. "Rights? You're talking to me about rights?" His eyes turned savagely angry, but it passed quickly as he sat back in the chair, which creaked in the barren room. "I understand that you killed that farmer that took you in near here. You or that boy, kilt a white man. You've both been on the run, until you were captured and brought back."

"That farmer was drunk and tried to rape me."

"Did he now?" He moved in the chair, causing its joints to complain again. "This is why we advocate temperance?" It was a question he seemed to be asking himself. "Split the man's head open with an axe. The important thing is you have been brought to justice. I don't know whether I should feed you to the men out in the barnyard or save you."

"Save me?"

"Keep you to myself, at least until you—both of you—are in custody."

"Custody? You—you and these men in robes? We were in the custody of a lawman. Do you know what happened to him?"

He ignored this. "You will be brought to justice. All in due time."

"What are you going to do with me?"

"Well, let's see." He paused to pour himself another glass of whiskey. This time he only drank down half and held the glass in both hands as he rested his elbows on his knees. He was clearly trying to make up his mind. "There's going to be a parade in Otter Creek." He smiled briefly at her reaction. "Yes, I think you'll be part of the festivities. We'll present you to the folks. Let them decide what to do with you. This fellow, Harlan Nau, he was one of them. Let them have a say."

"The police captain said we'd be given a lawyer in court."

"Well." He drank off the rest of the whiskey and studied the empty glass a moment as though he didn't know how it had gotten into his hands. "The folks in Otter Creek, they can settle this. It's their right, don't you think?" He put the glass on the windowsill, again turning it until it was positioned just so. Then he looked out the window at the activity down in the yard. It was getting dark, and some of the men had lit torches, which cast tall, monstrous shadows on the barn. "This happens all over the country, people taking charge of their own justice system. Lawyers, courts, and judges, all that's unnecessary. The people, they know what's right."

"You're talking about lynchings."

He tilted his head, still gazing out the window. "I'm talking about punishment, swift and final."

"It's not right. You need proof, you need evidence."

Now he turned to her. Something had happened to his eyes. She wasn't sure but she thought it was the whiskey. He didn't seem quite the same as when she'd come in the room. And then he stood up, quickly, causing the legs of the chair to scrape loudly on the floorboards. "Evidence? The man's dead. Proof? They only need to take one look at you." He moved toward her. "You see, it's not for me to say. It's the people, it's for them to decide. They want to hang you, that's what they'll do. I can't stop them. I won't stop them. My role is to deliver you. They want the power to decide these things. I'll give it to them." He came closer, so close she could smell the whiskey. "I deliver you and wash my hands, like your Pontius Pilate."

He grabbed her arm and pulled her over to the window. "Look out there," he said, nearly shouting. "You see that? That's what we need."

His hand was tight on her upper arm as he pushed until her forehead was up against the windowpanes. She could see then, in the field behind the barn, the men standing around with torches, their shadows shifting and dancing, while others worked on the enormous wooden cross laid out on the ground.

Mercy tried to pull herself free from his grip, but he yanked her back from the window, working his arms around her as he shuffled toward the bed. As they struggled, her hands flew up slapping and scratching at his face, but then he caught one wrist in his hand, and raising it to his mouth he sank his teeth into the soft flesh at the base of her thumb.

Nineteen

Rope opened his eyes and stared out at the road. For a few moments, everything—where he'd been, where he was going—was all a blank, a mystery, and he wondered how he'd got here in this automobile.

"We're almost to Lansing," Kincaid said. "Another hour or so, we'll be in Otter Creek."

"Since I've been out here, I have no idea where I am. Where is Lansing?"

"Raise your hand. Your left hand."

"What?"

"People usually use their right hand. But in your case, hold up your left hand, palm away from you." When Rope hesitated, he said, "Go ahead. It's a map of Michigan's Lower Peninsula." Rope stared at the back of his left hand. "The farm you worked on, it's not far from your wrist. The Mackinac Straits are up above the tip of your middle finger. We're now a little below the middle of your hand."

They had driven through the night, though twice Kincaid pulled over so he could sleep. Short naps, half hour or so. Said he slept that way for years during the war. And they had a flat tire after Kincaid swerved to miss hitting a deer.

Working together by flashlight, they jacked up the Chevrolet and replaced the tire. After that, Rope slept fitfully as the engine droned on into the night. They encountered flooded roads, which required taking detours that wound through hills. Even at that, they had to turn around twice and backtrack because of downed trees. Now, finally, they were out of that cold northern land. To Rope's surprise, he missed it. A harsh, unforgiving place, but something about it held the promise of an abundance he could not name. Something to do with the water, with the distance to the horizon. The land here was flat, and the horizon was interrupted by silos and barns and rows of trees bordering fields.

"How you going to find her?"

Kincaid didn't answer.

"Michigan, this is a big place. A big hand."

"We'll find her."

"And then what? You put both of us in jail."

"I told you: you will get legal counsel to represent you in court."

"You believe in it, justice."

"I believe it's better than the alternative."

"The people who have Mercy, they're the alternative," Rope said. "No counsel, no judge, and jury. We're already guilty." He looked out at cows grazing in a field. "How are we going to find her?" When Kincaid didn't answer, but just continued to stare out at the road, Rope raised his left hand again. "They left Mercy with that man who came to the farmhouse, Owen . . ."

"Dingley."

"That's right. The others, they called him a G-2. They said he had authority. And now he has her." Kincaid turned his head and considered Rope. It wasn't exactly confirmation, but he didn't refute the idea. "He'll bring her back down to Otter Creek?"

"I think so," Kincaid said. "Those men who held you up north, they and Dingley are Klansmen."

"And they have Mercy. Why?"

Kincaid looked back at the road. "They need her is why."

•

There were two candlestick telephones in the Otter Creek Police Department office, Ellie's and Kincaid's. When Ellie answered her phone, she turned in her swivel chair and glanced at Milt, who was stirring sugar into another cup of coffee. He'd lobbied for his own telephone, but it only led to Kincaid's usual spiel about budget priorities. He sat at Kincaid's desk and took up the phone in both hands. Something untrustworthy about telephones, with party lines and operators who could eaves drop.

He placed the receiver against his ear, wary that he might get an electric shock. This had happened too often. It was in the Lansing newspaper: just last year a farmer had been struck by lightning while using a telephone. These contraptions could be lethal. Milt held the speaker close to his mouth, careful to not touch it to his lips. "Deputy Waters here."

"How's your day been going?"

It was Dingley. Milt spun around in Kincaid's chair, so his back was to Ellie. "Let's see," he said. "This morning I nabbed a couple of kids playing hooky from school. The principal over there thinks my primary purpose is to act as truant officer."

"And you tracked them down?"

"Sure. When I was a kid I cut school so often I developed this sixth sense about where to hide out. These boys were in a shed behind the train station, with a pack of cigarettes and a girly magazine. Other than that, it's been a quiet day."

"Kincaid's not back yet?"

"No sign of him. Ellie says he called yesterday. He's on his way down."

"He got anything?" Dingley asked.

"Apparently not."

"Well." Dingley let it hang for a moment. Milt didn't like not being able to see the man when he spoke to you. No gestures, no eye contact, just a voice coming through this black cable that came out of the wall. "Wonder if this improves your day," Dingley's voice said. "We've got the girl."

Milt turned and looked over his shoulder. Ellie had her back to him, doing some paperwork at her desk. When things got this quiet, she was often engaged in a crossword puzzle in the newspaper. Whatever she was doing, she seemed to be preoccupied. Turning his back to her again, he said quietly. "Where?"

"She's safe."

"You want to bring her in?"

Dingley snorted, as though that was the furthest thing from his mind.

"What do you mean 'we'? 'We got her?'"

"Listen, Milt. I told you we have a network here in Michigan. We found her, I brought her down here, and for the time being she's, well, let's say she's safe." He was choosing his words carefully. Something he wasn't saying. "This all can work to your advantage."

Milt was staring at the open door that led to the cells in the back of the station. "What do you mean 'safe'? Why don't I just lock her up?" Dingley exhaled and Milt imagined him smoking a cigarette. "What's going on?" Milt asked.

"You're just going to have to play along," Dingley said.

"I want to see her."

"Tell you what. I'll come by the station in, say, an hour and pick you up." He waited.

Silence on a telephone was cruel, intolerable, and Milt finally said, "All right."

Dingley hung up. Milt put the phone down on Kincaid's desk and placed the receiver on its hook. Ellie had swiveled around to face him, making no attempt to conceal her suspicious nature.

"Who was that?"

"That?" Milt could tell she already anticipated a lie, and not a very good one. "Another kid. I've got to find another kid playing hooky, is all."

•

The truck had traveled at least a dozen miles over country roads, passing fields, wooded hills. At first, Mercy refused to speak to him. Mink. Dingley had called his younger brother Mink. He hummed blissfully, mindless of any tune. Grossly overweight in bib overalls. Head shaved to black stubble, revealing a topography of scars, and one a broad ridge curling down into the soft creases of his forehead.

But then she said, "Mink. Why do they call you that?" The smirk on his plump face was an awful thing. She could see the child he must have been and the marginal adult he'd become, not a little deranged and prone to violence. "It's a small animal, isn't it?"

"It was my hair," he said. "When I had some, it was dark and oily looking, like it was wet because I'd just crawled up out of the creek. Since we were boys, folks have said Owen and Mink come from the same tree, different limb." He snorted, indicating an attempt at humor was forthcoming. "Mines a lower, thicker branch."

Mercy was sorry she'd asked, so she held her piece, watching the land roll by slowly. When he turned the truck into a faint two-track and downshifted, they climbed a steep wooded hill until they reached a tarpaper shed in a clearing. The muddy ground, carved with tire tracks, was strewn with pails, barrels, and crates of bottles.

"What is this place?"

"It's your new home," Mink said. "For the time being."

Mercy nodded toward the contraption beyond the shed. Copper vat and tubing. "Is that a still?"

"It's an alky cooker," Mink said with pride. "Just moved it up here." He reached across her and untied the rope that bound her to the door handle. He leaned hard against her.

"Your brother told you to behave," she said. "I heard him."

Mink straightened up, surprised she had dared to challenge, and then as he pressed against her once more, grinning, his breath rancid. "Well, he ain't here, is he?" He giggled, a high chortling sound, something she imagined from an animal in a rain forest. "It be just you and me. So you behave and maybe I'll behave."

Though her wrists were still bound, she managed to push him away, and he giggled again as she got out of the truck. Mud oozed beneath a thin crust of frost, making each step difficult as they moved toward the shed. Beneath his overalls, the wide middle of him tended to float and jounce, reminding her of a carnival clown.

When they got closer to the still, she said, "What is that smell?"

He giggled again. "Money."

The shed door was held shut by a stick run through a rusted iron hasp. He removed the stick, tugged open the door, and, placing a hand on her shoulder, forced her to duck into a room with a tamped dirt floor. No windows, a table and two straight-back chairs by a potbelly stove in the center of the room. Along the back wall, two cots piled with soiled blankets. "This be my getaway for years," he chortled. "Nice fishing down at the stream, and in the fall you got your deer begging to be taken before the misery of winter."

"I'm staying here with you, alone?"

"Orphans can't be choosy, especially ones who think they can slay the Dragon. You're lucky they didn't tear you apart back there. My brother, you know, he saved you." Mink shoved her toward one of the cots and forced her to sit down. He stood before her, his bloated waist close, too close to her face, his hands stuffed in the front pockets of his bib. "Remember, try anything and all bets are off. I'll finish what the Grand Dragon started."

He went to the door and ducked out. Leaning in the opening, blocking its harsh light, he said, "Now, you're gonna stay put while I attend to business.

Any trouble out of you, I'll pull that coat and dress off and tie you up to a tree. Smear you with lard head to toe. Get it? Animals out here, they love the smell of lard. Can pick up the scent miles away." He grinned as he shut the door, and then she heard the hasp being closed and the stick being jammed into the ring.

She looked around the room. A few pots and pans hung on wall pegs, but nothing else. No utensils, nothing sharp, nothing that would slice through hemp. On the dirt floor by the table was a long wooden box, the lid secured with another hasp, held fast with a padlock. Then, exhausted, her racing heart only now beginning to quiet, she lay back on the cot and with both hands bound by rope pulled the foul-smelling blanket over her.

The stiffness seemed to rise and take hold of her joints and muscles, the pain concentrated in her right shoulder, her right forearm, her left hand where she had been bitten. Children bite. She had seen it many times among the orphans. When there was a fight, they would often resort to their teeth, wild with fury and fear. A bite tended to stop them from going further. They would back off from each other, crying, attending to their wounds, aided by friends.

Children bite. But a man, a grown man. This was something else. It wasn't like with the farmer. Harlan Nau's relentless urgency was fueled by whiskey-lust. This time, with the Dragon, there was whiskey, too. But this was something predatory, feral, driven by a need to destroy. He was the Grand Dragon, driven not just by lust, but hatred. She remembered the first bite, when this man, this Grand Dragon smelling of drink and cigarettes, grabbed her left hand and bit her below the thumb. It throbbed now, but the ache in her shoulder was worse. Carefully she pulled the fabric of her overcoat away from the dried blood on her forearm. She recalled his arms around her as he had dragged her toward the bed, and when she tried to pull herself away, he sank his teeth into her shoulder. She screamed then, which only made him more determined. They fell on the bed, where he was clutching at her dress, but then she managed to get free. As she got up, he grabbed her arm with both hands and bit her forearm. He made sounds she'd never heard before, something from a rabid animal. When he tried to get to his feet, he was so drunk he took hold of the iron bedpost for support. And there were other noises, which she came to realize was a fist pounding on the door. And voices, men's voices, but she could not understand what they were saying. And then this man, this Dragon, let go of the bedpost and came at her again, and she kicked him. Hard. Harder than when she kicked Rope, there on the railroad tracks. Kicked the Dragon so that it drove the wind out of him as he doubled over and staggered backwards, until he collapsed on the bed. When the door burst open two men in robes and those tall hoods rushed in and took hold of her arms. The Dragon writhed on the bed, his hand between his legs, curled up and howling. She didn't want to leave, she wanted another chance at him, and she fought against the grip on her arms, but the men were too strong, and they dragged her out of the room and down the hall. Shouting, everyone shouting then, while the Dragon cried out, a howling beast. He swore he would kill her, and she believed that's what they were about to do.

Then, nothing. She could not remember how she got down the stairs and out of the house. She found herself lying on the ground in the barnyard, next to a truck, with robed men about now, some brandishing torches. She thought she was screaming, but her voice was lost in the chaos. They jostled each other, closing in, shouting and cursing. "The little bitch attacked the Old Man! String her up right now!" They were lifting her up off the ground, when Owen Dingley forced his way through the mob. Mercy, stunned, bitten, was only half alert, but there were arguments, until Dingley convinced the others to back off, and when they did there were just the two of them, Dingley and his brother. He called him Mink, talking to him as though he were a half-wit, and then they put her coat on her before shoving her into the truck, and tied her wrists to the door handle. The others, the robed, hooded men jeered, and seemed on the verge of swarming around the truck as Mink climbed in behind the steering wheel. As he drove away from the stone house he hooted and hollered, elated, as though he'd won the contest, taken the grand prize.

Mercy slept there on the soiled cot, for how long she did not know, until she was awakened by a sound outside the shed—a familiar, repetitive sound, reminding her of Nau Farm. She got up and went to the opposite wall, where light came through a gap in the boards. She could see Mink, by a pile of wood, pick up a log, stand it on end on a wood block, and swing the short-handled axe down, splitting it into two halves that clattered on the ground. She watched him build the fire under the copper vat, splitting wood, adding kindling. Once he got the fire going, the air became heavy with smoke. He continued to chop wood, often needing several strokes to split a log.

·

Kincaid found Ellie Landis sitting behind her desk, looking relieved to see him.

Before he could ask, she said, "No, I haven't seen Milt since earlier today." She looked Rope over a moment. It wasn't clear whether she wanted to mother him or spank him. "At least you didn't come back empty-handed. What about the girl?"

Kincaid merely shook his head.

"What you want to do with this one? We have plenty of vacancies. He looks cold, hungry, and exhausted. We could put him in a cell, with plenty of blankets."

"No," Kincaid said, turning to Rope. "For the time being, I'm keeping you with me." The boy nodded, but it wasn't enough for Kincaid. "You understand what that means? You are in my custody."

"Yes, sir."

Kincaid looked at Ellie. "And what about Lois?"

"Your neighbor, Myra, found her at the house, in a bad way. Mitch drove Doc Evers out there."

"What kind of bad way?" But Kincaid suspected he already knew.

Ellie shrugged. "Well, it's the old bugaboo."

Kincaid and Rope drove through town to the DeVries's house. Mitch rode a wagon around town and the nag's reins were tied to the trunk of the maple that loomed above the front yard. As Kincaid and Rope got out of the Chevrolet, Mitch came out on the porch. By way of greeting, he raised his cane.

Myra Noyes stood behind him in the vestibule, an impossibly thin woman in her sixties. Bobbed hair, enormous veins on the back of her gnarled hands. Hard of hearing. "I came over this morning for coffee, like I do most every morning," she nearly shouted as Kincaid led Rope up the porch steps. "Since you've been gone, Lois has . . . fallen on old habits. Started the day after you left. Only got worse."

Mitch pulled on his full white beard. "She doesn't have the stamina for it no more. Certainly not that stuff the Dingley boys cook up."

"Dingley's?" Kincaid said. "You're sure?"

"Found two bottles in the kitchen," Mitch said. "Another empty out in the trash."

"Any idea where she's getting it?"

Both Mitch and Myra shook their heads. "Doc Evers is up there with her," Myra said.

Mitch studied Rope. "This your new deputy?"

"Not exactly." Kincaid went into the vestibule but paused at the bottom of the staircase. He looked back at Rope. "You could, you know. But you won't."

"I won't," Rope said.

"I know, because I'd find you again." Kincaid turned to Myra and raised his voice a bit. "What this boy could use is something to eat."

Mitch said, "Feed the lad? He and I are starving!"

Kincaid went up the stairs to Lois's room, where Doc Evers was closing his leather bag. Lois appeared to be asleep, lost beneath one of her quilts that dated back to the last century.

"She was seeing snakes and God knows what else," Doc Evers said, picking up the bag. "I've given her something to make her sleep. It's Dingley's. That stuff could make you go blind, if it didn't kill you." He went to the door, where he hesitated. "My car is still at Nesbit's. Don't know what Lyle's doing to it. My bladder can't take another ride in that buckboard of Mitch's. Drive me over to Nesbit's, will you?"

"Sure," Kincaid said as the doctor went out into the hall. "I'll be down in a minute."

He sat in the rocking chair by the window. Lois always said that Allison favored her father, but it wasn't true. Had she lived, had she had a full life, Kincaid believed Allison would eventually look like her mother, her head propped on a pillow, her closed eyelids darkened with age. Lois was someone people called vivacious. She'd once told Kincaid her father was an alcoholic, and his father before him. Throughout the decades of marriage, of raising Allison, there was the drink. She could go for months without a drop, and then she said there would be periods—days, weeks—that were black holes. No recollection at all. When Allison was pregnant, and then fell ill with the influenza, Lois took care of her daughter until the end. Then there was her husband, the judge, whose health declined following his daughter's death. Through it all, Lois was vigilant, and afterwards, when it was just the two of them together in the house Kincaid watched for signs. Occasionally, he'd find a bottle stashed in the back of a closet or in a cabinet. The most ingenious hiding place was beneath a full pile of clothes in the laundry hamper. It was like dealing with a child. She would deny it all, and then she'd go for spells where there were no signs, no evidence. But he knew that every day the threat was there.

She stirred, turning on her side, facing away from Kincaid. "I saw them," she said.

"Saw who, Lois?"

"Doc says my vision's been impaired. That's been happening for years. But I saw both of them, right here in this room. Allison and the judge. She wasn't pregnant. She was a girl. Wearing her favorite pinafore. Her hair almost down

to her waist. She was holding the judge's hand when they came into the room."
Lois turned so she was staring at the ceiling. "He sat there in the rocker, and
she climbed up on his lap the way she would. I asked her . . . I asked her . . ."

Kincaid waited. "What," he said finally. "What did you ask her, Lois?"

"Benny, her pony. I asked her if it was time to feed Benny." Lois's gaze
drifted toward Kincaid. "She didn't answer. Just got down off the judge's knee
and ran out of the room. And I could hear it, the barn door, the way the hinges
groan." She closed her eyes. "The judge said, 'She loves that pony. Practically
lives out in the barn with her.' Then he got up out of the chair and left the room.
I asked him to stay but he didn't seem to hear me. His shoes on the stairs . . .
had a way of coming down hard on his left foot. Injured it when he was a boy.
Riding accident. He was petrified Allison would get thrown from that horse.
But she never did. No, never."

Lois turned on her side again, and her breathing lengthened.

Kincaid got up from the rocking chair, which Allison's grandfather, a Civil
War veteran, had built. Most everything in the house had come down through
the generations. He moved toward the door, carefully, so the floorboards wouldn't
creak. He paused next to the bureau and picked up a slip of paper on the floor:
a redemption ticket from Van Nal's Tailor Shop. Amid the hairbrush, comb,
and bottles of perfume were two more tickets. Three trips to the tailor's since
he'd been gone. He put the slip on the bureau with the others, looked toward
the bed once more, and then went downstairs.

•

Mercy heard an engine struggling up the hill, an ominous sound. Through the
crack in the wall, she watched a truck jounce over the mud ruts in the clearing.
As the driver and Owen Dingley got out of the cab, Mink began unloading crates
from the truck bed. Empty bottles clinked as he stacked the crates on the ground
by the still. The fire beneath the vat was now sending a column of smoke aloft,
obscuring the fall sky.

When Owen Dingley and the driver started walking toward the shed, Mercy
rushed back to the cot. They ducked inside the shed, but it was difficult to see
them, backed by the light from the open door.

"It was a long way up north to get her," Dingley said.

"Too bad about the boy," the other man said. "I could really use both of them."

"Maybe, but this is what we've got, Milt."

The man called Milt came over to the cot, and Mercy could see him better: tweed coat in need of mending, unshaven jowls, tired eyes weighed down with misgivings and resentment. He leaned down for a closer look at her, and then reached out and pulled the collar of her dress away from her shoulder, revealing the bite mark. He seemed genuinely curious, so she held up her swollen hand for his inspection. "The Grand Dragon?" He was not speaking to her.

Dingley snorted. "You might say he has a taste for the ladies."

Milt straightened up and turned his head toward Dingley. Mercy couldn't read his face in the dim light. "The Old Man's done this before? What's he plan to do with her tomorrow?"

"Says he wants to let the people of Otter Creek decide. After the parade, when we're gathered in the fairgrounds, he'll speak. We're building the stage now. He wants you to bring her up there, on cue. Present her, so to speak. That's your role, and after tomorrow my guess is Otter Creek will be wanting a new police chief. You deliver her and then I guess he'll ask what they want to do. Who knows, they may want to hang her, they may want him to auction her off. He wants them to decide."

"You can't do that," Mercy said.

Milt seemed surprised that she had spoken. "We can't? Isn't it long overdue?"

Mercy sat up on the cot, causing him to back away. Loudly she said, "It's not right."

"That's for you to say?"

"There are laws."

"True," Dingley said. "There are laws. And there are laws." He leaned against the door frame, causing the light in the shed to shift, making it even more difficult to see. "And Milt here, he is the law."

"What?" Mercy said. Milt seemed to stand a little taller. "No," she said. "Kincaid, the captain, he's the law." And she could see it, Milt's fear and disgust combining like two currents converging to make a white-water eddy in a stream.

"Our law," Dingley said. "Milt represents our law."

"You can't do this." Mercy collapsed against the wall behind her. For a moment she thought her eyes were about to moisten, spill over. But she refused to cry before these men. "You can't."

"Well," Dingley said, "if you'd rather, we could just feed you to the Dragon."

"You sons of—"

"Now, now," Dingley said. To Milt, he said, "Didn't I say she's got some spunk?"

Milt stepped toward the cot again, leaned down, cautiously, as if he expected her to reveal her claws and strike. "You have to understand the circumstances that you're in."

"What circumstances? Ever since I came to Michigan I've been in circumstances."

"You and that boy killed Harlan Nau."

Mercy wished she could see his face better. "No."

"You swung that axe," he insisted. "Or maybe the boy, we don't know. Doesn't matter."

"I tell you like I told that Dragon of yours, that farmer, Harlan Nau, tried to rape me."

"Uh-huh." He seemed neither surprised nor interested. "It's no cause to go killing a white man." He started to turn away but then looked at her again. "Estelle, Harlan's wife? She just wanted children in the house again, someone to care for after losing their own to the influenza. Know what happened to her?"

"She never cared for me. Just made me do chores."

"Distraught, she was. Cut herself with a steak knife and bled to death." He walked back toward Owen. "Wish we had the boy, is all."

"She's all we got," Dingley said, turning in the doorway. "She'll have to do."

They ducked outside, closed the door, and secured the hasp.

In the dark, Mercy pulled the blanket up over her aching shoulder and lay down on her side. She thought she might cry then. Or scream. She did neither. Instead, she concentrated on the bites. Each one, until they were hers.

•

Milt and Owen walked back to the truck, where Mink had finished unloading the crates.

Owen took out a pack of cigarettes and passed them around. "Got to make an example of her. It's what people round here want."

Mink sat on the lowered tailgate. "She ain't good enough for no courtroom. Gotta be something allows people to see we mean business. Lotta people'd string her up in a heartbeat."

Milt said, "That what you got in mind, Owen?"

"It's up to the Old Man. Wait till you see how he works a crowd, brings them to his way of thinking."

But Milt knew it was all up to Owen, as well. Had been that way since they were kids. Mink would just wait for his brother to determine his next task, whether it was bullying some kid after school or unloading the truck. "You've worked it out with him, haven't you?" Milt said. "You and the Grand Dragon."

Owen gazed out at the woods as though he were counting the trees. Finally, he said, "They did it a couple years ago over in Duluth. Black boys working for a traveling circus raped a white girl. The police locked them up and thousands broke them out of the jail and hanged them in the town square." He drew on his cigarette. "And you know what they did to that fellow last just month in Chicago? What was his name? William, yes, William Bell. Now that was some swift justice."

Mink squinted through cigarette smoke. "What you be thinking, Milt? You can't go doing that to no girl? Well, you tell that to Harlan, and to Estelle. There's one way to make sure nothing like this happens around here again. Locking up this little girl, it ain't enough. That's what your Kincaid will do. We need different. We need to settle up the score. Quick, while it's still fresh in people's minds."

"A lynching," Milt said. "Jesus."

Owen turned away from the woods. "Listen. We need you. You're the authority. Rather than breaking into the jail, we need the police to deliver her. You're on our side."

"I hear you." Milt dropped his cigarette and heeled it into the mud. In that moment, that common gesture of extinguishing a cigarette, he became aware of an internal sense of motion, a pull akin to a magnetic field, a force he could not resist. There was the fear of being left behind, weak and isolated, and there was the need to be accepted, and he believed he had no choice but to allow himself to be carried along, as a matter of survival. He said it again, with greater conviction, "I hear you."

"Okay. Let's get back to town." Owen went up to the cab of the truck and opened the passenger door. He looked at his brother before getting in. "I'll be back for the girl tomorrow." Glancing toward the shed, he said, "Remember, no funny business." When his brother didn't answer immediately, he said sharply, "Mink?"

Mink lifted a haunch off the tailgate of the truck. "Yeah, yeah."

Milt got in behind the steering wheel and started the engine. "He all right out here alone with her?"

"He better be," Owen said.

Milt put the truck in gear. "Maybe we should bring her back to town with us?"

"And keep her where? No, we want her out of sight until it's time."

Milt eased out the clutch and worked the truck across the muddy clearing toward the two-track that went down through the woods.

"We got to do this thing right," Owen said. "We don't want damaged goods."

"Those bites," Milt said. "The Old Man, he really did that?"

Owen considered for a moment. "I grant you he's got some strong predilections."

Twenty

Rope was working on the second ham sandwich Myra had made for him when Kincaid came down the stairs. "I heard Mitch's wagon leave," Kincaid said to Myra.

"He's taking Doc Evers to Nesbit's to see about his car," she said. "You know Doc, too impatient to wait for anyone. Can I make you a sandwich?"

Kincaid shook his head. "Thanks, Myra, but we need to get going. You can check on Lois?"

"Sure."

He didn't look at Rope as he left the kitchen, but just said, "Let's go."

Rope stuffed the remainder of his sandwich in his mouth and followed Kincaid out to the car. As they drove into the village, Kincaid said nothing. Not one word. Something had happened to him while he was upstairs with the woman Myra called his lovely mother-in-law. Rope wasn't about to ask.

Mitch and Doc Evers were already at Nesbit's, talking to a boy who worked in the garage.

"My car's still not done," Doc Evers said this to Kincaid as though reporting a crime that warranted investigation. "Lyle isn't even here."

"Billy," Kincaid said to the boy, "Where is he?"

Billy was no more than a few years older than Rope. "Ain't seen Lyle since yesterday."

"How about Milt Waters?"

Billy shook his head. "He stops by most every day, but he's nowhere to be found, either."

"What we going to do about my car, Captain?" Doc Evers demanded.

"It's got problems I can't sort out," Billy said. "When Lyle gets back—"

"I got patients to see."

"I could take you around," Mitch offered.

"In that wagon of yours? Pulled by that flatulent old horse?" Doc Evers turned and started walking away, but before he reached the sidewalk, he stopped and said, "Oh, damn," and then climbed up onto Mitch's wagon. "Well, I don't have all day."

Mitch gave Kincaid a little smile, and then with effort hauled himself up on the bench next to Doc Evers. He took up the reins and turned the wagon into Main Street.

"That Doc Evers, he sure has a nose for diagnoses." Billy picked up a long iron bar and began working a tire off its rim. "That is one ripe horse."

Kincaid seemed unimpressed by this attempt at humor. As he watched the wagon move down the street, he said to Rope, "Remember what I said about you being in my custody?" Rope nodded. "That means you stay right here with Billy the comedian."

Rope nodded again.

"He tries to go anywhere, Billy, you have my permission to use that tire iron on him."

"This mean I'm deputized?"

Kincaid was clearly not in the mood for jokes. "Billy, you work in this garage all day and you see and hear things, and you just don't let on. Am I right?"

Billy stopped working, settling his iron on the concrete floor with a decisive clang. "What are you talking about, Captain?"

"Dingley's hooch," Kincaid said. His eyes drifted across the street, just for a moment, but it was long enough. "Van Nal's?" Kincaid asked.

Resigned, Billy gave the slightest dip of the head, not acknowledgment, but not denial, either.

"I see how this works now. Thanks, Billy." Kincaid started to leave the garage, but then stopped and looked back at Rope. "You stay put, hear?" He didn't wait for an answer but walked across the street.

As they watched Kincaid, Rope said to Billy, "What's he mean, seeing how this works?"

"You ain't from 'round here, are you?"

"No, I'm not."

"Where you from?"

"A long, long ways away."

"I guess so," Billy said. "Never been there myself."

.

Kincaid went up the steps to Van Nal's Tailor Shop and shoved open the front door, sounding the small brass bell that hung from the lintel. Van Nal stood behind the counter, looking like he'd long been expecting this moment, his dead-on eyes rheumy and defiant. "Morning, Captain," he said.

Kincaid said nothing but went to the rack of hanging garments and took down a wool overcoat and tossed it across the counter. Then another, and another, until he had piled up five men's coats.

"Don't believe any of those are yours," Van Nal said.

Kincaid ignored him as he picked up one coat. "Heavy," he said. He felt the pockets, and then found the source of extra weight. He picked up another coat and discovered the same, a lump sewn into the lining. As he was examining the third overcoat, the front door swung open, jiggling the brass bell again. Ernie Hagen, who ran the feed grain store down the street, came to the counter.

"One of these coats yours, Ernie?" Kincaid asked.

"Well, Captain, I don't believe so." He retreated toward the door.

"This one?" Kincaid picked up a gabardine coat.

"Never seen that coat before." Ernie looked at Van Nal as he put his hand on the doorknob. "Guess mine's not ready. I'll come back . . . another time."

"You do that," Kincaid said as Ernie slammed the door shut after him.

"Captain," Van Nal said, "you're scaring off my business."

"I'm going to close your business down, I don't get some answers." Kincaid picked up another coat and felt through it until he found the lump. "You sew the bottles in the lining."

"Bottles? I hadn't noticed."

"Dingley's. Where are the brothers making the stuff?"

"What stuff?"

Van Nal's wife Elif pushed through the curtain that concealed the back room. She had a thimble on her finger and another coat in her arms.

Kincaid took the coat from her, found the weight, and laid the garment out on the counter. "Would you like me to confiscate all these garments?" Van Nal was still defiant, while Elif looked petrified. "You want to tell me where they keep their still, or not?"

Van Nal folded his arms. His wife, looking as though she were about to plead guilty, rushed through the curtain to the back room, muttering something in Dutch. Or Flemish. Kincaid wasn't sure, but during the war he'd heard such accents in Europe.

"Well?" Kincaid said.

Van Nal continued to gaze out the window at the street. "You have no right to do that."

"I see." Kincaid took his revolver from his coat pocket, gripped it by the muzzle, and pounded the coats with the heel of the mahogany grip, breaking glass and releasing the pungent scent of whiskey. Four, five coats, hammered until the material was soaked with liquor. It felt good to hit something so hard, and he continued to hammer the coats until he was sure he had broken all the bottles sewn into the linings.

Elif came out through the curtain again and offered Kincaid two more coats. "Here is all of them."

"For today," Kincaid said.

"For today, this is so," she sounded relieved.

Kincaid took the coats from her, dropped them on the counter. "I'll be back," he said. "The still. You need to tell me."

Van Nal would not look at him, but there was something in his eyes, an acquiescence bordering on surrender, which led Kincaid to shove his revolver in his holster. He opened the door, engaging the bell, and looking up he was tempted to take the butt of his revolver to it.

"Wait, Captain." Elif turned to her husband and raised her voice, "Tell him . . . it must end now." She said something angrily in her native tongue. "I have told you how many times? No money is worth this."

Without looking at Kincaid, Van Nal said, "You take the county road toward Sutton Corners. Go about eight miles. There's a logging road that winds up into the hills east of there. It's up in the woods a good two miles or so in."

Kincaid stepped outside the tailor's shop and pulled the door shut, hard, so the glass rattled in their panes, and bits of dried putty rained down on the brick steps.

Rope and Billy were standing outside the garage. They must have heard the commotion in the tailor's shop. As he walked to his car, Kincaid said, "You finished with that tire?"

Billy nodded.

"Then why don't you two come with me. Bring that tire iron, a shovel. And, if you've got one, a sledge."

•

Billy sat up front with his collection of tools. Rope got in the back seat because he was the youngest, and he was from a long, long ways away.

"William Barnes," Kincaid said as he put the car into gear. At first, Rope thought this was a formal introduction. Billy must have thought so too since he turned and gave Rope a curt nod. He had a mole above his left eyebrow and what appeared to be a smudge of grease darkened his hollowed cheek. "I have a job to do that requires your assistance," Kincaid went on. "In order to do so I need to deputize you. Temporarily. It requires that you follow orders. Do you agree?"

Turning to Kincaid, Billy looked as though this honor was long overdue. "Sure, Captain." His smile revealed oversized, crooked teeth. "As deputy, don't I receive compensation?"

"Depends," Kincaid said. "On the job done."

Billy nodded toward Rope in the back seat. "He still in custody?"

"He is in protective custody." Kincaid thought about this a moment. "He needs to stay put."

Over his shoulder, Billy said, "Deputy William Barnes is keeping my eye on you, son."

They rode in silence then, passing through farmland beneath wooded hills. On straightaways, Kincaid floored it, until he downshifted as they came into the next bend in the road. They must have been a good eight or ten miles outside of town when he turned onto a two-track lane that wound up into the hills.

He eased the Chevrolet over ridges and potholes, tall grass ticking against the underside of the chassis. It occurred to Rope that this was not just a matter of protecting the automobile, but a predatory means of approach. When they neared the crest of the hill, Kincaid rolled the car to a halt and shut down the engine.

A half mile off to the left a column of smoke rose above the trees into the still air.

"Bring the tools." Kincaid got out of the car, closing the door gently. "Quietly, now."

He led them through the woods, the ground mostly pine needle carpet. Billy had a tire iron and a pickaxe, while Rope carried the sledgehammer on his shoulder. The land descended toward the sound of a running stream, which they crossed on a fallen tree trunk, and then they began their ascent, as though drawn by the smell of smoke which now shrouded the forest. When they reached the next ridge, Kincaid lifted his hand and they stopped at the edge of a clearing. He opened his overcoat and unholstered his revolver. The smoke was so heavy that Rope couldn't figure out what they were looking at until Billy whispered, "Dingley's still."

They moved forward, pausing behind tree trunks. At fifty yards Rope could make out a shed, a truck, and a rusted metal contraption unlike anything he'd ever seen. A large man in soiled overalls was loading wooden crates into the truck bed. He paused to tap out a cigarette and was about to strike a match when he sensed movement in the woods. He looked in their direction and one of the crates fell off the tailgate, bottles breaking at his feet.

Kincaid broke into a run, and Billy and Rope followed him into the clearing. The man ran toward the shed and picked up a shotgun that was leaning against the wall. He swung around and the first discharge cut through the branches overhead, sending pine needles drifting down on Rope's head. The second shot kicked up dirt to Billy's left. They continued forward through the smoke as he dropped the rifle and ran to the truck.

Kincaid raised both arms and took aim as the man opened the door and climbed in behind the steering wheel. One shot and Kincaid flattened the rear tire on the left side of the truck. "Mink!" he shouted. "You're not going anywhere. Now get out."

Mink did as he was told, also holding his hands up as he considered the broken bottles on the ground. "That's a lot of money soaking into the ground." Looking at Billy and Rope, he said, "Captain, this is your idea of a posse?"

"All the posse I need. Where's your brother?"

"Who?"

"Owen, your bother?" Kincaid waited. "Mink, this operation isn't all your idea, is it?"

Mink didn't look sure if he had been insulted or not. "I ain't seen him." Then he shook his head, disappointed. "Captain, you just brung yourself a heap of trouble. Lot of people round here going to be unhappy when the local supply dries up."

Kincaid lowered his gun. For a moment no one seemed to know what to do, and then Mink turned and jogged around behind the shed.

Billy said, "I ran track in high school, Captain. Want me to go after him?"

They could hear Mink crashing down the hill though brush.

"No, don't bother," Kincaid said. "We got the hooch." He looked at Rope. "Give Billy a hand putting on that spare tire."

"Damn," Billy said. "I didn't think changing tires was in a deputy's job description."

"It is if you're going to drive that rig down off this hill," Kincaid said. "I'll get my car and you follow me back to town."

Billy leaned into the truck bed and began removing the spare tire that was lashed to the fence. He looked at the crates in the truck bed. "We could all make a decent profit selling this stuff."

"An interesting proposition," Kincaid said. "But I believe it would be tampering with evidence."

"And a dereliction of my duties as a sworn in deputy?" Billy said.

"Something like that." Kincaid returned his revolver to its holster as he examined the still. "Before you go, put those tools to good use and bust this thing up."

Billy laughed. "We will do a first-rate bang-up job."

But Kincaid seemed in no mood for humor. He turned his head, drawn by a rapping sound coming from the shed. He removed the stick that secured the hasp, opened the door, and Mercy staggered out of the shed, blinking from the light, her wrists bound.

•

Mercy sat next to Rope in the back seat, while Captain Kincaid drove the Chevrolet back to Otter Creek. Billy followed them in the truck loaded with crates of bottled whiskey. As the countryside gave way to clusters of houses at the edge of town, Mercy felt it rising, a taut anxiety. They were returning, going back to where this all began.

She knew that Rope was staring at her hand, but she ignored him. "Those are tooth marks?" She didn't answer. "What happened?"

"Apparently, I was bitten." She rather enjoyed Rope's look of disbelief. "By a Grand Dragon."

"The Grand Dragon?" Kincaid said. "Here?"

"That's right."

"Grand Dragon?" Rope wasn't sure how to form the question. "What's he look like?"

In the front seat Kincaid turned his head, waiting for her reply. "Hungry, he looks hungry." She studied the captain's profile and thought she detected a faint smile. He was different from the others, though she wasn't sure how. "Where are you taking us?"

"Well," Kincaid said, "now that you're in my custody . . ."

"Jail?" Rope said. "A jail cell?"

Kincaid didn't answer.

"Years in an orphanage seemed prison enough," Mercy said. "A clean prison." When Kincaid tilted his head inquiringly, she added, "The nuns insisted that we keep it that way. We scrubbed and scoured every inch of that building. In Worcester, you can tell an orphan girl by her hands."

Her left hand was swollen, and her wrists were still raw from the rope, which Kincaid had untied before she got in the back seat of his car. What did this mean? A sign of trust in this police captain. To do what? To do what he set out to do, bring them both back to Otter Creek? Put them in a jail cell, where they would wait until they were brought before a court, a judge, and jury? Face justice?

No. Trust was a luxury. Justice an illusion.

"You're taking us in," she said, "because that's what you set out to do." She raised her voice. "Two orphans—nobodies, who got off a train in Michigan, you think we'll get a fair trial?"

Kincaid shifted gears and kept his eyes on the road as they entered the village.

•

Rope and Mercy got out of the Chevrolet in front of the police station. He followed her up the stairs to the front door, while Kincaid told Billy to take the truck around to the back of the building and unload the crates of Dingley's whiskey into the cellar.

Mercy watched Kincaid climb the stairs. In the car, she'd been angry, but now she looked weary, exhausted. "Are we under arrest?"

"You haven't been formally charged. Yet."

"We're under protective custody," Rope said.

"That some sort of inside joke?" Mercy asked.

"Perhaps." Kincaid ushered Rope and Mercy into the office.

Ellie was seated at the front desk. "Well, Captain, now you have 'em both." She glanced out the window and watched Billy drive the truck down the alley next to the station. "And it appears you found the still. Now *that* will disappoint a lot of folks around here."

"I suppose it will," Kincaid said. "No sign of Milt yet?"

She shook her head. "What you want to do with these two?"

"For the time being, we will put them in cells. They're minors. Extra blankets, and have some food sent down from Jake's. Anything they want."

"Anything?" She looked at Rope and then Mercy, doubtful. "I hear the perch is on special. That all right with you?" When they both nodded, she said, "I guess what we're running here is a five-star hotel. I will have the bellhop attend to your luggage. Now, if you'll be so kind as to follow me."

Ellie got up from her desk and led them through a low gate in an oak railing to an open door at the back of the station. There were four cells, two on each side of the corridor. "Young lady," she said, taking a set of keys off a wall hook, "I'm going to give you the honeymoon suite. It's a little more spacious and private. And the view of the alley captures the light nicely at sunset." After Mercy stepped inside the cell, Ellie closed the door and locked it. "Now," she said to Rope, her voice dismissive, "Your accommodations are a bit more modest." At the end of the corridor, she motioned for him to enter the cell on the left, which was not half the size of Mercy's. There was a cot with one blanket and a pillow, a washbasin, and chamber pot. She closed the door and locked it. "I'll get you both more blankets and place your order with the chef."

She walked down the corridor and out into the office. Rope had never been behind bars before. He put his hands on them. The iron was cold. He could not see Mercy, only her fingers, which were also gripping the bars on her cell.

"You don't strike me as having much of a sense of humor," she said. "I guess this is your idea of an inside joke." She waited. "For once, you could come back with something witty, something funny." After a moment, she said, "Guess not."

"You ever had perch?"

"Is that supposed to be witty?"

"No. I was wondering about the fish."

"Of course, you were. Cod, pollock, haddock, sure. No meat on Fridays, the nuns always had fish. But perch, no." Her hands disappeared from the bars. He could hear her stretch out on the cot and unfurl a blanket. "How do they do it, here in Michigan?" she asked.

"Do what? Cook perch?"

"No. Execute people."

"Jesus. I don't know."

"I hope they don't do what they did to him." She snorted, attempting a laugh. "I believe they burn crosses out here. Let's hope they don't nail people to them. Some places now use an electric chair. I'll bet out here they hang you."

"Don't think about it."

"What am I supposed to think about?"

"Think about perch," he said. "Besides, you didn't do anything. Harlan Nau was trying to . . . you know. You didn't do anything to him. You didn't have that axe in your hands. They're not going to hang you."

"Are you that ignorant?"

"Am I what?"

"Ignorant. You watch. They will determine that I was an accessory. You know, an accessory to murder? They will find that we planned the whole thing. They will say that I lured him up there so you could kill him."

"Why would they think that?"

"Because he was white, and I'm not."

Rope went over to his cot and sat down. "They need proof."

"No, they don't," she said. He could hear her blanket rustle as she turned on her side. "They do not need proof." By the way her voice reverberated, he knew she was facing the brick wall. "You are the most ignorant boy I ever met."

•

There was a horizontal slot in the cell door. Ellie passed the plate, covered with a linen napkin, through to Mercy. "Just a spoon, honey. No knives and forks. We are a high-security hotel." She went down to the end of the corridor and gave Rope his plate. "We had a fella, Norman Something, used to be a regular in here most Saturday nights. Last time we checked him in he was so stewed he took his fork and hacked away at an artery in his neck. Fortunately, his aim was lousy. He only managed to leave an ugly tattoo on his cheek."

"At the orphanage," Mercy said, "the nuns had one rule during meals: no talking."

"I was just making conversation," Ellie offered.

"No, you weren't." Mercy sat on her cot and removed the napkin. The perch, small fillets in fried batter, smelled better than anything she could remember. Years of institutional meals, she had developed a fierce skepticism and distrust of food. She didn't use the spoon but picked up a fillet with her fingers. Ellie leaned against the wall, folding her beefy arms over her ample chest.

"The nuns also used to do that," Mercy said.

"What's that, honey?"

"Monitor our meals. Watch everything we did."

"That so?"

"This is . . . it's fantastic," Rope said, chewing.

Mercy took a bite of the fillet. The batter, the fish, it was like nothing she'd ever tasted. The fish at the orphanage was usually overcooked unseasoned mush, which required cautious chewing: bones and cartilage. "I guess we can talk while we eat," she said. "It's not like you can punish us, since we're already in jail."

"Catholics," Ellie said. "You're a strange bunch."

Mercy ate some mashed potatoes with the spoon. "Much of the time we had to make a vow of silence. And make little sacrifices during the day. Offer our headache to Jesus, that sort of thing. Just about everything you do is a sin. Even thinking about most things is a sin."

"The nuns," Ellie said, "they believe in corporal punishment, don't they? Rulers, spankings—"

"Worse," Mercy said. "They like to hit you where the bruises don't show."

Rope added, "We had one sister who could really work your ribs. Expert, like a prize fighter." Mercy could hear him scraping the last of the mashed from his plate. "And don't get me started on the priests," he said. "'Course, I never had a problem with them myself. They go after the weak boys, the soft, pretty ones."

"It'd be a desperate priest to go after the likes of you," Mercy said.

"Thank you," Rope said. "I knew my looks were good for something."

"I don't believe it," Mercy said. "That's almost witty."

"It's a crying shame, young children and all," Ellie said. "Bet you're glad to be out of there."

Mercy picked up another fillet with her fingers. "This beats the orphanage by a mile."

Ellie went down to Rope's cell. "Downed that in a hurry."

"Thank you, ma'am."

Mercy finished her dinner and brought the clean plate, spoon, and napkin to the cell door, where she passed it through to Ellie. "Yes, much obliged. Ordinarily, we'd say prayers in thanks for our meal, or maybe sing a hymn."

"Sing all you want," Ellie said. When Mercy shook her head, Ellie started down the corridor, but then hesitated. "Suppose," she said. "Suppose the story you told the captain turns out to be true. Suppose you didn't do in Harlan like everyone thinks. If you get out of here, what all you gonna do?"

Mercy stared at the woman, and then shrugged.

"Well," Ellie said as she went through the door to the office. "We'll just see, won't we?"

Mercy heard Rope lie down on his cot. She needed to move, unaccustomed to a full stomach, so she walked back and forth in her cell, four steps one way, turn, and four steps the other way.

She did the circuit perhaps two dozen times, when Rope said, "What would you do?"

"Not sure." Mercy continued to walk, back and forth. "But I'd walk in a straight line without turning every four steps."

Twenty-One

Milt gazed out Dingley's kitchen window at the men gathered in the barnyard, most of them standing about, trying to look important, while a few did the real work, wielding hammers, saws, and taking measurements with a folding rule. At Owen's instructions, they had pried two rotting timbers from the barn walls and laid them out on the tamped earth behind the house. While a notch was fashioned into the longer timber with adze and chisel, they argued about every detail, particularly the fastening of the cross-piece. It was too thick to be nailed, so why not simply lash the two timbers together? No, rope burns quickly—the whole thing might come apart within minutes. Eventually, four holes were augered in the cross-piece, and wooden dowels, cut from a broken rake handle and smeared with axle grease, were driven through the joint with mallets.

Owen had been working the telephone, talking to other Klaverns. When he hung up, he said, "They'll be coming in from all over. I thought we might get a hundred or so, but it looks like we could more than double that."

"Great," Milt said, looking at the boxes stacked on the kitchen floor. "What's all this?"

"Robes and hoods." Owen held up one hand, spreading his fingers wide.

"Five? Dollars?"

"More, if you want a better cut of material." Owen gestured toward another box. "Jackknives, pendants, pins, household items, you name it. All emblazoned with the cross in the circle."

"What's your cut?"

"Depends. The more I sell, the better my percentage."

"Your moonshine runs throughout the county, and you sell these robes and stuff," Milt said. "You always knew how to make a buck."

Owen shrugged. "After the parade tomorrow, and the Grand Dragon's appearance, they'll be a surge of new memberships." He tapped a carton that was on a kitchen chair. "This one's for you. Let's find you something that fits. Of course, being born in Canada you need the red robe of an American Krusader."

Before Milt could respond, Owen lifted a folded garment out of the carton, held it up, so it would unfurl almost to the floor. "I think the length is good and the shoulders shouldn't be too snug." Draping the robe over his forearm, he placed the tall, pointed hood on Milt's head. "Perfect."

"I don't have five dollars."

"Don't worry about the five dollars." Owen refolded the robe and handed it to Milt, and then glanced out the window at the barnyard. "Look at those boys. They lack direction. Can hardly do a simple task without supervision. They need guidance. That's what the Klan provides. Guidance."

Milt nodded toward the boxes on the floor. "And pendants and pins."

Owen grinned, regarding Milt as though they shared a hard-won secret. "Membership. It's all about merchandise and hooch."

Milt crossed the kitchen so he could see his reflection in the mirror that hung on the wall. The high peaked hood suggested a dunce and he wasn't sure how he felt about the red. "Most of the others, they'll be wearing white?"

"They will," Owen said.

"Right. One hundred percent. Americans."

Outside the clatter of tools was interrupted by the sound of an approaching engine as a Model T rattled up the dirt two-track, and Milt followed Owen out the kitchen door and into the yard. Mink climbed out of the automobile, his overalls muddy, his face scratched and bleeding. The men parted as he made his way toward the farmhouse, where he stopped before his brother, looking like a boy who expected a reprimand.

"I ran several miles through them hills." For all his size Mink had a high, chortling voice with an oddly musical timbre. He glanced over his shoulder toward the Model T. "Lucky, Jake Slater picked me up."

Owen showed no concern for his brother's condition. "What about the still?"

The crowd of men behind Mink fell silent.

"As I was making my way down the hill through the woods, I could hear them busting it up," Mink said, and the register of his voice rose even higher. "It's not the feds, it's that Kincaid!"

Owen leaned close to his brother, so the others couldn't hear. "And the girl?"

Mink shook his head.

Turning to Milt, Owen appeared as though a long-held conviction was at last justified. "See why we need you, Milt? Members of the town council, that's one thing. We got our parade permit. But Kincaid, the police captain, that's another story entirely."

There was a tapping sound, up high behind them. Turning, they looked up at D. C. Stephenson, who was rapping his knuckles on a second-floor window.

"I'll go see what the Old Man wants." Owen started toward the house, but then stopped and looked back at the others. "Go on, finish your carpentering. Milt, Mink, you come with me."

As they walked toward the kitchen door, Mink said, "The Old Man looks hung over, you ask me."

"That he is," Owen said. He was seething. "You had to lose the still and the girl?"

"Kincaid had a posse! They came out of the woods, three of them. He shot out the tire on the truck. I barely got away."

"What posse?" Milt asked.

"I don't know," Mink whined. "There was lots of smoke, and I didn't stick around to take names."

This only seemed to fuel Owen's anger. They went in the house and before they climbed the stairs, he turned to his brother. "You wait here. You don't want to be up there when he learns you lost that girl."

Mink looked like he was being unfairly accused and was about to protest when Owen put up his hand and said, "Just stay here. If I can't square things with the Old Man, you'll want to make yourself scarce." As he climbed the stairs, Owen said over his shoulder to Milt, "Been this way since we were boys. Mink gets himself in trouble, and I'm the one who bails him out."

•

Kincaid came in from the office and leaned against the corridor wall. For minutes he stared into the cells, not exactly looking at Mercy and Rope but seeming to test the atmosphere, as though expecting to detect the source of an unidentified smell. Mercy was a pacer, back and forth, while the boy sat on his cot, elbows on his knees, head bent so that he stared at the floor. The girl finally stood still, glaring out through the bars at Kincaid.

"Legal counsel," she said. "Aren't we going to see a lawyer?"

Kincaid nodded but didn't speak. While he stared at them a long moment, Ellie came and stood in the doorway to the corridor.

Rope got to his feet. "You said we'd get a court-appointed attorney."

"I did," Kincaid allowed. "But you haven't been charged yet."

"What does that mean?" Rope said, gripping a bar with his left hand.

Kincaid straightened up and took the cell keys down from the hook on the wall. "It means you haven't been formally charged yet."

He let Mercy and Rope out of their cells.

"What's this?" Mercy sounded alarmed.

Kincaid said, "We're just going for a ride."

"Again?" She stepped out of her cell and held her arms out, wrists together.

"Put your arms down," Kincaid said. "No cuffs."

"So where are we going?" Rope said.

"Come with me." Kincaid led them out into the office. He went to the closet by the front door and took out Harlan Nau's axe, which was wrapped in butcher's paper and bound with twine. He went outside and led them down the steps to his Chevrolet, parked in front of the station.

"We want to know where we're going," Mercy said.

Kincaid opened the passenger door for them. "We're going to Nau Farm."

Mercy said, "I don't want to go back there."

"I understand," Kincaid said. "But it's necessary."

They maintained a tense silence during the drive out of town. When they reached the farm, Lyle let them in the kitchen, considering Rope and Mercy, and then the axe in Kincaid's hand. "What we got here, Captain?"

"I want to go over a few things. Details regarding what happened to Harlan. Where's Hannah?"

"Upstairs, putting things away. We're still unpacking. What details?"

"Let's go up," Kincaid said. "I want to see the attic again."

"With them?" Hannah's tremulous voice came from the top of the stairs. She might have been referring to a couple of yard dogs that were never allowed in the house. "Really Captain, I don't see why they need to come in here."

"Everybody," Kincaid said, gesturing with his free hand toward the staircase. "Upstairs, if you please."

They climbed to the second floor, walked to the attic stairs at the back of the hall.

Except Hannah. "I'm staying down here. My legs just ain't up to it."

"All right, Hannah," Kincaid said.

"Captain," Lyle said, "I don't appreciate your treating us like we are the guilty party here."

"Nothing of the sort," Kincaid said.

Hannah said, "And bringing that axe in here?"

"I just want to go over everything one more time."

Kincaid now gestured toward the attic stairs and followed them up. Looking back, he saw Hannah sit on a straight back chair in the nearest bedroom. She folded her hands in her lap, refusing to look at him.

It was nearly dark in the attic. Kincaid went to one gable end and drew aside the tattered curtain, admitting a shaft of weak sunlight across the pine floorboards. The cot was still at the far end, its thin mattress stripped of sheets and blankets. "You washed everything?" he said, walking over to the cot.

"There was a lot of blood," Lyle said. "We scrubbed the bedding but eventually realized it was best to just throw it out."

"Where?"

"Well, not throw out. We burned it in the incinerator can around behind the barn."

Kincaid looked down at the floor. "And here? Looks like it's been sanded."

"It was the only way to get the blood out, yes," Lyle said. "It was Estelle's request. She couldn't stand the sight of his blood remaining all over everything."

"The sight of it?" Kincaid said. "She came up here?"

"Yes, once. Soon after it happened."

From down on the second floor, Hannah said, "She was weak from the hospital stay, the operation and all. My sister could barely manage the stairs. We tried to talk her out of it, but she was adamant. She wanted to see where it happened."

Kincaid looked up at Lyle. "And what did she see?"

"Blood. So much . . . blood." Lyle, shaking his head in wonder and disbelief, folded his arms. "I thought she was going to have a heart attack right up here. She insisted we describe how we found him, and then asked that we clean it up."

"We?" Kincaid said. "Who found him?"

"I did," Lyle said. "I told you that in the first place."

"I know. You just said we."

Lyle looked away as though he couldn't bother to answer.

"So tell me again, Lyle, exactly what did you find when you came up here?"

"Well," he said, walking toward the cot, "Harlan was here, sort of propped up on the floor. With the axe, you know."

"Buried in his skull," Kincaid said. "That's how you found him."

"Yes."

When Kincaid turned, Mercy stared back at him, insulted, while Rope wouldn't look up from the floor. "They say something different, Lyle."

Lyle considered them with disbelief, or perhaps pity.

Hannah could be heard now, struggling to climb the attic stairs. She stopped on the top tread, breathing heavily. "What do you expect?" Her voice was shaking. "Of course, they say something different. They ain't going to admit to it."

"They say that Harlan was drunk. He'd been drinking the entire time Estelle was in the hospital." Kincaid pointed at the cot. "He came up here while Mercy was in bed. He dropped his overalls while he was trying to get at her. That's how he was found, with his pants down. Isn't that right?" he said looking at Mercy. She nodded. "They were both on the cot. There was a struggle."

"You sure she didn't invite him up here?" Lyle asked.

Kincaid ignored this. "Her clothes were torn. The dress she's wearing under that coat is pinned together. It was rape, or attempted rape. I can't be certain which because a doctor never got to do a medical examination."

"Of her?" Hannah said. "Of *this*?"

"It was attempted rape," Mercy said. "He tried but never got that far. Attempted."

"I just bet it was," Hannah said.

"They struggled, here on the cot," Kincaid continued. "Harlan's overalls were down, Mercy's clothing torn. And then . . . and then Rope comes up the stairs."

"With that axe," Lyle said.

No one spoke. The only sound was of flies, drawn to the light coming through the far window, buzzing as they tried to find a way through the panes of glass.

"You came up here," Kincaid said to Rope. "Why did you bring this?" He held out the axe and tore the twine and butcher's paper away, letting it drift to the floor.

"I was down in the shed on the back of the house," Rope said. "That's where I slept. I kept the axe outside the door. I split wood. Every day, I split wood." Rope seemed to understand that he wasn't really answering the question. "I heard them. I heard Mercy and Harlan upstairs somewhere. I could tell there was a problem from their voices. He was a problem. He'd been that way while his wife was gone, and it got worse every day."

"You heard them, so you came up here," Kincaid said. "And what did you find?"

"They were there on the cot. He was on top, and she was . . . her clothes were torn. When he saw me, he got off her and she got up from the cot. She went downstairs. Right away. Holding her dress up, she walked past me and down the stairs."

"Was anything said?" Kincaid asked. "Between you and Harlan?"

Rope shook his head.

"Mercy," Kincaid said. "She didn't say anything?"

Rope hesitated a moment, and then shook his head again.

"What?" Kincaid said. "What aren't you telling me?"

"She said—" Rope looked at Mercy, and then back at Kincaid. "When she walked by me to the stairs she said, 'I could kill him.'"

"Well, there you are," Lyle said. "They was both in on it, you ask me."

Kincaid stared at Rope. "That's what she said?"

Rope nodded. "That's what she said, yes."

"And then what did you do?"

Rope now seemed to be having difficulty breathing. "I hit him." He inhaled, deeply. "With the axe. But it was with the blunt side, not the blade. He went down. Stunned, there by the cot. I thought of finishing it. But the way he looked, I didn't. Besides, I could hear Mercy going down through the house. I knew she'd leave. There'd be no stopping her, and I wanted to catch up to her." He took a long slow draught of air, desperate to fill his lungs.

Kincaid held up the axe. "So what did you do with this?"

"I dropped it. I just dropped it, right about here where I'm standing, and went down the stairs after her."

"I've heard enough," Hannah said as she carefully turned and started to make her way down to the second floor, the stair treads creaking under her weight.

"You dropped the axe," Kincaid said.

"I'll say he did." Lyle moved toward the stairs. "Let me help you, dear."

Kincaid dropped the axe on the floor, the maple handle clattering on the wood.

Lyle and Hannah paused on the stairs.

Rope stared at the axe, and said, "Not like that," and then he got down on his knees and crawled about, his face close to the floor. Kincaid could see dust motes swirling in the air.

"I didn't drop it," Rope said, distracted as he searched the floor. "Not like that."

"What, then?" Kincaid asked.

"I flung it down," Rope said. "You know, like you do with an axe, and the blade, it sets in the wood. I was in the habit of doing it out in the yard. I like doing it, setting the blade so the handle was easy to grab a hold of next time." He bent over until his face was almost touching the floor and crawled forward slowly. "Here. The blade, it went in *here*. It sank in good, see?"

Kincaid went over and looked at the crease in the floorboard. Then he picked up the axe, leaned over, and fit the blade into the wood, pushing it until the handle stood up from the floor at an angle. He looked at Lyle who was part way down the stairs. Hannah slowly eased herself down until she was sitting on the stair tread. Kincaid could only see the back of her head.

"It don't mean a thing," Lyle said. "These old floorboards got all sorts of cracks in 'em."

"This is no crack," Kincaid said. "It's a perfect fit."

"I say it don't mean a thing."

Next to him, Hannah continued to look down the staircase. Her shoulders, Kincaid thought, were moving. Just the slightest tremor.

•

Mercy went to the cot. Her legs felt weak, and she needed to sit down. They had been wandering in this cold wilderness called Michigan, orphans in exile, and now they were back in this place where it all began. There was something true and reliable about Rope. She had come to understand that. He was quiet, often hard and unyielding, and she wasn't sure what she felt about him, but she cared about him. She might even love him—she really didn't know. Now he was kneeling on the floor, staring at the axe that fit perfectly into the crevice the blade had made in the wood, and Mercy believed him. He did not slay the man. That's the word they often used in the Bible. Slay, slew. By the thousands in battles. With knives and swords and hatchets. With pikes and spears and lances. With axes. Cruel, torturous weapons. Weapons of reckoning, of vengeance. Goliath, the Philistine. Holofernes, the Assyrian. John, and his brother James. Sharp blades stained with blood. Sacrificial blood, the blood of reprisal.

She had said, *I could kill him,* and perhaps, if the axe had been in her hands at that moment, she could have, but Rope didn't.

He did not kill Harlan Nau.

•

How many times had Rope raised this axe to split wood? He knew the blade's heft, he knew the handle's balance point. In order to get a clean split, you had to strike the log along its grain. His first day on the farm Harlan had said there was only one way to do it. He demonstrated for Rope how to set the log on the block just so, line up the grain, and then raising the axe above his head with both hands, bringing the blade down and cleanly splitting the wood in two. He did it several times: one blow.

Then he handed the axe to Rope. Harlan Nau expected this orphan just off the train to fail. Since he'd lost his fingers to the factory machine in Haverhill, Rope recognized that most people expected him to fail. He was defective, eternally flawed. Few things in this world were done—done properly—with one hand. The first few times he swung the axe, Rope was off the mark. He hit the log too far to one side or the blade did not find the grain. He had used his right hand as a guide, cradling the handle with his remaining thumb as he raised the axe. It was no good. Harlan Nau peered off at the distant fields, and there was no need for him to say what was on his mind.

But then Rope said he wanted to try it one-handed. This man, this Michigan farmer glanced at him, shaking his head slowly. Rope set the next log on the block and repositioned his body, turning so he could raise the axe over his left shoulder, not his head. He looked at the grain. He raised the axe, and then swung down, the blade driving through the wood. A satisfactory sound, split wood, clattering on the cold, hard ground, a kind of applause.

Nau was not impressed.

Rope did it again.

And again.

And again.

He split five logs cleanly, one stroke each time.

Nau shrugged, nodded toward the pile of logs waiting to be split and stacked, and then wandered off toward the barn.

Repetition, no matter if it was a machine stamping out leather in a shoe factory or if it was splitting logs, was a necessary part of survival. Repetition fed you, clothed you. If you couldn't do a thing properly again and again, you wouldn't have a place in this world. You'd starve. You'd die. Repetition was salvation. Hours on end, splitting logs here in rural Michigan, his shoulders and back sore at first, until his muscles hardened and became attuned to the moment of concentration when he brought the blade down in true alignment with the wood's grain.

Rope's face was inches above the attic floor, and he could see hair embedded in the dried blood on the blade. He raised himself up, leaning back on his haunches. He turned to Mercy, on the cot. She looked ill, but her eyes offered him something he couldn't quite comprehend. They gave him hope. And courage, which he needed there, kneeling on the floor where this terrible thing had happened.

Staring up at Kincaid, he said, "I did not do this. There was no blood on the blade. I flung it down. Here. It stuck in the wood, here, splitting the grain, see? I did not kill that man."

"I know." The captain's voice was quiet. "Why, Lyle? You came up here, found the axe here. Why'd you finish Harlan off?"

Lyle Nesbit withdrew his hands from his trouser pockets and folded his arms. Flies beat against the window glass.

"Was it the farm?" Kincaid asked. "With Harlan gone and Estelle probably not long for this world, the place would go to Hannah. Is that it?"

Lyle turned his head away. More silence except for the frantic, desperate flies beating against the glass. "He was in a bad way, you could see that. I could have let him go, and it wouldn't take long. He was in agony, and I put him out of his misery. It was my doing."

"No." On the stairs, Hannah shifted her weight, causing the tread beneath her to creak. "Not entirely," she said. "He did it for me. But it wasn't really about the land." She stood up, slowly, and turned to face Kincaid. For a moment, she considered the axe, jutting out of the floorboard. "This goes back, Captain. A long ways back. Estelle was my sister. People often mistook us for one another. Harlan took a shine to me. I was fourteen, going on fifteen. I would not let things go too far, if you know what I mean, but he was insistent. Once, it was after a social, he showed up with a flask, like boys did, and when the evening was breaking up he offered to drive me home in his buggy. It was one of the few times that liquor has ever passed my lips. He stopped the buggy by where the stream runs through Knut Andersson's pasture, and you can figure out the rest. I was mortified. I thought for a while that I might be pregnant. I refused his further advances. This angered him because, you know, he believed he had earned rights." Hannah looked toward the cot, and it was as though she could see Harlan Nau, his body bloodied and fallen. "To my horror, some months later he takes up with Estelle. She was such a little fool. You could see it back then in the way she gazed at herself in the mirror. I warned her, I told her about Harlan and me. But there was this sense of competition between us sisters. I developed what you might call a deep resentment toward Estelle, one I could never voice, because you could not admit to having given yourself away like that. When I took up with Lyle, I was saved, it seemed. He understood that I bore this burden, and in time he guessed at its source. He asked me about Harlan, and I told him. I passed the anger and disgust I felt for Estelle and Harlan—and for myself—on to Lyle. But he married me, and we bore it together. For years. Their farm, it was bigger, more profitable. They had two children. We had none. And I'd miscarried twice. When their boy and girl died of influenza it was a kind of vindication for me. I can't justify it, but there it is. And when Lyle came down the stairs after finding Harlan, I knew, I knew it wasn't the way he was telling it to Estelle. It wasn't until later that I fully understood. But at that very moment when he came down to the kitchen and said that Harlan was left for dead, his head split open with an axe, and she said it had to be them, them two orphans—at that moment, I knew that's not the way it really went. It was in Lyle's eyes. He made it right, Captain. He had waited all this time. Years. And then he made it right."

5

Ghost Parade

Twenty-Two

Milt stood with his back against the bedroom door, trying to remain invisible. The Grand Dragon was irate—irate and drunk. As he paced the room, he shouted, and then he became quiet, whispering, muttering, only to suddenly bellow again. Frequently, he returned to the pint of Dingley's on the chair, sometimes refilling his glass, sometimes drinking straight from the bottle. His rant often made little sense to Milt, complaining about people he'd never heard of, often mentioning Indiana, boasting he owned the state and everyone in it. And he would own Michigan, too, every senator, every councilman, every judge, every cop, even the governor. His outrage, his embarrassment, his disgust worked in circles, coming back always to *them* and *they*, his opponents who actually thought he could be denied. He went on and on, his anger billowing, feeding on itself, and at the center of it, at the core of it was this orphan girl off a train from back East, who was now gone, taken, stolen from him.

Owen Dingley remained steadfast, calm. He spoke quietly, offered explanations, gave assurances that everything would work out. Klansmen were coming into Otter Creek in droves, and the preparations for the parade were nearly complete. The girl was insignificant, incidental. Each time the Grand Dragon mentioned her, Dingley said she would be found. He had wisely told his brother Mink to wait out in the hall.

The tirade lasted a good twenty minutes before the Grand Dragon stopped pacing and turned to Milt, glaring at him as though he'd just realized there was a third man in the room. "And this is?" His voice was a small hiss, leaking out through tight lips.

"Milt Waters," Dingley said. "The police deputy."

The Grand Dragon's white shirt was untucked and his necktie askew. He raised an arm and wiped his sweating face with his sleeve. "The deputy?"

"Soon to be the chief of police."

Stephenson cocked his head, not seeming to understand what he'd heard, but then he smiled as he came closer to Milt. His clothes, his breath smelled of sweat, tobacco, and whiskey. "You lose that girl, deputy?"

"No, I did not."

"You did not. You going to get her back for me?"

"I could do that."

"You could?"

"I will, yes." The Grand Dragon didn't seem satisfied. Milt added, "She is wanted, wanted for murder, and she will be brought into custody."

Stephenson finished what was in his glass. "You know where she is?"

Milt nodded. "The police chief took her." He glanced at Dingley. "When he raided the still."

For the first time since Milt had entered the room, the Grand Dragon appeared reasonable. He nodded, even smiling for a moment. "You get her from the captain . . ."

"Kincaid," Milt offered.

"And we make you captain." He seemed pleased, reminding Milt of a child who has been talked down from a tantrum. "You know . . . did I tell you that I own every politician, every police chief in Indiana?"

Milt nodded.

"It's true, I do. You realize that this would never happen down there? No police chief would think of raiding a still without my say so." He considered his empty glass a moment. "And as for the girl. Well, that's another story." He walked around the bed to the chair and poured more Dingley's in his glass. After he drank it down, he seemed composed, almost serene. "All right Deputy . . . Waters. You want to be chief of police around here, you find me that girl." The

Grand Dragon looked to Dingley for confirmation. "We have several members of the town council, correct?"

Dingley nodded. "They've cleared the way for the parade, everything upright and legal."

Stephenson seemed to find this amusing. "Permits. Always the permits. Signed and sealed." He tipped his head, a dismissive gesture. "You deliver the girl, and your town council will make you chief, hear?" He picked up the pint of Dingley's and as he filled his glass he said in a soft, exhausted voice, "Now leave me be, both of you." Dingley moved toward the door. Milt turned the knob. "And have somebody send another bottle of this stuff up here," the Grand Dragon said. "This is some of the worst hooch I've ever tasted. Makes me wonder if Michigan is worth the trouble."

•

In the kitchen at Nau Farm, Mercy watched Kincaid place the handcuffs on Lyle's wrists and lock them.

"These really necessary?" Lyle asked.

"I suppose not," Kincaid said. "They're a precaution."

"I'm not going to try to run or anything."

"I know, Lyle. But up north I handcuffed this boy and girl so I'm in the habit."

"Just being fair?"

"You could look at it that way." Kincaid turned to Hannah, who was sitting at the kitchen table, daubing the tears in her eyes. "I'm going to ask Ellie to check on you," he said to her. "Just to see that you're all right."

"You're not going to lock me up, too?"

"No, I'm not, Hannah. Whatever your role is in this, you didn't swing that axe."

Hannah ignored him then. She ignored all of them, even Lyle. She was already alone. Mercy had been alone in that kitchen, often waiting for something to cook on the stove. It was not a good place to be alone. She hoped never to set foot in the Nau farmhouse ever again.

The captain opened the kitchen door and led them out to his car. They rode to the police station in silence, Mercy sitting in the back seat with Rope. Up front, Lyle didn't seem perturbed in the least, considering that his wrists were handcuffed.

When Kincaid stopped the car in front of the station, he said, "Why don't you two wait here while I take him in?"

"Do we have to?" Mercy asked. "I mean, are we still under arrest?"

"No," he said as he got out of the car. "It's merely a suggestion. You're both free to do as you please."

Lyle got out but before he shut the passenger door he leaned in, his bound hands gripping the back of the front seat. "Free?" He grinned at Mercy, and then Rope, and then back at Mercy. A hostile, demented grin. "Your kind ain't never gonna be free." He kicked the door shut and led the captain up the porch steps to the station.

Mercy sat next to Rope, neither of them speaking, neither of them moving. For the first time since boarding the train in Worcester she was frightened. It started back in the farmhouse kitchen and had been swelling within her as they drove into town. This wasn't like how she'd felt before. Then, she'd been anxious. She'd been confused. And she'd been exhausted, hungry, and cold. When Harlan Nau attacked her on that cot, she thought she might die if she didn't fight back. You read about it in newspapers and magazines: women, girls, raped and killed. When Harlan Nau's weight came down on her she realized this could be his intent, which was why she fought so hard. You fight for your life. Every minute, you fight to survive. After she fled the attic, her anger drew from a well of energy that maintained her through her journey north to the Mackinac Straits in search of her aunt. Since being in Michigan there had not been one moment of peace.

But now, suddenly, there was this new thing. Fear. Kincaid was saying that he had no hold on them. They could stay, they could go. They could do as they wished. They were free. Free to do as they pleased. Perhaps Lyle Nesbit was right. They could never be free. It created an enormous, featureless void. No dimensions, no limits. Nothing to see, nothing to grasp. What was it, to be free?

"So?" she said.

"So."

They sat again for a minute, silent.

"You know," she said, "when we were on that train I wanted to get off once we reached Michigan. That was my plan. I had this letter from my aunt, and the purpose of my getting on that train was to find her. Every time we were taken off the train and lined up on the platform, I wanted to be taken. By somebody, anybody. And I thought of running off, but I didn't. Town after town, we'd stop, and I didn't have the nerve to just light out. I was afraid. I wasn't free to run off, and I was afraid in a certain way." She looked out the window at the front of the police station. "But this, this is worse."

"We don't need to run," he offered. "We could get out of this car and just start walking."

"Walk? Where?"

He didn't answer.

"What direction?"

"Well, we could . . . go back east?"

"No."

"All right. North?"

"No."

"Not south."

"I am definitely not going south," she said.

He had turned to look at her, but she continued to stare out the window of the Chevrolet. "Whatever we do," he said, "we do it together."

She wasn't sure. "Are you asking me or telling me?"

"The man just said we were free. I guess I'm asking you."

"Maybe that's what frightens me most," she said.

"Is that it? You're afraid . . . of me? You want to go on, on your own?"

"I don't know," she said. "What I want right now is for you to stop asking me questions."

"All right."

"I want a moment's peace. I want to just sit here. Till something comes to us."

He was about to say something. Instead, he just nodded.

•

At first, Ellie was baffled, but when Kincaid explained that Lyle and Hannah Nesbit had confessed to what really had happened at Nau Farm, she came around.

Her husband Mitch was in his usual place on the bench by the front door. "I'm not entirely surprised," he said as Ellie put Lyle in a cell. "He and Harlan were brothers-in-law, and I always sensed there was a history of unpleasantness there."

When Ellie sat behind her desk again, she nodded toward the street, meaning the occupants in Kincaid's Chevrolet. "What about them?"

"Up to them. We have no hold on them." Kincaid opened the front door. "Make sure Lyle gets fed and has plenty of blankets. Then call the county prosecutors' office, tell them we have him in custody, and that I'll call later to see how they want to proceed."

Ellie reached for the telephone. "Jake's Diner is doing a brisk business. Three dinner specials in one day. Been awhile since anyone's cracked a murder case around here. So much excitement for our little hamlet." She saw Kincaid's confusion, and added, "You haven't heard?"

"Heard what?"

"About the parade." She waited. "Town councilors were next door in town hall this morning. They got a signed permit, so it's all perfectly legal. These folks move fast. They'll be marching down Main Street to the fairgrounds tomorrow. I understand it's more dramatic at night. Torchlight, and all."

Kincaid paused at the front door. "The KKK. Here?"

She nodded. "I hear they're coming from all over." She nodded toward the street. "Those two kids, particularly the girl, ought to make themselves scarce."

Kincaid began to open the door, but then turned back to Ellie at her desk. "You have any idea where Milt has disappeared to?"

Ellie shook her head. "He's been scarce for days."

"Can one of you babysit Lyle for a while tonight?"

Mitch raised his hand off the knob of his cane. "Long as I get my usual fee, a free meal out of Jake's."

Ellie swiveled in her chair and stared at her husband, perhaps in mock surprise. "And I was going to cook your favorite."

"Sure you were." Mitch chuckled. "Just hope Jake's hasn't run out of perch."

"I'll be back later," Kincaid said. He went out on the porch and took the steps down to his car. He would not have been surprised to see the sedan empty. They could be long gone. Two orphans who knew how to make tracks. But they were there, in the back seat, both fast asleep. Mercy's cheek was on the boy's shoulder, while his head was thrown back and turned to the side, his mouth open.

Kincaid drove out of the village toward his house, while they were huddled together like a couple of sleeping puppies.

•

At the police station, Milt parked his truck behind Mitch Landis's wagon. No sign of the captain's Chevrolet. The lights were on in the station, but when he went inside the office was empty. Until he heard someone stirring down the hall of cells. There were shuffling footsteps, alternating with the tap of a cane, and Mitch came into the office. He looked half asleep.

"Those cots," he said, "don't do wonders for this old back." When he saw Milt's face, he added, "I'm doing your job, deputy, minding the store."

"Those two kids back there?" Milt nodded in the direction of the cells.

Mitch went to his usual place on the bench by the front door and eased himself down, folding his hands atop his cane. "No kids here."

"Who's back there?"

"Lyle."

"Lyle?"

"Confessed."

Milt went through the door to the hall and saw Lyle in the first cell, on his back beneath a blanket, sound asleep. Confessed? To murdering Harlan Nau? Milt was tempted to wake Lyle up and demand an explanation. Instead, he went back out into the office, where Mitch was staring out the front window as the captain's Chevrolet pulled up to the curb.

"Best I pick up Ellie down at the grocery and make for home," Mitch said as he got up off the bench. He opened the front door and went out on the porch as Kincaid came up the steps. "Captain, your prisoner has been fed, watered, and put to bed," he announced cheerfully. "I reckon you and your deputy have some catching up to do." He hobbled down the steps to his horse-drawn wagon. The rich scent of fresh road apples filled the office.

Kincaid came into the office and closed the door. He sat on the bench and crossed his legs at the knee. He might have been waiting for the train to arrive.

Milt went to his desk and rather than sitting in the chair, angled a haunch on the front corner.

"Haven't seen you in a while, Milt."

"You're the one went trapsing way up north after those two kids."

Kincaid ran a thumb along the bench armrest. "What you been up to while I've been gone?"

Milt looked back toward the door to the cells and then considered Kincaid. "Lyle? Confessed to killing Harlan? I don't believe it."

Kincaid didn't look entirely convinced. "I know you and Lyle go back a long way. But I suspect, when you think it through, you might come around to it."

"That so? Don't count on it." Milt folded his arms. "Where are those orphan kids?"

"They weren't charged with anything, so they were free to go."

"Go where?"

Kincaid appeared to give this serious consideration. "Why?"

Milt stood up, but he didn't really know what to do beyond that. He toyed with the buttons on his uniform jacket.

"We've contacted the prosecutor's office," Kincaid said. "They said someone will be here later today or tomorrow to set things in motion."

"I asked you about those kids."

"I heard you. Does it matter?"

"You just let them go? You actually think this will stick on Lyle?"

Kincaid shrugged. "It's up to the lawyers and the court now. Hannah corroborated his story. She's out at Nau Farm, pretty upset, as you can imagine."

Milt looked away in disgust. "This . . . this will not stand."

"It's not for you to determine," Kincaid said. "What I suggest is you get yourself a good night's rest because I understand there's going to be a parade here tomorrow and we're going to have to keep order." He waited. "You do know about the Klan, about their parade?"

"Everybody knows about it," Milt said unable to keep the heat out of his voice. "What exactly are you and I going to do to 'keep order.'"

"I think there should be a presence, don't you?"

"A police presence?"

Kincaid nodded.

"You going to stay here the night?"

"Somebody's got to look after our guest. I expect Lyle will be moved to the county jail by tomorrow."

"You wouldn't want me to stay here tonight, would you?"

For the first time Kincaid smiled, almost. "Probably not the best idea, Milt."

"You're damn right. The temptation might be too great." Milt went to the front door and opened it. "After you went all the way up there, those kids, they're gone? How far could they get?"

"They got all the way up to the Mackinac Straits. Impressive, when you think about it."

"Uh-huh. You brought them back down here, and then let them go."

"Why're you so concerned with them, Milt?"

Milt went out on the porch, not bothering to pull the door shut behind him. He went down the steps, his boots clattering on the wood. As he walked to his truck, he heard the station door close. Just the faint click of the latch.

Twenty-Three

Mrs. DeVries was in the kitchen early, where she cooked Mercy and Rope a breakfast of bacon, eggs, and biscuits. She appeared frail but invigorated by the simple fact that she was out of bed and functioning in the world again.

"The captain," Mercy said when she brought her plate to the sink, "he didn't come home last night?"

Mrs. DeVries had liver spots on her hands, and her knuckles were large and deformed. Mercy had seen arthritis in some of the older nuns in Worcester. "You cooked," she said. "I'll clean up."

Mrs. DeVries leaned against the counter, pulling her cardigan tight with her folded arms. "He called. When they have a prisoner, someone has to spend the night in the station. For some reason, it wasn't Milt Waters, the deputy. Jim didn't say why. So he spent the night at the station, yes." She studied Rope, sitting at the kitchen table. "He wants you to do a few chores. You're both welcome to stay here, but you'll have to earn your keep."

"Thank you." Rope got to his feet. "What chores?"

"The captain mentioned that there was firewood that needs to be split and brought in," Mrs. DeVries said. "I understand you know how to handle an axe." Mercy looked up from the soapy dishes in the sink. Rope looked befuddled, accused. Then Mrs. DeVries laughed, a hoarse sound that rose from withered lungs. "Properly. Otherwise, you'd have spent the night in that jail cell."

"Yes, ma'am," Rope said as he went to the kitchen door.

Turning to Mercy, she added. "I have a job I do every few days. You come with me and help."

Mrs. DeVries was guided by a quiet, intent form of anticipation. She lent Mercy a heavy coat and a pair of boots, noting that it was the coldest morning yet in November. They walked two blocks from the house, entered a stand of woods, and followed a meandering path that brought them to a cemetery.

Mrs. Kincaid quietly greeted several others, apparent regulars who came to replace flowers and tidy up ancestral plots.

"Often after Jim goes to the station, I come here." She stopped walking and looked at several stones. "My parents, and my grandparents. And this is my husband, the judge. The great sadness of his life is that he outlived his daughter." With effort, she bent down and began to clear leaves and twigs from Allison DeVries Kincaid's stone. "In the fall," Mrs. DeVries said, "the leaves from the maples are a never-ending chore."

Together, they began to clear the ground around the family plot.

"From the dormitory windows at the orphanage in Worcester," Mercy said, "we could see a cemetery across the street. Old stones, so weathered you could barely read the names. When I was little, I thought it was strange, having a family plot. But at some point, I realized it might be reassuring." Mrs. DeVries straightened up, leaves in both hands. "The knowing, I mean," Mercy added. "Knowing who came before you. Knowing where you'll end up."

"You must wonder why." Mrs. DeVries walked over to the trunk of the nearest tree, deposited the leaves, and brushed off her hands. Returning, she said, "Why certain children are like you and Rope?"

"Why we're orphans?" Mercy asked. "We weren't wanted. None of us are. We were given up. Or we were taken from our mothers. Or they died in childbirth, and there was no one else to take us. Most of us had no idea about our mothers. I knew a little, learning about her by chance, which is why I got on the train that brought me to Michigan. And our fathers? They often didn't even know we were born. Or if they did, it didn't mean they were going to become fathers. As for grandparents and great-grand parents, there's none of that. You don't have a lineage. You're not part of a family history. No plot waits for you."

"I can't imagine." To Mercy's surprise, Mrs. DeVries gathered her long coat about her and sat down on her husband's headstone.

"Not being wanted? Tossed away?" Mercy shook her head. "Early on, I came to believe that we were meant to be this way. You're just here, not certain how you got here, and no idea where you're going. It's who we are, who I am."

"I come here often because it makes me feel . . . like I belong. Perhaps a cemetery is the opposite of an orphanage. It's the ground, the trees, the sky. Cold and hard in winter, changing with the seasons, but a sense of permanence and belonging I can't really explain. When I'm here, I know where I am. In this moment. And I know it won't last. There is just this moment. Here, there are no illusions. You can't look at these stones and lie to yourself. When my husband died, there was a sense of relief—he'd been ill a long time. When your child dies, it changes time for you."

"Captain Kincaid, he comes here?"

"Sometimes." She looked out across the cemetery, ignoring the slight breeze that drew her gray hair across her face. In that moment, Mercy thought she could see Mrs. DeVries as a younger woman. Time had pared her down, leaving the bones of her face smooth and angular, her eyes large and moist. "But when I come here, I have to admit it's also frightening. You think of all the things that can go wrong. I try to leave it here, the worry, the dread, the fears. Bury them, so to speak." She smiled to herself, remembering. "Not that I'm very successful."

They walked out of the cemetery, returning to the path through the woods. Bare branches clattered overhead. Squirrels rustled the leaves, chattered as they raced up trees. Cold leafy air. "Since coming to Michigan," Mercy said, "it's been like a foreign land. But this also brings something else, something I've never had before. I haven't been able to figure it out until now. I'm not confined here. I've felt like I'm headed toward something. Whatever it is, it's stronger than I am. I don't know where it's leading me, and it won't let go."

Mrs. Kincaid placed her arm through Mercy's. "As I said at the house, you can stay here with us, as long as you need."

"Thank you."

Mrs. Kincaid pulled her closer. "You are not confined here, true. But it helps to have a destination." She smiled, looking over her shoulder toward the cemetery. "I just paid a visit to mine."

•

During the night, Kincaid had dozed at his desk but eventually gave in and went into one of the open cells and slept on the cot, despite Lyle's deep snoring. He was awakened by the smell of Ellie's coffee brewing. Two men sent by the county prosecutor arrived and took Lyle to the county jail. Soon after they left, two town councilors led D. W. Stephenson into the station. Like Stephenson, Seth Nichols and Nolan James were wearing topcoats, suits, and fedoras, which caused Ellie to glance at Kincaid with a raised eyebrow.

Kincaid responded by saying, "Ellie, perhaps these gentlemen would like some coffee?"

Nolan James held up a palm, his hand scarred and calloused from decades of working his land. "Thanks all the same, Ellie. We're not here for a social visit."

"I trust you're here to inquire about Lyle Nesbit," Kincaid said.

Seth Nichols was barely five feet tall, but he had a booming voice that he had long believed qualified him to dominate public meetings. "You locked him up for Harlan's murder?"

Behind the two councilors, Stephenson stared at Kincaid, the hard, steady gaze of a man accustomed to getting his way with just a look. Kincaid considered Stephenson for a long moment, and then made a point of addressing Seth and Nolan. "Lyle confessed."

"Well, that just ain't right," Seth said.

Nolan added, "You gotta let him out."

"Afraid it's too late for that." Both councilors appeared aghast. Stephenson was about to speak, but Kincaid said, "Prosecutor's office already had him taken to the county jail."

Nolan and Seth were at a loss, and they turned to Stephenson. Based on his bloodless pallor and bleary eyes, it was clear he was desperately hungover.

"So," Stephenson said, "you got nobody back there in your cells?" Kincaid nodded. "What about those two you tracked down? Those orphans who were out there at the farm when Harlan Nau was murdered?"

"No reason to hold them," Kincaid said.

Stephenson pursed his lips in disbelief. "Where are they?"

"Set free," Kincaid said. "What's your interest in them?"

Stephenson appeared to recalculate, and he looked away as though wondering how he'd ever found himself in such a situation. He shook his head and started for the door.

Seth nearly shouted, "We'll have to take this up with the council."

"As I said, it's in the county prosecutor's hands now."

"You went way up north to nab those two, and then you pin it on Lyle Nesbit? Captain Kincaid, this . . . this is not right."

"That's for the court to decide," Kincaid said.

For a moment the two councilors were silent, until Nolan realized that Stephenson was standing by the door, looking impatient. Ellie could barely conceal a smile as Nolan rushed to the door and opened it so Stephenson could step out on to the porch.

Seth Nichols continued to stare up at Kincaid. He appeared to be waiting for something, an explanation, or perhaps an apology. Quietly, urgently, Nolan said, "Seth. Come on."

They left the station and Kincaid went to the front windows and watched them walk single file down the porch steps. Nolan opened the door to a Dodge sedan, but Stephenson didn't get in, instead looking across the street as Milt's Ford truck pulled up to the curb. Milt got out of the truck, dressed in uniform. He crossed the street, and Stephenson stopped him on the sidewalk. Nolan and Seth gathered round. There was much gesturing, especially on Stephenson's part, and though Kincaid could hear their voices, he couldn't understand what was being said. Whatever it was, Milt stood there, nearly at military attention, while he took the pasting. Stephenson finally turned and allowed Nolan to open the car door for him. Milt remained on the sidewalk, looking chastised and undecided as he watched the three men drive away.

Kincaid went to his desk, sipped his coffee, and waited. Ellie, though she pretended to be busy at her desk, occasionally raised her head from her paperwork and glanced toward the front door.

•

Milt could feel the slightest tremor in his hands, and his blood seemed to be percolating, creating a throbbing pulse in his right temple. It reminded him of when he was a boy and his mother would scold him, or his father, before he disappeared, took his belt to Milt's backside. It wasn't fear or pain, in this case, it was embarrassment, and the sense that he'd been unjustly singled out for punishment.

He watched the Dodge head east down Main Street, until it turned the corner beyond Jake's Diner. How did Stephenson do it? He carried himself in a manner that demanded others to comply. It was evident as soon as he looked at you. Here on the sidewalk, the man had thrown a tantrum. Both Nolan and Seth were afraid, and both men were enthralled. Most likely, they were relieved, too, that Stephenson's anger hadn't been directed toward them. He gestured with his arms, spittle issuing from his mouth, his voice rose and fell, one minute imploring, the next pleading. He hollered and moaned. He pounded fist into palm, and at one point he even stamped his feet like a child determined to get his way.

Milt stood there and took it. He was in uniform, which often provided a kind of protection. His cap, the hard brim pulled low on his forehead, the jacket with gold buttons and bound by the leather holster, the jodhpurs and his freshly polished boots, they often shielded him, causing people—citizens—to be cautious and submissive.

But this was D. C. Stephenson, the Grand Dragon of Indiana. Grand Dragons don't request, they don't ask. They state what they expect you to do to get them what they want. They let you know that there are no excuses, that failure will have consequences. The Grand Dragon knew what Milt wanted, and he made it clear that only upon his say so Otter Creek's town council, led by Nolan and Bert, would name Milt chief of police.

Milt turned and looked at the police station. When he had crossed the street from his truck, he had seen Kincaid, standing at the window. He must have witnessed the entire exchange with Stephenson. Now Kincaid was gone, most likely sitting at his desk, waiting. If Milt climbed the porch stairs and entered the station, he'd be met with silence, and with that stare. Very different from Stephenson's, but in its own way just as effective. No shouting, no conniptions, no demands. Kincaid would bludgeon him with reserve and disappointment. It would be equally devastating, if not more so.

Milt's boots seemed to have sunk into the sidewalk concrete. He might never be able to move from this spot, this moment. There was a choice here, between two men. He began walking, crossing the street to his truck. He got in and drove down Main Street, no particular destination in mind. He just drove, out of the village and past farmhouses, pastures, grazing horses, and cows. He saw none of it.

Instead, he saw them gathered in the fairgrounds, hundreds of Klansmen in their robes, and a vast audience of people, many of them folks Milt had known all his life. It is night and they come bearing torches. The solemn wavering light, the blackest shadows. There would be a trial. This is the Old Man's purpose. At the conclusion of the parade, he wants a trial. The people's court: the Grand Dragon presides, and the people determine innocence or guilt. He interrogates the two orphans, presents evidence in the case. No need for lawyers, with their slick arguments, their fanciful turns of phrase. The Grand Dragon speaks plainly, in a voice everyone present can understand. They are united in their desire for justice for Harlan Nau's murder. The Grand Dragon lays bare the truth, and the girl admits that she lured Harlan into the attic, where the boy killed him with an axe, and then he turns to the crowd, Harlan's friends and neighbors, and he asks what is the just punishment for this crime?

At that moment, Milt is there on that stage, where he can see the fervor in their torchlit eyes. He is on up there because he found the boy and girl, he delivered them to the fairgrounds. That is his role, his purpose. He has captured the boy and the girl and brought them to justice for this crime against the very existence of Otter Creek. In response to the Grand Dragon, they raise their voices, all of them knowing that they had regained something essential, something necessary to their lives. Milt has seen this in photographs in newspapers: justice determined by the people. With the guilty hanging from a tree, people, men, women, and children, stare toward the camera, their eyes illuminated, their faces grim but resolute: This is what is necessary to protect ourselves. This is what needs to be done if towns like Otter Creek are to survive. Strangers cannot take the life of one of our own and not suffer the consequences. At some point, you have to act, otherwise everything you believe in will be stripped away. It takes courage. It takes belief, in yourself, in knowing right from wrong.

•

After Mrs. DeVries hung the telephone earpiece on its hook, she said to Rope, "He needs you."

"Me?"

She nodded. "At the station." Looking at Mercy, who was sweeping the kitchen floor, she said, "And you need to stay in the house."

"Why?"

Mrs. DeVries clearly did not like her instructions being questioned. "The captain thinks it would be wise." Yet she seemed to understand that this wouldn't be enough to satisfy Mercy, so she added, "It seems we're being invaded."

It was a twenty-minute walk from the house to the station in the center of the village. By the time Rope reached Main Street, he understood: the Klan was streaming into town. They came in trucks, cars, and two busses passed Rope. One group came on horseback. All men, many wearing robes, some also wearing their pointed hoods. Some wearing masks draped from their hoods. There was a hierarchy: most robes were white but there were some that were silver and a few that were gray and black. They were everywhere. Sitting on benches, loitering in doorways, standing in groups on sidewalks, smoking cigarettes and cigars.

When Rope entered the police station, Ellie said, "Ghosts!" Her sarcasm had a gleeful edge to it. "It'll be a lovely fall evening for a ghost parade!"

Billy Barnes had also been summoned by Kincaid, and he and Rope stood before the captain, watching him lay out two five-dollar bills on the front edge of his desk.

"Today, you're both deputized," Kincaid said.

"What's the assignment, captain?" Billy asked. "Another still?"

"Crowd control," Kincaid said. "No tools necessary. Just be visible. The town is going to be filled with strangers. There'll be some drinking, no doubt, but they've got a permit for this parade and the use of the fairgrounds, so we just want to establish a police presence and maintain order. You don't have to do anything." He looked them both up and down with a wry, assessing stare. "Except look the part." He almost smiled, as he gestured with a thumb toward the back of the station. "Otter Creek used to have a larger force. In the closet you'll find some gear. Jackets, caps, whatever fits. Outfit yourselves as best you can."

Billy picked up the two five-dollar bills and handed one to Rope. "Honestly, I love Abe Lincoln." He looked at Kincaid, perturbed. "What about weapons, you know, in case things get out of hand?"

"You, armed?" Kincaid shook his head. "Just try to look the part."

"Can you do that? Put us in uniform?" Rope asked.

"I'm the police chief, aren't I? But considering the disposition of the town council it may not be for long. Don't expect to make a career of it."

•

When Mrs. DeVries went upstairs for her afternoon lie down, Mercy decided to sit out on the Kincaid's front porch swing. It felt like the times at the orphanage when she and one or two other girls would sneak into the cellar to smoke cigarettes. The lure of off-limits, the thrill of defiance. The stark November sun and the air, thick with the smell of decaying leaves, was a relief after the hours of chores in the house. From the direction of the village fairgrounds, she could hear the report of hammers and the warble and clap of boards as they were stacked together.

Mercy took notice of the Ford the second time it came down the street, slow enough that she could see four men inside. They wore white pointed hoods and masks with large irregular eye holes. When the car came to a stop at the curb, Mercy got up from the porch swing. In the orphanage, she had learned that sometimes just standing up and showing that you were ready could cause a bully to have second thoughts.

Defiantly, she walked out to the edge of the porch, folding her arms. The hooded men sat motionless in the car, their enormous black eyes staring at her.

"I'm through with running." She said it quietly, to herself. "You heard the captain. We are free." And then louder, she said, "You can't hide from me." And even louder, "I see each one of you. I see you!"

The doors to the car, front and back, opened and three men climbed out, leaving the driver behind the wheel. They crossed the front lawn, three abreast, their robes swaying about their legs. Their masks held ghoulish expressions of determination and resolve.

Mercy dropped her arms at her sides, her fists protruding from the sleeves of her borrowed coat.

The three men stopped at the foot of the porch steps. "Where's the boy?" one of them asked.

"What boy?"

The man came up the steps and said, "The one that helped you do in Harlan Nau." He grabbed Mercy by the arm, but then quickly let go and retreated to the yard, his hands up. All three men seemed to freeze.

"Move aside, honey." Behind Mercy, Mrs. DeVries's voice was frail yet firm. "I need a clear shot."

Mercy stepped to her left and turned toward the open front door, where Mrs. DeVries stood with a rifle at her side. "Leave the child alone," she said. When they did not move, she raised the gun and took aim. "I don't see men in my yard, I see grouse. Get off my property. Now."

The three men looked at each other, and then backed away toward the Ford idling in the road. They had difficulty gathering the hems of their robes as they climbed into the car, which pulled into the road before all the doors were shut.

Mrs. DeVries lowered the rifle. "I said to stay in the house."

"I'm sorry . . . I just wanted some fresh air."

"Those men disturbed my nap." Mrs. DeVries turned to go back in the house. "I just hope I can get back to sleep."

"You hunted grouse."

"So?"

"Did you eat them?"

"Good Lord, child," Mrs. DeVries muttered. "Where did you come from?"

Twenty-Four

Toward the end of his tour in France, Kincaid was put on military police duty, which, if nothing else, gave him a notion about what he might do after he returned to the states. MPs were often called on to break up drunken brawls and occasionally search for a soldier who had gone AWOL. They were also assigned to marches, parades, occasions when heads of state made an appearance, purportedly to boost morale. Easy duty it was, troops marching by a review stand filled with stout men with waxed mustaches and women gripping their parasols and feathery hats in the wind. The MPs often established a betting pool to see who could determine the number of soldiers on parade during such occasions of state. Kincaid had an eye for calculating men in groups, and he won the pool several times, which usually consisted of devalued francs and American cigarettes.

It was a perfect fall afternoon, the chill in the air offset by warm sun, when the Klan paraded through the village. Kincade disliked parades but was impressed by the numbers the Klan had mustered for the march. At least three-hundred members of the KKK passed by on Main Street. Klansmen, Klanswomen, and children also dressed in robes and pointed hoods. Some of them did not wear masks because this was the new Ku Klux Klan, and people lining the street would applaud when a local dignitary—a judge, a lawyer, a schoolteacher, or a newspaper editor—passed by in the ranks. There were at least two dozen equestrian Klansmen, several crudely designed floats promoting American values, a fire truck, an ambulance, and one automobile, Owen Dingley's Dodge sedan, which transported the guest of honor, the Grand Dragon from Indiana, D. C. Stephenson. The parade ended at the fairgrounds, where there was a picnic, which included clowns and games for children. The carnival atmosphere, not to mention the free food and beverage, drew a large crowd. Early evening speeches were scheduled to be given from the stage that was still under construction. Kincaid wandered through the fairgrounds, and occasionally he would see Billy and Rope, both trying to look the part in their ill-fitting police uniforms.

During the parade and the picnic, there had been no incidents. Police presence didn't seem necessary. As it was getting dark, Kincaid walked back to the police station.

Ellie was sitting behind her desk, though it was after five o'clock. "Where you been?"

"Watching the parade. Problem?"

"You best get home. Lois just called and she's frantic. That girl, she's gone missing."

•

Rope maintained a position at the Main Street entrance to the fairgrounds. He found it interesting how the crowd reacted to his presence, to the uniform. Most people altered their course to keep their distance. Those who walked close by tended to avoid looking directly at him. Except children. They often stared at him as though trying to figure out what they were looking at, and one girl lingered, her eyes spiked with curiosity, ignoring her mother's reprimands until she was taken by the hand and pulled away.

The crowd had a smell, reminding him of public gatherings back in Haverhill. Despite it being a chilly, overcast November afternoon, there was the earthy smell of the grass crushed underfoot, and the air, smokey from grilled meat and cigars, was sweetened by cola cut with whiskey. One of the few times someone acknowledged Rope was when an elderly woman, tall but stooped, approached him with a bottle of Vernors. "Dear, you must be parched. Don't worry, they're giving drinks away." When he tried to decline her offer, she added, "It'll be dark in an hour. People are taking the little ones home. Tonight, you'll see." He must have looked perplexed because she smiled, revealing brown-stained teeth. "Then it'll be mostly Klansmen, and the picnic will be over, I tell you."

Rope became particularly conscious of the way he stood. It didn't seem right to lean against the fence that ringed the fairgrounds and, though his feet and back were tired, he thought he shouldn't look for a place to sit. So he stood, not exactly at attention but maintaining a straight posture, which by late afternoon brought a deep ache to his muscles. After a couple of hours, he learned to alternate putting his weight on one leg, letting the other rest.

At dusk, a women's church choir gathered on the stage and sang "Onward Christian Soldiers." Rope watched Captain Kincaid's Chevrolet move slowly through the crowd on Main Street until it stopped in the fairgrounds' entrance.

"How're you doing?" Kincaid asked.

"Fine. The crowd's thinning out. I guess there will be a pause for a couple of hours before the evening events begin."

Kincaid didn't seem to be listening as he surveyed the fairgrounds. Finally, he said, "I've got to go back to my house. You take a break. Ellie's got sandwiches and coffee for you at the station." He reached down and shifted into gear, but then he put the car in neutral again. "Listen, and listen carefully. Mrs. DeVries called and said she doesn't know where Mercy is. I want you to stay here in the village. I'll see what's going on. I need you and Billy to stick around while this crowd's here. She's probably gone for a walk or something."

"She was not supposed to leave the house."

Kincaid stared out through the windshield. "Just stay here, understand?"

Rope didn't answer until Kincaid turned and looked at him. He nodded, and then stepped back as Kincaid put the car in gear again.

•

At first, it seemed too easy.

After cruising aimlessly in his truck, Milt had driven back into the village, which was filling up with Klansmen. They came in cars, trucks, and busses. They rode in on horseback. Some walked, appearing out of the countryside as though they were on a sacred pilgrimage. They must have numbered in the hundreds. There was a festive air around the fairgrounds as they waited in large groups to form up for the parade. The stage was being completed, with a large tent erected behind it, to house dignitaries, people like the Old Man and the pack that accompanied him, not to mention locals—councilmen, judges, ministers, journalists, and school administrators—who would join the Grand Dragon on stage.

Milt entered the tent, where Klansmen were gathered around food and beverage laid out on tables. He found Mink in one corner, his back to the crowd while he and a few others worked on bottles of spiked Coca-Cola. Milt could smell the whiskey before he even reached them.

Mink wore his bib overalls, but the other men were in their Klan robes. They eyed Milt's approach, assessing his police uniform, and it was clear they had tacitly decided to stop discussing whatever it was that made them look so concerned. Mink, half-lit, went through introductions, but Milt registered no names, only where these Klansmen came from: Grand Rapids, Newaygo, Mason, Dimondale, St. John's. Who they were or where they were from really didn't matter—they were here now, and their heightened sense of purpose was further elevated by the Dingley's in their green bottles of Coke. Quickly, these men, bulky in their flowing robes, ventured off, seeing others to talk to or claiming they wanted to get at the food before it all disappeared.

The last to leave was a fellow from Newaygo, who said, "Who's gonna break it to the Old Man? He ain't gonna be happy about it."

"Break what?" Milt asked.

Mink sipped his Coca-Cola, wincing before he spoke. "The Old Man wanted her, but we thought she was long gone, because Kincaid released both of those kids. And then they saw the girl."

Newaygo nodded his head, regretful, even contrite.

"Mercy?" Milt said. "Where?"

"Sitting on the porch out at Judge DeVries's place." Mink took a moment to scan the crowded tent, as though to be sure this conversation was private. "Four of them, in a car," he said quietly. "They get out and are this close to grabbing her, when Lois DeVries comes out of the house." He glanced at Milt, smiling at the irony of it. "With a rifle. She used to bird hunt, I remember." He took a drink from his green Coke bottle and shook his head again.

"Might be old," Newaygo said, "but with a gun in her hands, she means business."

"The judge's wife's always been a handful," Mink said. "And a good customer, too."

"So, the girl's still out there at DeVries's place?" Milt asked.

"I guess," Newaygo said.

Milt said, "What does the Old Man want with her, anyway?"

Mink shrugged. "I got me a few ideas."

"Yeah, but I mean here, tonight." Milt tilted his head in the direction of the stage beyond the canvas tent wall. "He intended to, I don't know, use her somehow?"

"Maybe set up a game of African Dodger," Newaygo said. "Like at a carnival. You get three baseballs for a nickel. Stick her head in the hole cut in the canvas and throw strikes." He laughed. "The novelty would be that it's a girl they're hitting. Imagine the line of boys waiting their turn."

"Use her?" Mink said. "That's one way of putting it. I can think of some others."

"I'm not talking about some carnival game," Milt said. "I'm talking about an example."

Newaygo, chastised, looked off toward the crowd at the food tables.

Mink didn't seem to follow, and he stared down into the neck of his Coke bottle. "Of what?"

"Well," Milt said, "I thought he wanted to get her up there on the stage and present her to the crowd. This is why we're here, right? This is what we're fighting against. This is why Harlan Nau isn't here with us tonight. Know what I mean?"

Mink looked up from his drink, his eyes bright. "Yeah. I get your meaning. He could do that." After another swig, he said, "There could be a . . ."

"A trial." Milt paused to let that sink in. "Let the people decide. No slippery lawyers, no lenient judges. No half-baked sentence. Let Otter Creek determine—"

"Her—her and that boy—if they could find him, too," Mink said. "Like my brother said out at the still, they could lynch 'em. Now that would be something."

Milt said, "I don't know if it really might go that far, but we could make a point."

Mink didn't seem sure what the point would be, and after a moment of deep thought, he said, "Why the hell couldn't they hang 'em, if they was guilty?" He stared hard at Newaygo, and then at Milt. "And they are guilty. That's not the issue, right?"

"It's what's to be done about it," Newaygo offered. They were silent for a moment, and then he said, "Now, I'm going to get in line at the trough before all that chicken's gone." He made a little gesture with his hand, and then started to work his way through the crowd.

"What was that, with the hand?" Milt said. "A Klan sign?"

"Yup," Mink said. "They have plenty. I don't go in for all that, the passwords, and signs. Boys' stuff. Most of these fellas wouldn't know what to do, if they had the chance, you know?" He drained his spiked Coke. "Those four that tried to nab that girl. Maybe if they hadn't been wearing those get-ups they might have pulled it off. Those hoods and all only announce your intentions. Me, I'd go out there and just be friendly-like and charm that girl off the porch before the old lady got a sniff of what's goin' on." He dropped his empty Coke bottle in the trampled grass.

For a long moment, Milt stared down at several empty green bottles at Mink's feet. "I got a better idea."

"What's that?"

"Maybe they were just wearing the wrong get-up." He raised his head.

Mink was staring at him. Getting it, slowly. "You go out there, I'm going with you."

It was dark when they left the fairgrounds, got in Milt's truck, and drove through the village. Neither spoke until they were a block from the DeVries's house. There was no sign of the Chevrolet.

"Kincaid's not here," Milt said. "Listen. You stay here in the truck. I'll go up to the door and knock. There's nothing alarming about that. I'll tell the girl we need her in the village."

"You need a why. What will you tell her?"

Milt pulled over to the curb. "We need her at the station," he said. "I don't know why, exactly. Kincaid's orders. I'm just the deputy, you know?"

"The girl, she knows you?"

"Only saw me the one time out at the still. I wasn't in uniform. That's what she'll see, this uniform." Glancing at Mink, he said, "So you make yourself invisible."

"What if old lady DeVries answers the door?"

"She likes me . . . like I was a stray cat that needs milk."

"People shoot strays."

"Well, then. That's why you came along, Mink, so you can protect me. You're a bigger target."

"I could have stayed back at the fairgrounds." Mink opened the passenger door, saying, "I'll hide behind that tree in the yard. Once you get her in the truck, I'll jump in, make sure she doesn't get out." He closed the door and began walking toward the DeVries's house, keeping to the dark front yards of the neighbors' houses.

Milt drove slowly down the block, parked the truck in front of the DeVries's house, and went up on the dark porch. The only light in the house came from the left, the living room. He tapped the brass knocker, and after a moment heard footsteps coming to the front door. Cautiously, he thought. And he realized that maybe most of the lights were out because of what had happened earlier. As soon as the front door opened, he could be looking down the barrel of a rifle.

The footsteps stopped on the other side of the door. There was silence.

"Mrs. DeVries," he said. "It's Deputy Waters."

Still, silence. Until he heard the bolt thrown and the doorknob turn. The door opened only a couple of inches. It was the girl's face, which he could barely see in the dark, just the faint gleam of her right eye.

"You must be Mercy," he said. "Is Mrs. DeVries in?"

"She's upstairs, sleeping." The one eye, large. He remembered when they were in the shack out by the still, her eyes too big for her dark face. Eyes that cast their own light, penetrating the dark.

"Well, I don't want to disturb her. But we need you down at the station."

"Why?"

"The captain didn't say, only just bring you down there."

"He heard about what happened?"

"About those Klansmen, yeah, we heard something, but it's not exactly clear what happened. I think that's why he wants to see you."

The eye shifted, looking beyond him as it scanned the front yard. Not seeing anything, she stared at him again. She still hadn't opened the door more than a couple of inches.

"I believe it's for your own protection," he said.

She surveyed his uniform, and then she looked at his face for a long moment. The only thing to do was stare right back into that bright eye, which he did, until she blinked. "You want to take me to the station? Now?"

"The sooner the better, don't you think?"

"One minute." She closed the door, but he didn't hear the bolt thrown. He stood in the dark of the porch, trying to hear if she was climbing the stairs or if she was calling up to Mrs. DeVries. He heard nothing.

When the door opened again, Mercy was wearing a long overcoat. She started to step out on to the porch, but then hesitated. "I should tell Mrs. DeVries where I'm going," she said. "She shouldn't wake up and find me gone without any word."

Milt nodded. "I suppose you're right. Where is she?"

"Upstairs in her room."

"Sleeping. I suppose what happened earlier tuckered her out." He waited while she thought it through. There was indirect light coming from the living room, which caught the side of the girl's face. Those eyes—suspicious green eyes, the green of Mink's Coke bottles. "We could call her from the station," he suggested. "That would let her sleep longer."

She considered this briefly. "She was quite exhausted and could use the sleep." She stepped out onto the porch and pulled the door closed carefully, not to make noise.

Milt followed her down the porch steps, along the front walk, to the curb. There was no sign of Mink, but it was dark, almost too dark. Milt opened the passenger door and Mercy climbed into the truck, and after a moment he closed the door. He almost wanted to look around and see what Mink was up to, but he walked around the front of the truck and got in behind the steering wheel. After he started the engine and was about to shift into first gear, the passenger door opened. The girl let out a yelp as Mink slid onto the bench seat, crowding her between the two men. She started to speak, but Mink covered her mouth with his hand. And then he hollered, taking his hand away from her face. "She bit me! The little—" He slapped her once, hard, and then a second time.

•

After being struck twice, Mercy was dazed as the truck rattled down the road. Dazed so much that her head lolled against the back of the seat. Squeezed between the two men, she was overwhelmed with a sense floating, of letting go. Not hopelessness, but adrift in the swelling pain that flooded the side of her head. She knew that the massive weight next to her was the man called Mink, who had held her in the shack in the woods.

Slowly her vision sharpened, allowing her to realize that the truck was approaching the village lights. It was a clear, moonless night, the sky awash in stars, and they were accompanied by distant music, a marching band consisting of out of tune horns, drums not quite in sync. On the sidewalks of Otter Creek, she saw the robes, the hoods, and then the truck turned off the road, crossed an expanse of grass, skirting an enormous crowd, hundreds of ghosts amassed before a wooden stage.

When the truck stopped next to the large tent that had been erected behind the stage, Mink's arm rose up and his hand gripped the back of her neck tightly.

"No yellin', no screamin'. One peep out of you and I'll snap this twig." He gave her neck a squeeze that sent a shot of pain down her tendons and into her shoulders.

They got out of the truck, Mink's hand still clutching her neck, and she was guided into the tent. The policeman led the way. He walked with an assertive stride, enhanced by his tall riding boots and the bulging contour of his jodhpurs. There were Klansmen in the tent, dozens of them, and they fell silent as they watched her being walked toward a group of men standing by long tables covered with the remnants of a feast. Platters and large bowls cleaned out seemingly by a starving horde. And then they stopped walking, Mink's hand signaling with a pinch before he released her neck.

She stood before several Klansmen, all in robes, hoods, and masks. One had his back to her. From his posture, from the strict attention the others paid him, it was clear that he was the leader. Slowly, he turned around. He was not wearing a mask. She knew him, knew that face, and she remembered how he had bitten her earlier, the sharp ache still pulsating through the base of her thumb. He had full cheeks and a dimpled chin. His pale skin was glazed with perspiration. He seemed excited, thrilled even, and she suspected he was quite drunk.

He looked from her to the policeman, approvingly. "Well done, Deputy Waters."

Then he gathered his robe so that he could raise an arm. A signal. Another robe nearby said loudly, "All right, it's showtime. Everyone outside."

Quietly, obediently, they filed out of the tent through a raised flap. In their robes and hoods, they were as a different species, alien, foreign, a reverse order of nuns—not the beamy women, their breasts and wide hips draped in swaying black habits, but bulky, masculine figures in white.

When the tent was empty, Mercy turned to the Grand Dragon. He was speaking quietly to the two Klansmen who flanked him. Beyond them, in the corner, Mink was donning a robe, which swelled over his massive belly.

"I left mine in my truck," Milt said, almost apologetically.

"That's all right, Deputy." The Grand Dragon's voice was kindly, as though he were trying to ease the fears of a child. "It's appropriate that you're in uniform. This audience needs to see that we have the law on our side. You will accompany me up to the stage. In fact, I'd like you to lead the way." He looked back at the two Klansmen briefly. "You keep her here until she's sent for." He and the deputy began to walk toward the open flap in the tent wall.

"You're really going to go through with this?" Mercy asked.

The Grand Dragon stopped and came back to her, staring at the ground in thought. "Well," he said, reflectively, "a crime has been committed, a capital crime. So, something needs to be done. I think we should let our brethren decide that."

"Decide what?"

He raised his eyes. Small, gray, voracious. "Your sentence. Your punishment."

"Trial? You're going to put me on trial out there?"

"Shouldn't they have a say in this? It was their friend, their neighbor who was killed."

"That man, Lyle, Harlan's brother-in-law, he confessed."

"Did he now?" His voice was light, playful.

"I heard him. At the farm, he confessed to the whole thing."

"You heard him?"

"Yes. He told Captain Kincaid. His wife was there, Estelle's sister, and Rope."

"I see. Tell me, was a lawyer present? Did he have legal counsel?"

This had not occurred to Mercy. "No. No, but I'm sure—"

"You heard this confession. Captain Kincaid heard it. Well, I'm not so sure about that. Doesn't sound like this purported confession is valid. Perhaps it was made under duress, under false pretenses. This happens, you know, in our flawed legal system." The Grand Dragon's face changed, his penetrating stare curious, beckoning. "And what about this boy, Rope, I believe he's called. You know where he is?" She shook her head. "Shouldn't he be here, with you? Weren't you in on this together? Perhaps he was the one who swung the axe. You going to take the fall for him? You see, that's what they must decide, all these people in Otter Creek. Culpability. Guilt. It's their decision, don't you understand? That's what we are offering them. Justice of their own making."

"You can't do this."

At first, he looked as though he couldn't believe what he'd heard, but then he smiled. "Oh, but I can. The Grand Dragon can. This is why he's here. It's only fair. It's only right." As he turned away from Mercy, he glanced over at the two Klansmen. His voice was flat, issuing instructions. "Keep her here until I call for her, and then bring her up on stage."

Twenty-Five

Kincaid's mother-in-law opened the front door as he came up the porch steps. She was wearing her bathrobe. "After what happened earlier, I went up for a lie down."

"Tell me about earlier."

Mrs. DeVries folded her arms against the evening chill. "They came up the front walk, dressed in those ridiculous outfits." She looked up and down the dark road.

"And you persuaded them to leave?"

"With the aid of my hunting rifle."

"You're cold. Let's get inside."

She didn't move but continued to stare out into the dark. "You don't suppose she just went for a walk?"

Kincaid took Lois by the upper arm and gently guided her into the vestibule, closing the door behind him. "Where would she walk to?"

"I don't know. She said she wouldn't leave the house while I was upstairs. The only time we went out was when we walked to the cemetery this morning." She moved toward the kitchen, slippers making a slow shuffle rhythm on the hardwood floor. "I'll heat up some coffee."

"Why would she go back to the cemetery?"

"No idea. She helped me clean the graves. Seemed curious about family, not having any of her own. Maybe she just got tired of being cooped up in the house." She pushed through the swinging door to the kitchen.

"How did she seem after these men came to the house?"

"Quiet. I thought she understood that she shouldn't venture out." From the shelf above the stove, she took down the box of matches. "Tell you one thing, she wasn't afraid. Nothing scares that child."

"I should go," Kincaid said, holding the swinging door half-open. "Have a look around."

She struck a match, which brought a glow to her eyes. "Well, I'll have coffee here when you come back. When anyone comes back. And where's that boy, Rope?"

"Helping me out in the village." She stared at him as she continued to hold the burning match. "I needed a semblance of crowd control during the parade and at the fairgrounds."

His mother-in-law removed a pack of Luckies from the pocket of her robe and lit a cigarette, waving out the match just as the flame reached her bony fingers. "No sign of Milt, still, so you put that boy in uniform?"

"Him and Billy Barnes, the fellow that works at Nesbit's garage."

"Some police force." She shook her head as she exhaled smoke. "And what about Milt?"

"Don't know what I'm going to do about him." A blue cloud drifted toward him. She went for days only smoking in her room or outdoors, knowing that the smoke bothered him, but now he was tempted to ask her for a cigarette. "I'll have a look around for Mercy." He began to turn to go out through the swinging door but paused to look back at his mother-in-law. "You'll be okay?"

"I haven't put the rifle away, so I'll be fine." She wasn't really answering his question, and she added, "I'm just making coffee, Jim. No Dingley's. Just coffee."

•

Something happened to the crowd when the Grand Dragon began to speak—it reminded Rope of Mass, when the congregation becomes still, silent, not just attentive but devout. But here they had torches. Hundreds, illuminated by torchlight. Standing at the fairgrounds entrance, Rope wanted to move closer so he could hear and see better, but he felt it was his responsibility to maintain his post.

At first, only phrases reached Rope. The Grand Dragon talked about family and community, about what was ours: our land, our homes, our children, our jobs. He talked about all these things as though they were about to be lost or stolen. Rope had none of these things, except his makeshift police uniform and the promise of a few dollars for being visible until this crowd dispersed. The man, the Grand Dragon, reminded him of some priests as they gave their sermons during Mass. There was a rhythm to their speech, a cadence akin to song. Occasionally he would resort to rhyme. Or he would fall into a litany, a repetition of words, hammering home an idea, a feeling. The good, the wholesome, the honest—all these things that we value. His voice rose and fell but was forever climbing, musical, if increasingly hoarse, reaching into a higher register as though he might actually pull the audience closer and then, miraculously, lift them up, make them one. And they were, they were unified in their stillness, their devotion.

But then, just when he had them, the Grand Dragon paused. He was adept at managing the wide sleeves of his robe and, pushing them back, raised his arms above he head, his face bathed in a sheen of sweat. He kept his hands aloft and was silent, and it seemed that time itself had stopped.

Rope scanned the crowd. No one moved. No one spoke.

He could feel it, this unnamable thing that bound them together in that field. They were waiting.

•

There were just three of them in the vast tent, three men in robes, hoods, and masks. Mercy looked at them. They looked at her. They seemed to be waiting. For a sign, a signal.

The largest one was Mink. At first, she thought he was uncomfortable in his robe, but then she realized he was drunk. He had been drunk when they drove into town, but now he had reached the point where he appeared to be doing a little dance to maintain his balance. He giggled often, his voice muffled by his mask.

The other two Klansmen merely stared at her. Their large eyeholes gave them distinct personalities. To the left of Mink, a slighter man with a somber mask, which she expected to shed tears, and to Mink's right was the Klansman with broad shoulders who had come up the DeVries's porch steps for her. His eyeholes were irregular, one haughty eye larger than the other, suggesting that he was leering at her, angry that he even had to endure her presence.

They did not speak to her or to each other, and she realized they were listening to the Grand Dragon, whose voice seemed to descend from the vaulted roof of the giant tent. She tried to block it out, the voice, their eyes, the rancid smell of food left on the tables. Instead, she was reminded of the nuns in the Worcester orphanage, of times when as a girl she would be able to observe them, not when they were tending to the children, but when they were together, a flock of aliens in black habits. She recalled that they often spoke French amongst themselves, that their voices tended to slur and clatter, and they almost seemed to be singing. Mercy had learned to decipher their emotions by how they moved, particularly the hands, those pale, fluttering appendages that would suddenly come out of hiding in all that black, floating, gliding, seeming to coax the strange words out of them. Wrists articulated anger and regret; fingers wrote intentions in the air. Seeing the nuns this way, knowing that they weren't always the brooding, heavy presence intended to keep the children at bay, Mercy learned to not fear them. As she got older, she learned to stare back at them, whereas others would lower their eyes in submission.

This is what she did now: she stared at all three Klansmen. She looked directly at those enlarged holes, jagged edges cut from white cloth, and occasionally she caught a glimpse of a human eye, lurking in the darkness behind the mask.

•

Milt took up a position near the bottom of the stairs that led up to the stage. He felt conspicuous in his police uniform, but he understood his role. Owen Dingley, who was up on the stage, had explained it to Milt: at certain point during the Grand Dragon's speech a signal would be given, and the girl would be brought out from the tent; Milt would walk her up the stairs to the stage and hand her over to Dingley, who would then convey her to the center of the stage. Like the Grand Dragon, Dingley did not wear a mask. It seemed that this was the highest point of honor, the greatest tribute, to wear the hood and robe but to leave the face revealed. This was a performance, Dingley had suggested, a carefully orchestrated spectacle, and Milt's part in the drama was to represent law and order.

Stephenson, the Grand Dragon standing at the podium, appeared to be in a trance. Milt was reminded of a performer who had sung the same tune so many times that the words and melody came forth effortlessly. No need to think about what he was doing, what he was saying. Instead, he was watching, calculating the response from the audience. His hands, his arms seemed to orchestrate their reaction, while his voice, lilting, lifting, sought an opening in their collective mind. It was a power Milt had never witnessed before: the Grand Dragon was in complete control of the crowd. Several hundred Klansmen in robes, and perhaps an equal number of people in street clothes, most wearing coats, hats, and scarves in the cold November night. They were all silent, they were all still. It seemed to Milt that they were all waiting.

And he was waiting for the signal, for the girl to be delivered from the tent, for law and order to play its role. Milt didn't like standing there beneath the stage, but he told himself his moment was about to come. For that, he must wait.

•

Kincaid parked the Chevrolet outside the cemetery gates. He took his flashlight and walked among the stones, drawn toward the knoll in the northeast corner. After Allison died, he came here every day. For months. He hated it. He would see the same people here, tending to the stones, replacing flowers. It wasn't that such gestures were empty, they were futile. Nothing would bring the dead back. Not tears, nor flowers, nor prayers. It was futile gardening: they came here with rakes and clippers and brooms, and they tended their plots as though they expected to bring forth a rich and bountiful harvest.

He stopped coming. He knew Lois visited the cemetery several times a week. He could not go. They never spoke of it directly. She would mention that the first leaves were coming down or, in spring, a dusting of pollen created a yellow haze so fine it highlighted the etchings in the stones. Snow, she once said, was beautiful but sad. "When it's my turn," she had whispered over her dinner plate, "I will miss the snow."

He found the stones with ease, even in the dark. He could only bear to shine the flashlight on Allison's stone for a moment: 1892–1921. The years were somehow more difficult to read than her name. A name carved in stone had meaning, carrying those letters on into the future. The name meant something to her when she was alive. It placed her in the world. It identified her. It was right that the name should continue after she was gone. But the years, they were meaningless to the dead. What difference now if you were dead after twenty-nine years or, like her father the judge, sixty-nine?

After his brief glimpse of the stone in the flashlight beam, he scanned the knoll, watching for movement. A ghost. A girl. Something, anything. But there was nothing but cold, still air.

He began walking back toward the car. Mercy had nearly been hauled off the front porch by robed Klansmen. Kincaid suspected he knew what had happened to her. She had done it before, the logical, sensible thing, the desire for preservation:

she had fled. Somehow, on foot probably, she had gotten out of Otter Creek once again. She was free. She had taken him at his word. There was no threat that she couldn't escape. He envied her. He had never been, would never be so free. He was tied to his life. There was something brave, something determined and bold about Mercy. She did not have to stay. She did not have to wait. She could always flee. Somewhere he had read, or heard, *All wanderers are not lost.* Mercy could always wander but she would never be lost.

•

The other two Klansmen had gone out to watch the Grand Dragon's speech, after telling Mink they would let him know when it was time.

"Time for what?" Mercy asked.

"Time?" Mink said. "We have plenty of time." He moved closer, a white apparition in the dim light of the torch laid across the top of a trash barrel by the nearest food table. "I've heard the Grand Dragon's speeches before. He takes his time, likes to work the crowd up slowly, until they're ready."

"Ready?"

"For the trial." He loomed over her. "He wants to be sure they arrive at the right verdict."

"And do what?"

He shrugged. "It's up to them. Maybe there'll be a lynching. Happens, you know." His mask shook as he giggled. "Or maybe they'll eat you. And if they don't, he will."

"Eat me."

"Oh yes. That's what he does. Eats them."

"Them?"

"You think I'm kidding. Girls. Girls like you. After all, he is the Grand Dragon." He took a step closer. "But not yet. There's still time."

"Time for what?"

"For me. I need some recourse."

"Recourse?" It was the wrong word.

He was like a child, singular in his attention. As he came toward her, she stepped back until her hip bumped into the corner of a table. She could feel the heat from the torch. There was nowhere to go.

"When you held me at the still out in the woods," she said, "your brother Owen, he told you to leave me alone, didn't he? Where is he now?"

"He's up on the stage with all the big shots." There was no giggle. "So he's not here, is he?"

Mink reached down with one hand, took hold of his robe, and raised it up, revealing his bib overalls, an oddly delicate gesture, performed with the mock flourish of a magician. His other hand began unfastening the buttons of his overalls.

Mercy glanced over her shoulder, toward the tent flap. It was down. Outside, the Grand Dragon's voice had paused—even his pauses were dramatic. The silence of the crowd, the moment of anticipation, felt heavy, suspended in the night air. There was only the flickering light of the torch, the faint crackle of the flame, which was nearly extinguished. The tent was on the verge of darkness.

She looked at Mink. "You don't mean that, recourse."

"Let me show you want I mean."

"It's the wrong word."

Her insistence caused his hand to hesitate at his buttons. "Doesn't matter," he said. Then he seemed to turn his head in the direction of the stage, beyond the tent wall. "They talk and talk. It's all just words. I don't need words." His hand began to fidget again as he unfastened the last button. "Know what I need?" His hand disappeared inside his overalls.

Mercy turned her head again, searching the table. Bowls and plates, filled with scraps of food. Meat, bread, something that looked like it had been coleslaw, limp slivers of carrots, soggy ribbons of cabbage. It was difficult to see in the failing torch light. There was a wooden spoon, crumpled napkins. Nothing heavy, nothing sharp.

She looked down at Mink's hand, which had disappeared inside his overalls and was engaged in a difficult, intimate operation. "Here we are," he said as he yanked himself free.

Mercy turned her head away again, in the other direction, toward the trash barrel, the heat from the torch warming her face, as the Grand Dragon shouted, "The time is now!" and a great cheer burst from the crowd.

She picked up the torch and waved the burning end at Mink. His other hand let go of his robe, but it was too late. The weak flame quickly took on new life as it consumed the hem of the robe. The crowd's voice swelled, and Mink's shrieks were lost as Mercy ran toward the back wall of the tent, where she fell to her knees, lifted the heavy canvas, and rolled out into the cold night air.

It was dark and the dewy grass was slippery. She got to her feet by grabbing hold of the door handle of a truck—the policeman's truck that had delivered her to the fairgrounds. She made her way along the side of the truck until she could see around the corner of the tent. The crowd was cheering, many with arms raised in adulation, and they had not yet noticed the smoke that escaped from inside the tent. As she turned, Mercy saw a carton on the floor in the truck, its lid dislodged and material—red material that looked almost black in the dim light—draped over the side of the box.

•

At first, Rope sensed something about the crowd. The tenor of its voice shifted in a matter of seconds: first confusion, then alarm, and then panic as people started to move away from the stage. The Grand Dragon was still speaking, but it was clear that other Klansmen on the stage were trying to identify the source of the problem. Their tall, pointed hoods tipped back as they looked skyward, and it took Rope a minute to see that they were looking at the smoke that was obscuring the starry fall sky. The tent peaks, which mimicked the Klansmen's hoods, began to glow from within, and just as voices shouted *Fire!* Rope saw the first flames leap off the canvas top.

Suddenly, everyone was moving, running, pulling others along, or pushing them out of their way. One of the tent peaks burst into flames, and there was the sound of cracking wood from within, which brought screams as people ran past Rope, through the fairground entrance, and into the street. There was no controlling them, no cautioning them to flee in a calm, orderly fashion. People, shoved aside and knocked down, were trampled. To avoid being swept along with the crowd, Rope clung to one of the entrance gateposts.

He looked for Billy, the other uniform, but could not see him anywhere. The stage was now bare, the tent behind it aglow as sparks spewed into the dark sky. And something else happened, which Rope could not at first comprehend. There were men, mostly Klansmen, ghostly in their white robes, jostling and shoving their way through the crowd, wielding sticks and clubs. It was as though the fire had allowed them to realize their true intent. It made no sense, but somehow Rope saw that it was the true purpose of the entire event. This was the reason for the robes, the hoods, the masks. There was no law, no order. The Klansmen were free—free to do damage. They beat anyone in their way. What they could not control, they would destroy. They worked in small groups, and when one of them extended an arm, pointing in Rope's direction, several others fell in behind him as they walked swiftly toward the fairgrounds' entrance.

•

There was shouting, and shoving, as Milt watched the men on the stage fight their way down the steps. The heat from the fire was already intense. Dingley led the Grand Dragon down to the ground, clutching his forearm as though he were a blind man. With his free hand, he grabbed Milt's shoulder. "We have to get him out of here!"

"My truck," Milt shouted. "It's behind the tent!" He took Stephenson's other arm, and they pulled the man through the crowd. He seemed dazed, drunk, unable to walk a straight line. At one point, he dragged his feet, forcing Milt and Dingley to stop while he leaned over and vomited into the trampled grass. They continued around the side of the tent, hot as a furnace, and when they reached the truck, Milt said, "Quickly, before the whole thing goes up." He opened the driver's door, while Dingley maneuvered Stephenson to the other side of the truck and into the cab.

When they were all in the truck, Milt started the engine, grateful that it turned over on the first try, and then he said, "What about your brother? Wasn't Mink in the tent with the girl?"

Dingley pointed toward the field at the back of the fairgrounds. "Go! Just get us out of here!"

There were people running past the truck, making it difficult for Milt to drive forward. He put the truck into gear and started to pull away from the tent, just as flames began to lick its back wall. In the light from the fire, he could see the carton on the floor, crushed beneath the Grand Dragon's feet. The robe and hood, red because he was an American Krusader, were gone.

•

The fire brought on absolute mayhem and hysteria. Mercy had never seen anything like it. People running everywhere, fleeing in panic. Groups of Klansmen were beating people at random, using fists, sticks, and clubs. No reason, really, but they were doing it because they could. It was why they were here.

She worked her way through the smoke toward the darkness at the back of the fairgrounds. Something about the red fabric of her robe, hood, and mask caused people to avoid her. Upon seeing her approach, people would raise their hands in surrender, backing away. She understood their fear: the Klan outfit provided authority, anonymous power. It made her invisible. It was her salvation.

A high wooden fence enclosed the back of the fairgrounds. One section of boards had been torn away, and she slipped through the opening, and then ran past houses on the edge of the village. When she started across a field she slowed to a walk, corn stubble snagging on the bottom of her robe. In the distance she could hear the screams and shouts coming from the fairgrounds, reminding her of biblical stories about the fall of Jericho—all that was needed were the trumpets.

She found the cemetery, and after following the path through the woods, she came within sight of the DeVries's house. The vestibule was dark. She climbed the porch steps and let herself in, and as she closed the door a light came on and she was startled by the reflection in the window—someone standing by the door to the kitchen. She turned around and looked at Mrs. DeVries, the stock of her rifle pressed against her shoulder as she sighted down the barrel.

"You dare come back to this house?"

Twenty-Six

Kincaid couldn't find Rope or Billy anywhere in the smoke that shrouded Main Street. He heard people but he could barely see them: coughing, yelling, calling for children. In the fairgrounds, the tent smoldered, and the stage was engulfed in crackling flames. The clop of horse's hooves approached, and then Mitch Landis emerged from the haze with several men and women in his wagon, all bloodied.

"I'm taking them to the school, where Doc Evers has set up an infirmary," Mitch said. "He got several doctors and nurses to come in from surrounding towns. But he's not there, he's at his office. You might want to get over there." Mitch slapped the reins, and his mare began pulling the wagon down the road.

Kincaid returned to his car and drove to Doc Evers's office, where the smell of burnt flesh reminded him of the fields in France. He found the doctor working on Mink Dingley, applying gauze to his bare chest and enormous belly.

"How did this happen?" Kincaid asked.

The side of Mink's face was blackened and his right eye closed. He said something, his voice barely a whisper. Kincaid leaned close, holding his breath against the smell. "That little—"

"Mercy? How?" Mink's left eye only gazed up at Kincaid. "Where is she now?" Mink looked away. "What about Stephenson? Where's he?"

Mink's eye came back to him. He coughed as a shudder ran through his body. "He should have eaten that little girl when he had the chance."

"What? Where is he, Mink?"

"Who cares? You think you can do anything to him? The Grand Dragon?" Mink turned his head away. "Been staying out to the farm."

He closed his left eye. Kincaid straightened up and looked at Doc Evers.

"We need to get him to the hospital in Lansing," the doctor said. "I only have so much morphine." He nodded toward the door to his smaller examination room. "Go look in on you deputy. He's beat up pretty bad."

Kincaid went into the room, where he found Rope lying on an examination table. His face was bloody, swollen, and his right arm was in a sling.

"They just came at me," Rope said through thick lips. "It was the uniform."

"What about Billy?"

"Lost track of him. Crowd went crazy, and those men, they just . . ."

"Can you walk? I'll get you home."

Rope's bloodshot eyes sought him. "Home?"

"You stay with us as long as you want, understand?"

"Where's Mercy?" The boy could only whisper.

"I don't know," Kincaid said. "She wasn't at the house. What has Doc Evers said about you?"

"Dunno, I may have a cracked rib or two, and my shoulder's not right." Rope sat up with effort and slid off the table. "We need to find her." Standing, he had difficulty keeping his balance.

"I'll take you home first, and then . . ."

"No."

Kincaid didn't bother to argue. He took Rope by his good arm and helped him out the door.

They drove slowly through the village, which was quiet now. The sidewalks were empty, except for a few dogs sniffing about for food. Kincaid drove by the entrance to the fairgrounds. A wooden cross had been erected next to the stage. It was meant to be set on fire at the conclusion of the rally, but it remained untouched while smoke billowed into the night sky from the stage and the collapsed tent.

When they reached the police station, Kincaid pulled over to the curb. Billy was sitting on the front steps, smoking a cigarette. He came down to the sidewalk.

"You all right?" Kincaid asked.

"Remember, I ran track in high school," Billy said. "Those boys couldn't keep up. It's been quiet the past hour. I've been minding the store."

"Don't suppose you've seen Deputy Waters?"

Billy shook his head. He looked down Main Street, the air still hazy with smoke from the fairgrounds. "All those Klansmen," he said. "They just disappear into the night?"

"You get on home, Billy, and get some rest."

"What about the uniform? My clothes are in the station."

"Tomorrow morning, you come back to the station," Kincaid said. "Eight o'clock sharp, in uniform."

Billy grinned broadly. "Yes, sir."

•

At Dingley's farm, Milt sat on the stoop outside the kitchen door, surveying the men and trucks in the barnyard. He was reminded of his fascination with the carnival that used to come through Otter Creek every summer. As much as he liked the games, the shows, and the rides, he was drawn to the night they were packing up to move on to the next town. It was like that in the barnyard, but most of the men were still in their robes and hoods, an army of ghosts packing trucks and vans, which then rumbled out into the night, headed for the next stop on the Grand Dragon's tour of Michigan. Dingley's hooch was flowing freely, and chores were performed with a bold, tipsy swagger. There was shouting, there were arguments, and one brief scuffle between two men who had a disagreement over a missing toolbox.

Dingley's farmhouse, its windows illuminated by kerosene lanterns, presided over their labors. The light, the long shadows created a palpable tension. The men behaved as though they were being observed from the house, which seemed threatening and ominous. They knew that Stephenson was in there, brooding, incensed at what had happened at the fairgrounds. Someone would take the blame, certainly. No man wanted to be a scapegoat. No man wanted to be found responsible and suffer the consequences. But someone, to be sure, would be sacrificed. They knew how it worked: this was, after all, the Grand Dragon.

Finally, Owen Dingley came back out the kitchen door.

Milt knew it would come to this. "He wants to see me."

Owen nodded. He led Milt into the house and up the staircase. As always, there were men, the generals of this robed and hooded army, standing about, talking quietly. They were solemn, and they considered Milt's passing with the curiosity one affords a condemned man on his way to the gallows.

On the second floor, a guard opened a door, letting Milt and Dingley into a bedroom. Stephenson lay on his back in the iron-frame bed. His suit, white shirt, and tie lay in a pile on the floorboards, as though a man had dissolved there. The bottle of Dingley's hooch and a glass sat as witness on the wooden chair next to the bed. Stephenson wore only boxer shorts, black socks held up with garters, and a sleeveless undershirt. The man was fat.

"I come through towns all over the Midwest." He was so drunk he had difficulty sitting up in the bed. "But I never been to one like Otter Creek." He reached for the glass on the chair, nearly tipping it over before clutching it tentatively in his fingers. "Why is that, Deputy Waters?"

"I guess things just got out of control," Milt said.

"Did they now?" Stephenson took a drink and then rested the glass on his stomach. "Tell me, what precipitated things getting out of hand?"

"Well . . . they just did. They just went, you know, that way."

Stephenson's eyes drifted toward Owen for moment, and then he looked at Milt, taking in his uniform. "I was under the impression that you represented law and order round here." He sipped whiskey, and seemed to reconsider, as though deciding on a different approach. "After I went up on stage, what exactly happened in that tent?"

Milt didn't answer.

"You don't know?"

"No, I don't."

"Can you explain why you don't know?"

Milt shifted his weight to his other foot.

"You were left there in the tent, to guard that girl."

After a moment, Milt said, "There were several of us."

"How many?"

"Well. Three, four if you include me. Then two of them went out to watch you speak." He glanced toward Owen. "Leaving me. Me and Owen's brother."

He hesitated. There was no getting around the next part. "Then I stepped outside the tent to catch some of your speech."

"Leaving the girl . . . with Mink," Stephenson said. "And then?"

"And then, well, I don't know, there was smoke, and a fire. And all hell broke loose."

"Because?"

"I don't know . . ."

"Because you abandoned your duty." Stephenson finished what was in his glass and, with effort, reached for the bottle on the chair. "You're the one in the police uniform. You're the one who was responsible for the girl, who would keep her at bay until it was time to deliver her up to the stage. No?"

Milt started to speak, but then said nothing.

"The other policemen, it would have been better to have them assume these duties," Stephenson said as he refilled his glass.

"What other policemen?"

He looked up from the bottle, startled. "You didn't know about the police in the fairgrounds?" He turned to Owen and shook his head wearily. "There were two that I noticed."

"Two? Policemen?"

Stephenson almost smiled. "Are you surprised, deputy?"

Owen said, "I saw them, too. Neither of them was Kincaid. In the torch light I couldn't tell who they were, only that they were policemen. Where did they come from?"

"I have no idea," Milt said.

"I believe you don't," Stephenson said. He took a drink from his replenished glass. "Whoever they were, they were out there in the crowd, apparently doing their job. Something you neglected to do."

Milt cleared his throat. "I did not know—I was not told—that the girl was my responsibility. I delivered her to the fairgrounds, something your men failed to do earlier in the day, and I—"

Stephenson put the bottle back on the chair, banging it hard on the wooden seat, sounding like a gavel. "Do not talk to me about other men's failures, deputy. They are Klansmen. One-hundred percent Americans. You . . ." He again looked at Owen. "He was given a red robe, am I right? You are Canadian? You're not even American-born, have I got that right?"

Milt said nothing. There was a moment when he thought he would simply turn and leave the room.

But Owen said, "The robe and hood I gave him, the red outfit, when we drove away from the fire it was missing from your truck."

Stephenson said, "And what do you suppose happened to it?"

"Draw your own conclusions," Milt said.

Stephenson sat up, alert, incensed. "You're telling me to draw my own conclusions?" Something was happening to his face. His skin was turning blue, and his eyes were bulging. "I'll tell you what happened to that robe. That girl used it to get away."

"Some of the men saw her," Owen said. "They saw the red robe, hood, and mask leaving the fairgrounds. They didn't know who it was, just a Klansman in red." Then, almost as an afterthought, he added, "And my brother was seen being carried out of the tent. Word has it he was taken to Doc Evers's. I don't know if he's alive or dead."

Stephenson got up off the bed and had difficulty putting the glass down next to the bottle on the chair. He tended to veer sideways as he came across the room. Shorter than Milt by several inches, he had the vicious gaze of a watch dog. "In the morning, I will leave Otter Creek and never return . . . that is a certainty. They call me the Old Man. Know why? Because they are my boys. My boys, deputy, will find you. See, this is all about protection, and you have failed to understand that. Protection of what is ours, what is rightfully ours. We are threatened, so we need to protect those rights, and each other. You should have stayed in the tent with Owen's brother and that girl. But you didn't, you didn't do your duty. Tell me, what will you do, Deputy Waters? Whatever it is, everywhere you go in this town you will be looking over your shoulder." Stephenson took hold of the lapel of Milt's police jacket, fingering it for a moment as though determining the quality of the material. "There will be retribution. We need examples. We were going to make an example of that girl. Instead, you will be our example. Do you understand that?"

Milt stood perfectly still.

Stephenson turned away, seeking the refuge of the bed. "Now get him—" He made a little shooing motion with his hand.

•

Mercy boarded the train. The conductor, his mouth concealed beneath the cow-catcher mustache, asked her destination. When she didn't answer immediately, he said, *Worcester?* She shook her head. *So, you're not going back. Ah, then it must be Chicago. Then why don't you join the others?* He gestured with one hand, directing her into the carriage, which was finely appointed with kerosine lanterns and varnished mahogany. All the passengers were children, sitting two to a bench, and they all wore robes and high-pointed hoods. No masks. White children, staring at her with eyes that said *Don't sit near me.* She had no choice: there was only one vacant seat. She walked down the aisle and sat next to a heavy girl who was peeling a banana. On the bench across from her sat two boys, identical twins. They gazed at her with pallid blue eyes, then looked at each other, and shook their heads.

The train began to move. All Mercy could see out the windows was black smoke drifting back from the engine. *Where are you headed?* she said to the twins.

They both seemed surprised that she had dared address them, or perhaps that she could speak at all.

Mercy turned to the girl beside her. *Chicago,* she said as she inserted the banana into her mouth.

Encouraged, the twins leaned toward Mercy. *We are going to the stock yards.* They spoke together, their voices unified so that one seemed an echo of the other. *To be fed to the hogs.*

Why? What have you done?

We got on the train to look for our families, that's what we have done.

She was about to explain about her aunt and why she had come to Michigan, when the boys looked past her, their blue eyes startled, frightened. Turning, she saw a woman coming down the aisle—not walking but gliding on air. A beautiful plait of hair surrounded her dark face. Mercy knew it was her Aunt Andrea.

I've finally found you.

The woman stopped in the aisle and seemed to hover above Mercy and smiled. *I am not your aunt.*

Mother?

But the woman had already continued to drift down the aisle toward the back of the carriage. Mercy got to her feet and began to follow, until the train suddenly went into a steep descent. It wasn't a hill, but the train seemed to be falling. She was pulled back up the aisle, watching her aunt get smaller. The train began to tilt and spin, causing all the children to float out of their seats. Their robes billowed as they clutched at each other, trying not to be thrown toward the back of the carriage. The smoke from the engine was pouring in the open windows. There was the sound of burning wood, and a smell, an awful smell. Mercy could no longer see her aunt, and she reached out desperately, trying to keep from falling through the smoke.

She heard her name spoken, once, twice, and she opened her eyes.

"Mercy, I think you were dreaming. Was it a nightmare?"

Mercy was lying on a couch, clutching the blanket to her chest. She was in the DeVries's living room, the old woman leaning over her, and across the room Kincaid and Rope looked concerned.

"The train," Mercy said to Rope. "It was taking us to the stockyards in Chicago."

He nodded.

"Well, that's one train you'll never be on again," Mrs. DeVries said. "Now I've soup on the stove. Why don't we all eat?"

Mercy got up off the couch. Her balance was uncertain. She still felt as though she were on the train, falling through the air. Mrs. DeVries took her arm, but Mercy said, "I'll be okay, thank you."

Mrs. DeVries let go of her arm, and said to Kincaid, "I nearly shot the poor girl. I thought one of the Klansmen had come back." She pointed to the red garment, draped over the wingback chair by the fireplace. "I came into the vestibule with my rifle, and there he was, but he pulled back the mask and it was Mercy. Thank God I didn't shoot her when she came through that door in that robe." She laughed. "I wasn't imagining it, and I haven't touched the Dingley's."

The captain said to Mercy, "You were in the tent at the fairgrounds?"

"Yes."

"Why?"

"I'm not sure. They came for me here at the house. A policeman . . ." She watched Kincaid turn his head slightly. "I didn't know him, but he was in uniform, so I went with him because he said you wanted to see me at the station. Then another man got in the truck, the one who held me out in the woods, and they took me to the tent. They wanted to put me on trial, letting the people decide my punishment."

"There was a fire," Kincaid said.

"I got out of the tent, found that red outfit, and walked here. That man— Mink—he . . ."

"He's alive," Kincaid said. "All I know is he's in the hospital."

•

They had come by Milt's house two, maybe three times during the night. A car, gliding slowly down the street. Though it was dark, he could see the shape of the hoods. The last time the Ford stopped at the end of the front walk, he expected the men to get out. He sat in his mother's favorite chair at the living room window, his revolver resting on his thigh, waiting. A head turned. They were conferring. They had to know that he was armed, that they would eat lead before they reached the front door. If old lady DeVries could fend off a bunch of Klansmen with a hunting rifle, they must know what they'd be in for approaching Deputy Waters's house in the middle of the night.

That last time the Ford sped away. Decisively. He sensed it meant they wouldn't be back. But this wasn't over. They would find another approach. What did the Grand Dragon say? *Everywhere you go in this town, you will be looking over your shoulder.*

Milt believed it. There was something relentless about these men. My boys, Stephenson, the Old Man, called them. Like dogs, working their quarry, they would find a way. They used deception, distraction, they would strike when it was least expected. He would probably never know what hit him. It was no way to live, thinking—no, believing—that any moment could be your last. A sip of coffee, a forkful of blueberry pie, pausing to tie a shoelace, and then, like that, it was over, done.

At first light, he left by the back door.

Twenty-Seven

Kincaid was up Sunday morning before anyone else, and he drove into town, slowly, assessing the damage left behind by the Klan. The streets and sidewalks were strewn with debris. Fencing had been knocked off kilter, slats and pickets torn away. Paper wrappers, swaths of newspaper scuttled along on the November breeze. Dogs scavenged around overturned trash barrels. On Main Street, he passed Herb and Mary Napier in front of their hardware store, sweeping up broken glass. Herb paused to rest both hands on the top of his broom handle as he watched the Chevrolet roll by.

Kincaid found Milt in the police station, wearing a fedora and a heavy tweed overcoat with the collar turned up. A suitcase, the leather stained and frayed, waited patiently on the floor next to his desk. Kincaid felt a moment's relief at the realization that he would not have to tell Milt he was fired. They were well beyond that. Milt's expression, difficult to pin down, reminded Kincaid of Herb Napier. Both men seemed harnessed by a combination of fear, despair, and vengeful anger, which made them stony and resolute. Kincaid had questions, lots of them, but if he took the wrong tack he'd hit a fierce headwind. Better to let Milt take things in a direction of his own choosing.

"I been thinking about my truck," he said. "What it might be worth."

"How you getting to where you're going?"

"Not in that old Ford, that's for sure. I'll take the train."

"How far?"

"West. Got relations in Des Moines. And I know people in Albuquerque."

"I see. Doubt that truck's got that kind of miles left in it."

"Good for getting around town, you know, hauling stuff."

Kincaid nodded. "How much you asking?"

For a moment, the old shrewdness came into Milt's face. He was a man who liked to dicker and deal. "Well, I been thinking forty-five would be fair." As an afterthought, he added, "Wouldn't give to a stranger for less'n fifty."

"Forty-five." Kincaid tried to sound noncommittal. "So, this is not a visit you're paying out west?"

"Nope. You're going to have to find yourself a new deputy."

"I suppose."

"I figure you been thinkin' on it already." Milt waited, and when Kincaid didn't respond, he said, "Then there's my house."

"I'm not in the market for a house."

"I gather that. I left a note on Ellie's desk. If anybody can find a buyer for that place, it's her and Mitch. The place, it needs work. It was my mother's, and her family going back to that granddaddy who was in the Iron Brigade and lost a leg at Gettysburg." For a moment, Milt seemed uncertain until he resolved some internal debate. "It'll take time, but I'd rather Ellie not sell the house to somebody who wants to just knock it down."

"No, you don't want that. Besides, maybe you want to hold it in case you decide to come back."

"'Fraid you don't understand the situation. I can't come back."

"Sounds like you're being threatened, Milt. Is that it?"

"Who's gonna protect me? You?" He gazed about the office, and then came back to Kincaid, looking as though he'd just realized he was there. "Those two kids, they really didn't finish off Harlan?"

"No."

"How'd you know?"

"Something about them when I came upon them up north," Kincaid said. "A hunch."

"They just didn't act guilty."

"And Lyle did?"

"Not till he confessed. They—both he and Hannah—seemed relieved."

"Lyle," Milt said, almost to himself. "Guess I always knew he had this streak in him. Call it a potential. A couple of times he made reference to Estelle and Hannah, leading me to wonder if something wasn't buried way back in there." Milt looked squarely at Kincaid. "So what happens to them, the kids."

"Up to them."

"They out to the Judge DeVries's place?"

"For the time being."

Milt nodded. He did so instead of something he might have said.

"What?" Kincaid asked.

"Nothing."

"What?"

"It's just that this might not be the safest place for those two kids." He waited, and then added, "But then what's safe? Where's safe? This business with the Klan, it's . . ." He decided to leave it at that.

"Going to be lots of work around town today, if shops are going to be open for business tomorrow morning. When I drove past Napier's Hardware, Herb and Mary were already sweeping up. I saw something. Call it tenacity."

It was difficult to read Milt's face. Remorse? Embarrassment? "They got a reason to stay," he said. "To dig in." He glanced toward the front windows. "It's a good little place, Otter Creek. It'll look out for itself. Always has."

"You don't have to go," Kincaid said.

This appeared to stop something in Milt, alter his line of thinking. He was caught unawares, and he could barely conceal it. But then he said, "Yeah, I do. I grew up here. Time I move on—it's long past due."

"We protect ourselves. You know that. I know you believe that, Milt. It's why you worked in this office all these years." Milt looked undecided, like he might just spill the beans entirely. "The Klan, they got something on you?"

"They said they'd finagle it so I'd be police captain. Withdrawn now. They're the kind that need someone to blame. Now it's me." Clearly, he didn't want to dwell on it. "Any word on Mink?"

"Don't know," Kincaid said. "I believe he was sent up to a hospital in Lansing. Burned pretty bad."

"Burns," Milt said. "If they don't kill you, they scar you for life." He still looked like there was something more he couldn't keep a lid on, and once he walked out the door it would be too late.

"What is it, Milt?" Kincaid said again.

"You should have let them go. That black girl and the boy, you should never have chased after them."

"And let it stand that they were guilty?"

"It would have been easier on folks around here. You don't understand us, do you?"

"Maybe. But I understand my job."

Milt looked away, stung, studying the office one more time. "You ain't better'n me, no matter what you think." When Kincaid was about to speak, he shook his head. "We're more alike than you know—you just don't want to admit it." He turned to Kincaid now. "We both got our damage. My ex. You, the war, it must have taken a toll, and losing your wife, pregnant and all. A lot of damage. But you're the kind that keeps on, no matter what." He leaned over and picked up his suitcase by its leather handle. "The train pulls in just before eight."

"Can I give you a lift to the station?"

"I'd prefer the walk." But he didn't move. "You interested in that truck, I'll send you my address once I get settled. Back door to the house hasn't had a lock since I was a kid. Keys are in the kitchen." He almost smiled. "Forty-five dollars, I know you're good for it." He shifted the suitcase over to his left hand and held out his right. Kincaid took it. It was a firm hand, and Milt didn't let go. "For what it's worth," he said, "that shouldn't have happened last night. They got a right to their point of view, but their execution is wrong."

He released Kincaid's hand and left the station. Kincaid went to the front window and watched as cars, trucks, and wagons moved through the village now, while shopkeepers washed down their section of sidewalk. Milt walked up Main Street in the direction of the train station like it didn't mean anything to him.

•

First thing in the morning, Rope shoveled coal into the furnace in the cellar, and then went out to the woodpile behind the house, loaded the barrow, and built a fire in the stove in the kitchen. He welcomed the sense of routine at the start of the day. It was what he needed, routine. Kincaid had assured Rope and Mercy that they were free. Mercy welcomed her freedom, but Rope found the notion oddly constrictive. He wasn't sure what it meant. In Haverhill, between the orphanage and the factory work, he'd always lived by imposed routine, but now he realized it would be necessary to devise one. It meant making choices, coming to decisions, and acting upon them. He'd rather not think about it. Better to shovel coal and tend to the stove on this cold November morning.

He heard footsteps on the second floor. Kincaid had left early—half asleep, Rope had heard the Chevrolet leave—so by the pace of the steps overhead, it could only be Mercy. He listened to her bare feet move along the floorboards toward the head of the stairs, and then she spoke his name. Not Rope. Lincoln.

She said it as second time, with urgency. "*Lincoln.*"

He left the kitchen, pushing through the swinging door and into the vestibule, where he could look up and see her in a blue bathrobe, hands gripping the newel post.

"Come quick," she said, and then turned and rushed back down the hallway.

He took the stairs in twos, followed her toward the back of the house, to the last door on the left, which was open. Mrs. DeVries was lying on the floor in her nightgown.

"What happened?" he said.

"I don't know, but we have to get her back in bed and call a doctor."

The woman's eyes were open, but she didn't seem to be seeing. Her mouth was slack and something was affecting the muscles on the right side of her face, as though an unseen force were tugging down on the skin.

He got his arms beneath her. She was remarkably light, all bones, it seemed, and completely unresponsive, her limbs almost liquid the way they hung over his forearms as he lifted her off the floor. He laid her out on her back on the bed, and Mercy drew the covers over her.

"What is it?" he asked.

"Not sure," she said. "Something like this happened to one of the nuns in Worcester. She was never the same." Mercy rushed out the bedroom door, her voice echoing in the hallway. "There must be a doctor's phone number down in that book by the telephone."

Rope looked at Mrs. DeVries, who was staring at his shoulder, her eyes not moving. He could hear her shallow breathing but could not see any movement. "We'll get help," he said to her, though it seemed pointless.

From the hallway, he felt the first hint of heat rising up from the woodstove in the kitchen.

•

A truck and a Dodge sedan were parked in Dingley's barnyard. The two men loading suitcases and boxes into the trunk of the sedan were Perry Neilson and Bert Coombs. When Kincaid got out of his car, they walked toward him, shoulder to shoulder, blocking him from getting any closer to Dingley and D. C. Stephenson, who were on the stoop outside the kitchen door.

"This is private property," Neilson said to Kincaid. "Can't let you by without an appointment."

Neilson and Coombs had spent most of their lives falling into things. Jobs, marriages, things that didn't last long. Otherwise, they could usually be found in Jake's Diner or shooting pool at places like TJ's Billiards Room. Both large men, Neilson wore a newsboy cap that sagged over his right ear, Coombs a bowler in need of brushing. Last Kincaid knew they both lived under Ma Neilson's roof.

"Perry, Bert," Kincaid said amiably. "I hardly recognize you without your robes and hoods on."

Bert leaned forward, but at the sound of Owen Dingley's voice he held back. "It's all right, fellas. Let the captain through."

When they reluctantly stepped aside, Kincaid approached the house. Owen came halfway down the steps, as if to run interference for D. C. Stephenson, who smoked a cigarette as he rested a haunch on the railing.

"Mink, how's he doing?" Kincaid asked.

"He's up to the hospital in Lansing now," Dingley said. "Doc Evers thinks he'll make it."

"I'm glad to hear it."

"Sure you are." Dingley's eyes were full of blame. "You set that girl free. It's all her doing."

"Really? What was she doing in that tent?"

"According to Mink, she started that fire," Dingley said. "What are you going to do about it?"

"Do? She was there against her will, is my understanding."

"You'd have to take that up with your deputy."

"I have," Kincaid said. "He and your brother brought her to the fairgrounds. You had plans for her?"

Stephenson flicked his cigarette butt into the barnyard, indicating that he was prepared, with great reluctance, to join the conversation. "It was a peaceful public assembly."

"You haven't seen the condition of the village this morning." Kincaid took a step toward the stairs, causing Dingley to back up. "She says you were going to put her on trial."

Stephenson was staring off toward the road with studied disinterest. "Suppose we had. Wonder what the verdict would be."

"Depends on what she was accused of. And then there's the matter of proof, which requires evidence."

"Problem with the legal system in this country is it's lost its urgency," Stephenson said. "It's become slow, ponderous." He gazed down the steps at Kincaid. "Remember when that anarchist shot President McKinley in Buffalo back in, what, aught-one? Leon whatever-his-name was. His trial lasted two days. Two days. And a month later he went to the electric chair in Auburn, New York. That, Captain, is justice."

"That's what you had in mind?" Kincaid said. "A trial and an execution, a form of entertainment?"

"Folks in Otter Creek might find it educational," Stephenson said, his eyes roaming, as though he were speaking to a crowd. "But electricity is still scarce in little bergs like this." He looked down at Kincaid in earnest. "Lynching would be quicker."

Dingley took a step closer to Kincaid. "And like the man said, it was a peaceful public assembly, until that little bitch set the place on fire." He came even closer, too close, leaning forward. "Now, are you here on my property in some official capacity?"

Kincaid placed a hand on Dingley's chest, and for a moment the two men remained that way. When Dingley took the slightest step back, Kincaid removed his hand and looked up at Stephenson. "You heading out of this 'little berg' soon."

"That is an absolute certainty," Stephenson said. "Owen has kindly offered to drive me to Muskegon."

"That's what I came to hear," Kincaid said. "And that I won't see you in this town again."

"It's up to the Grand Dragon," Dingley said. "It's a free country. And he has plenty of folks who share his beliefs."

Kincaid said, "There'll be no executions in Otter Creek, no trial by mob. There will be no lynchings. Enough blood was spilt last night."

Dingley glanced toward Perry and Bert, and then back at Kincaid.

"We got nothing to do with that," Perry said.

"No?" Kincaid said. "Lots of injured folks were treated last night, and one of my deputies was beaten."

Dingley seemed to find this humorous. "You have more than one?"

"I didn't have enough last night. It was Klansmen, bands of them working over the crowd as they left the fairgrounds. Your Grand Dragon gave them a taste for blood."

"Why don't you round up your suspects and leave us be?" Dingley said.

"Tell you what I will do," Kincaid said. "After your Grand Dragon is gone, I will keep a close eye on Klan members here, fellows like you and Perry and Bert, because you know at some point somebody's going to slip up, somebody's going to say something that will make all their brethren nervous. Once that happens, they start to talk, and they start thinking about protecting themselves. And eventually, they will sort themselves out, revealing who the perpetrators were. It's common enough with herds." He looked up at Stephenson on the kitchen stoop. "You fancy yourself as something of a shepherd? A successful shepherd banks on the herd sticking together. But they don't, not always, particularly when the shepherd has left them alone in the pasture. When a threat, some predator, arrives, say a wolf or, since we are in Michigan, even a wolverine, what happens to your herd? It's basic instinct. They scatter, they run, the flock breaks up, and everyone is just out to save his own hide."

With a little effort, Stephenson lifted a haunch off the stoop railing. "You don't look much like a wolverine to me." He stared as though he were alone with his thoughts. "But you sound quite certain about this basic instinct."

"In this case, I am quite certain," Kincaid said. "Because what happened in Otter Creek won't be that easily forgotten. People were injured, badly hurt. And they're upset. They'll clean up the village today and be open for business tomorrow, but they won't forget. Somebody, eventually, will be held accountable." When Stephenson turned his head slightly, Kincaid added, "But you, you'll be long gone, so for the time being the Grand Dragon has nothing to worry about."

"For the time being?" Stephenson said.

"Time will tell," Kincaid said. "The anonymity of the robes, hoods, and masks, it protects you. But maybe that won't be enough. When they begin to put those hoods and robes away, you won't know who you can trust."

For the first time Stephenson appeared to be engaged, determined to correct some misunderstanding. "This is about more than robes, much more."

"That, Mr. Stephenson, is an absolute, 100 percent certainty." Kincaid nodded toward Neilson and Coombs. "Taking your lackeys with you?"

"Well," Stephenson said, "they'd be welcome, and they'd be a big help to our cause, no doubt, but this is their home. There's much good work they can do right here in Otter Creek."

Kincaid glanced back at Neilson and Coombs, who feigned embarrassment and humility as if they'd received a pat on the head. "It's best you stay close to home," Kincaid said to them. "At the moment, I got one deputy with a bum shoulder and cracked ribs. Local members of the Klan may be needed for questioning."

"Are Bert and Perry suspects, Captain?" Stephenson asked.

"Suspects?" Kincaid studied Neilson and Coombs long enough that they both looked away. "Hard to say at this point. I've just begun to gather evidence."

"Evidence?" Stephenson said.

"Folks who were beaten claim that the perpetrators were dressed in Klan garb. That boils it down to several hundred suspects." Kincaid looked back at Neilson and Coombs again. "But there was enough blood spilt that it's possible that traces of blood might be found on their robes." Neilson and Coombs glanced at each other. "I need to start somewhere, so I could confiscate the robes from your boys here. Check them for signs of blood. It would be a rather scientific investigation, much like they do in the cities these days. You know, they even take fingerprints now?"

"Imagine that." Stephenson said. "Fingerprints."

"But, of course," Kincaid said, "if Perry and Bert were smart, they'd have already done something about their robes, if they had anything to do with last night's assaults. They might have already washed the robes and hoods." He looked at both men. "Or perhaps the garments might be misplaced, lost. Burned, even. You're all so fond of fires."

"Well," Stephenson said as he walked past Kincaid to the Dodge. "I wish you luck with your investigation, Captain. If anyone can do it, you can. Since coming to Otter Creek, I have been given to appreciate that the police captain is most thorough and determined."

Dingley followed Stephenson to the car. "Yes, you have a job ahead of you, all those robes to collect. And I suppose you'll have to get some judge to sign a search warrant."

"Owen, I think you might have a future in law enforcement," Kincaid said.

Dingley and Stephenson stood next to the automobile, staring at the one suitcase that remained on the ground. Dingley turned to Neilson and Coombs, who did not move. It was a long moment.

"You want a hand with that?" Kincaid said finally.

"No, thanks. I got it." Dingley picked up the suitcase, placed it in the trunk, and closed the lid.

He opened the passenger door for Stephenson, trying not to look like a chauffeur, and then he came around and got in behind the steering wheel and started the engine. As the Dodge pulled away, neither Perry nor Bert turned to watch because they would not take their eyes off Kincaid.

"Your robes," Kincaid asked. "Don't suppose you gave them to your mother, Perry, for that good woman to launder. Where are they?"

Bert looked at Perry, who said, "Ain't you supposed to get you your search warrant first."

"Oh sure. But we could clear this up quickly if you just provided me with the robes. Voluntarily."

"Voluntarily."

"Right. That way I don't have to go rummaging through your things, your car . . . your mother's house."

Perry shook his head, but Bert nodded toward the Ford truck across the barnyard, and said, "They're in the truck." When Perry looked at him, his voice lifted in a whine, "I told you we should do something about them."

Perry cleared his throat, preparing a different tack. "If there is what you call evidence on these robes, what does that mean? What would we be charged with?"

"I'd have to think about that, Perry, and consult with the county prosecutor. I mentioned assaulting a police officer. We could start there. I suppose other charges would depend on how injured people fare."

Bert's eyes swelled with regret. "We didn't do nothing, not at first," he blurted. He took a deep breath and for a moment Kincaid expected that he might start crying. "We was told to keep order in the crowd during the parade. When that fire started, and people started running, things just got out of hand. Most of those Klan boys was from out of town, you know. They went into a frenzy, and it opened something up, if you know what I mean."

Reluctantly, Perry nodded his head. "We didn't intend, I mean, we didn't think . . ."

"I know that," Kincaid said. "Let's have a look at those robes."

They went to the truck, and Perry took a heap of robes from the front seat. Kincaid examined the robes, and said, "Those look like blood stains, wouldn't you say?"

"You can't prove it's from last night."

"I'm not a man of science, Perry, but I can take these over to Doc Evers's office, and no doubt he'd be able to determine if it is blood. Human blood. What do you say? Care to make a little wager?"

Bert sat down on the running board and stared up at the barn. "If we was to confess, would things go easier for us?"

"I'm sure it would," Kincaid said. "It's largely up to the prosecutor, but I would recommend leniency. We just need to go over to the station so you can make a statement."

Bert put his elbows on his knees and lowered his head. "You want us to finger Owen and Stephenson."

"I'm not going to tell you what to say." Kincaid folded up the robes and tucked them under his arm. "I just want to know who might be responsible for last night's violence."

Bert raised his head, aiming a shrewd eye at Kincaid. "And if both Owen and Stephenson are named in our confession, what happens to them?"

"That is an interesting question, Bert." Kincaid leaned against the back of the truck fender. "I expect that the state police, and maybe even the federal authorities, would have to be notified. Stephenson is from out of state, and that may be a factor. But you know—you and I know—that Owen and Stephenson are the kind that usually get off these things. Nothing sticks to them. It would be a shame if the whole thing gets hung on you fellas."

Perry leaned over and expressed his skepticism by spitting in the dirt. "Hear that sound, Bert?"

"Sound?" Bert said. "What sound?"

"Sort of a baaing." Perry wiped his mouth with the sleeve of his coat. "Baaing. You know, like sheep."

Twenty-Eight

For several weeks it had been their habit to sit on the porch swing after dinner. Winter coats, wool hats, scarves, boots. Cold fresh air, the rattle of fallen leaves. Mercy liked the fact that they seldom spoke. Shared silence felt like trust.

For once, Rope broke the silence. "Since that Klan parade," he said, "it's been . . ."

He didn't finish, which was not unusual. He didn't need to.

"I know," she said. "I haven't been able to decide."

"But now you have?"

"Now I have, yes." She waited. "And you, too?"

He didn't answer, but out of the corner of her eye she saw him nod.

They watched the dark, stitched by the bare maple branches entwined above the road in front of the DeVries's house. Behind them, they could hear the radio in the living room, a murmured delivery of the day's news, which Kincaid listened to every night. News from Washington, Europe, places that would be difficult to find on a map. Every night the same deep voice, which seemed to both push them away and draw them closer to the rest of the world. Kincaid,

Mercy had come to realize, felt it was his duty to listen in, to pay attention. The world was a troubled place, and there was always a chance he might be needed.

She couldn't wait any longer, so she went first. "Michigan seemed so far away. Then we got on that train. And here we are."

"You said it was what you wanted."

"I know. I'm not sure what I thought I would find. My aunt? Something, anything about my mother? I end up with a photograph of them as girls in Jamaica. But here, here is what I got. And here is where I've decided to stay."

"You have." It wasn't a question.

"Surprised?"

"Yes. And no."

"It's Mrs. DeVries," she said.

"Sure. Just in these few weeks you can see the change. She needs you."

"She's so frail. But she insists on doing as much as she can. And her mind never quits."

"I listen to how you two talk," he said. "Neither ever runs out of words."

"This morning she asked me if I pray. I told her that in the orphanage the nuns made sure we prayed all the time. Since leaving, not so much, not the way we used to, down on our knees, hands clasped. I told her that sometimes I wondered if there was a different God in Michigan. I thought this might disturb her. But, no, she just said, 'Here, what you do with your life is the prayer.'"

"If you weren't here, she'd be in this house alone most of the time, talking to herself."

"It goes both ways."

"How long will you stay?"

"Who knows?" Mercy said. "Whenever she mentions spring, it's 'if I see the crocuses bloom.'"

"She could be wrong."

"With her determination, she could be very wrong. But right now, I can't up and leave."

Again, Rope nodded. "I heard her mention school to you."

"I may enroll in the high school after the holidays. If . . ."

"It's a big if."

"I know. I doubt that people our age around here are ready for me. Mrs. DeVries says not to worry, that most people will be all right, and those who aren't, well, she still has her hunting rifle."

"In the village, I get these looks," he said. "I'm that boy off the train, so I must have killed Harlan Nau." When she didn't answer, he said, "It's worse for you."

Mercy wanted to let it go, but she felt a gnawing doubt building in her. "So. You're going?"

He took a moment. She imagined him fashioning a thought the way he would tie a knot, pulling on the ends, allowing it to tighten and become strong. "When I do chores at the police station, I have lots of time to talk to Mitch Landis. He sits on that bench for hours, reading the paper while his wife works. He's like a loyal old dog, waiting by the door. He tells these stories about his younger days working on ore boats up and down the lakes. I'm not sure when he's making it up and when it's for real. He says when you're in a storm on the lake, it's always the worst anyone has ever seen, until you survive it so crewmates can tell stories about worse storms. He loves to tell these stories."

"And you want some of your own stories to tell someday."

"I suppose."

"He's warning you. It's a hard way to go. But you love it—the water, the boats."

"Guess so."

"I could see it when we were on that ferry crossing the straits. That's when I first really saw you, had a sense of who you were. Before that you were this strange boy who kept following me, and I wasn't sure what to make of you." She took hold of his hand, his right hand. The nubs of his missing fingers were cold, so she slid their hands into her coat pocket. The first time she'd held it, she could tell he was uneasy, but after a few times of massaging the enlarged knuckles, the bulbous stumps, he came around to welcoming her touch. Along with goodnight kisses before leaving the porch, it was the extent of their intimacy, but the hand, his hand felt like a promise, an assurance. After the hand, one day the rest might follow.

But tonight, she sensed in him a tension, a reluctance. She knew this because she knew the hand. "What?" she said. "What is it?"

"I've been wanting to tell you . . . for several days." He began to withdraw his hand from her pocket, but she held it tightly until he relaxed in her grip. "Mitch has given me the name of a man in Detroit. They crewed together for years. His friend still works for one of the shipping companies. Does office duty now. Mitch says he can get me work in the yards doing maintenance on the boats through the winter, and then in the spring there's a good chance I could crew on a boat." He paused, anticipating the next question. "Sometime after New Year's I'll take the train to Detroit." After a moment, he said, "We could write."

She began to turn toward him but decided to face the dark. "Have you ever written a letter to anyone?"

"Never had the need."

"The way you talk, you might start with postcards. Ones with pretty pictures of all the places your boat will take you. And how do you send a letter to a sailor on a boat that's always moving about the Great Lakes?"

"Mitch explained that. In Detroit, there's a boat called the *Wescott* that comes out to the ships as they pass on the river and delivers letters and packages. He says they call it 'pail mail' because they hoist it up to their decks in buckets."

"So, you're planning on writing?"

"I could."

"And you expect packages?"

"I didn't say that."

She smiled. "No packages?"

"A letter would be just fine, you know, now and then."

"If I have something to say, maybe I'll write."

"You came out here looking for your aunt. You found a photograph of your mother and her sister, both gone." He waited, and she knew that what he had to say next would be difficult. "But you are not alone now. I'm not that easy to get rid of. I'll be back."

"How do you know?"

"Well. I guess I don't. But I think I will."

"I meant how do you know I want you to come back?"

"Guess I don't. I'd have to come back to find out, wouldn't I?"

They didn't say anything, as though they'd reached a dilemma that couldn't be defined in words, and staring out into the night seemed the only solution. His hand was warm now. She squeezed it once, and when she let go, he withdrew it from her pocket.

She wasn't sure, but then she decided to tell him. "Trains."

After a moment, he said, "That first time we spoke, when I gave you something for dinner wrapped in a napkin. On the train, remember? You said you dreamed of the train."

"I often dream about trains. You ever have dreams that haunt you?"

"I forget them soon as I'm awake. Don't know why."

"I've had dreams ever since I can remember, but even before we came out here on that train I'd wake up in a sweat. Sometimes I think I must have been talking to myself or to people in my dreams. But this one was different because I get off the train." She took her hand out of her pocket and examined the toothmarks. "These scars," she said, "they'll never go away. And this dream I had last night, it was . . ."

"You remember it?"

"Most of it. At the beginning there's a train—always the train. It pulls into a station, and I get off. And when I step down on to the platform there's the Grand Dragon. He looks like that man D. C. Stephenson, but not entirely. Worse, if that's possible. He's on his hands and knees, and his face is smeared with blood, flesh hanging from his mouth. A group of Klansmen in their robes and hoods surround him. As the train leaves the station, the smoke from the engine makes it difficult to see, but then I realize that they're watching him eat a woman lying on the platform. Her clothes are torn, and he's biting her all over. It is so real. The men stand around him, urging him to devour her, all of her. As he bites into her flesh, he becomes bigger and bigger, but suddenly her moans, these terrible moans, stop, and she lies there, dead. And then . . ."

Rope's head was lowered, pensive. "And then?"

"The Klansmen all back away from the Dragon, and as they do so he gets smaller. His voice, everything, shrinks as he pleads with them to stay, but they walk on down the railroad tracks, many of them pulling off their robes and hoods, throwing them aside in disgust. The dead woman is not even thirty, and her eyes are still open, and her wounds give off this smell. And the Dragon, the Grand Dragon, he's now just a little old man who won't stop pleading, like a spoiled child. Without those men around him, he's nothing. And then he looks at me like it's my fault. He moves toward me, but something stops him, and I don't know how—but then it's a dream—we're in the police station, and he's in one of the cells, reaching out toward me through the bars. Then I woke up. Soaked in sweat."

Rope didn't say anything. She was relieved.

Her feet were getting cold. She got off the swing and walked in place. The floorboards creaked beneath her weight, a rhythmic sound that was accompanied by the newscaster talking about the possibility of snow along the Michigan-Ohio border.

"I guess he's right," Rope said.

His voice broke her out of a spell. "Who is?"

"The man on the radio. Look, snowflakes."

Mercy watched one drift out of the dark, a messenger fluttering to earth. Then she saw another, and another, and then suddenly they descended through the darkness with the lightness of sifted flour. A new sound rose from the front yard, the gentle rattle of snow striking fallen leaves. From within the house, silence as Kincaid switched off the radio.

She went down the porch steps, where she detected the slightest breeze. The air was colder, a hard cold, and the snow fell faster, big flakes now.

"Where are we going?" he said, coming down the stairs after her.

"Right now, does it matter?" Her fingers sought his coat pocket and gripped his warm, familiar hand. "Let's just walk, wander a bit."

Mercy tilted her face upward and she could feel the snow, minute points of cold on her skin. Turning her head, she saw that he was doing the same thing, his eyes closed, snow collecting on his lashes, and for a moment she could see the face of the man he would become. They walked out beneath a canopy of branches now etched with snow, escaping the pale light cast by the house, and disappeared into the shelter of night.

• • •